Wishes, Lies, & Fireflies
A Sewing Circle Suspense

Claire Yezbak Fadden

ISBN: 978-0-9988645-9-4
Editors: Chris Hall, Barb Wilson
Book Cover: Liz Bank Design
Format: Enterprise Book Services, LLC
Publisher: Brightwood Books

Disclaimer
This story is a work of fiction. Names, characters, and incidents are either products of the author's imagination or are used fictitiously. Any resemblance to actual events, locales, organizations or persons, living or dead, is entirely coincidental.

For every sister who is a friend.
For every friend who is a sister.

For Yoohoo and Yukhta.

Always for Nick.

Chapter One
Spring 1958

Addie Burhan blew a lingering puff of smoke across the dining room, a tacit protest to her sister Beth's three-cent raise. Playing poker on Thursday night with her and their three best friends, Helene, Mabel, and Peg, highlighted Addie's week.

The gentle sound of Johnny Mathis played softly in the background as Addie eyed the ladies gathered around the diminutive cherrywood table. *Does the glow of love still grow?* Well, in friendships, it did. Addie treasured these ladies nearly as much as she loved her sister. Her Sewing Circle. Their card-playing night had turned into a standing date to relax, laugh, complain. And share secrets.

The Circlers were good at keeping secrets.

Addie gazed around the room, delaying the game for a moment longer if only to annoy Beth. That's when their mother's Fostoria crystal came into view. Beth had prominently displayed the rarely-used pieces in her china closet.

A warm smile slipped across Addie's lips. Her big sister had laid claim to the goblets and footed dessert bowls, while Addie chose the tea glasses and tumblers, both daughters equally needing these small pieces of their mother's memory to remain alive in their homes.

Addie returned her attention to Beth's show cards—a three, a five, a nine, and a queen. She took another drag on her cigarette and exhaled slowly. Seriously, someone would have to teach her big sister the finer points of seven-card stud, but that person wouldn't be Addie.

At least not tonight.

"Are you in?" Beth finally asked.

Addie glanced at the pennies and nickels piled in the center and attempted a quick calculation. There might be as much as fifty cents.

Addie eyed Beth's tapping shoe. "You have pocket deuces, and you're gonna up the ante on that?" *She's definitely bluffing.* And judging by the nervous vibration of her shaking leg, she was bluffing big time.

Beth shrugged. "Better to have pocket somethings instead of that mess you got showing. I see a lot of red. Too bad it's not from the same suit."

Helene, Mabel, and Peg had already folded, turning their cards face down in front of them. Helene and Mabel sat back and giggled at what had become a weekly clash between siblings. Peg, the peacemaker, sipped her tea, waiting anxiously for the altercation to end.

"Will you accept a postage stamp or a five-cent Mr. Clean coupon?" Addie offered, stubbing out the butt in an ashtray and reaching for the nearby pack to light another.

Beth didn't respond. Instead, she forked into her homemade cherry supreme. She held the dessert in front of her lips for a moment before sliding the gooey, whipped-cream-covered dollop into her mouth. She sighed. "Delicious."

Addie rolled her eyes and tossed in three cents. Her just-lit cigarette dangled from the corner of her mouth. "Mom's favorite dessert won't save you. Show 'em," she demanded, whiffs of smoke escaping with each word.

Beth set her fork down slowly on the side of the dish, fanned out the three cards she had secreted in her hand, and placed them on the table. Two fives and a queen.

"Baby sister, that's what you call a full boat. Not a deuce in the bunch," Beth announced, pride dripping off every word like honey.

"How in the…" Addie's voice trailed off. *When had Beth learned to really play cards?* Times were changing.

As if she read Addie's mind, Beth explained, "Last week, after losing that big pot to Helene, I realized I bounce my leg when I'm bluffing." Beth raked some thirty coins toward her. "So today, I did the opposite. Worked, huh?"

Addie shook her head in disbelief. "Well, hell, now I'm going to have to figure out another way to pay for my Easter hat."

Beth narrowed her eyes and glared. "What are you talking about?"

"Since we started this group, I could always count on you to contribute ten or fifteen cents each week to my bottom line."

The twinkle that winning had put into Beth's eyes dulled. "What?"

"You have a terrible poker face," Helene chimed in. "I'm afraid we've all taken advantage a time or two."

Beth placed a hand over her heart and gasped. "Deception from the most important women in my life. Wow. Now who can I trust?"

"All's fair in love and poker, dearie." Mabel's grin brightened against her smooth, alabaster skin. "We're best friends—except when we shuffle."

"That's when all bets are off," Peg added, unaware of the pun and equally oblivious that her jaw no longer clenched in anxiety.

Beth cheerfully separated her newly earned pennies from the nickels. "Well, if that's how things are, I guess I'll live with it. Or I could quit, and you'd have to play four-handed."

"No fun in that," Peg said.

Addie tapped her flaming red fingernails against the table, a wicked grin playing on her lips. "We could find another equally naïve card player," Addie suggested.

"Oh! Like Nora!" Helene shouted and clapped her hands.

Addie's heart slammed against her chest at the mention of her former friend. One hand covertly gripped the hem of Beth's Irish linen cloth. *Not Nora. Anyone but Nora.*

Helene continued, "You know she's back in town. I've missed her. She'd be a great addition."

"Hey, I didn't say I was quitting," Beth hastened to add. "Just don't like the idea that *yinz* took advantage of me."

"Sorrrry," Helene said. "It's just that you're so…"

"So gullible," Addie supplied, recovering from the jolt of panic Nora Gallatin's name spun her into. "You believe everyone about everything, even when the facts point otherwise."

"Well, maybe I prefer to think the best of people."

"You definitely do, big sis," Addie agreed, looking at her watch. "I have time for one more hand. Another chance to get some of my money back from you?"

"It's only nine," Mabel said. "We usually play until ten."

"I have to get up early to make Ahren's lunch. Tomorrow, he's delivering way out in Willetburgh, across the state line. Want to make sure he has something proper to eat."

"Well, aren't you the perfect wife?" Helene rolled her eyes. "Makes the rest of us look bad."

"I pack a lunch for Cal," Peg said defensively.

"Of course you do, dearie," Beth answered. "But Addie, this is new...catering to Ahren. What's up?"

Addie pouted and looked at each of her friends. "Is there a law against taking care of your husband?"

Helen huffed. Beth and Mabel laughed. "No law I know of," Peg declared after a minute.

Addie slid the ashtray nearer. "Are we playing or what?" she asked, desperately wanting to move the conversation along.

"Guess so. My deal," Beth said. "Same game, deuces in the hole are wild. Ante up."

"You were joking about Nora, weren't you?" Addie asked, her stare fixed on Helene.

"Not really."

"Well, I say no! There's no flipping way I can be around that woman. I don't want her anywhere near me." Addie raised a cigarette to her lips. She flicked her lighter several times before the flame finally caught. She sucked in the comforting smoke and blew out as though her vote settled the entire matter.

"That's your third cigarette in as many minutes," Helene said.

"Never you mind how much I smoke or how fast, hell on wheels," Addie chided.

"My, we're a bit touchy tonight," Mabel said. "All at the mention of Nora's name. Make this my last hand. I need to get back to the motel."

Addie averted her eyes from Helene. She didn't want to see the *now-look-what-you've-done* glare certain to be on exhibit. Instead, she set her burning cigarette in the ashtray and picked up the two cards in front of her. *Pocket deuces.*

Her gaze slid to Beth's, but the look painted on her sister's face sent a nervous flutter to the base of Addie's stomach.

Clearly, the Nora matter was anything but over.
God, help me.

Chapter Two

Addie glared at her image in the full-length mirror anchored to her bedroom wall. She was rapidly approaching forty, and every bit of her age showed on her figure. She smoothed out her swing dress. At least the full skirt made her waist look small.

She leaned in to examine the dark bags forming under her eyes and blamed them on the past three sleepless nights. How could the Sewing Circle gals even consider bringing Nora back? The question hounded Addie. She could barely think of anything else.

She shook off her anger and instead ran to her vanity to apply a pancake foundation, temporarily concealing the circles under her lower lashes. She finished the look off with a smattering of loose powder. Pleased with the repairs, Addie snapped the compact shut. A few quick swipes at her chestnut curls and she'd be ready. At the last minute, she grabbed her grandmother's pearl necklace, the one Beth loved, from the jewelry box on her dresser. She stood for a moment inspecting the beads before racing down the stairs into the living room.

"We're going to be late," she shouted to her husband, Ahren, as she shoved a window nearest the front door closed. Spring had arrived in southwestern Pennsylvania, but the afternoon's gentle breeze billowing her bark cloth drapes had turned cold by early evening. She tugged the panels together, glad that soon the day's light would extend beyond six o'clock.

"Lucas!" she shouted. "Where are you?"

"Right here, Mom. Don't have a hissy fit," her son replied in that derisive tone mastered by teenagers.

Addie wheeled around to take in his six-foot frame draped over an overstuffed chair, his stocking feet dangling off an armrest. A Mallo Cup candy wrapper and his high-top sneakers were discarded on the floor nearby. A musical show, *American Bandstand* maybe, blared through their Westinghouse console in the corner.

"Don't start with your attitude," Addie said. "You've got chocolate and marshmallow all over your mouth. Turn off the television, get your shoes on, and let's go. It's your cousin's confirmation day."

"Yeah, I know," Luke answered, licking the corners of his mouth. "I was at the church this morning, remember?" He grabbed his shoes, laced them, then stood.

"Honey, will you get the dessert from the refrigerator?" she asked Ahren, standing in the doorway.

"You didn't make that awful green thing, did you?" Luke's voice boomed from behind her. "I hope there's something else for dessert if you did."

Addie frowned. "I'll have you know that everyone loves my lime Jell-O ring. Besides, your Aunt Beth will have lots of other goodies. She always does. She's really the cook in the family. You, my handsome son, got the mother who makes reservations for dinner."

"And delicious reservations they always are," added Ahren.

Addie curtsied. "How did I get so lucky to marry you?" She handed him the string of pearls—not real ones, of course, but a high-quality imitation, their mother had always said. "Can you help with the clasp?" She lifted her curls from the nape of her neck. "Maybe I should try an Italian cut," she suggested, and turned back toward him. "Then someone might mistake me for Sophia Loren or Elizabeth Taylor."

Ahren spun her around and planted a small kiss against her skin before hooking the necklace in place. "Don't lop off your curls," he said, tucking an errant one behind her ear. "They make you more beautiful than a movie star." The couple stood that way, with Ahren behind her, his hands bracketing her waist as he nuzzled her.

Ahren always said the right thing at the right time. She'd never have to worry about him straying. That's why she had picked him

7

over Barry. Mom and Dad had approved since he was Lebanese. Barry wasn't, but he was rich—something Ahren would never be.

She didn't regret her choice. Her life had turned out fine being married to a five-foot-six high school running back. Not NFL quality. He never anticipated hearing from the Steelers, but Ahren was the guy who'd always been chosen for pickup games at Rockyburgh Park.

More importantly, he treated her like a queen. Something she wished was true about her sister Beth's husband, Ted.

Addie attempted another curtsy, but this time, she wobbled on her kitten heels, nearly toppling them both.

"Whoa." Ahren grabbed her waist tighter. "You all right, honey?"

"Never been better," she giggled, turning to face him. A slight hiccup escaped, so she covered her mouth, giggling harder. "I tried a new recipe that called for a splash of sherry."

"Wow, that sounds great..." Luke began, but his father's glare stopped him.

"You added alcohol to the dessert the kids will be eating?" Ahren said. "Do you think that's wise?"

The dissention in his words swept through her. These were the times she loved Ahren the least. He couldn't mask the disdain and disappointment with her for even the slightest variation off the beaten path.

Addie never liked paths—beaten or otherwise. She wanted to explore the road not taken, brave her own course, but being married to Ahren prevented even the slightest meandering.

Her husband accepted the tried-and-true—tradition and routine. "That's the way we've always done it" was justification enough not to change a single thing. Even relocating a table lamp was cause for extensive discussion. And usually, the lamp stayed right where it was.

Yes, Ahren was a housewife's dream—stable, reliable, steadfast...

And as boring a man as anyone would ever meet.

"We can't always be wise like you, honey," she said, pinning a hat to her head and grabbing her purse. "Let's go."

Addie tried to recall one time in their nineteen-year marriage that Ahren had done anything that wasn't wise, measured, or careful. He'd never been spontaneous, not even in their early years.

But she couldn't blame him. She'd already been pregnant when they'd exchanged "I do's." Luke had arrived *a few weeks early*, and being a mother had consumed Addie, overriding her adventurous side for years.

Still, the fact that Ahren never made plans for the two of them to be alone irked her. Either set of grandparents could have watched Luke, but Ahren hadn't ever seemed to crave that closeness the way she did. He was happy to collapse in his easy chair, inhale the pot roast she'd made, and watch the evening news.

Ahren couldn't come up with an original idea if his bosses paid him for one. That's why he drove a route for Gallatin Coal and Fuel. There wasn't anything creative about delivering coal to furnaces in the greater Keystone area. All he had to do was attach the truck's chute through the window and wait for the lumps to tumble into the customer's basement. And then repeat every other week.

It was a steady job with one large problem: no one needed coal during the hot summers.

The dog days started as soon as school let out in June and often stretched past Indian summer. They had to make Ahren's six or seven months of salary last for twelve because, by Labor Day, they usually had spent their paltry savings. No way could they survive until October, when the weather would finally cool. When their fridge stopped working last March, Addie had started giving piano lessons to the locals.

After confirming that Ahren held the dessert, she *whooshed* out the door, skirts swirling in her wake. She breathed in the crisp air, cool against her skin, and strode to the car.

It had been nearly a month since Addie learned of Barry Gallatin's return. She hadn't seen him; still, thoughts of the man who had never quite moved out of her life echoed. As she stood by the coupe waiting for Ahren and Luke, troubling thoughts of another woman's husband invaded her like hornets buzzing in her ears.

And nighttime magnified the lie. A lie she kept buried to remain Ahren's loving wife and Luke's caring mother.

***

Beth Jacobsen replaced the lid on a pot of cabbage rolls steaming on the gas range before swatting at her son Joel, who tried to fork a delicacy from inside the Dutch oven. "Stop," she directed. "Everyone will be here soon. We'll sit for dinner, and you can eat as many as you want then."

"Come on, Mom. You know there won't be any left for me once the family gets here—especially after Aunt Addie, Uncle Ahren, and Luke fill up."

Beth swatted at him again. "Don't talk like that about your godparents. Who stood behind you today as you said your vows and became an adult in the church?"

Joel stared at his empty fork. Beth guessed that he was strategizing how to connect its tines to a pig-in-a-blanket.

"That's right." Beth huffed. "Your Uncle Ahren. Now, go comb your hair and get ready for your party."

"I don't want a party. I just want to eat." Joel raked a hand through his unruly waves.

Beth straightened her apron before herding her youngest through the kitchen's swinging door. "I'm not arguing with you." She kissed his cheek before whispering, "And I'll put some pigs-in-a-blanket aside for you."

"Thanks, Mommy," Joel said and turned, nearly knocking his sister over as he raced to his room.

"What's his problem?" Opal said, looking over her shoulder.

"He's a hungry boy." Beth motioned at the cotton napkins in Opal's hands. "Put those on the buffet and make them look nice. Then can you chop the vegetables for the tabouleh?"

Beth pulled a stack of green melamine plates from the cabinet and followed Opal to the dining room. "Where's Ruby? That girl always disappears when there's work to be done."

Only two minutes separated her daughters in age, but those two minutes made Opal the much older twin. She was reliable, whereas Ruby was flighty as a feather boa and just about as useful.

"I need both of you to give me a hand. The family will be here in less an hour."

Opal fanned out the napkins in a lovely arc, seemingly nonplussed that, once again, Ruby had gotten away with goofing off. "She'll be down after she takes the curlers out of her hair."

"What? Who's she trying to impress? Her cousin won't care."

"True, but Dante is coming, and she wants to look especially nice for him." Opal patted her napkin arrangement beside the Fostoria crystal goblets that only saw daylight on the most special occasions.

"I didn't know Opal invited all the Gallatins. I told her she could invite Genna." Beth grabbed tomatoes, cucumbers, and fresh parsley from the refrigerator, handed them to her daughter, and pointed to the cutting board. "That's how many more people?" She counted out loaves of Syrian bread.

"Oh, not the whole family. Just Genna and Dante. He's giving her a ride over, so Ruby suggested he stay for dinner."

A growing uneasiness in her stomach doubled. Addie would have a kitten knowing any Gallatin would be here, much less two of them. Beth hadn't dared tell her sister that she'd seen Nora twice in the past month, both times at Woolworths. They'd exchanged pleasantries, but neither woman had made an attempt to rekindle their long-ago friendship.

Beth owed Addie that much.

Opal looked up from the piles of chopped vegetables cluttering the counter. "Ruby's liked Dante for as long as I can remember."

Beth shook her head. At this rate, Ruby would be married as soon as she graduated from high school. "How can that be? She was five or six when Nora and Barry moved to Pittsburgh, and they've only been back since January."

"Don't know. What I do know is that since she and Genna became best friends, all I hear is 'Dante, Dante, Dante. He's so tall and handsome.'" Opal rolled her eyes.

"Is that so? Well, of course he's tall. Barry was over six feet when we were in ninth grade."

"You went to school with Dante's dad?"

Beth swung around so quickly that Opal jumped back. "What are you talking about? We all went to school together; me, your Aunt Addie, Ahren, your dad...all of us. We were a gang until folks started getting married, and Barry moved to Pittsburgh."

Ruby appeared in the kitchen doorway, her hair a tousle of curls and a brightness of young love surrounding her. "Why did he move?"

"So glad you could join us." Beth pointed to the sink, where a colander full of green beans waited to be cleaned and trimmed. "Want to lend a hand?"

Ruby grabbed a pink paisley-print apron from a nearby hook, slipped it over her head, and tied the sash. "So why did Dante's family move?" she asked again, chopping the ends off the string beans.

11

"Why does anybody do anything? Money." Beth laughed. "By then, Mr. Gallatin had succeeded in the coal industry. He moved his corporate offices to the big city and didn't look back to our little town, where he'd left folks without jobs, including your grandfather. Mostly, he wanted his only son, the heir apparent, living closer so he could run the business."

"*Air a parent?* What's that?"

"It means he's next in line to inherit Gallatin Coal and Fuel, right, Mom?"

"It's h-e-i-r, not a-i-r. And yes, Opal, you are right."

"I kind of remember them living here," Ruby said. "I'm really glad they're back."

"Are you glad the *whole* family is back? Or just Dante?" Opal giggled.

"Smart aleck," Ruby hissed, snapping a bean pod in two.

"It was tough for some people when the company relocated," Beth said, not really addressing the girls. "Might take time for folks to warm up to Barry and Nora."

Ruby giggled. "I'll warm up to Dante." A flighty coquettishness painted her words as though nursing a crush on Tab Hunter or Frankie Avalon.

"Fixing the green beans is help enough," Beth said, wiping her hands together.

"Did you know that Mom went to school with Dante's parents?" Opal asked.

Ruby twirled around as though royalty had entered the dreary kitchen. "Really, Mom? You ran with the Gallatins?" Ruby asked, eyes wide.

"We were friends," Beth said, emphasizing *were*.

"That's so cool," Ruby said.

"It was at the time. Now get back to the beans."

Beth purposely downplayed the importance of Nora. From kindergarten through high school, the two had been closer than petals on a flower. Until Barry had proposed to Nora. Weeks later, Addie got engaged to Ahren.

Nora and Addie had been bridesmaids in each other's weddings, and Beth was the maid of honor to both. Not long after the last handfuls of rice had been thrown and the tiered cakes cut, the friendships splintered.

Years later, when Nora was pregnant with their third child, Barry had followed his father to Sewickley, a wealthy Pittsburgh suburb. So why had they moved back to this sleepy hamlet? Rumors suggested that Nora wanted to be closer to her sickly mother.

Was there another, more ominous reason?

Funny how the drama from years ago reappeared. They'd been so young and naïve.

We should leave the past in the past and invite Nora to join the Sewing Circle, and then we'd have the girls back together.

As soon as the thought crossed her mind, her stomach clenched. *Addie would never permit it.*

"Why is Dante coming to your brother's confirmation party?" Beth asked finally. "And why didn't you ask me? You know I worry about having enough food."

"Mom, you always have enough food. We could invite the football team, and there would be leftovers," Opal declared.

Beth ignored Opal's response, keeping her gaze trained on Ruby, who peered out at her from behind a fringe of black eyelashes.

"I told you, he's giving Genna a ride. It would be rude—" Opal finally answered while Ruby stood silent.

"I don't like you chasing boys," Beth admonished. "It's just not done."

"Well, if you're Ruby Jacobsen, it is." Opal laughed.

Ruby sent a glower in Opal's direction.

"You better not embarrass me with Nora."

The twins giggled.

"I mean it. We've been friends a long time." Sadly, though, the length of time wasn't an accurate indicator of the *quality* of that friendship. "I won't have her thinking my daughters are boy crazy."

"Not *daughters*." Opal waggled a finger. "*Daughter*. The one you named Ruby."

"I don't have time for this," Beth said, placing her hands on her hips. "We have people coming for dinner, and all I have ready are the grape leaves and the cabbage rolls."

"You made cabbage rolls, too?" Opal smacked her forehead. "Of course you did. Because your son won't eat *mishees*."

The snarl in Opal's voice made Beth wince. "He doesn't like grape leaves, and this *is* his party. He's the one who got confirmed."

"It's always about your son," she singsonged, using a jovial tone to mask this open secret.

In Middle Eastern families like the one Beth grew up in, boys were valued above girls, men above women. Her husband, a mixture of Danish and German, seemed to warm to the practice.

"Don't start. Go check on your father. See if he's awake, but don't disturb him." Hopefully, he'd slept off last night's overindulgence in the beer garden.

"Okay, Mom. And you know I'm kidding, right?" She left, not waiting for a response.

There'd been a tinge of humor in Opal's voice but also a trace of truth. From the time when Beth was a young girl to her life now as a married woman, the gears turned around the menfolk. She wouldn't validate this truth to Opal and Ruby.

Well, not before they got married.

She wanted her daughters to see the world as a limitless canvas with more colors than just pink or blue for them to paint with. But that was a discussion for another day. She had ambrosia salad to make and the *lubee*—green bean and tomato stew—to cook. No time to let her mind consider the world's injustices.

Beth grabbed the red and yellow hook-and-loop potholders Joel had made in summer camp and opened the oven door to check on the pan of grape leaves baking inside, praying they would stretch to serve ten instead of eight.

Chapter Three

"Can I drive?" Luke asked, dangling Addie's keys to the Chevy Bel Air from his finger.

"Yeah, sure," his dad replied, grabbing them and unlocking the doors. "When you start making the payments."

Luke huffed and climbed into the backseat. "Can we at least put the top down?"

"For this short ride? By the time we get to Beth's—"

Ignoring Ahren, Addie reached across the seat and pushed a button on the dashboard. Seconds later, the roof disappeared, revealing a dimming sky.

Ahren cast a dismissive look at his wife. "Guess we have enough time after all."

"That's much better," Addie declared, jostling her hair a bit to feel the rapidly cooling wind travel through her strands. "Fresh air. Just what we need." She turned slightly to give her son a wink before taking in the breeze grazing her face and rushing past. Inside the Chevy, the impossible seemed possible.

They'd owned the car only a few months, and it was the center of one of the few fights she and Ahren had had during their years together. They argued over the purchase, of course. Ahren had been reluctant to buy another car when the payment would be nearly thirty dollars a month. Their ten-year-old Dodge ran fine.

If they had to spend money on a luxury like a convertible, at least she could pick a reasonable color—say Shadow Gray or Horizon Blue, Ahren had argued.

Fortunately for Addie, the used car lot was fresh out of boring colors.

"This baby is barely four years old, hardly any miles," the salesman had said, opening the driver-side door and encouraging Addie to slide in behind the steering wheel. Once inside the Rosemary Red automobile with a matching red-and-white interior, Addie made up her mind.

Ahren hated the idea of red, even though he had agreed that Addie looked amazing in the color. But Addie had insisted.

"What did you get Joel for a gift?" Luke asked.

"Why do you want to know?" Ahren bristled.

"You and Mom are his godparents, so you should get him something great."

"We got him that plastic flying saucer thing he asked for. Frizzy, I think it's called."

"You got him a Frisbee, Mom. Not a *frizzy*. Is that what's in the box?" Luke said, pointing to the odd-shaped gift placed in between her and his father in the front seat.

"Yes. The darn thing cost ninety-eight cents and didn't come with a box." Addie cringed at the cost. She'd have to sit through nearly three thirty-minute lessons with the Nader girl, Macy, practicing her tedious version of Beethoven's "Für Elise" to pay for a toy that looked like a plastic plate.

"Anything else?" Luke pried further.

Addie knew what he was getting at. "Of course, we're giving him an envelope," she answered, referring to the cash tucked inside the card she had signed earlier.

Luke was right. Since they were both Joel's godparents, the gift needed to be more than a buck or two—more than the paltry five dollars Ahren thought they could spare. The man barely made over the one-dollar minimum wage. Most of that went to their seventy-five-dollar mortgage, so Ahren was being generous.

Still, an occasion as important as what confirmation signified in the Maronite Catholic Church deserved more. Ten dollars seemed just about right, but doubling the cash meant little meat in the spaghetti sauce she'd be simmering tomorrow. Ten dollars was a hefty sum for a twelve-year-old and a sizable amount to pull out of the family budget.

Addie would have to book a few extra students when she'd rather be doing anything other than helping an eight-year-old find middle C. She hated pinching pennies, figuring out ways to stretch a meal, mend a shirt, or hold off buying Luke a new pair of sneakers when his big toe poked out of his high tops.

She was good at saving money, just like Beth, when she wanted to. Their mother had taught them well. But forced frugality clashed with Addie's innate extravagance. Another reason why she often found herself daydreaming about how her life might have been easier had she married Barry.

Addie suspected that Nora didn't look at the price tag before trying clothes on at Kaufmann's.

Addie turned on the car radio, and Luke stopped asking questions. The Everly Brothers' "Wake Up Little Susie" belted through the speakers. She closed her eyes, soaking in the harmony of Phil's and Don's voices.

Her decisions as a nineteen-year-old, a year older than her son, led to love, not money. They led her to Ahren, a man as consistent as the Bible.

Still, she couldn't help but daydream about a life as Mrs. Barry Gallatin.

***

Beth dried her hands on a dish towel and tossed it on the sink before entering the dining room to give the table a final inspection. Opal had done a wonderful job arranging everything to look special before heading into the living room to read. Ruby, on the other hand, had haphazardly finished the green beans and ran to her bedroom to change her clothes for what might be the fifth time. Beth couldn't be sure.

Beth tucked an errant strand behind her ear and realized she should go upstairs, comb her hair, and assess Ted's state. The man's temperament had four gears: charming, partially drunk, fully drunk, and belligerent. *Please, God, let him turn the dial to charming and stay there, if only for tonight.* Ted had slept through the actual ceremony but promised that he'd be on his best behavior for dinner.

Sadly, Ted wasn't particularly good at keeping promises.

Beth glanced to where Opal sat, ready to compliment her efforts, when a realization hit. A body that once belonged to her little girl was now inhabited by a soon-to-be woman. Beth knew the day would come, and in some ways, she prayed for it.

The effort to cover for Ted in the evenings and on weekends was exhausting. She didn't want her daughters to think his volatile behavior was something they should accept when they took a husband. And she definitely didn't want Joel growing up to be that kind of man.

The ear-bashing timbre of Ruby hurrying down the wooden staircase, her heels crashing against each plank, interrupted her thoughts. Her daughter ran straight to the front room, pulled up the shade, and parked herself in front of the bay window, bending so far forward that her face nearly touched the glass.

Beth checked her Timex. Addie and her family should be arriving any minute.

Ted had lost his parents many years ago. His spinster sister lived in Baltimore, some three hundred miles away, and rarely visited. Having Addie so close was a blessing. Next to her husband and children, she was all the family Beth had. The longing Beth held for her mother and father stabbed the deepest at gatherings like these.

"Stop staring," Opal said. "He'll get here when he gets here."

"I know," Ruby replied, dismissing her sister's order. "I tried to phone Genna, but that nasty old Mrs. Doyle wouldn't hang up and let me make a call. Not even for five minutes. Said she was talking to her son."

"Party lines are no party," Opal decreed. "Mom, when can we get our own phone?"

"What are you two hollering about?" Beth asked.

"We can't make a single call. That old biddy is always on the phone."

"Don't talk about Mrs. Doyle. She's probably lonely," Beth replied, noticing that Ruby hadn't budged from the window.

"Lonely? She has a bunch of grandkids," Opal said.

Beth laughed. Gladys Doyle had been her mother's best friend; Irish Catholic and always pregnant. It was hard to believe that her children had grown and moved out of the area. Not one of the eight stayed behind to care for their widowed mother. No wonder she was always on the phone. Sadly, the Jacobsens were unlucky enough to share a party line with this next-door neighbor—an uneven partnership, to say the least.

"She listens in on my conversations," Ruby added. "We need a private line."

"When you have sixty cents to pay each month, we'll get one. In the meantime, you're not hanging in the window like a doll for sale."

Ruby didn't move.

"I mean now!" Beth directed.

Ruby turned toward her mother, and Beth let out a gulp. "What in the world!"

"We'll be out of Kleenex for a while." Opal howled, pointing to her sister's bust.

Ruby smoothed her cashmere sweater so it clung to every curve.

"Change that top. You look ridiculous."

"But—"

"Before everyone gets here and you make a fool of yourself," Beth boomed.

Ruby stood her ground until her mother reached inside her bosom and removed a wad of tissue.

"Go," Beth ordered, waving the balled-up paper like a weapon. "Don't come back until you're wearing something presentable."

"What's all the ruckus?" Ted stood in the doorway. He combed his fingers through his brown hair. Two days of stubble dotted his face. A somewhat wrinkled plaid shirt and blue jeans completed his disheveled look.

"It's nothing, dear. Girl stuff." Beth turned back to Ruby with a pleading look. *Please don't do anything to rile your father.*

Ruby nodded as she headed past Ted, arms tight across her chest, and slowly climbed the steps leading to the room she shared with Opal. Beth knew this wasn't the end of the stuffing-her-bra battle.

"I'll help her pick out something," Opal volunteered, hustling toward the exit, obviously not wanting to stay in the same room as her parents.

"Thanks, honey," Beth said. "And check on our guest of honor."

"Those daughters of yours don't let a man sleep," Ted grumbled as he took the space in the chair Opal had vacated. "Noisy and disrespectful tarts. I tell you, Beth. You need to do something, or we'll end up with two hussies, and who knows what else they'll bring into our home."

Beth decided against debating such a ludicrous assessment of their children. Ted wouldn't even remember the encounter by tomorrow. Instead, she offered him a glass of water.

"Water!" Ted snorted. "Aw, little lady, come here." He patted his knee, and when Beth got close enough, he grabbed her arm and spun her into his lap. "Baby doll, you know I love you."

He kissed her hard, making her glad she hadn't fixed her face. Her red lipstick would have smeared across her mouth resembling a clown's. "And you know the last thing I want is water." He grabbed her waist and lifted her off him. "Open me a bottle of Iron City."

He slapped her bottom half-jokingly, but the smack was hardly a love tap.

Beth got the message. Ted would not be managed. Not by his wife or anyone else. Even in his charming phase, if the man wanted to drink, he would drink.

Now, the best she could hope for was that Ted's dial would turn slowly and not reach belligerent until after Joel's party was over.

Chapter Four

Beth stared out her kitchen window. Both hands firmly gripped the rim of the porcelain-covered cast-iron sink while she waited for the water to fill the basin. A mounting anger raked through her, anger so intense that her legs nearly gave way, threatening to send her crumpling to the ground if she let go. How would she ever regain her composure?

She ignored the dinner dishes piled on the drainboard, awaiting their turn to be dipped into the soapy water, which was about to overflow. *Steady now,* she thought, turning off the faucet. *Stay calm.* In an hour, everything would be done; the gifts opened, guests heading home. *Please God, give me the strength to keep this smile on my face.*

"Everything tasted delicious," Addie said, pushing through the swinging door, her hands containing more dirty plates. "You always put on a nice spread, just like Mom. Lord knows she loved these celebrations."

Beth didn't turn around to meet her sister's gaze. She simply moved aside, allowing Addie to add to the pile. "I'm surprised with your blurry vision that you even noticed," Beth snarked.

"What's that supposed to mean? Are you mad at me?" When no reply came, Addie moved toward the refrigerator. "Want me to serve the Jell-O mold?"

"Sure, Adele Frances, serve the dessert," Beth replied, her attention now captured by a goldfinch perched on a buckeye tree branch illuminated by a street lamp. Late spring showcased their

21

black-and-yellow coloring reminding her of the Pirates and Steelers uniforms. This songbird definitely belonged. She made a mental note to buy sunflower seeds for her bird feeder.

"What's eating you?" Addie asked, obviously annoyed that Beth had called her by her full name. "Did Ted do something to upset you?"

Beth spun around and locked eyes on her little sister. "Ted always does something to upset me. I expect him to get drunk. I plan for him to ruin things. But you...you..." Her voice cracked a bit. "I don't need you showing up soused."

Addie placed her Tupperware container on the blue Formica tabletop. "You exaggerate everything. I had a little sherry, that's all. Hardly enough to sign me up for AA."

"You had more than a little," Beth accused, turning again toward the window. "I smelled your breath when you got here. And your glass hasn't been empty since."

Addie lowered her voice so the family in the dining room wouldn't hear. "Loosen up. I had a nip or two."

"I don't have the luxury of sipping sherry. I have to keep all the wheels in motion," Beth said, disappointment coloring her words. "And the least you can do is not derail the car."

"And you could have told me that Genna Gallatin would be here," Addie hissed, removing the seal and inverting the plastic mold onto a serving platter.

"It slipped my mind."

"Slipped your mind?" Addie mocked, still speaking in hushed tones. "You know how hard this is on me."

Beth moved to where Addie stood. "Twenty years have passed. You moved on. Barry moved on. Nora moved on. That stale, old teenage romance can't be causing you to drown your sorrows in dessert wine!"

"Some wounds never heal." Addie looked down and focused her attention on the wobbly gelatin.

Beth pressed on. "Because you keep poking at them, keeping them bleeding. You and Nora are grown women. Mothers. Time to leave the high school drama behind. We're moving into another phase of our lives. Your son is going away to college soon, only coming home once in a while on the weekends. Don't ruin today because of some stupid teenage stuff from so long ago."

Addie busied herself with controlling the jiggling mound of lime gelatin on the dish. "I'm barely over the fact that Helene wants to take Nora into our collective bosoms. And then, I run into precious Genna. You could have warned me," she said, her eyes drilling into her sister's.

Beth blinked. Addie was right. She should have told her.

"And, well," Addie continued, "I overreacted."

"That's one way of putting it." Beth framed her hips with her hands. "What do you care if they live here? Barry hasn't meant anything to you in decades."

"Yeah, I know. Lots of water under the bridge. Time to let things go," Addie said, stepping closer to Beth. "She took Barry away from me, and you—"

"And I what? Took her side? You were serious about Ahren. By then, you'd decided to marry him, not Barry, so what was I supposed to do? Give up my best friend in loyalty to you? Nora has the right to be happy, too."

Addie cast her gaze down. "Oh, I'm sure she's happy."

"Addie, honey. You made your choice. I remember the night you told me that Ahren had asked you to marry him. You said Barry would never be the right guy. He's the kind of man who would never be true."

Addie turned away, waving her hands in the air to dispel the image of Barry cheating on her. "He picked Nora, so what else could I do but pick Ahren?"

Beth sighed. "You married a good man."

Addie nodded, tears streaming down her cheeks.

Beth moved closer, encircling her sister in a gentle hug. "You made the right choice. You know that," she said several moments later, tipping Addie's chin.

She looked straight into her sister's camel-brown eyes rimmed with hazel green, hoping to convince her of this truth. "You said you couldn't trust Barry after what he did. You will never have those worries with Ahren," Beth said. "You're with the right fella."

Addie swiped at an errant tear. "The right thing isn't always the right thing, if you know what I mean." She gave her sister a half-smile.

"I know." Beth hugged her sister and held the embrace until Addie pulled away.

"Let's get dessert on the table," she said.

Beth grabbed an extra wineglass and held open the swinging door for her sister to pass. "I'll join you in a toast."

"And what are we toasting, sister dear?"

"Why us, of course. The two Reuben girls," Beth said, lifting her glass.

"Can I toast, too?" Opal asked, appearing in the doorway. "I'm not a Reuben girl, but—"

Beth laughed. "Great idea. We'll drink to the women in our family. You and Ruby can join us in a few years."

Opal frowned. "Mom," she said, drawing out the word, "Ruby might want to start now. She's really upset that Dante didn't show."

"He was supposed to be here, too?" Addie asked, her voice filled with growing alarm.

Beth offered an apologetic nod and turned back to Opal. "Help your aunt with dessert plates and forks. I'll grab a bottle of port. We're all out of sherry."

***

"Give me the car keys," Addie said.

Ahren swiped her hand away. "Yeah, right. Not after the way you and Beth have been guzzling."

"I don't want to drive. I'm not a fool. Let Luke drive us home. He needs the practice."

"Luke? I don't think he's interested." Ahren grinned. "He's been talking to that Gallatin girl. What's her name? Ginny?"

"Genna. Her name is Genna. And you know that as well as I do." Addie reached for her jacket hanging on a nearby coat rack. "You're still jealous of Barry," she teased. "After all these years, you pretend not to know the names of his children."

"I don't need to remember their names. I don't have anything to do with that family, and I hope you don't either."

Nothing except that Gallatin is the company name on your paycheck, Addie wanted to say but knew tossing that barb wouldn't make her feel any better. Hurting Ahren wasn't the remedy for the panic growing in her heart.

Ahren placed his gray fedora on his head and moved toward his son. "Luke, we need to get going. Your mother wants you to take the wheel on the drive home."

"Nah, Dad. I told Genna I'd walk her home. Her brother can't pick her up like he promised."

Addie scurried to where Luke and Genna stood. "How will *you* get home?"

"Same way. I'll walk. We don't live that far away from the Estates," Luke answered, referring to the wealthy side of town.

"Too far," Addie said, louder than she meant to. "It's probably five—"

Ahren interrupted. "Leave the boy be. He'll get himself home. He's eighteen, if you'd remember."

Addie had no problem keeping track of Luke's age or a million other details about her only child. She knew blue was his favorite color, that he ate his Cheerios without milk, and that he liked his eggs over medium. "No runny white part," he had admonished her years ago.

She also knew that he had applied to Notre Dame—the only college he'd ever been interested in attending. And her heart crashed as he opened his acceptance letter, complete with a full basketball scholarship to a school some four hundred miles from home.

Her son, stretching now to six-two, had led Keystone High to the state championship a couple of months before. After that, getting into Notre Dame was a slam dunk.

Today, though, Addie couldn't deny that she'd learned something new about her son on the edge of manhood—the type of young lady he found attractive.

She eyed Genna, a slip of a girl who hardly said a word throughout the evening. Tall and willowy like her father, Genna's olive complexion, green eyes, and ebony curls were a strong nod to her mother's Italian heritage. Of course Luke's head was turned. Probably every boy in eleventh grade was taken with her beauty. The new girl in town. They were the same age that she and Barry had been when they first fell in love.

But Luke couldn't fall in love with Genna. Of course not.

In two months, he'd be moving to South Bend, Indiana. Genna would remain in Keystone to start her senior year.

This would-be romance would fizzle as quickly as it started.

Chapter Five

"Sorry I'm late," Addie said to no one in particular. She quickly tossed her coat on Mabel Bergen's living room sofa and scurried to the dining room, where four women waited. She slid into the high-backed chair next to Beth. "Luke borrowed my car, and I had to wait until Ahren got home from work so I could catch a ride in the coal truck."

Four blank faces stared at her from around the table. Her sister and their friends would forget almost anything except being late to play cards.

Addie tugged open her coin purse and fished out two crumpled dollar bills. "Anyone have change?"

Helene groaned, Peg frowned, and Mabel made her way to the sideboard, where an old cigar box was kept for just this purpose. "How much do you need?"

Addie held up the bills, one in each hand. "Break it up between pennies and nickels." The icy stares intensified. "Whatever you have will be perfect, Mabel," she reworded.

"Seriously, Addie, you show up late. *And* you didn't bring change." Beth's complaint was said with a smile, but the message was clear.

Addie scooted the pile of coins closer to her and handed Mabel two bills. "Thanks, May."

"You can count it if you like," Mabel said of the change, slipping the folding money into the cigar box.

26

"Not necessary." Addie dismissed the thought. "Let's get to shuffling."

"Yes, let's." Helene Maddock, the least tolerant of the group, repeated the directive. *She really is hell on wheels,* Addie thought. Helene slid the stack toward Mabel, who split the deck into two even piles. Helene then restacked the cards and dealt, her fire-engine red fingernails gleaming with each toss of a card. "Seven-card stud, deuces and the dealer are wild," she announced, dealing two cards face-down and one card up, beginning with Addie.

The ladies shared a low, lazy giggle, Helene's repetitive attempt at humor and their polite laughter expected. Addie sighed, relieved that no one had mentioned Nora.

At least not yet.

"Bethie, will you drop me home later?" Addie whispered into her sister's ear several hands later. "I don't want Ahren to wait up. He starts work so early."

"Sure," Beth said, a quizzical look on her face. "Why is he getting up so early? Are people still getting coal delivered? Seems like business would be slowing down with summer right around the corner."

Addie agreed. "He's taken on an extra job. And well, I'd rather have him asleep when I get home. That way he won't expect...you know."

A raucous, unladylike chortle swept around the table. Addie, turning red at the realization that everyone had heard, looked up at a sea of laughing faces.

"We all hope the husbands are asleep when we get home, for one reason or another," Helene assured. "The bet's to you, Addie. You in or out?"

"In." Addie hurried to toss three pennies into the pot.

"Got a hand like a foot," Beth said, adding her three-cent ante.

"I'll stay to see one more card," Peg said. Mabel tossed her coins in without a word.

"Pot's right," Helene said before dealing the next card face up.

***

Ninety minutes later, Addie looked at her watch and her dwindling cache of coins. She stood and stretched her arms above her head. The ladies played for nearly two hours straight before deciding to take a break. The usual teasing banter took place hand after hand, but no one had mentioned Nora. Addie exhaled a breath of gratitude. "Mabel, let me help you serve dessert," she offered.

"I hope you ladies enjoy," Mabel said as she and Addie set plates on the table.

"Your famous lemon chiffon pie?" Peg said with satisfaction, scooping up a taste. "Can I take a slice home to Cal? He loves anything you bake, but this is his favorite. All that lemony cream cheese, whipped cream on a graham cracker crust."

"Me too," Helene said, asking for her husband. "Adam will enjoy it if I don't eat both pieces before he gets a chance."

"You're the big winner so far tonight," Beth said to Peg, passing her the deck.

"Throw in two books of Green Stamps, and I might have won enough to get a mixer," Peg said, referring to the trading stamps they'd collected since they were little girls.

"Coffee, anyone?" Mabel asked.

Four hands shot up.

"This is pretty tasty," Beth agreed after putting a forkful in her mouth. "So much better than licking stamps."

"There's a glass punch bowl with sixteen matching cups in their catalog. I have to have it," Helene said. "But I need another book and a half. I wish more places gave them out."

"They have them at Rascal's Grocery and at the A&P," Addie said. "What about at the butcher shop?"

"At Pete's? Are you kidding?" Beth laughed. "He ain't about to add any extra giveaways."

"Speaking of Pete, guess who I ran into at his shop today? Nora Gallatin's housekeeper, that's who," Peg answered before allowing any guesses.

Addie's legs weakened at the mention of the name, and she nearly spilled her coffee, having trouble getting the cup to sit inside the saucer correctly.

"Her housekeeper?" the group said in disbelief.

"Yeah. You know Vernie Slaughter? Well, she told me she's their full-time housekeeper. The woman barely moved back into town and already has *help*," Peg added, emphasizing the word.

"Can you imagine?" Mabel sucked on her Pall Mall and slowly blew out smoke. "Having a housekeeper. Someone to do your errands. All the things you hate doing, like standing in line at Pete's."

A housekeeper. *That was a luxury no one could afford,* Addie thought. *Except the Gallatins.*

"Do we have time for one more hand?" Addie asked, helping Mabel gather the plates and cups, hoping to change the subject.

"It's nearly ten." Mabel grinned, nudging Addie with her elbow. "But you want to stay out later, right?"

Addie didn't answer. Instead, she took her seat and mindlessly stacked what few pennies and nickels remained in front of her.

"Since this is the last game, let's make it interesting. How about we play Murph's?" Mabel asked.

"Didn't we ban that game?" Addie joked, referring to the homage to Murphy's, the local five-and-dime store.

"Murph's is fine," Helene snarked. "Anything to get the game going."

Peg cut the cards, and Mabel shouted as she dealt, "Fives and tens are wild."

"We know," Helene barked, tossing a nickel toward the table's center.

"What else did Vernie tell you?" Addie hated asking, but she had to know what they talked about.

"That she was glad to have the job. We spent the rest of our time complaining about the price of pork chops," Peg said. "Forty-three cents a pound. Pete might as well be a highway bandit."

"They're thirty-five cents at Rascal's, but they're not the thick cut Ted likes," Beth volunteered.

"I told that to Pete," Mabel said, straightening the cards in her hand. "Know what he told me? 'Then go buy them at Rascal's.'"

The bet came around to Helene, and she raised a penny. "Sounds like Pete," she said, punctuating her critique with a huff.

Addie added an agreeable huff of her own. "I'll see your raise and bump a nickel," she answered, increasing the bet just for spite.

"Well, aren't you the spendthrift," Beth chimed, tossing her cards onto the table.

"Too rich for my blood," Mabel added, sliding her cards toward the pot splayed in the middle of her crocheted tablecloth.

Peg flipped her cards on top of Mabel's. "Seems like our friendly game is changing," she said, reaching for her purse. "Good thing this was the last game. I should get going. Cal's not feeling well, and he's home with all three kids."

"Well, let me get you that slice," Mabel said, moving toward the kitchen.

"Thanks, hon. He'll be in a snit if I stay out much later."

In a snit meant Cal might knock her around a bit if he had a mind to. Addie didn't want to be among the group consoling Peg Thomas next Thursday if Cal used her as a punching bag. Too many Sewing Circles had revolved around bruises and black eyes attributed to Peg bumping into walls and tripping over carpet. Things seemed to have improved recently, though, once Cal got that promotion at the post office.

Still, against her better judgment, Addie pushed her informal inquisition about Nora.

"Why did she leave Pittsburgh, anyway?" Addie asked, hoping her voice sounded nonchalant, the opposite sensation of her pounding pulse.

"Something to do with her mom," Peg said, jingling her car keys. "Vernie didn't say, and I haven't had a chance to talk with Nora in person."

"What will that woman do with her extra time?" Mabel asked, returning with Cal's dessert.

"Join our group?" suggested Helene.

"Yeah. Playing six-handed would be better," Beth said.

Peg waggled a finger but kept moving toward Mabel's front door, keeping her opinion to herself.

Addie's blood turned cold, a revisit to the panic she endured last Thursday. "She's got a maid, for Chrissake. We have nothing in common anymore."

"Nora's one of us," Helene said. "She always will be."

"Nora's not part of us," Addie sniped.

Mabel handed the dessert plate to Peg and turned to face Addie. "I can't imagine why you'd say such a thing. You still holding that flame for Barry?"

Mabel's tone was light, but that didn't stop Addie from wanting to slap that glib grin from her face. Mabel knew nothing about what had happened that summer.

Addie, on the other hand, had thought of nothing else over the past eighteen years. How could she sit at Nora's dining room table, sipping iced tea from her crystal glasses, and pretend otherwise?

Addie exhaled. Her own sister would renew her friendship with this chippie and invite her back into their clique. Maybe Nora would have the decency to decline the offer Beth was assuredly going to make.

They couldn't let her into their inner circle. They just couldn't.

Beth had come up with the idea of playing cards nearly a decade ago, long after Nora had moved away. A standing date with Addie, Helene, Mabel, and Peg, every Thursday, no matter what. Originally, they told their husbands that the ladies were sewing baby blankets.

That story blew up a few months later. After an evening at the local beer garden, Ted stumbled home, only to see the *hags*—his nickname for Beth's friends—packing up their coins.

Addie couldn't sleep that night, worried that Ted would take his anger out on Beth. She'd called her sister first thing and let out a relieved sigh at Beth's voice, with a bit of a lilt, answering the phone.

"Can you talk?" Addie had asked.

"Sure. Ted's left for work."

"Are you okay?" Addie had spilled the question quickly so that the answer could come quicker.

"Ted might be an alcoholic, but he's not a hitter like Cal."

"Small relief," Addie said. "So he wasn't mad that we're playing cards instead of sewing blankets?"

"He snarked at me as soon as *yinz* pulled down the street," Beth said. "'Never saw baby blankets sewn with a deck of cards.' I didn't answer; just kept cleaning up."

"What did he do then?"

"He asked how we thread our needles with pennies and nickels, then laughed and went upstairs to sleep it off. He thought women playing cards was funny."

"Funny, as in humorous?"

"Yep," Beth added, letting out an annoyed grunt. "He just kept shaking his head as though men were the only ones capable of drawing to an inside straight."

Addie hadn't been offended. In fact, she'd been so relieved that her heart had resumed a normal beat. "Thank God. Will he tell the other husbands? Ahren won't care, but Adam, Bert, and Cal might."

"No, he doesn't talk to any of those guys, only Ahren. They rarely go to the Red Stone for a beer or call him if their sink is clogged," Beth had said, referring to her husband's plumbing business. "But the girls better tell their husbands anyway. You know how hard it is to keep a secret in this small town."

Addie knew about keeping secrets, ones much greater than a sham Sewing Circle. She tucked what change was left from her original two dollars into her coin purse while Mabel gathered the remaining coffee cups and overflowing ashtrays.

"Next week at your place," she shouted after Helene, who was halfway out the front door, close on the heels of Peg.

"You still riding with me?" Beth asked Addie.

"Still am," she answered, retrieving her coat. She hugged Mabel goodbye and followed her sister to her car.

***

Beth sat behind the steering wheel, waiting for Addie to finish her goodbyes. The night was silent except for the occasional chirping of crickets by the creek behind Mabel's house. Beth thought she saw a few fireflies skitter by her front windshield, but it was too early. Lightning bugs liked warmer, humid weather. She'd have to wait until June to enjoy their flashes of light, the way she and Addie had done in their childhood.

Beth tooted the horn, and Addie gave her a wave as if to say *one minute*. She closed her eyes and thoughts of the innocent conversation she'd had with Momma Garza last Sunday after mass surfaced. "My little girl is home," the now-gray-haired lady had said.

Seeing how much the woman she respected for her entire life had aged sent a spear of pain into Beth. Momma Garza had taught her how to pluck her eyebrows.

"She's not so little anymore now with children of her own, but she's back to take care of me," she had said, pride lacing her words.

Beth grinned. She couldn't imagine anyone having the fortitude to take care of the formidable Mrs. Garza. But the years had passed, and the strong woman who had waited up for her and Nora after a spring fling dance had morphed into a frail grandmother. Still, Beth couldn't forget the wrath she had unleashed when they missed their ten o'clock curfew.

Sofia Garza drove to the high school gymnasium only to find four teenagers in the parking lot, making out in a Nash Rambler. A half-empty bottle of cheap whiskey was on the floorboard by Beth's feet.

The yelling, scolding, and hour-long lecture still rang in her ears. Even the boys stood straight while releasing a volcano of apologies. Sofia had told Beth's parents what she'd found. Frances and Del grounded Beth for what seemed like months, but was actually only two weekends.

How could a woman behind that terse chastising now need help?

What was that boy's name? Beth scratched her head as though rubbing her scalp would bubble up the memory. *Artie. Wonder where he is now.*

She remembered how her thighs stuck to the vinyl seats on that unusually warm April night. And how quickly she buttoned her blouse when she saw Momma Garza's bullet-brown eyes peer into the passenger-side window. Nora was in the backseat with Barry, just like she had always been—except for that summer after Addie's senior year.

The summer that had changed them.

When Beth first saw Sofia Garza again, she'd hugged her with such enthusiasm that the seventy-year-old gasped for air. "So sorry," she said. "I'm just so happy to have Nora back in town."

Sofia bobbed her head. "I feel exactly the same; just don't have the same vim and vigor you have, Bethie."

Beth hugged her again. It had been decades since Mrs. Garza had called her Bethie.

Nora's and Beth's bond started in second grade when Beth had forgotten her lunch, and Sister Mary Margaret asked for a volunteer to share theirs. Nora's hand was the first one to shoot up— practically before Sister had finished her sentence.

As they split a peanut-butter and jelly sandwich, sliced pears, and one of Nora's mother's home-baked *pizzelle* cookies, the seeds of friendship sprouted. They had been like Damon and Pythias. Inseparable, committed, trusted.

Up until Nora married Barry, and Addie married Ahren.

Beth hoped that, once again, she'd be able to renew her relationship with her one-time trusted confidante and pal. These things took time, but they could rebuild their friendship. Addie would just have to accept that. Or so Beth had prayed.

But the heaviness Addie brought with her when she entered the car forced Beth to admit a different truth. Judging from how she had probed Peg for every detail, Addie wasn't about to forgive and

33

forget. She yanked on every last thread holding those ancient wounds together.

"Mabel always makes that same dessert," Addie said, slamming the car door.

"A dessert our waists don't need but our mouths are happy to eat." Beth put her key in the ignition, where it awaited her to start the car. She rolled the window down instead. "You got a cigarette?"

The evening sky was dark, but not so dark to mask Addie's eyebrows arching in surprise. "I thought you quit."

"I did. Last Lent, but sometimes I need a drag or two."

Addie passed her a Lucky Strike. She clicked open the lid of her silver lighter and flicked the flint wheel. Sparks ignited the wick, and seconds later, Beth blew smoke out her mouth in a billowy puff. "Okay, let's hear it."

"Hear what?"

"Cut the crap. You've been dying to tell me everything wrong with Nora and why she's not welcome."

Addie lit her own cigarette, rolled down her window, and blew a puff of smoke into the atmosphere. "For God's sake, Beth. You know what she did to me. What he did to me. How could you even consider being her friend again? After all these years."

"Exactly, after all…these…years." For as strong and smart as Addie had proven to be, Beth couldn't understand how a high-school broken heart had ruined her little sister in small ways. Not that most folks would notice. Giant chunks of Addie's soul had been ripped out and died somewhere during the summer of 1939. Only her stubborn streak survived.

"You're my sister. That's a bond that can't be changed, broken, or diminished. I will always love you. I will always be here for you."

Addie shook her head. "Yeah, I know. You love your family, but you choose your friends. Isn't that what Nora always said?"

"Sure, she said that because she didn't have a sister. Just a mess of brothers who never gave her the time of day until she married well."

Addie huffed. "That she did."

"You know I love you above anyone else, except my kids, of course." Beth rested her case. "What?" she finally asked when no response came.

"I'm waiting for the *but*…"

"There is no *but*," Beth said.

"Then why are we having this conversation?"

Beth didn't answer.

"I'll tell you why. Because you want to pick up where you left off eighteen years ago. I don't…I can't."

"We're different people now," Beth pleaded. "This isn't high school anymore. This is real life."

"Real life. You want to know what's real life? Having your heart squashed by the man you thought loved you and then finding out that he dumped you for your sister's best friend."

Addie tapped the ash off her cigarette, sending residue cascading into the darkening night. "I couldn't even come crying to you." She swallowed. "I turned to Ahren." The words were whispered so quietly Beth could barely hear.

"Playing the heartbroken damsel was your choice. And now you want to blame Nora. Well, baby sister, that ship has sailed. Grow up. And move the hell on."

Addie sucked on the end of her cigarette, filling her lungs before releasing a long, slow stream of smoke through her lips. "You are inviting her to join us?"

"Don't know yet. Either way, this has nothing to do with Barry Gallatin breaking your heart during senior year. Who knows? Maybe she doesn't want anything to do with me, you, or the ladies."

"I doubt that," Addie said. "But I can hope."

"Hope what? That you'll spend the rest of your days envying a life you chose not to live?" Beth tossed her extinguished cigarette butt out the window, turned the key, and the engine jumped to life. "Is that what you want? I hope not. You have a husband who adores you and a son who needs you. And frankly, all of us who love you deserve better than the meager effort you've shown lately."

"You are so dramatic. How do you know what choices I made? This isn't a movie where you get to make big, sweeping statements about my life."

"That's not fair—"

"Fair? You think this is about what's fair?" Beth watched Addie's eyes fire with rage. "You think you know me, but sister, you don't. You haven't known me. I think you never knew me at all."

Beth turned from Addie, moved the gear shift into drive, and pulled away from the curb.

Maybe she didn't know everything there was to know about her sister and that summer. The events after Addie's graduation blurred together. Had she missed something? Something important. Something seminal in Addie's life.

She could keep guessing or ask Addie to tell. But tonight wasn't the time. She'd wait for the right moment. That much she did know.

Addie was as stubborn as a red wine stain on a white silk blouse. Unless you handled her carefully and used the right amount of coaxing, Addie wouldn't budge.

Driving down the quiet street, Beth decided to be patient. With Nora back in town, the long-buried truth, the reason why Addie had never embraced her life, would surface.

And yes, whatever reality faced Addie, Beth would be there for her.

***

Addie quietly turned the key and the knob at the same time, and the front door creaked open, barely wide enough to slip through. Ahren, the lightest sleeper she knew, would awaken at the slightest noise. She wondered if every husband was the same way. She'd ask the girls their opinions at next week's card game.

Ahren had left the ceramic urn-shaped table lamp on, putting their entry awash in a soft light. She hooked her purse and jacket on the brass coat tree rack in the corner, slipped off her kitten heels, and crept up the wooden stairs, careful not to place her entire weight on each step.

Does everything sound louder at night? she thought, climbing to the top. The tiniest noise clattered in her ears. *Probably just nerves.*

Her dress and slip dropped to the bathroom floor. She'd gather them in the morning, she decided, forgoing removing her makeup.

She reached for her robe and tiptoed down the hall past Luke's room, where a stream of light peeked out from beneath his door. *He's home.* Her heart released a cloud of tension. *He's safe.*

Without turning on her bedroom light, she climbed under the covers and gazed at where Ahren slept. He wasn't snoring. This was good and bad news.

"How did the game go?" he asked, his eyes closed.

"You're still awake," she said.

Ahren shifted to his side, facing her. "Of course I am. How could I sleep until I knew you were home?"

"I told you not to wait up," she snapped. "You have to get up early and—"

"Let me worry about me," Ahren said. "And worry about you. That's what I do." He kissed her quickly on her open mouth. "Now I can sleep." He settled back into his pillow. Moments later, a quiet, rhythmic snuffle began.

Asleep. Addie was grateful. Not for the reason she had given the girls earlier. She loved sex with Ahren. He was a patient, generous, and adventurous lover. Her only complaint was that their sex life wasn't as active as it once was.

In the years after Luke was born, they would make love like rabbits, hoping to add a baby brother or sister to the family. Addie enjoyed this part of marriage. Sex was so much better when you weren't an eighteen-year-old girl splayed in the backseat of a Studebaker. Sex was better with commitment. Something a young girl didn't realize, couldn't realize, until she became a woman and a mother.

Knowing that sleep would take a while to visit, Addie plumped her pillow and gazed out her bedroom window. Fortunately for her, her first student wasn't until three that afternoon. *Please, God, let Macy show some improvement. If I have to review the basics one more time, the keyboard cover might slam down with that girl's fingers still on the keys.* Of course, she wouldn't do anything to hurt a student. Still, the idea had appeal.

Addie punched her pillow again and tugged at the quill of a feather poking through the linen pillowcase.

Barry Gallatin is back.

She struggled to think of something else, anything else. Still, Barry's face resurfaced in the space between her thoughts and swirled in front of her eyes.

She hadn't seen him in a dozen years, but she'd recognize the lanky body and that unruly curl of his brown hair. Maybe now there were gray streaks sprinkled in and more meat added to his once-sparse frame. No matter. She'd know her first love from across a room, a street, a football field.

Did he ever grow in that spotty mustache? She absentmindedly ran a finger across the skin above her upper lip and recalled the irritation where Barry's uneven stubble had scratched her skin when they kissed. "This is like making out with sandpaper," she had said. He'd pulled away, insulted at her words.

"Does this mustache make me look older?" he had asked Addie weeks later after they had made love.

Barry was older. Two years older. He had been in college while Addie still struggled with Mrs. Harmond's home economics assignments. Barry Gallatin had a bright future; at the time, Addie believed he was her future.

Had growing a mustache simply been a passing phase of a teenager transforming into a man? Or was it a signature element of his appearance? Like Clark Gable and Yosemite Sam.

Stop thinking about Barry.

Ahren's snores increased in sound and frequency.

Turning away, she pulled the blanket up over her ears. She needed sleep but she didn't want to fall out pondering what might have been. She could deny her feelings. She'd been doing that for nearly two decades with no resolution or relief. The next day, the next hour, the next minute, her thoughts would return, bombarding her with memories of that summer when the man who said he'd always love her married another woman.

She couldn't let Nora into the Sewing Circle. Her only safe bastion. Nothing, even childbirth or alcoholic husbands, canceled their weekly card-playing therapy sessions.

She remembered how pregnant Peg had waited until after they finished their game before calling her husband. An hour later, she had given birth to their third child.

The Sewing Circle had been her oasis when all she imagined was desert.

Nora could not be a part of this. Not today. Not ever.

How could she convince Beth without revealing the improbable bond that kept her heart permanently entwined with Barry's? It wasn't envy. She wasn't jealous of Nora. In many ways, she pitied the woman.

As long as they didn't cross paths, she could manage.

When Barry moved to Pittsburgh, she had breathed a canyon-sized sigh of relief. She could continue to hide the truth of that summer.

Now everything had changed. This new reality hung over her like a guillotine ready to fall. How could she save her family and

Barry's without the truth being exposed for every Keystonian to scrutinize and pass judgment?

She couldn't. Wouldn't let that happen. Not to her. And especially not to Luke.

The sooner the school year ended, and he was on his way to Indiana, the better for everyone. Somehow, she had to keep the status quo until he left for college.

But how?

Chapter Six

Beth wiped sleep from her eyes and turned off the flame under the frying pan where she scrambled eggs. Staying up late had caught up to her. Perhaps after she got the kids off to school, she'd take a nap. She reached for a loaf of bread and turned toward the toaster on the far side of the counter.

"What are you doing?" she barked, watching Ted riffle through her pocketbook.

"You got a five-spot, baby?" he asked.

"Stay out of my purse." The snarl in her voice was so sharp and unexpected, Ted placed the bag on the kitchen table and put his hands up in surrender.

"Sorry. You get the money for me," he demanded. "I need to pay back Abner from last night."

"With my money."

"What money you got? You don't work. I work, cleaning out folks' clogged lines and leaky sinks. When you get a job, then you'll have *your* money. Until then, it's my money, and I let you have some. Right now, I want five dollars back."

"Keep your voice down. The kids will hear."

"Don't care." Ted reached into the purse and extracted Beth's wallet.

"That's grocery money." Beth seized the case from his grasp. "Why do you owe Abner anything anyway?"

"Because while you were out with the *hags* gambling away the mortgage, I was forced to entertain myself at the Red Stone. And by forced, I mean I bought a round for the guys but came up a bit short." Ted chortled. "I gotta go. Are you going to give me that money or…"

Beth didn't want to get to the *or*. The twins and Joel would be downstairs any minute looking for breakfast. She couldn't let them hear this argument. Not that today would be the first time they'd overheard their parents fighting.

Her husband buttoned his blue uniform shirt and tucked the tails into his waistband. The patch sewn above the pocket was coming loose; *TED* embroidered in a hard-to-read script in case a customer wanted to address him by his given name instead of *Hey, Buddy*. She recalled their first date and him telling her he was named after his great-grandfather Theodore, but she could call him Teddy like a loveable, cuddly stuffed bear.

"Want me to run a stitch?" she asked, pointing to where the thread pulled away from the patch.

"No. I don't want you to run a goddamn stitch. I want you to give me five dollars."

Beth unclasped her wallet and fished out five ones. Ted snatched the bills and stuffed them in his front pocket. "See you for dinner," he said, sending a kiss in the air that landed somewhere between them.

A second later, the back door slammed.

Teddy. These days there was nothing soft and cuddly about the man. *But maybe he was right about me getting a job. Wasn't Clara down the street selling Avon? Maybe I could be an Avon lady.*

Opal was the first to push her way through the swinging door, Ruby on her heels. Joel slunk in a few seconds later. She cringed. They had been waiting for their father to leave.

"Smells good in here," Joel said, heading toward the stove. "Are these ready?"

"Fix yourself a plate," she directed. Beth avoided eye contact and busied herself making sandwiches. Bologna, cheese, and ketchup. She cut them in her trademark triangles, the way the kids liked, and covered them in plastic wrap. Alongside each sandwich she placed a banana, a homemade chocolate chip cookie, and a paper napkin.

"I'll skip the eggs, just toast," Opal said, opening the loaf of Wonder Bread her mother had left on the counter.

"I'm not hungry," Ruby said. "I'll eat my banana after first period."

"I want toast, too," Joel added.

"What's happening at school today?" she asked anyone willing to engage in small talk.

Joel shrugged, but Ruby was eager to share what could be considered exciting news to an eleventh grader. "Luke asked Genna to the senior prom," she effused. "Juniors can't go unless a senior asks them." She added this small detail, elevating the importance of the invitation.

"That's very nice of Luke to ask the new girl," Beth said.

"Nice hasn't anything to do with it," Opal chimed. "He could hardly take his eyes off her at Joel's party. Auntie Addie didn't seem happy about that."

"Aw, your aunt isn't happy about most things right now," Beth replied, recalling their conversation from the night before. *Wait until she hears this. She might well blow a gasket if she has any left.*

"Anyhow, he planned to ask Shari Short. She's a shoo-in for prom queen, but he switched and asked Genna. Shari is fuming. Now she has to go with Bart Majors, and everyone knows what a bore he is."

"How do you know so much about this?" Opal asked. "You don't even know Shari Short."

"Do so. We have American lit together."

"I'm in that class too," Opal reminded. "She's never said as much as howdy to me."

"That's 'cause you're not a people person, Opal. Get your nose out of your books and you'd make friends."

"Like Shari who didn't know you existed last week. Hardly," she said, buttering her toast seconds before Joel nabbed them.

"Hey! Mom, look at what—"

"You can make more. And don't burn them this time." Joel pointed to the blackened edges of a slice he'd bitten into.

"Ruby, have you thought about a career in gossip reporting? You could replace Hedda Hopper or Walter Winchell when they retire," Beth said, eyeing Opal placing two fresh slices of bread in the toaster.

"That would be fun," she answered, a prideful air taking over her voice.

42

"But you'd have to learn how to spell," Opal poked. "And figure out those bothersome details like grammar and punctuation."

Ruby shoved her sister's shoulder. "You know so much. You're just jealous that Genna is friends with me."

"She's your friend because Luke is our cousin. She was trying to sweat information out of me last week during gym class."

"Girls." Beth stood between them. "Stop this. Stay out of your cousin's affairs. Eat your breakfast, those of you who are having some, grab your lunches, and start walking to school."

"Aw, Mom, can you drive us? Otherwise, we'll be late," Ruby whined.

"Okay. If you're ready. I have to be at the church by eight, and I don't want to be late either."

"Are you meeting with the *hags*?" Joel chirped.

"Don't use that word."

"Dad does!"

"Your father has a lot of bad habits I don't want you to imitate," Beth said. "Calling people insulting names is one of them. If you want a ride, grab your stuff and get in the car."

"Brilliant," Ruby whispered into Joel's ear. "Get Mom all upset. You're such a loser."

"Ruby! What did I just say about name-calling? The three of you are going to be the death of me." Beth took off her apron and tossed it in their direction. "I'm starting the car. If you're not in a seat when I pull out of the driveway, then you'd better be ready to hit the shoe-leather express."

"So corny, Mom," Ruby said, a laugh lifting the edges of her words.

"Corny but true." Beth left the kitchen, an unsettled niggle vibrating in her chest.

Luke and Genna. That can only lead to trouble. I'd better tell Addie before she hears about this through the grapevine.

***

Stuck in the church hall basement separating other people's treasures from their junk was the last place Addie wanted to be. But that's where she was this Friday morning. Ahren had kissed her goodbye early and wished her a good day, saying he'd be home after work. She didn't worry that he would stop off at the bar for a few, like Ted always did. She was incredibly lucky to be married to him.

"How you raise money for the church building fund from folks' junk is a mystery to me," he had said before disappearing out their bedroom door. He was right, of course. Still, every year St. Gregory's held their bazaar, and as far as Addie was concerned, that was the bizarre part.

"Where do you want me to put these?" she asked Mabel.

"Over there, I guess, for now," she answered, a small tower of pots and pans at her feet. "All this stuff. How will we ever get through everything by next Saturday?"

Addie placed the box of old clothes in the corner of the church hall, along with some twenty others in similar condition. She clapped her hands in a brushing motion, attempting to remove the dust and invisible cooties that surely rode along with these castoffs. Some people just didn't understand—if the garment was so dilapidated you wouldn't wear it, no one else would either. *Don't donate it. Just throw the dang thing away.*

"Who else is coming to help?" she asked, her hair falling out of a loose bun gathered at the nape of her neck.

"Your sister should have been here already. Helene said she had time to help on Monday."

"And Peg?" Addie inquired.

"Well, Peg is lucky to get out for Sewing Circle, so I didn't even bother to ask."

"For the life of me, Mabel, I don't understand why you volunteered to organize this mess. This is the most thankless job of all the thankless jobs."

She laughed. "You should be grateful instead of criticizing me. Your name was next on the list. Father Yusuf was about to lasso you into managing this paradise." Mabel made a sweeping motion with her arm to highlight the mountains of broken appliances, worn-out clothing, and dated pocketbooks littering the room.

"I would have had the sense to say no!"

"Of course you would have. And then, you'd have been the chairman of the fall fundraiser. Face it, Addie. That man doesn't give up. And we're lucky he doesn't. We'd still be waiting to build this hall if he hadn't gotten the congregation working together."

"I know. Next he'll be hounding us to raise money to refinish the basketball court."

"And replace the hoops because Luke wore out the boards this season." Mabel laughed. "You and Ahren must be happy about him getting into Notre Dame."

"We are. He's still gonna have to get a part-time job, even with the scholarship money." Addie breathed deeply. That scholarship was the only reason they could consider college for Luke. Any college. "I can stay for another hour or so. I don't have any lessons until this afternoon. What else can I help with?"

"Can you go through that box over there, the one with the costume jewelry? See if there's anything worth something. Put the good things in one pile. The rest we can sell for a dollar a handful."

Addie dumped the carton filled with a mountain of tangled necklaces, bracelets, and rings—the kind that would turn your skin green if you wore them too long. "Where did all this stuff come from? No one has this much costume jewelry at home."

"True. Old Mrs. Nassar bought old stock from a secondhand dealer for her store but never bothered to sell any. She donated the pieces instead. Said the church needed the money more than she did."

"You mean she unloaded the goods. Judging by what's in here, we may have to pay folks to take this gaudy stuff." She held up a brooch designed in the shape of a flamingo. The pin nearly covered the palm of her hand. "What would you wear this with?"

Mabel stopped what she was doing long enough to look. "Oh dear me. I didn't know you could put that many pink rhinestones on a pin. Must weigh a ton."

Addie moved her open hand cradling the brooch in a slight up-and-down motion as though assaying the piece. "Definitely would tear a hole in any sweater or scarf you pinned it to. Maybe we give this stuff away. You know—free with purchase." The two laughed.

"We won't hear the end of it from Mrs. Nassar's sons."

"Ain't that the truth. Those boys defend their momma like she's the Blessed Mother on loan to Earth."

"The mouth on you," Mabel chided.

Addie laid the pin down next to some equally tacky baubles. "They think she's as pure as the driven snow. Untouched by man or beast. Not sure how they wrap their minds around the fact that they wouldn't be alive if that were true."

"Maybe a second and a third virgin birth," Mabel chortled.

45

"Now who's got the mouth? You blaspheming hussy." Addie raised her eyebrows in exaggerated shock.

"Makes two of us."

"Good thing we're volunteering to do the Lord's work as penance for our evil ways."

Mabel rolled her eyes. "Surely something in there is valuable, relatively speaking."

Addie sniggered, holding up a pair of hoop earrings that resembled spiderwebs. "Value is in the eyes of the beholder. Maybe we could reschedule the sale to before Halloween. Some of this stuff is guaranteed scary."

Mabel hooted. "All kitchen items go on these two tables," she directed and busied herself with a box of donated dishware. "I'll set these up on that table yonder. This is a nice set for someone just starting out. Maybe Luke could use it when he moves."

"That won't be for a few years," Addie said. "He'll be living in the dorms for now. Who knows what he'll do once he graduates? He may not even come back here. He's gonna discover a whole new world."

"Think he's good enough to become a pro?" Mabel asked.

"Maybe. I don't know if he's interested in that. But getting a college degree, now that will be something. He'll be able to get out of Keystone and not work for the coal industry." *And the Gallatins.*

"Your boy is so tall. Basketball may be his ticket." Mabel plunked a stack of saucers next to a matching set of teacups. "What do you feed him? Whatever it is, Ahren's momma didn't give him any."

Addie ignored the jab at her husband's height, the focus of many discussions over the years.

"Who's clomping down the steps? Why, I bet it's my big sister. And look, Mabel, she's out of breath. Thought you were in better shape than that," Addie said, her hands on her hips.

"Sorry I'm late," Beth said once she hit the bottom step. "And I'm not out of shape, I'll have you know. I was rushing. Seems like all I do is rush around these days."

"Don't worry," Mabel said. "Addie's been keeping me company unearthing the Nassar family's buried treasures."

Addie scoffed. "These things should have stayed buried. Can I interest you in a glitzy flamingo pin? Hardly worn. In fact, I'll guess it's never been worn."

Beth moved to where Addie stood pointing at the brooch on the table. "Reminds me of something Ted bought when we were in Florida for our honeymoon. I buried it in the bottom of my jewelry box. I'd be happy to donate mine if you think we could sell the pair."

Addie and Mabel couldn't contain their laughter. "We'd be lucky to sell one," Mabel said. "Addie suggested that we slip a piece of this junk jewelry in every bag when the customer isn't looking."

Tears of laughter streamed down Addie's cheeks, and she swiped them away. "We're not supposed to be having this much fun," she said, barely containing herself.

"No fun allowed here," Beth declared, sending the trio into another round of raucous guffaws.

"We're going to the devil, the lot of us."

"Well, we'll be in good company," Mabel said, taking control. "Beth, start sorting clothes. Men's. Women's. Children. Do the best you can, and we'll help when we get done with these boxes."

"Absolutely," Beth agreed, dumping her purse on a nearby chair.

"But wouldn't it be more fun to help me in the baubles department," Addie taunted, dangling two fringed earrings in front of her chest as though they were nipple tassels.

"Pretty much anything is more fun than rummaging through other folks' old clothes," Beth said before looking at her sister. "What in God's name are you doing?"

"I'm Gypsy Rose Lee," Addie declared, swinging her hips and twirling the earrings as though they were attached to her breasts.

"Va-va-vooooom!" Mabel howled. "You missed your calling. Should have been a stripper instead of a piano teacher."

"You really can keep them spinning," Beth said. "Mom and Dad would have been so proud to have a burlesque star in the family."

Addie took a bow. "Knew I could be a star somewhere," she said, setting the earrings down on the table before retrieving the next piece of showy jewelry to display. "I thought you'd be here at eight."

Beth scowled. "I meant to be, but my morning went sideways. The kids were late for school, so I had to give them a ride, and then Joel's teacher asked if I could spare thirty minutes to help her with reading circles. Glenn Morgan's mother was supposed to be there and had to cancel at the last second."

"It's no problem," Mabel said. "We still have another week to get ready."

"I hate being late. And I hate not living up to my promises." Beth grounded the words in such an exaggerated way that Addie knew there was more to her sister's reasons for being tardy.

"Well, one thing we can do," Addie interrupted, "is ask more than our friends to volunteer. How many women are part of the church's ladies' guild?"

"I don't know," Mabel said.

"There's more than five names on that roster."

"Adele Frances. Stop picking on Mabel."

"I'm not picking on anyone. I'm angry that it's always our small group doing the large work of this church." Addie nearly snorted, feeling a step above those lackadaisical women who showed up for mass and disappeared just as quickly.

"We need to expand our circle," Beth said.

The hairs on the back of Addie's neck stood on end. "What do you mean?"

"I'm not talking about the Sewing Circle, silly. I mean our circle of volunteers. Maybe more of the ladies would step up if we didn't appear so closed off. Could be it's our fault that some of the gals don't join in."

"That's ridiculous," Mabel said. "Why would we want to keep all this fun to ourselves?"

"Just sayin', things appear a bit different when you're on the outside looking in. We see it as no one will help. Maybe they see it as we're simply fine without them." Beth stared, forcing Addie to turn away.

"People aren't helping because they don't want to," Addie snapped. "Otherwise, they'd be here. Mabel posted sign-up sheets at all the masses. The same names appeared. The same names that always show up."

Beth unpacked a box filled with scarves and shawls. "Who donates these treasures?" she asked no one in particular. "We might actually sell some." Beth twirled, modeling a burgundy shawl with lace appliqués.

"Is that satin?" Mabel asked.

"Feels more like silk. Definitely wouldn't keep you warm," Beth replied, swirling the fabric around like a matador taunting a bull.

"That's lovely," Addie said. "Are there any more like it?"

"So we can dress alike?" Beth teased. "I always hated that when we were little."

"No, I don't want to look like you," Addie retorted. "Wonder if there are more nice pieces in that pile."

Beth rummaged, then held up two handfuls of silky scarves. "There are a few."

"Maybe this bazaar won't be a bust after all," Mabel said, relief dotting her words.

"You're open to recruiting more hands?" Beth asked, picking up the thread of their conversation.

"Of course," Addie answered for herself and Mabel. "We're not crazy."

"Great. I'm going to reach out to Nora and see if she has anything to donate and if she'd help us set up on bazaar day."

Beth's declaration flew past Addie's ears with such force that she reached for the banquet table to steady herself.

"Nice setup, but nope. No Nora. Get it? There's no Nora," she said, slicing her gaze from Beth to Mabel. "No Nora."

"If Addie's uncomfortable, then we need to find volunteers other than…" Mabel said supportively.

Beth continued separating the shawls and scarves into piles. "Addie, you're being childish."

Addie's pulse quickened so much she consciously took a deep, extended breath before answering. "Maybe so, but I can't pretend to like her, and I won't pretend that what happened—even though for you it's ancient history—doesn't matter. It mattered then. It matters now."

"Then what are you going to do on prom night?" Beth said as though detonating a grenade.

"What are you talking about?"

"You always go to the girl's house with Luke to take a photo of him and his date."

"Yes…and your point?"

"You'll have to speak to Nora then."

"Why in the world would I need to talk to Nora? Shari Short—" Addie swallowed.

"Luke didn't tell you he asked Gemma to the dance?"

49

Addie's head swam with denial. Beth had to be lying. But she knew her sister wouldn't cavalierly toss a bomb like that without reason.

How would she know? How *could* she know?

Opal and Ruby. Girls talk to their mothers; boys don't—other than to ask: "What's for dinner?" How did this relationship move along so fast? Luke had dumped the head cheerleader for a girl who just moved back into town? A girl he could never have?

Addie tossed a handful of rope necklaces into a box. "I've got to go."

"You said you were available until this afternoon," Mabel protested.

"Just remembered something I need to do." Addie grabbed her coat and purse and headed toward the stairs, but Beth blocked her way.

"I didn't mean to upset you. Thought you'd want to know, and I thought Luke might not tell you."

"Yeah, like you dropping the news on me with your velvet fist is so much better."

"Please." Beth moved closer, but Addie put her hand up.

"I'm not mad at the messenger. I just need to work a few things out, okay?"

"Luke going to a dance with Barry's daughter isn't the end of the world." Beth sounded so much like their mother when she put on her authoritarian voice that Addie's jaw tightened.

"Don't lecture me about something you don't understand."

"I don't want you driving while you're upset."

"I'm fine. I'll call you later tonight, okay?"

"If I don't hear from you by eight, I'm coming to your house."

Addie turned to Mabel. "Sorry to leave you in the lurch, but Beth is a great belly dancer. Ask her to entertain you with that pile of scarves she's sorting."

She dashed out, not waiting for either woman's response.

Chapter Seven

Addie reached her car in the church parking lot and leaned against the door, still sifting through Beth's words. A spring breeze swept by, doing little to minimize the bubbles of sweat gathering along her brows and upper lip. She placed her hand on her chest, attempting to quell her pounding heart. *You'll have to speak to Nora.*

Maybe that was the answer. Not telling Nora the truth, of course, but using her to convince Genna to not go to the dance with Luke out of respect for Addie.

She could imagine how that conversation would go down. Addie would come out looking like a loser who couldn't recover from a high-school broken heart. And Genna would still go to the dance with Luke. No teenage girl ever listened to her mother about anything that had to do with boys. Ever.

What else could she do? Forbid Luke from going to the prom with a pretty girl? Because that's all her son would see when he looked at Genna. A beautiful young woman, a new conquest. Maybe that was the attraction. She was someone new, a sparkly distraction from the girls he had known. She would seem glamorous having lived in a big city. Before long, their friendship would turn stale. Genna would join the other giddy young ladies and become boring and unexciting to Luke.

That was the outcome Addie sought. She didn't have time to wait, though, for things to unfurl naturally. And there was the added worry that this relationship wasn't a passing fling.

Addie needed to get Luke on his way to Notre Dame before he decided he was in love with Genna. He wouldn't be leaving until the end of June—two months away—two months too long for her to keep them apart.

Why couldn't Nora and Barry have waited another year before moving back?

By next April, Luke would have nearly finished his freshman year, met women from other parts of the country, and not been interested in the new girl at Keystone High. He would have been on his way to a new life, a better life than he would have known had he stayed in southwestern Pennsylvania.

The town gossips said Nora had returned to care for her mother. Even Mrs. Garza had told Beth the same. A noble motivation to be sure.

But Barry Gallatin never did anything that didn't benefit Barry Gallatin. His mother-in-law's well-being wouldn't have been a strong enough enticement for him to relocate in his hometown and all the history he wanted to stay in the past.

There had to be another reason, a more compelling incentive. What was Barry getting out of this?

As she drove with the top down, Addie could think of nothing else. The stream of scenarios flowing through her mind entertained every possibility from the absurd to the criminal.

Could Barry be involved in something illegal? Embezzlement, perhaps?

An affair with a major client's wife? Maybe Nora triggered this quick return.

Something happened. Something big to pull their three children out of school before the end of the semester, but what? And how could she find out?

Their oldest son, Dante, was in the same grade as Luke. Poor kid. Had to finish his senior year at a new school.

Maybe he's part of the puzzle. At the very least, he could answer some questions if I could get a chance to talk to him.

Addie would get to the bottom of Barry's relocation. She could count on Keystone's army of wagging tongues. Someone knew the truth, and she'd be damned if she couldn't figure out who did.

None of that mattered now, though. She needed to squelch Luke and Genna's romance and fast.

As she pulled onto Main Street heading toward home, the fragments of a plan formed, causing Addie's mouth to tip up in the slightest of smiles.

A minute later, she unlocked her front door and hurried through. She headed toward the parlor, where the telephone directory sat perched on a small wooden stand under their rotary phone. She thumbed through the tissue-paper-thin pages until she found the number.

Addie dialed and breathed a sigh of relief when her call was answered. Maybe solving this would be easier than she thought.

***

Later that day, Addie sat on the piano bench alongside her newest student, helping the teen with proper placement on the keys.

"There, dear. That's what I call your piano hand," Addie said, admiring Shari's slender fingers formed in a *C* shape. "It will feel awkward for a while, but the more you practice, the more comfortable you will feel. Before you know it, this will become second nature."

"I hope so. Right now, I feel like a clod," Shari said, turning frequently to glance over her shoulder. Her blonde ponytail nearly swatted Addie's face each time the girl swung around to get a view of the door.

She needed Shari to stay put until Luke got home. When she invited her, Addie had mentioned Luke. Not anything specific, but just enough encouragement to make Shari believe that her former boyfriend was behind the idea. What was taking him so long? Practice for the spring league should have ended forty minutes ago.

Addie continued her ploy of experienced teacher to novice pupil, noticing for the first time how shaky her own hands were next to Shari's. "Everyone is unsure of themselves at first."

Shari nodded, her anxiety seeming to build with every moment.

"Being nervous is part of the process," Addie continued, tilting her body so she faced the girl. "It must be much harder to lead all those cheers in front of bleachers full of your friends and family. You never stumble or miss a beat."

Shari beamed at the compliment. "Thank you, Mrs. Burhan, for offering to teach me for free. I've always wanted to learn, but somehow…"

Buttering up Shari Short was taking more energy than she would have suspected. The pressure of running this gambit by having her in their home without Luke's knowledge mounted.

This meeting would go one of two ways. She mentally crossed her fingers that her son's reaction would favor her will and not go off the rails to where she would have no choice other than to tell Luke the truth.

"I'm happy to teach you," Addie said. "So let's get started. I'm going to play a four-note ditty, and I want you to replicate the pattern."

"I'm not sure what you mean," Shari said.

"Here, I'll show you. And remember, this is supposed to be fun." Addie played a simple musical arrangement. "Now your turn."

Addie jumped at the sound of a slamming door.

"Mom, I'm home," Luke hollered, speeding through the living room. He stopped when he spotted Shari and his mother seated at the piano near the picture window.

"What are you doing here?" Annoyance permeated Luke's voice, but Addie couldn't tell who he was irked with.

Shari stuttered. "Well, uh, your mom invited me. She's teaching me how to play," she added quickly, pointing at the keyboard.

"I see that." Luke turned toward his mother. "Can I talk to you?"

"Sure, honey. I'll be done with Shari in about twenty minutes."

"I mean now!"

Addie flinched at the harshness in Luke's words. "You're behaving rudely. I'll not have you—"

"Fine, then I'll just say it in front of Shari. Why did you invite her here? She's not my girlfriend anymore."

"I offered to instruct our neighbor. That's what I do. I teach piano." Addie replied, realizing the cruel mistake she had made inviting this innocent girl into her melodrama.

Luke tapped his sneaker against the floor as though stalling for time. Finally he said, "Shari, it's best that you leave. I'm sorry my mom pulled you into this."

"Pulled her into what?" Addie demanded.

Luke stared his mother down. "You know. I don't know how you found out so fast, but it doesn't matter," he said. "This is none of your business, Mom."

He turned to face Shari, who quickly gathered her belongings. "Shar, we've had some laughs, and you're swell and all...but I like Genna, and that's who I'm taking to the prom."

"Well, Luke Burhan, if you think I came over here to beg you to take me to the dance, then you're sorely mistaken." Shari painted each word in layers of indignation. "I only agreed to this, well...I don't know why I agreed, except for maybe I thought we might talk. But it seems that your mind is made up." Shari raced toward the front door.

"Shari, honey, please allow me to apologize for my impolite son. He wasn't raised like that, and I don't know what's gotten into him."

Shari's lower lip quivered; her eyes glistened with unspilled tears.

What have I done? Addie thought, realizing she hadn't considered Shari's feelings in her scheme. She couldn't distract Luke with another pretty girl, especially one he had history with.

"Really, dear, if you would like to learn to play, I would be so happy to teach you," Addie continued, following the stunned lass out the door and onto the porch.

"I don't think so," Shari said, tears now streaming.

"I'm so sorry," Addie said, no other words coming to mind. "I had no idea."

Shari bobbed her head and set out down the street as fast as her feet would allow.

When Addie turned around, Luke's tall figure filled the door frame. She had never seen such a scowl on his face, a mixture of anger and cynicism glowering through. She didn't know which emotion pierced her soul more—her son's rage or his disappointment—although for what she had done, she deserved both.

"How could you?"

"How could I what?" There was no acceptable answer for the ruse she had concocted. Yes, she was as much a domineering, meddlesome mother as all her friends, but even they would condemn this as going too far.

"Stop messing in my life. You don't have say over who I see. And you certainly can't invite girls over here and try to set me up with them. Especially an ex-girlfriend."

"Luke, I don't know—"

"Save it." Luke snapped, backing inside. "You're not being fair to me or to Shari," he barked once Addie appeared in the entry.

"I didn't know that you and Shari had..."

"Of course you did. I'm guessing that Aunt Beth told you." Addie remained still.

"I thought so. Even for you, this is too much." His voice grew in fury and disbelief.

"Luke, I..."

"I know you liked her dad a long time ago, but seriously, that was before I was even born."

Addie folded her hands and stared at the ground. There was no defense. No words to right this wrong. She stood there listening to him rant, a rant, under different conditions, he had every right to unleash.

"I'm not going to stop seeing Genna because her daddy broke your heart."

Addie's head snapped back. "Who told you that?"

"You did, pretty much every time you say how things could have been different had you married Barry Gallatin."

Addie's blood pressure rose some ten points at the truth coming out of her son's mouth. "I have never said anything—"

"Not to me, but to Dad, over and over. I can hear when you fight."

Addie plopped into a nearby chair and lowered her head, both hands pressed firm against herself as though her heart would explode through her chest if she moved them.

Breathe.

Her precious son had heard everything. She pictured how his frightened little face must have looked when he was five and again at ten. Did he hold his hands over his ears? Did he cry? Every kid worried when their parents fought.

Parents fight. That's part of the landscape of families, Addie told herself. She also knew that minimizing her previous actions wouldn't help.

She needed to fix this, but how? Her chest, now a drumbeat of anxiety, pounded. How could she explain to her eighteen-year-old son about the woman she was at his age?

Impossible. She was in an impossible situation.

Addie took another deep breath. When she looked up, Luke stood before her, not with the face of a child, but a grown man.

And for the first time, she clearly saw his real father burnishing through. That tenacity, that stubborn streak.

She braced for him to yell, but instead, his voice was soft.

"I don't know how else to say this. I like Genna. I really like her. There is something about her I can't put my finger on. She's like no other girl I've ever known." Luke paused as though giving his mother time to absorb his words. The serious flash in his eyes made Addie's stomach clench.

She would have to tell him. She would be the one to shatter his heart into a million pieces.

"I don't have anything against Genna," Addie began.

"If you gave her half a chance, you'd probably like her—if for a second you could forget that her last name is Gallatin."

"Luke, I know you think I'm foolish."

"I don't know what to think. I can't talk about this anymore," he said, regaining his earlier anger. "Promise that you'll *never* invite a girl over without talking to me first."

"I promise." Addie hesitated. "Luke—"

He was gone before she could continue.

What now? Dear God, what do I do?

How many lives might I ruin to save Luke from my terrible mistake?

Chapter Eight

Addie stood silent, shocked at the intensity of Luke's reaction. Obviously, she had underestimated her son's attraction to Genna.

It's not too late. It can't be.

She jumped at the vicious slamming of the front door and scurried to peer through the partially opened sheers in the living room. She watched Luke hustle down the sidewalk. He fled in the same direction Shari had taken.

Addie was fairly certain he wasn't going after her, though. If she guessed, Luke was headed to his best friend Bucky's house, a safe haven to cool off and perhaps rethink his actions. Addie could only hope, but she knew hope didn't get you the results you wanted. You had to do more than cross your fingers and wish. You had to act.

But what could she do? Forbid him to leave the house until he started college? The mere idea was a joke. She and Ahren had cultivated Luke to be a free thinker, to choose the road not taken. Their efforts to instill an independent mindset in their son had paid off—until now.

Addie had witnessed her son's temper at every age and tantrum level. She had been the object of his aggression and disappointment on many occasions.

But today's words—how he said them and their strong meaning—foretold the thinking of a boy-turning-man.

She and Ahren had prepared Luke for this day and the world as they knew it. A world that challenged you to pursue your dreams, not wait for them to arrive, helter-skelter, on their own.

She'd witnessed how compromise had changed Ahren. She wouldn't let Luke make that same mistake.

A pang of sorrow pierced Addie's heart. This horrible timing had turned her into Luke's enemy. The clingy mother who couldn't let go of her son; a broken woman not mature enough to handle a youthful heartbreak.

She yanked off her shoes and raced out the door, her stocking feet drumming against the pavement, but gave up after two blocks. He moved too quickly, and she wasn't sure what to say, even if she caught up to him.

Addie bent over and held on to her thighs, panting. It took her a few moments to gather herself before turning around. As she strolled back to her house, a cacophony of solutions bombarded her brain, but the same one continued to rise to the fore.

How could the right answer be so wrong?

Addie grabbed her keys and headed toward the car, but stopped on the front porch, hopelessly wishing for another alternative— one less distasteful—to magically appear. She lifted her gaze to the dusk-painted sky and prayed for a simpler remedy to a problem that was anything but simple.

She glanced at her watch. *A quarter till six.* If she was going to do this, she needed to leave now, before Ahren got home. As she jammed the key into the ignition, the distinct rumble of a coal truck pulling up to the curb filled the air. But before she could put the car in gear and back out of the driveway, she heard a rap on the car fender.

Addie rolled the window down and took in the familiar figure, his clothes coated with black dust. Ahren stood alongside the car, his tired eyes staring back.

"You're going out?" he asked, disappointment ever so slight in his words.

"Not for long. I've gotta run to Beth's. There's leftover chicken in the refrigerator if you get hungry," she said, gushing her excuse before she lost her nerve.

"And Luke?" Ahren asked, scratching his head.

"He's at a friend's house. He'll be home after dinner," Addie replied, hoping that was somewhat close to the truth.

She blew him a kiss, put the car in reverse, and backed out. She waved as she pointed her car in the opposite direction of Beth's. *A weary Ahren won't notice,* she hoped.

Addie forced air through her lungs in deliberate gulps and exhaled hard, willing calm to replace the panic surging inside. Her hands shook, and just the least little bit of sweat gathered under her nose. She swiped at the beads and continued her deep breathing.

Before long, rows of simple clapboard houses of her friends and neighbors appeared. Just the thought of these folks brought a grin to her lips. These modest homes erected side by side, each with a small, neatly mowed lawn, anchored the stability of the town she had grown up in. These people were the heart and soul of Keystone, the very definition of hometown.

A peacefulness cloaked her, and her heart rate relaxed. This little city was her birthplace, her refuge. Barry and Nora had abandoned this town and its people years ago. As far as Addie was concerned, they forfeited their claim to its sweet sanctuary now.

The farther she drove toward the outskirts, the more the landscape changed, and the frequency of buildings thinned. Clusters of cozy homes whose backyards touched each other were now replaced with great expanses between dwellings, rolling lawns so deep and wide all you could see was the driveway leading up to a great house.

Before long, Addie pulled to the side of the road and parked. Still not certain how she'd start this conversation, she quieted the engine and remained in the car. Across the way stood Barry and Nora's residence, magnificent and stately. From her vantage point, Addie took in the lights emanating from the second floor as well as the lantern illuminating the portico. A single car rested idle in the semicircular driveway.

"I have no other choice," she declared to the emptiness inside her vehicle. "I'll just tell them the truth. They'll be upset, maybe even mad, but they'll get over the hurt and see things for what they are." She reached for her purse and sucked in an even breath.

Somewhere deep inside, she would find the nerve to talk to Barry. Things would be easier if Nora weren't there, but if she were...well, that couldn't be helped.

They are both reasonable people. They used to live in the big city, after all. This sort of thing is commonplace in metropolitan circles, right? Addie knew she was stalling the inevitable with this mental pep talk. She tipped her head against the seat and closed her eyes to clear her mind and organize her speech.

Where do I start? What if he wants to know why I didn't tell him before? How do I keep him from telling Luke? And Ahren? Poor, dear Ahren. What will he do when he finds out? Because he will find out. There has to be another way. Any other way that won't hurt the people I love.

Addie opened her eyes at the sharp rev of a car engine. She looked out her window in time to see Barry speed past, the red taillights of his Cadillac dimming in the night as he disappeared down the street.

Damn, did I doze off? She glanced at her watch. An hour had passed since she parked.

Addie slammed her palm against the steering wheel in frustration, but a small twitter of relief released in her chest. Maybe this was for the best. Tonight wasn't the right time. She didn't have the right words.

She started her car, resigned that this news could wait one more day. And maybe in that time, things would change, and she wouldn't have to reveal her choice of so many years ago.

As Addie pulled onto the street headed in the opposite direction from Barry, another question whirled in her mind.

Where was he going?

***

Beth leaned against the dining room china closet, telephone receiver to her ear, stretching the cord from the kitchen wall phone about as far as the coil would allow. *Answer the phone,* she pleaded into the handset, praying Addie would pick up. The clattery ring repeated with no answer.

She had been phoning since six thirty. Now, half past eight, the nighttime had swept in like a graying mist. Beth searched out the dining-room window as though Addie might appear. The street, blanketed in inky darkness, stared back. The sparse light offered from the streetlamp did little to illuminate Addie's whereabouts.

Where are you? Why isn't anyone answering the phone?

She hung up at the sound of Ted's voice in the kitchen. "Where's your mother?" he asked Opal. "She home?"

"Of course I'm home. Where else would I be?" Beth said, storming into the kitchen, returning the beige receiver into the cradle where the base hung near the door. "Where have *you* been?"

"Don't start with me." Ted opened their refrigerator, stared inside as though searching for something he couldn't find. He grabbed a beer and popped the cap with a Labatt's bottle opener, a prized promotional giveaway that he kept in his front pants pocket.

"I have homework," Opal had declared before hurrying out.

"Great, now you're scaring the kids." Ted laughed, dropping into the kitchen chair recently vacated by their daughter. "I'm hungry. Got anything to eat?"

"Your plate's warming in the oven," Beth said, sliding her hand into an oven mitt. She set meatloaf, green beans, and mashed potatoes on the table in front of him.

Ted took a pull from his beer. "Aw, sweetie, you made my favorites." He reached for her arm, yanked her to him, and patted her butt.

"Not now, Ted," she hissed. "The kids are still awake."

"It's good for them to see their parents being affectionate."

The odor of sour mash and burnt hops permeated Beth's nostrils as he spoke, making her turn her head.

"Don't look away," Ted growled, shifting Beth's face toward his.

She accepted his sloppy kiss and moved to the other side of the kitchen. "Later, Ted," she directed, hoping he'd pass out before she made the climb upstairs to their bedroom in an hour.

"Who were you on the phone with?" Ted asked, inadvertently showing a mouthful of food.

"No one."

"Aw, honey, don't lie to me. I heard you." Ted put his fork down and grabbed the beer. He took a swig and waited.

"So now you're jealous?" Beth immediately regretted her gibe, not certain how much her husband had drunk before coming home. If he'd been mixing in whiskey with his beer—the way his breath smelled—he might blow his top.

Beth chased her cheeky retort with a vague explanation. "I wasn't talking to anyone. I called Addie, but she didn't answer."

"Isn't it late to be calling? She's probably asleep," Ted said. "Maybe she's sleeping off all that port she drank at Joel's party."

Beth had forgotten how much wine her sister consumed that evening. Was that the beginning of all this? The night she met Genna Gallatin? "Actually, Ted, I'm getting worried about her."

"You're worried about Addie. That's a laugh."

"I know you two don't always get along, but—"

"Not so." Ted waggled an inebriated finger back and forth.

Beth breathed a relieved huff, recognizing this happy-drunk gesture.

Operating under the right balance of alcohol pulsing through his veins, a happy-drunk Ted could be very insightful. He offered perceptive, shrewd, and often intuitive opinions that occasionally escaped Beth.

"That broad is tough as nails," Ted continued, "and she scares the crap out of me." He chuckled and took a swig. "Imagine what she does to poor Ahren."

Beth frowned. "Stop. I really mean it. She was supposed to call me tonight, but she didn't. She's so upset about Nora and Barry's moving back that she isn't behaving normal."

"Huh. How can you tell what's normal for Addie? She's always acting crazy in some way or another."

"This is different. She's behaving irrationally about simple stuff, things that don't really matter," Beth defended.

"Your sister always makes too much out of every goddamn thing. I'm so glad you're not that way. We wouldn't still be married if you were," Ted declared. "But with Ahren, well, that's a different story. He's so pussy-whipped."

"Stop being vulgar!" Beth shouted. "You're talking about my sister, remember?"

"I definitely remember. We both know who wears the pants in that family. Addie pretty much does what she wants to do. She's selfish. If she didn't call you, well, that suits her fine. Don't ruin our evening because of her." Ted finished the last swallow from his beer, released an extended yawn, and stared at Beth as though his summary of her sister's shortcomings answered every question.

Two of the most important people in her world were bullheaded, obstinate, and stubborn. Neither backed down from anything. Theirs was an oil-and-vinegar relationship. Addie and Ted were forced together because of family, but as soon as they could, they'd separate.

She cleared Ted's dinner plate and empty beer bottle. "Get some rest. I'll be up in a little bit," she said. *After I get hold of my sister.*

"Okay." Ted rose slowly as though waiting for his feet to stabilize underneath him. "I've had a tough day. I might be asleep before you." He pecked her cheek. "Nice dinner," he added before leaving.

Beth waited a beat, listening to the sound of Ted's steps fade. She scurried to the phone and redialed the familiar number. It rang once, twice, three times before a voice said, "Hello."

"Ahren?" Beth asked.

"Oh, hi, Beth," he said, punctuating his reply with a long yawn.

"Can I speak to Addie?"

"Addie?" He yawned again, not as long or as loud as the first time. "Huh, she's not home. She took off before dinner. Thought she was with you," Ahren said, confused now that he was more awake.

Beth hesitated to answer. What could she say? How could she cover for Addie? And where in the heck was her sister anyway?

"You still there?"

"Yes, Ahren, I'm here."

"Oh wait. I hear the front door closing. Addie, honey?" Ahren asked. Beth couldn't decipher the mumbled response. "Your sister's on the phone."

Beth's heart pounded harder, waiting a full minute or more before hearing Addie's voice.

"It's awfully late to be calling," Addie said, her tone as smooth as silk. "Is everything all right?"

Beth wanted to come through the telephone line at her. "Where have you been?" she growled, her pulse struggling to regain normalcy.

"Glad to hear it."

"Hear what?" Beth snapped. "You said you'd call tonight, and you didn't. What's going on?"

"Great. Can't talk now. We'll talk in the morning. Good night," Addie said, emphasizing *night* with a lilt.

Beth stared at the receiver seething at her sister's inconsiderate attitude.

Ted's right. Addie does damn well what Addie wants to do. Her promises don't mean a thing.

Beth finished straightening up the kitchen and headed toward her bedroom, feeling guilty for judging her little sister so harshly. Addie was a free spirit, that's true, but she wouldn't knowingly worry or upset Beth.

What are you afraid to tell me?
Or is it something I should already know?

Chapter Nine

The next morning through her kitchen window, Beth took in the golden rays dusting her backyard and imagined where wildflowers would soon bloom. Black-eyed Susans with a smattering of wild bergamot would be the first to explode against the barren ground, leaving winter a distant memory.

She finished the breakfast dishes and made a vague excuse to Opal, Ruby, and Joel about running an errand. Ted was still sleeping off last night's booze, so before he woke, she drove straight to Addie's house and pounded on the door three times before her sister answered, still in her bathrobe and slippers.

"You can't hang up on me in person. I want to know what's going on," Beth demanded, pushing her way into the house.

"Well, good morning to you, too," Addie said, running a hand through her obviously uncombed hair. "Why are you here so early?"

"Early? It's after eight. Why are you still in your pjs?"

"Because it's Saturday? People sleep in on Saturdays, so can you lower your voice? Ahren and Luke are still in bed."

Beth huffed. "Well maybe you should get dressed then, and we can go out for a cup of coffee. You have some explaining to do."

Addie remained silent as though digging her heels in like she did when they were children, taking the contrary position. The discussion could be about ice cream flavors or radio shows, it didn't matter. Beth knew her sister would put up a fuss just because she could. Not once did she make things easy.

Beth tugged the sides of her cardigan sweater together, realizing that the air carried a chill. She lowered her voice. "Why did you tell Ahren you were at my house last night?"

Addie rolled her eyes, but Beth knew the question had jarred her sister. "Okay. Okay. Let me get dressed. I'll meet you at Smithey's in fifteen minutes."

"I'll wait here," she said, not agreeing to cool her heels at the corner coffee shop, hoping Addie showed.

Addie sighed resolutely. "If you weren't my sister…"

"If I weren't your sister, I wouldn't be worried sick. Go put some clothes on." Beth crossed her arms and tapped her foot, the way their mother used to do when the girls were goofing off.

Addie raced up the staircase. Seconds later, Beth overheard her giving Ahren another excuse for her leaving and him complaining slightly that she had been gone with Beth the night before.

After what seemed to be an excessive amount of time, Addie emerged in a matching sweater set and capris, her makeup impeccable. She bounded down the steps, her unruly chestnut curls bouncing against the top of her head. The sisters had the same hair color, but Beth still preferred Addie's tresses to her own.

"What took you so long?" Beth asked, glancing at the shabby housedress under her sweater she'd thrown on an hour before.

"Unlike you, I don't appear in public looking any old way." Addie slipped her pocketbook onto her arm. "Are you driving or am I?"

Beth grabbed her by the other arm. "Let's walk and talk. More private that way."

***

The pair wasn't five feet from Addie's front porch before Beth lit into her. "What is going on with you?"

"Me?" Addie pulled away.

"Yes, you. You're being so secretive and, well, erratic," Beth snapped. "And that's saying something because you're generally unpredictable, but this is…the way you're acting…there's a guarded air about you."

Addie stared away from her sister's puzzled expression and blinked, anything to avoid giving an answer. She increased her gait. Maybe if she hurried, Beth would stop the inquisition, although she knew that wouldn't happen.

Beth continued, "What can be so bad that you're sneaking around? Lying to Ahren?"

"I'm not sneaking around. I just needed a little time, ya know? Time to sort my thoughts out and…"

"About what? Luke's new girlfriend?" Beth stopped suddenly, causing Addie to alter her pace and trip on the uneven sidewalk. "You okay?" she asked, reaching for her sister's shoulder to steady her.

"Fine. I'm fine. Will you stop asking?"

"See? That's what I mean. You fly off the handle at any little comment."

Addie stared at her shoes, not moving forward or back, delaying the inevitable. How could she lie to Beth? Again. What she needed was time, time to devise a better plan.

"Addie, please. You're scaring me. What is wrong?"

She's asking because she cares. And I can't tell her the truth for the same reason. Not after all these years. I've got to tell her something. But what?

Beth waited and waited. Addie knew Beth would win the waiting game. Her big sister had the patience of a champ. Beth's ability to manipulate her into saying and doing whatever she wanted was legendary. They'd been dancing to this song since Addie was in diapers.

Beth, perfect Beth, always getting what she wants. Always making the right choice, the best decision. How would she feel once she learned of the choice Addie had made?

Before Addie could dream up a response, Beth gasped.

"Oh. My. God. Why didn't I see this before?"

"What are you babbling about now?" Addie asked, watching the color drain from her sister's olive complexion.

"You're having an affair with Barry."

"Are you crazy? You of anyone should know that's the last thing I'd ever do. I'm hurt that you'd even think that of me," Addie protested, feigning offense. But Beth appeared unconvinced.

"Ever since they moved back, you've acted like a squirrel greedily gathering nuts. Like you have to protect everything that's yours."

"What in the world are you talking about?"

"Every time I bring the Gallatins up, bring Nora up, you flip out."

Addie couldn't deny the fact, but Beth's conclusion, now that was a different matter. "I tried to tell you that—"

"Hi, girls!" A sweet voice pierced the air. "Where are you headed this fine morning?"

The sisters swiveled to take in their friend's approach.

"We'll finish this later," Beth hissed under her breath. "Peg." Her greeting held a lighter tone, and Addie breathed an inward sigh for this reprieve.

Peg may have saved Addie for the moment, but Beth was tenacious when she wanted to be. And today, she really wanted to be. She wouldn't let up until she got answers. Addie toyed with going along with the affair story. *Might be better for her to think of me as an adulteress than to find out who I really am.*

Beth opened her arms wide to accept Peg's hug. "You've already been to the market?"

Peg shifted the nearly-full paper sack to her left arm, accepting Beth's hug. She moved toward Addie for a quick embrace and stepped back. "Just needed a few things, so I ran to Cowan's," she said, pointing to the items.

"They open early on Saturday," Addie stated.

"Yeah. A whole hour before the supermarket. Lucky for me. I was out of eggs. And of course, Cal wanted an omelet for breakfast."

Peg smiled, unintentionally highlighting the purplish bruise on her cheek. The swelling, the size of a dollar pancake, slowly morphed into an ugly mixture of magenta-green.

"Better get going. See you on Thursday." Peg turned to leave, then stopped. "Hey," she said conspiratorially. "Wanna know the real reason the Gallatins moved back?"

Addie's heart seized.

"What are you talking about?" Beth asked.

"Well, I was just chatting with old Mrs. Cowan, and it seems there were some problems with their older son Dante. She didn't know any details."

"That sounds ridiculous," Beth said.

"I hadn't heard that." *But it wouldn't surprise me.* Dante Gallatin had left his younger sister stranded at Beth's. *He sounded like the kind of kid who could cause trouble,* she thought, feeding into her need to judge him—and by association, Barry and Nora.

"They're here to help Nora's mother," Beth defended a little too quickly.

"Possibly. And," Peg emphasized, "for their kid to get a fresh start. Banished to Keystone."

"Sounds like the name of a bad romance novel," Addie muttered.

Peg tittered a laugh. "Poor Nora. All that money and all this heartbreak. I guess the two go together."

Beth kept quiet, but Addie could read her mind. Mrs. Garza either didn't know the truth, or she was covering for her daughter to save face. Either could be true.

"I better scoot," Peg said, dashing down the sidewalk. "You know Cal doesn't like to wait."

"How does she stay upbeat being married to that abusive jerk?" Beth questioned after Peg was out of earshot. "Did you see the size of that welt? He slapped her a good one."

Addie had concern for Peg. Clearly, her husband beat her, and Peg blithely hastened back to him to make a cozy breakfast. Had she read about wives of domestic abuse in an article in *Homekeeper* or *Women and Hearth*? Probably neither, because no one talked about these things.

Still, she had learned somewhere about abused women taking the blame for their husbands' unhappiness. Peg deserved to be pummeled for the sin of running out of eggs. Cal's abusive behavior was her fault. Her shortcomings caused the omelet disaster. If she were a better wife, Cal wouldn't hit her. What utter bullshit.

Yes, Addie should help Peg escape her abusive husband and find a better, safer life. A life where she wasn't used as a punching bag. Addie should have sympathy for Peg, but she couldn't, not today. What small trace of sympathy she possessed she reserved for herself.

Addie turned on her heel and strode away from her sister. "I need to get home. I can't go to coffee with you and explain my life."

"Whatever the problem, running away from me won't help." Beth's words trailed behind.

"I'm not running away from you," Addie shouted over her shoulder. *I'm running to something. I'm running to fix this. I'm the only person who can.*

Addie increased her pace as though every second she wasted would have to be accounted for in some grand reckoning.

She should have stormed into Barry's house last night and laid out the situation. She'd lost precious time, and now the clock was running out.

Chapter Ten

Addie collapsed on the bottom step of her front porch and yanked off her penny loafers. Her feet hurt. Running without socks wasn't wise.

"Everything all right with your sister?" Ahren asked from his seat in the glider, where he nursed a cup of coffee. "Seems like she's having a few crises this week. Ted?"

Addie jolted at his voice. She turned to see what most would say was a man quietly enjoying the new day from the comfort of his veranda. She hadn't noticed him sitting in the shadows. Addie knew Ahren much better than most. He didn't spend Saturday mornings idly sipping coffee as robins chirped, heralding spring's arrival after a long, cold Pennsylvania winter.

He was worried, and she couldn't put her finger on the cause. He might be concerned about the amount of time she spent with Beth, but he never had been before. There was something more ominous hectoring Ahren; so ominous he did everything he could to appear calm. And that made Addie nervous.

"No. Well, not any more than usual," she corrected, infusing a cavalier note into her answer. "I needed some extra time with my sister, that's all. Does that bother you?"

Ahren took another sip and swallowed as though seeing his wife through fresh eyes. The sweep of his gaze gave Addie a chill. A good chill, one she hadn't experienced in a long time. After all these years laced with a few arguments, she loved this man. He wasn't strong, but with him, she was safe. He wasn't rich, but she never went without. She wouldn't claim he was handsome but to call him good-looking didn't stretch the truth.

If only their beginnings hadn't been spoiled. If only she hadn't fallen for Barry before she dated him, their marriage could have been one of the epic romances of all time. Ahren. She had grown to love him, maybe a bit too much. She couldn't let him know how she had deceived him, not in the usual way people may think. But in a more consequential, profound betrayal.

"It's just that since Nora came back, you've been…well, elusive."

"Not you, too," Addie said, still rubbing her feet and searching for signs of a blister.

"Luke told me about your argument. That doesn't sound like you, honey. You never get in Luke's business about girls. About everything else, yes. But this Genna thing…I think you need to back off."

"You're right." Addie picked up her shoes and trotted up the few steps, stopping in front of Ahren. "I'm overreacting. He's leaving for college soon, and well, we'll be all alone in this house. I didn't think this day would come so quickly."

Ahren placed his coffee on the side table and stood. He took the shoes from Addie, tossed them on the glider, and held both of her hands in his, inching her toward him. "You sure that's all?"

She turned away from his onyx-tinged eyes drilling a hole in her. "What else could it be?"

"Honey, come on. You've not been the same since that family moved to town. Everyone has noticed. Tell me what's wrong. Maybe I can help."

A ripple of fire lapped through her chest.

If only things were that simple. Tell Ahren the truth. That would fix everything. He'd put a stop to Luke's romantic fancies with Genna. And it might well come to that.

But she wasn't prepared for that outcome today. She had to try one last thing. Plead with Barry to be reasonable, to be a man, to be fair. Sadly, she'd never seen him be any of those things.

Addie tugged her hands free. "Uh, I need to change into some more comfortable shoes. Promised Mabel I'd help her today to get ready for the bazaar."

"Mabel?"

"Beth and I ran into her on our way to the coffee shop," Addie lied, conveniently swapping Mabel for Peg.

"Why is it always you? Can't someone else fill in today?" Ahren pleaded in that relaxed tone he had mastered, making the appeal seem more casual than she suspected he meant.

"No one else is stepping up." Addie shifted toward the door. "I'll be home early, though," she said, leaning up to kiss Ahren and lingering a second.

"I'm here when you're ready to talk," Ahren said as she hurried to her room. She clutched her throat and released a silent sob.

You were here nineteen years ago when I needed you. You've always been here. But will you stay with me after you learn what I've done?

***

Heading to her car parked catty-corner across the street from Addie's home, Beth fought an unsteadiness growing inside. After that conversation, her foundation had been knocked about and set adrift like a dinghy cut loose from its tether.

She and Addie had always worked their way through troubles. They never locked the other out. The sisters, no matter their differences, supported each other and presented a united front against any enemy or problem.

If Addie hadn't been there for Beth all these years, drying her tears and slipping her a few bucks when Ted drank away the mortgage money, Beth didn't know where she and her children would be. Addie didn't back down from anything, even though in some cases Beth wished she had.

As Beth strolled, she shifted the recent events around in her mind like puzzle pieces, hoping to make sense of her sister's erratic behavior. With each step, the clearer the picture became. A queasy dread gurgled inside her chest as she painstakingly traced the beginnings to Barry's return.

What had forced him to retreat to a place he once said was a movie theater short of a hick town? Beth couldn't help imagining the wild variations that story would manifest on the city's street corners. Folks would fill in the blanks to craft a tale they wanted to believe. Peg was proof of that.

But Beth had made an assumption, too, proving her to be no better than the town gossips she often complained about. She immediately regretted sharing her suspicions but couldn't help but wonder if Addie had protested a bit too much, claiming offense and outrage at the allegation.

From her vantage point, Beth spotted her sister and Ahren holding hands on their front porch. What were they talking about? She wasn't close enough to hear. She started to approach when something held her back. Instead, she waved and hollered, but neither acknowledged her.

Maybe they don't see me, Beth thought, taking slower strides in their direction. She reached her car and stood in the street, absentmindedly fingering her keys, hoping they would turn around. They never did. Instead, Addie kissed Ahren and went inside.

Beth got into her car. On the drive home, she took a small measure of comfort from that short display of love between Addie and her husband. Maybe she was wrong about the tryst with Barry. Beth had to confess that she knew so little about her sister these days. She had accused her of an affair based on decades-old information, information from when they were young and naïve.

Still, it was rare to see her and Ahren show any affection in public. Maybe these sweet, loving moments were abundant when they were alone. And maybe that's why she had witnessed this occurrence today. They didn't realize there had been an eavesdropper snooping into their private time.

Beth's brother-in-law put up with a lot being married to Addie. She didn't question his commitment, although she might have questioned his sanity. Addie's commitment to him was another matter. Ahren could never measure up to the man Addie thought she should have married. Seemed to Beth that no man could. Was all that for show? Was she still in love with Ahren after nearly twenty years of marriage? Was she ever in love with him?

Beth recalled Addie's wedding day. That morning, after she had found her retching into the toilet, Addie confided that she was pregnant. She and Ahren had only "done the deed" one time and not until after they were engaged. "How could I be so unlucky?" Addie had complained.

In the years to follow, Beth had often wondered how the couple could have been fertile enough to get pregnant the very first time they were together, then not be able to repeat the trick and give Luke a baby brother or sister.

She pulled into her driveway just as Ted trudged out the front door.

"Thought you'd be gone longer," he teased. "Things with Addie usually take a whole lot longer."

"You're going out?"

"Poker game. Me and the boys," he answered.

"Where?"

"The Italian Club. Can you give me a lift?"

Whenever Ted asked for a ride, Beth knew that meant heavy drinking. This time, she'd add in gambling money they didn't have to the price tag.

Beth climbed back into the car and reached across the seat to pull up on the knob and unlock the passenger-side door. She didn't complain or nag. She accepted this as part of keeping stability in her family. They couldn't afford for Ted to have another run-in with the police for drunk driving. If he lost his license, he couldn't make a living.

"I can't fix people's plumbing without my truck full of parts and pieces," he had told Deputy Parris, who had called Beth from the scene of Ted's accident. Fortunately, no one had been hurt and the damage to his plumbing truck limited to the bumper.

Deputy Parris had calmed her when she arrived at the crash site and gave her Ted's confiscated keys. He had also let Beth take Ted home that night to sleep it off. She remembered his name because she had associated it with going to Paris, France. A place where maybe her life would be better.

Not knowing where to turn, Beth had implored attorney Adam Maddock, Helene's husband, for help. He'd made a few telephone calls. Five days later, after paying a large cash fine, Ted's truck had been released from the impound yard.

No criminal charges ever emerged, and no article appeared in the *Keystone Herald* recapping the evening's events. Last July, she'd made the final payment on the line of credit she had taken out on their home to fund what she crossly referred to as *Ted's drinking expenses*.

Beth remained indebted to Adam for this mini-miracle. Somehow, he had saved Ted's business while keeping everything out of the papers. Her deepest gratitude, though, she saved for Helene, who held this secret—and countless other indiscretions—between the two of them. Not even her kids or Addie knew how close the family had come to financial ruin and humiliation.

Addie isn't the only one keeping secrets.

Ted climbed into the front seat, and before Beth could put the car in gear, he grabbed her purse. "Got a five or a ten?" he asked, slamming the unopened pocketbook against her chest. "I'd help myself, but you hate me going in your wallet."

Beth glanced at her husband, now acting like an eight-year-old and hoping Mommy would give him money for an ice-cream cone. She unfastened the gold-colored clasp on her bag and reached in. "I can spare a five," she said, careful to not let Ted see what the folds of her wallet held.

"That'll be good." He held his hand out, awaiting the greenback.

Beth snapped the clasp shut and squeezed her pocketbook in between her side and the car door, out of Ted's reach, before he decided a five-spot wouldn't be enough. She'd have to stop keeping the house money in her purse and start hiding small amounts where Ted wouldn't look. Shifting into reverse, she backed down the driveway.

Ted shoved the bill into his front pants pocket and observed Beth. "Honestly, doll, I half expected you to put one of those springy mousetraps inside to snap down on my hand." He laughed.

I would if I thought it would do any good.

After dodging a drunk driving charge, they had agreed that Beth would take control of their finances. "I'll be the breadwinner," Ted had said, "and you give out the dough." He made a joke of their agreement, a division of duties that soon led to nothing but grief for Beth.

Ted expected her to dole out cash as though she was a teller at Midville Bank. At first, she attempted to reason with him, tried to show him on paper just how far his paycheck went. These days, with Ted's increased drinking and decreased customer calls, the money barely made a trip around the corner. Still, Ted demanded that she make ends meet, even though he spent most of his time tugging those ends apart.

"Do you need me to pick you up later?" she asked, pulling into the Italian Club's sparse parking lot and stopping in front of the entrance.

"Naw. I'll catch a ride with one of the guys or walk. I'm getting pretty used to walking these days." Ted snaked his hand around Beth's neck and pulled her to him for a kiss. "I'll be home early," he said, winking. "Don't be asleep, okay, doll?"

Ted yanked the door handle open and spilled out of the car, not waiting for her reply.

Beth watched him wrestle with the wrought iron pulls to open the arched, oversized oak door. The weight of the impressive Tuscan-style carved panels proved to be a challenge to Ted's strength. This made Beth smile.

She wondered if the inside décor was as garish as the outside. She'd never find out. Only men were allowed in this club. One didn't need to be Italian, though; only bring enough cash to cover one's bar tab and any unsanctioned gambling debts.

Beth shifted the car into drive. Just as she was about to pull away, a tall man wearing a fedora approached, motioning for her to roll down the window. She slowly turned the hand crank, eyeing the figure, but sunlight backlit him, making it hard for her to discern his features. When she finally got the window down, he spoke.

"Hello there."

She recognized that voice immediately. *Barry Gallatin.*

"I thought that was you when I saw Ted walk in," Barry said. "You got a minute, Bethie?"

She cringed at him using her high-school nickname. "Wow, I'm surprised to see you."

"Why? You knew I'm around now, right?" he asked, seeming disappointed that Beth's welcome home wasn't warmer.

"Well, yes, I heard through the grapevine…" she stuttered. "Still, I didn't think I'd run into you."

"It's a small town, Bethie. You knew our paths would cross, especially since my daughter is dating your nephew."

"I'm in a bit of a hurry," Beth said, stunned at his boldness. "What did you want to talk to me about?"

"Nothing, really. Just saying hi to an old friend. Maybe I should change that to former friend. You don't seem to be the least bit happy to see me."

Beth glanced away.

Barry propped onto the door and poked his head partially into the car. "I am happy to see you, Beth. I am…but I really need to talk with Addie."

A surprised groan escaped her mouth. Beth took a moment to regain her composure. "You haven't seen her since you got back into town?" she stammered, incredulous at his request.

"No, I haven't. Not even sure how I could get hold of her. Guess I could look her number up in the phone book and call her house, but I didn't want to rile Ahren. They're still married, right?"

Beth recalled the last time she had seen Barry and Ahren together. A horrendous eruption of male bravado led to blame, threats, and finally, a bare-knuckle brawl.

"I'm not here to make any trouble. I need to talk to her, that's all. Bounce an idea off her," he said, more to himself. "Could you let her know? I mean, without making a big deal?"

Beth shifted nervously on the seat, distancing herself from Barry's face a few inches away.

"Talk about what?" she managed to ask, pushing every hurtful emotion down. This man had broken her sister's heart, torn apart their group of friends, and merrily skipped off to take his place among Pittsburgh's high society. He didn't send a backward glance at the damaged souls he'd left in his wake.

Bad memories rushed back, snippets of the devastation left when friends became enemies. Addie wouldn't take up with Barry again—not in this life or the next. What bothered Beth's sister was something more complicated and consequential.

How did she miss the clues? The realization made Beth's stomach tighten. Addie was in real trouble, and that trouble involved her son. An overwhelming urge to find Addie swept through her, but first she would dig for more information.

"You haven't seen her, or this town for that matter, in a decade. Maybe more," Beth said. "What could be so urgent now?"

Barry huffed and backed away slightly. "Oh, so now you're interested in what I have to say?"

"Your turning up is a little weird, wouldn't you agree? You're up to something. You're always up to something. Tell me what, and I'll see if I can help." Beth licked her lips as though wiping clean the words that left her mouth. The last thing she would do was help him.

Barry flashed his roguish grin, the one emphasizing the dimple on his cheek. The grin he'd employ when he wanted to appear humble and unpretentious.

"I'm protective of my sister," she answered, firing the sentence at him like an arrow.

"Well finally, something that's just like old times," he snarled. "Look, Beth, I'm not here to make trouble."

"Well, that would be a first. I don't know what you're up to or why you moved back home. I do know that anyone who gets caught in your orbit eventually ends up spun into the atmosphere to struggle on their own—"

"Stop right there."

"I will not," she snapped, jerking her car door open and using it like the blade of a snowplow to push him away. After he stepped back, she slammed the door and started her car. "I'll let Addie know you want to speak with her—if you let Nora know, too."

"It's nothing like that. This doesn't involve Nora."

Beth shifted the car into gear. "Addie is my sister. Nora used to be my friend. I won't have you hurting either one of them. Not anymore," she shouted out the window before pulling away, her tires screeching against the asphalt.

She glanced in her rearview mirror at the image of Barry standing alone, somewhat slumped. He appeared shrunken, perhaps beaten. The silhouette was no longer a match to the boastful, carefree teenager she had grown up with.

Once she was out of the parking lot and heading for home, she let out a huge gasp. *Oh, my God. Addie, what have you done this time?*

Instead of staying on Main Street, Beth turned at the next signal and made a beeline for her sister's house as though a three-alarm fire bell rang out in her head.

Chapter Eleven

Beth's heart pounded so loudly that she barely heard Ahren speak as he ushered her across the porch and into his house.

"Addie didn't mention that you were coming back to get her," he said, still nursing the same cup of coffee she had seen him with some forty minutes before. "You two don't make a move without the other." He added a laugh. "How much more is there to be done to get that junk sale of yours ready?"

She inhaled and searched around for her sister. Was he making polite small talk, or was he digging for information? Either way, she decided to play dumb. "What?"

"The bazaar. You and Addie are headed there again to work." He made a statement, but his tone was questioning.

Beth distractedly picked up the gist of his conversation. "Yes. Uh, that's right." She licked her lips, now suddenly dry and chafed. Yet another opportunity to cover for Addie. Beth decided the least she said, the better.

"That's what Addie told me, but she didn't say you were going, too. I thought she was the only volunteer helping Mabel."

"Like you said, I couldn't let her go without me." Beth feigned a smile and prayed Ahren would change the subject. He didn't.

"Addie said she ran into Mabel at the coffee shop and..." Ahren stopped at the sound of Addie bounding down the steps.

Thank God. Beth wasn't half the fabricator her sister was. The more Beth stretched the truth, the more the truth wrapped around her neck and yanked.

81

She sent an imploring look to Addie, hoping she wouldn't blow their story either.

At least not until Beth could get to the bottom of this.

***

After changing into sneakers and an outfit suitable for sorting rummage, Addie lingered in her bedroom, rearranging her shoes on the closet floor. This was her delay tactic of choice when putting off any unwelcome duty—getting together with Barry to discuss their past and their present topped that list. She used the stolen time to mentally try on different outcomes, envisioning situations that, once exposed, left no one in anguish.

Predictably, none came to mind.

Some thirty minutes later, she arrived at acceptance. She would call him from a phone booth so Ahren wouldn't hear her setting up a meeting. If Nora happened to answer, Addie would simply invent a story about talking to Barry about Ahren's job. Simple as that.

Nora would believe, or pretend to believe, this fib from a childhood playmate. Their friendship had disintegrated much like an old flag, decayed from weathering life's harsh elements. Addie hoped that Nora would hold memories of when their girlhood flag flew in pristine glory.

She scurried down the staircase and stopped halfway, surprised to find Beth standing in the foyer, deep in conversation with Ahren.

Dear God, why is she here? Again.

They both turned to where Addie stood. "You ready?" Beth asked.

Addie, not wanting to be caught in another lie, at least not in front of her husband, played along. "Yep." She didn't know what intuition had returned Beth to her front door. Still, she sent a prayer of gratitude to the heavens for the fortuitous circumstance.

"You girls are really putting in the hours. What time will you be back, honey?" Ahren asked Addie, who now stood in the foyer alongside Beth.

Addie reached for her purse, hoping her jumpiness was more in her imagination than in reality.

"Not sure." Addie turned to Beth. "Do you know?"

Addie watched annoyance flood Beth's face and inwardly chuckled. *That's what you get for showing up uninvited.*

"I guess until Mabel says we're done, or dinnertime, whichever comes first." Beth glowered at her sister before turning to Ahren with a smile. "Hopefully not more than a couple of hours." Addie linked arms with Beth. "I'll be back in time to start dinner for you and Luke," she said, not offering a goodbye peck or even a backward glance. She all but pulled Beth through the front door and toward the car before saying a word.

"What are you doing here?" she hissed.

Beth snapped her retort. "Bringing a message from Barry."

Addie fought the urge to scream and waited until they were inside Beth's car, well out of Ahren's earshot, before she even released a breath.

Halfway down the street, she croaked, "What message?"

Beth turned her head, and Addie took in the completeness of her sister's expression. She had perfected that official big-sister disdain, draped with a disapproving frown to frame her words. Beth turned back to face the road and waited a beat.

Addie knew she was punishing her. Payback for not confessing the whole story.

"He would like to talk with you," Beth finally admitted. "I guess about Luke dating his daughter."

Addie's blood pressure had regained a normal range only seconds before. Beth's unexpected reply bounced against her chest, boosting her heart rate into orbit like the Explorer I satellite. Addie's essence now propelled into a new galaxy, where worlds collided, her world and Barry's inexorably connected on a crash course she'd managed to avoid for so many years.

"Where are we going?" Addie finally managed to ask, avoiding providing additional details. "And why were you talking to Barry?"

"I'll answer all those questions, but first, you have to tell me what is going on. I guessed it had something to do with Barry. But now, after talking to him, I know you're worried about something more important than the dregs of an old romance."

Addie swiped a tear threatening to seep down her cheek. She might as well confess the truth. In a matter of hours, maybe minutes, everyone would know, too.

Still, she couldn't compel her voice to string together the words. *Luke is Barry's son.*

"Well?"

Addie stared out the window, formulating her confession, one she should have made many years ago. Would life have been easier if she had? Her choices had been limited. Pick the lady or the tiger. In her case, there was a tiger behind both doors. So she picked a husband, Ahren. But maybe she should have chosen the other door, the one truth stood behind.

Truth, justice, reality, whatever you called this karma, had tracked her down and would now have its day. Once word got out, Luke's life would be ruined.

And Ahren, her dear Ahren, would never forgive her.

Beth jerked the steering wheel to the right, turning down a little-used dirt road. She pulled onto the shoulder and shifted into park before killing the engine. "Okay," she said, a commanding tone piercing her voice. "Let's have it."

Addie licked her lips and fidgeted with the clasp on her handbag. *Delay and deflect.*

"Ad-dee?"

If I'm going to tell someone, it needs to be Barry. I need to tell him first. Then Ahren. And of course, Luke. He will be the hardest. They have to hear this from me.

Accepting what she needed to do, and the order in which to do it, gave Addie a strange sense of strength and purpose. She couldn't continue decorating the truth, stretching the facts into shapes that fit her narrative. The time had come to take responsibility for her decision and her willingness to renew the lie whenever necessary.

"Beth, I love you and trust you more than anyone in this world."

"Then—"

Addie put her hand up. "You must believe me. I'll tell you everything, but first I have something I need to do. There are a few things to straighten out."

"You have me worried sick. I don't know what to do. How to help you."

"Don't worry about me. I'm all right. Well, I will be." A tight, narrow, unconvincing smile set on her lips. "Barry and I need to talk, that much is obvious, but first tell me how you ran into him and what he said."

Beth relayed the details of her conversation in front of the Italian Club. Addie sat in rapt attention. *He suspects. He must suspect. Why else would he be looking for me?*

"Do you think he's still there?" Addie asked, not sure which answer she hoped Beth would give. Things might be easier if she could approach Barry on neutral ground, eliminating the need to call his home and perhaps lie to Nora.

The clock chronicling the romance between Luke and Genna kept ticking. Addie didn't want her mind to contemplate the impulses of a teenage boy, especially when that boy was her son. Obviously, the relationship he created with Genna would lead in one direction. She had to do something, put up some kind of roadblock before his attraction to her intersected with life's natural progression of affection, of touching, and…

No, she wouldn't think about that, about the two of them embracing, kissing…

Stop! They just started seeing each other.

Beth glanced at her watch. "That was less than an hour ago," she said. "If he's in the same card game with Ted, he'll still be there. But do you want to talk to him in front of the guys? In front of Ted?"

"Did Barry give you another way for me to contact him?"

"Well, no…"

"Then I don't have any choice. You don't want me to show up on his front doorstep, do you?"

"Of course not, but you won't be able to go inside the club."

"I won't?" Addie said, sitting a little straighter. "Watch me."

***

Addie practiced deep breathing as Beth pulled into the parking lot. "Second time today," she said.

"Huh?"

"This is the second time I've been here today. I'll park and wait for you."

"You don't have to. I'll be okay." Addie considered her sister's demeanor and attempted to reassure her. "Really, Beth. I'm fine. I'll say my piece and be on my way."

"Seriously, you expect me to drop you off and go about my business, cooking dinner and folding laundry? Have you met me?"

"Yes, I've met you. Such a pain in my behind. Don't you need to get home to your children? Remember them?"

"Yes, I do, so let's get this over with. I have a meatloaf to make."

Addie grimaced and willed her hands, practically strangling her purse, to steady. There wasn't time to debate. And she'd probably lose anyway. Beth was staying. All Addie could do was dictate the terms.

Her sister's eyes glimmered with a mixture of love and understanding, encouragement and faith sprinkled in as well, just like the time Addie had tried out for the lead in the school play and ended up being cast in the chorus. Beth consoled her and encouraged her to work a bit harder, to be prepared for next season. But Addie decided to lament her horribly unfair situation with a constant drumbeat of *oh, woe is me*.

After days of Addie feeling sorry for herself and threatening to quit drama class, Beth declared an end to her indulgent, self-inflicted misery. "If you want this bad enough, then do something instead of complaining," she had scolded. "I'm through listening while you wallow in self-pity." Beth's declaration snapped Addie out of her funk and into a plan for success. The following year, Addie acted the lead in the senior play.

All throughout her life, no matter the event, small or large, her sister supported her, encouraged her, cheered for her. Today was no different.

In that moment, Addie decided to tell Beth the whole truth as soon as she finished with Barry. Beth deserved to know, and selfishly, Addie understood how much she would need Beth's support while confessing everything to Ahren and Luke.

"If you stay, park on the far end, where Ahren won't recognize your car if he happens to drive by. You can pick me up over there, under that buckeye tree, when I'm done."

"I don't mind going in with you," Beth said, her offer cresting with jaunty promise.

"I know. This is something I need to do alone." *And if I don't go now, I may lose my courage.*

"You realize you may not get past the entry hall. I don't know how strict they are on this 'No Women Allowed' rule," Beth was saying as she watched a young man slip past their car. "Oh."

"Oh what?" Addie snapped, impatience now battling with anxiety to take the upper hand.

"See that boy?"

Addie nodded.

"Do you know who he is?"

"Uh, nooo." Addie extended the *o* in *no*, exasperated at Beth's latest delay tactic. "Should I?"

"That's Dante Gallatin, Barry and Nora's oldest."

Addie craned her neck to get a better view. She should have recognized him just from his tall frame and mop of wavy brown hair. *He's barely a month younger than Luke.* She turned back to face Beth.

"The boy Ruby has a crush on?"

"Yes."

"Would he tell us why the family moved back to Keystone?" Addie prodded.

"Why is the reason important?" Beth asked.

"Just curious," Addie retorted, faking indifference.

"Would the reason change the news you want to tell Barry?"

"Well, no. But it could affect his reaction and his actions to correct the matter." Addie quieted, realizing she had said too much.

Beth pounced. "Correct what matter?"

"If I hurry, I could stop that kid and ask," Addie said, reaching for the door handle.

"I have a pretty good idea of what you're going to tell Barry," Beth blurted. "You probably don't want to have that conversation with his son nearby, where he might hear."

Addie curled back into her seat. Beth was right, but she wouldn't let her off the hook that easily. "And what do you think I'm going to tell the man?"

"Just saying, right now might not be the perfect time to clear the air with Barry."

Addie exhaled, an acceptance slowly replacing the resolve she'd harnessed just moments ago. "Well, how else can I talk to him? I definitely don't want to have this conversation with Nora in the room," she said, anger now piled on the mountain of emotions threatening to explode.

Beth's eyes flashed.

Addie crossed her arms. Things had gotten out of hand. She shouldn't have come here with Beth. And why did Beth always seem to have the upper hand? How could she get the scoop on Barry?

"I'm sorry," Beth said, recoiling from her aggressive position. "This is your mess to clean up. Seems like I immediately go into big-sister mode. I apologize. I'll go home, but if you need a ride, call me."

Addie smiled, her eyes filling with looming tears. "You're right. Damn it, you're always right. This isn't the time or place. But I need to talk to him soon."

"Whatever you say."

Addie appreciated Beth's attempt to sound chipper. Nothing about this was happy and delaying the inevitable only made things worse. "Let's head over to the church for an hour. That way, when Ahren asks me how things went, I can tell him the truth for a change."

On the drive, Addie contemplated how to convince Barry to move his family again. Pennsylvania was a big state. He could pick another town, one that would separate his daughter hundreds of miles away from her son.

Deep down, though, she knew the Gallatins could move across the planet. If Luke and Genna wanted to be together, they'd find a way.

Still, she had to try.

Chapter Twelve

Addie and Beth found Mabel nearly swallowed up by piles of discarded winter coats, bulky and heavy. They both smiled as Mabel hugged them with earnest gratitude, shocked at their unexpected help. The trio had been occupied for over an hour, sorting through a fresh delivery of donations when Addie excused herself on the pretext of phoning Ahren.

On the drive over to St. Gregory's, she remembered the office telephone inside the church hall. A perfect place for both privacy and anonymity. She couldn't come up with a better plan to reach Barry without involving Nora, although Addie suspected that Nora would be involved soon.

Not wanting either woman to be within earshot, Addie waited until both Beth and Mabel were enmeshed in juicy gossip about the new Kresge's salesclerk—the one who wore low-cut sweaters.

Lucky for her, the janitor walked by when he did and agreed to place the call. She didn't want to chance the bartender recognizing her voice. She paged through the directory to find the number for the Italian Club. Ed dialed and asked for Barry Gallatin. Without a spec of curiosity, he handed Addie the receiver.

"They're looking for him," Ed declared and shuffled on his way to wipe down the church pews or whatever he did on a Saturday afternoon, not bothering to ask Addie a single question.

"Thank you, Ed," she said to his receding back. She put the receiver to her ear awaiting a *hello* from the other end.

The silence increased the anxiety building inside of Addie. Of course she wouldn't discuss any part of this over the phone, but they could plan to meet at a discreet spot somewhere outside the town limits. A place where neither of Barry's eighteen-year-old sons would walk in unexpectedly. Maybe she'd suggest the next town over. A remote coffee shop, where they could devise a plan to restore their families well-being with minimal collateral damage.

Would he refuse to meet in person? What if he didn't believe her? How could she prove her claim? Just by watching Luke, observing his mannerisms, his build, it was obvious.

That is, if someone was looking.

What if he wanted to discuss something completely different? Maybe Nora had complained that none of their old friends would have anything to do with her. Could Nora suspect why Addie had built an ice wall around their past?

The repercussions expanded in Addie's mind. Consequences whose tentacles stretched to entangle more lives than just hers. Addie's immediate impulse was to stop Luke from dating his half-sister. Naïvely, that seemed like a simple, direct goal. But now a realization she hadn't considered mushroomed in its place.

Her only child had siblings, a sister and two brothers. Siblings, that wondrous gift from God to be cherished and prized. Maybe not so much during the childhood years of rivalries and competition. But as a child grew from baby to teen to adult, their siblings were there. True, steady, reliable, and always on their side like no friend, acquaintance, or spouse could be.

How selfish I've been.

Addie saw Beth's eyes boring a hole in her. She waved, and her sister gestured back, a telling smile gracing her face. She suspected Beth knew what she was up to, who she was calling, and she approved.

Addie tapped the toe of her shoe against the faded linoleum. *What is taking so long?*

"Hello, sir." The voice on the other end finally spoke. "He's not here. Seems like he's left, but his son Dante is playing pool. Wanna speak to him?"

Addie hung up without responding, a mixture of disappointment and relief sprayed against her heart. What now? She glimpsed at the wall clock. Barely two hours had passed since

Barry spoke to Beth. That didn't seem long enough to finish a card game, but maybe Barry had stopped by for a beer instead.

Addie shook her head. *I'll go crazy if I spend one more minute trying to figure out Barry and his motives. I couldn't do it twenty years ago—fat chance of being successful now. I need to hear directly from him, not keep throwing guesses against the wall and praying something sticks.*

She glanced to where Beth and Mabel sat, willing her jittery innards to ebb. *There's nothing I can do about this right now.* She resumed her spot near her sister behind the stacks of used toys ready for pricing.

Why was Dante at the club?

He wasn't old enough to gamble or drink, but these local social clubs made exceptions for the kids of their members, she supposed. Not to admit women, of course, but to let young men roll dice and consume alcohol in a "safe" way.

Dante Gallatin. Luke's younger brother by a month.

How would she break that news? And whose world would be shattered?

***

Beth hovered near the gently-used toys—spinning tops, dollhouses, and pogo sticks—waiting for Addie to notice her. Finally she rested her palm on her sister's shoulder and wiggled her hand, as though waking her from a deep sleep. "Time to head home," she said as soothingly as her voice would allow.

Addie flinched, then lowered her head. "Sorry I wasn't much help today," she confessed, tossing a rag doll into a box.

Beth grinned. "We weren't even supposed to be here, remember? Mabel is thrilled we showed up at all."

"Still, I could have done more. I can't concentrate on anything. Not until I get—"

"Well, girls, I need to get out to the Silverwing and relieve Bert," Mabel hollered from the other side of the room.

"You working a shift at the motel?" Beth asked.

"Naw. Clarence had to take the day off and Bert filled in. I told him I'd bring dinner and give him a break." With her hat atop her head and her pocketbook in hand, she turned off the lights and moved toward the door. "I can't tell you how surprised and happy I was to see you both. You are true-blue pals." She blew them an enthusiastic kiss.

"We're still not close to being done," Addie lamented.

"We can finish up on Monday or Tuesday. Whatever we don't get to, I'll put aside for next year's bazaar and next year's chairman. Guarantee you it won't be me." Mabel sent a gleeful grin in the sisters' direction.

"That's a good idea. Otherwise we won't be ready in time," Beth agreed, joining her at the doorway. "Father Yusuf will be pleased with what we've done."

"He better be," Mabel declared. "Is Sewing Circle still on for Thursday?"

"Far as I know. We're at Helene's, right?"

"It's her turn," Addie chimed in, mustering more energy, Beth thought, than she had displayed in hours. "But she canceled the last two times. Some lame excuse about a lawyers' get-together."

A sense of gratefulness for Helene and her husband Adam rose from the recesses of Beth's chest. "If she can't host, we can play at my house," she said, finalizing the matter.

"That would be grand," Mabel said.

Addie snapped, "Helene always has an excuse. It has to do with her hoity-toity husband. He wants to run for judge next year, so he's rubbing elbows with the muckety-mucks."

"Adam Maddock is a fine attorney. He'd make a wonderful judge," Beth retorted immediately, taking a breath to tamp down the corners of her defensive response.

"As if you'd know," Addie screeched. "They act like they're so much better than us. So what if Helene married a lawyer? She's still *hell on wheels* to me."

Beth grinned at the memory. She had been eating a bologna sandwich at the school lunch table when Helene confessed that she didn't know how to roller-skate. "I don't even own a pair of skates," she half-bragged to her friends. The girls, maybe eleven or twelve at the time, took Helene's admission as a challenge.

That Saturday, the six headed to the Keystone Roller Rink committed to teaching Helene the childhood skill. Sadly, Helene spent most of her time creeping along the walls, afraid to let go, and when she finally did, she landed on her rump.

The girls immediately got bored with instructing, and their lesson deteriorated into skating past her, occasionally throwing out an encouraging word or two. Except Nora.

Nora stayed with Helene the entire afternoon, demonstrating how to walk like a duck with her heels together, toes pointed out, until she got her balance. Helene didn't master roller-skating, but to this day, she prized her hard-earned moniker, which she proudly modified to *Helene-on-wheels*.

Addie droned on, "I don't care how rich or famous or powerful her husband becomes. She's no better than the rest of us."

"Why are we arguing about this now?" Mabel asked. "Let's gossip about Helene on Thursday, when she's there to defend herself."

"She'd laugh this whole thing off. Rich or poor, Helene is Helene. Nothing will change that," Beth declared, scowling at her sister. "She's a good friend. Always has been."

Addie remained quiet. She waved goodbye to Mabel and followed Beth to her car.

"What was that about?" Beth scolded. "Running Helene down? She's your friend."

"Sorry. Guess I'm out of sorts." Addie leaned closer. "I tried calling Barry while he was at the club, but he had left. I don't know how to contact him now...not without Nora being around."

Beth watched Mabel's Dodge Coronet pull away. "Maybe you should call his house. I mean, after all, he came up to me and said he wanted to talk to you. He wasn't acting secretive or guarded, like you are."

Addie's eyes flared. "What do you mean?"

"You're skulking around as though being caught talking to Barry would make you guilty of a high crime. Then you'd really need to stay in Helene's good graces," she added, hoping to lighten the mood.

"I'm not skulking," Addie defended.

"Then why did you ask Ed to make the call?"

"How did you know that?" she cried indignantly.

"Doesn't take a brain trust to figure that out," Beth replied simply.

Addie let out what sounded like a *pfft* sound to Beth, dismissing her observation before continuing. "I...I just didn't want to get tongues wagging. You know Lenny DeMatteo. He's a worse gossip than the entire Sewing Circle put together; maybe the Ladies' Guild, too."

They both laughed at the truth in Addie's statement. If someone wanted to know what was going on in Keystone, all they had to do was pull up a stool, order a beer from Lenny, and pay attention. He had more news bulletins than the local CBS affiliate.

"Let's take a break for today. Maybe after a good night's sleep, an answer will materialize."

"Like a miracle?" Addie said. "The Blessed Mother will appear to me in my dreams? I'd like to believe that, but it hardly will happen."

"You are the most stubborn person I know." Beth's voice climbed. "What I'm telling you—if you'd stop for a second and listen—is to give this some space, stop pushing so hard. Let your mind rest, and you'll see things more clearly." She stared at Addie, who reminded her of a billowing sail whose wind had dissipated.

"I can't pray things will be okay like you do. Things don't just work out." Addie's statement bit into Beth.

"You could do a whole lot worse than to pray. Lashing out at Helene because her husband is successful isn't going to improve your situation. If anything, you'll make things harder. Keep your friends on your side, Addie. You don't need to alienate any of us. And offering up a few Hail Marys never hurt anyone."

Addie sniffed before allowing tears to trickle down her face. "I've messed everything up. I've ruined my life. Ahren's. Luke's and…and…"

Beth gathered her sister into her arms and held her while she wept. Addie's chest expanded and contracted with each grief-ridden sob.

Beth couldn't help but wonder if her sister cried for the sins of her past or for the wrongs she was preparing to make.

Chapter Thirteen

On Monday morning, Addie made scrambled eggs and bacon for breakfast, packed two brown bag lunches—Ahren's tuna salad on rye and Luke's ham and cheese on Wonder Bread—and left the house thirty minutes early for Mrs. Bergen's piano lesson. She marveled at Bert's sixty-six-year-old mother, who decided to take up piano. Still, she was grateful for a student who was available before three-thirty on school days and for the additional forty cents each week to add to the family kitty.

Her route took her past St. Gregory's, where, at the last minute, she complied with an overwhelming urge to stop. Addie fished a floral scarf from the backseat, where the babushka had lain since Joel's confirmation, and put the covering on her head. She secured it with a loose knot under her chin and scurried inside like a church mouse scampering for shelter.

She dipped her fingertips into the holy water font, made the sign of the cross, and walked toward the statue of the Blessed Mother, at whose feet a bank of votive candles glimmered. After a moment, she slipped a coin into the slot and lit one of the wicks. She took comfort from replicating this long-standing tradition her mother had venerated. *What the heck, lighting a candle wouldn't hurt.*

She knelt down in one of the empty pews and offered several Hail Marys as Beth had suggested. Not surprisingly, no immediate miracle took place. Still, she had to admit that her sister was right. Comfort surrounded her in this familiar house of worship, even if she was asking the Lord for the impossible. He was in the business of performing the impossible, right?

She glanced up in time to watch Father Yusuf stroll by. He straightened a few hymnals at the end of a pew across the way, bowed in her general direction, but didn't stop. She sent up another prayer of thanks for this small mercy. She wasn't in the mood to exchange pleasantries about yesterday's sermon. She'd come up short in that conversation since she had slept in Sunday morning, missing the nine o'clock and the eleven-thirty services.

Pleased with her prayerful appeal, Addie exited just as the daily mass goers arrived for an eight-thirty service. Her mother had been among these faithful men and women, never missing a day to pray and receive Communion.

What would Mom say if she knew I'd become a Christmas-and-Easter Catholic?

Addie knew the answer. Her mother would have hated her behavior, not just in her faith, but how she was living her life.

Or rather how she was living her lie.

Before today, when was the last time she had earnestly prayed; truly prayed? Sure, she went to mass when she had to. Wasn't she the picture of a good Catholic godmother watching Joel as he was confirmed?

No point in comparing piety with the pious, she decided, pushing her way through the heavy wooden doors. She propped one open long enough for Lenny DeMatteo and Mrs. Garza, Nora's mother, to skitter past, exchanging a quick greeting. Funny how the Italians preferred the Maronite Catholic mass to the traditional Latin mass at St. Mary of the Ocean.

Addie hustled to her car, yanking the scarf from her head. Now she would be late. Something, or someone, had drawn her to church today. She had to be here. She had to seek this refuge. Unburden her soul. Hopefully a few minutes wouldn't matter to Claudia Bergen.

She turned to see if Nora's mom or Lenny were watching her, but of course they weren't. By now they would have taken their usual places in their usual pews, consumed with their private prayer rituals. They took no notice of a woman they'd known since her girlhood. She blended into the scenery like butterfly weed, lovely but expected. Still, she couldn't shake the sensation of being observed.

Her heart pounded as she convinced herself that no one in the churchyard was reading her thoughts, as though they were Superman with X-ray vision. The old bartender, Lenny, didn't know what she was plotting. He came to this mass every morning. Of course she'd run into him.

And Momma Garza, the woman who had placed fresh-baked *pizzelle* cookies in each of Addie's child-sized hands every time she came to play. The waffle-like dessert reminded Addie of edible snowflakes. "Some for now and some for later," Nora's mother would say, wrapping up a small bundle in wax paper for Addie and Beth to take home.

Momma Garza, another casualty of my bad decisions.

She gunned the gas pedal, racing down the street, not fully halting at stop signs, only to still be five minutes late for Mrs. Bergen, who apparently was more than happy to take advantage of Addie's tardiness.

"Gave me time to get my scones out of the oven," she said as Addie opened up her valise and retrieved sheet music for beginners, taking in the scent coming from the kitchen.

Mrs. Bergen returned holding a serving tray piled with orange marmalade scones.

"A cup of coffee and one of your scones, just what I need," Addie agreed.

As she bit into the still-warm scone, a calm slowly replaced anxiety. Perhaps after the lesson, on her drive home, she would stop at the phone booth in front of Kresge's and call the Gallatin residence.

***

An hour later, Addie wandered around the women's department shopping for a new slip—or perhaps a nightgown? She'd forgotten which she had told the Kresge's salesgirl when she approached. Addie didn't need either. She was stalling, merely wasting time, digging for the courage to drop a nickel into the payphone.

"Adele, is that you?" A tinny voice sounded behind her. "Why, of course it is. I'd recognize you anywhere. Honey, it's Addie."

She hated being called Adele, and that's how she recognized the voice. Since her parents had died, only one person still called her Adele. Addie did her best to not let her mouth gape open as she turned to face Nora and Barry, hands full of what appeared to be towels and sheets.

"We just stopped in for a few things," Nora explained. "Still trying to get the new place presentable for company."

"Hi, Addie," Barry said, standing a few inches behind his wife. "It's good to see you."

Nora grinned, swinging from side to side as though enjoying the moment with her girlhood friend. "Between you and me, I'm hoping to join your Sewing Circle," she said with a wink.

"You don't have to hide the truth," Barry jested. "We all know it's an excuse for you ladies to play poker. And that's okay with me."

"Honey, would you mind going to the register and paying for these?" Nora asked, shoving a stack of linens at her husband. "I need to catch up with Addie."

"Sure. I'll meet you at the car," he said. Barry stood a few seconds too long, his stare trained on Addie. No one moved. His husky voice broke the silence. "It's great to see you after such a long time."

"It has been a while," she agreed. Awash in the insincerity of his words, Addie wondered why he was putting on this performance. Was this the same man who wished her dead, or worse, the last time they had spoken?

"Would love to hear about you and the family when you have the time," he continued. "Maybe you and Ahren can stop by the house for dinner."

Nora clapped her hands. "That's a marvelous idea, especially since our little Genna is starry-eyed for your Luke."

Addie gulped. *That's what this friendly reception is all about. Dear God, they think this budding relationship is a good thing, our kids as a couple.* Her timeline shrank as she contemplated their bright, welcoming faces aglow in grins, anticipating the grandchildren they might share with Addie and Ahren.

Her lungs tightened as though bricks pressed against them. Something must be said, and yesterday wouldn't have been soon enough. Try as she might, she couldn't form those words in front of Nora.

"Uh, yes, of course," Addie finally stuttered. "That would be lovely. I know Ahren would enjoy seeing you both. But, um, Barry, I did want to talk to you, you know, business-wise."

"Business-wise?" he questioned.

She leaned in conspiratorially. "About Ahren...his future with the company. If there's anything you can do to—"

Barry stiffened. "Well, I..."

"Not here, of course. Maybe I could stop by your office or meet for coffee? I don't want to bother Nora with the details."

Nora huffed. "Ever since we were kids, you two kept secrets. We're grown-ups now. Let's talk about it at dinner."

Addie stepped back, willing her brain to spin yet another lie. *After all, what's one more?* Lying had gotten her into this mess; maybe fresh lies would get her out.

"Nora, I don't want to bore you with our family matters." She pushed out a puff of air caught in the back of her throat. She had to keep talking, keep the ball moving forward. "Ahren would be furious if he even suspected. But we were friends, right? Friends help friends."

Barry shifted his weight, eyeing Addie with a new suspicion. "Did Beth mention that I ran into her the other day?"

"Yes, but I didn't know how to get hold of you."

"She's right, Barry. Our number's not in the book. You should have given it to Beth," Nora admonished before turning toward her friend. "You know you could have called my mom. She would love to talk to you. She says you've been distant these past few years."

Addie paused. She thought it curious that Nora and her mother were discussing her at all. She couldn't allow her curiosity to derail her mission. "Should have thought of that. I saw Momma this morning on her way into mass," Addie said.

"She still does that?" Barry asked, incredulous.

Both women smiled, as if this might be the dumbest question ever posed. "She's a mainstay at St. Gregory's," Addie answered, hoping to get back on track. "So, Barry, can we talk soon?"

"All right, you two," Nora interrupted. "Addie, I'll call to set up our dinner party. I have your number. You phone Barry at the office to see how he can help Ahren. I will keep your secret," she added, making a zipper motion across her lips.

Keeping secrets and telling lies pretty much amounted to the same thing. Addie would call his office that afternoon.

Chapter Fourteen

Why is Addie so adamantly against Luke and Genna?

Beth stared at the tepid Tetley as though an answer to this question would magically appear in the tea leaves. She had been wrestling with this thought off and on since she saw her sister Saturday afternoon.

Three days later, Beth was no closer to an answer. She needed to start dinner instead of wasting time at the kitchen table. Still, she couldn't get herself to move.

What was she missing?

The fascination with each other was a first crush. Luke and Genna were teenagers with their entire adult lives ahead of them. Their flame would die out as quickly as it had ignited, Beth convinced herself.

On the other hand, she mentally argued, Addie had been roughly the same age as Luke when she fell for Barry and then married Ahren. Maybe they weren't too young for real love. Was that what Addie feared? Being in-laws with the Gallatins, bound together forever as family? Sharing the joys of grandparenting with a man who had haplessly broken her heart? Surely people had survived worse.

She took a swig of the now-cold Earl Grey and hurriedly stood, as though the brew had fortified her decision.

"Hey, Ruby!" Beth moved toward the staircase and yelled for her daughter. "Come here for a minute."

"I'm sorry, I didn't mean to do it," Ruby hollered from the top of the landing. An I-got-caught-in-the-act panic rang through her voice.

Beth blew an exaggerated breath. *What now?* "Are you up to something?"

"Not really. And it wasn't my fault," she declared, stomping her foot to emphasize her innocence. "Well, not entirely. I'll fix it right now."

"Fix what? What in the heck are you confessing to?"

"Aren't you yelling at me for clogging the toilet?"

"You clogged the toilet? Our only toilet?" Beth scratched her head. "Honestly, Ruby. Your dad will blow a fuse."

"Guess I used too much paper. Don't know why Opal always has to tattle. I told her I'd clean—"

"No one tattled. And I wasn't yelling. I didn't even know... Oh, never mind. Your dad won't be home for a while. The last thing he'll want to do after fixing other folks' toilets is come home to a broken one. You better get the plunger and—"

"I know what to do, but really, Mom. Joel should have to help too. He was in there before me. It smelled sooooo bad. And you know how big his *huddah*—"

"Get down here, please, and stop discussing your brother's bowel movements. I need to ask you about something. You *and* Joel can clean the bathroom together after we're done."

Ruby bounded down the steps toward her mother as though she had been sprung from lockup.

Beth pointed to a dining room chair. "Sit, please."

Ruby obeyed but kept a steely eye trained on the doorway as if to ward off trouble.

Beth turned to see what held her daughter's interest but saw nothing. She pulled up a chair, hoping to probe for answers without alerting Ruby to what may seem like inappropriate curiosity.

Worse, Beth worried about how her inquiry might stir the pot. The last thing she wanted to do was cause unwarranted attention to Luke and Genna's relationship, possibly encouraging the kids to dig their heels in.

The image of her sister as a fractured mess on Saturday afternoon materialized in her mind's eye. Beth rubbed her palm along the goosebumps running up her arm, recalling the tormented quake of Addie's body. Beth had held her while buried, uncontrollable anguish escaped. From the relentless crying and horrific sobs, Beth knew the problem went deeper than a broken heart. If there was something she could do to lift this burden—whatever the burden turned out to be—she had to try.

"Look at me," Beth said, scooting her chair so close that their knees nearly touched. "Tell me about Genna. How did you get to be friends, and... Well, whatever you want to share."

"Oh." Ruby giggled.

"What's so funny?" Beth turned to see Opal and Joel peering from behind the doorjamb on the other side of the room. Sheets of pure glee painted their devilish expressions. "What in the world?"

"Joel's making a pig face, and Opal...well, Opal's regular face is plain funny," Ruby lamented.

"We have the same face, you moron," Opal taunted.

Ruby snorted. "It looks much better on me."

"Have you two been eavesdropping?" Beth demanded.

"No, ma'am," Joel squealed, and the pair scampered away toward the backyard.

"I hate being a twin," Ruby said. "They wanted to watch me get in big-time trouble. They should be in trouble, too."

"I already told you, you're not in trouble," Beth said, frustration mounting. "And I'll deal with your brother and sister later. Right now, tell me about Genna, her family... why they moved back."

Ruby didn't respond quickly, as though she, too, needed to debate how to phrase her answer. "Why the third degree?" she finally asked.

"Third degree?"

"That's what they say on *Perry Mason*," Ruby said of a new lawyer show the family had watched recently on television. "When you're trying to squeeze information out of people, you give them the third degree."

"I'm not forcing information out of you," Beth said, softening her words. "I just want to know what's going on in my daughter's life, that's all. You have a new friend, and I'm interested."

"You don't ask about any of my other friends," Ruby stated. "Not even the boys."

"Boys? What boys?"

"See? You don't even know if there's a boy in my life."

"Is there?"

"Well, no…but that's not the point. You're not interested in anything except that stupid C-minus in geography I got from Sister Mary Prudence."

Sadly, Ruby was right. Beth paid more attention to academics than to what was happening socially with any of her three children. She didn't delve into their personal lives; well, not yet. They'd never given her a reason to monitor them beyond the normal levels most parents maintained. If it wasn't for her concern about Addie, she wouldn't be quizzing Ruby at all.

Beth needed to find out something, *anything*. Next to calling Nora, Ruby was her best option.

"Does your interest in Genna have anything to do with her dating Luke?" Ruby asked, now being the one to pose a question.

Beth frowned. "Why do you ask?" she said, realizing that Ruby probably knew more about the Genna-Luke romance than anyone else on the planet.

"Well. Uh, you know. Auntie doesn't like Genna. Luke told us that she's trying to break them up."

"I'm sure you're exaggerating," Beth said.

"Am not." Ruby folded her arms across her chest for emphasis. "Aunt Addie invited that stale old Shari Short to their house. Said she was going to teach her how to play the piano. But the real reason was so she could get her back together with Luke. She's so stuck-up, everyone knows it, but Auntie would rather Luke take her to the prom instead of Genna."

"Oh, such drama. Your aunt wouldn't do something stupid like that," Beth said, fully believing her sister was capable of this stunt and far worse. "And even if she would do such a thing, it's probably because she's worried about Luke getting involved with someone he hardly knows. After all, he's leaving for college soon."

"Huh." Ruby huffed, and Beth knew there was more to this story than was being revealed. Hoping her daughter would supply the next chapter, Beth stayed quiet so Ruby would keep talking and maybe spill a bean or two.

"Aunt Addie and Genna's daddy were special friends in high school," Ruby finally said, raising her eyebrows to accent *special*.

"When we were kids, we all ran around together. Barry Gallatin was in our group. No big deal."

Ruby huffed again. She bent toward her mother but hesitated to continue.

"What are you huffing about?" Beth demanded, no longer amiable to the waiting game they had been playing.

Ruby scooted a millimeter closer and bent her head toward her mother's ear as though warding off unwanted listeners. "Genna told me that Aunt Addie still likes her dad and is jealous of her mom. That's why she won't let them date."

"And you believe that?" Beth sputtered out, forgetting her pledge of silence.

"Well, yeah." Ruby scrunched her face, then continued her juicy tale, annoyed at the interruption. "But Luke said he didn't care what Aunt Addie said. He told his mom that he was eighteen and could do what he wanted. And if he wanted to see Genna, he'd see Genna." Ruby sat back in her chair as though delivering the closing arguments in a murder case.

Where do these kids get such crazy ideas? But maybe their assumption wasn't too far from the truth. Whatever was going on with Addie started right after Luke showed interest in Genna. Before that, Addie didn't care where the Gallatins lived, as long as they left Ahren alone at work.

A niggle whirred in the back of Beth's mind. Something obvious yet hidden emerged. She pushed the unsettling idea down. A notion that first sparked in her mind when she saw Dante in the Italian Club parking lot.

For a brief second, he had reminded her of Luke.

"So you and Genna have become good friends. She confides in you?" Beth asked, deciding to take a lighter tack.

"Well, yeah. We're best friends."

"What happened to Sally and Mandy? Do you girls still get together?"

"Sure, we still do stuff. It's just that, well…this is gonna sound bad, but Genna has a big brother."

"The one you were waiting for the afternoon of Joel's party? The boy who was supposed to pick up his sister and didn't? That fellow?"

"Yes. Dante was cute and all. I wanted to get to know him." Ruby turned away, seemingly embarrassed at her actions. "Well, that's when Genna and I first became friends."

"You struck up a friendship to get close to Dante? Ruby Marie, that's not a nice thing to do."

"I know, and I can't tell Genna because, even though Dante turned out to be a jerk, Genna is really terrific. I'm glad we're friends, and we might not have been if I hadn't thought I liked her brother."

"Thought?" Beth asked. "But you don't anymore?"

"Like I said, he's a jerk. He's not nice to people," Ruby declared. "Especially Genna. He did something really awful, and that's why the family left Pittsburgh, right smack in the middle of the school year."

Beth took in a breath. She didn't want to press too hard or too fast, but this could be the missing link she's been looking for. "What do you mean?"

"Just that I overheard Genna's mom talking about cleaning up another one of Dante's messes when I was at their house a couple of days ago. She wasn't talking about the kind of mess Joel and I made." Ruby clucked. "It was something bad, and when Mrs. Gallatin saw Genna and I near where she was standing, she stopped speaking."

"Who was she talking to?"

"I don't know. She was on the phone. She never said a name, or if she did, I didn't hear her." Ruby motioned to leave. "That's really all I know, Mom. Genna doesn't talk about Dante, except to say that he plays nasty tricks on her and on Roman."

"Roman?"

"Her younger brother. He's a grade behind Joel."

"What kind of tricks?"

"More like pranks, I guess, but they make Genna cry sometimes. Maybe that's why she likes Luke. He's so sweet and nice. He doesn't do mean things to get a laugh."

Beth nodded that the conversation was over. "Finish cleaning up the disaster in the bathroom," she directed, lacing her words with lightness. "And don't worry. I won't say anything to Dad."

Ruby gave her mom a thank-you hug and hurried off.

Beth watched her leave, now convinced that there was more going on than a simple case of star-crossed teens.

***

First thing Monday morning, Addie called the Keystone office of Gallatin Coal and Fuel only to be told that Mr. Barton Gallatin wasn't accepting appointments. His secretary would submit her request, and if a suitable time could be arranged, she would be notified. The hours had dragged since. She busied herself around the house with menial tasks, hoping to distract from the wait.

The familiar drum of a basketball bouncing against her floor broke her train of thought. "Luke, honey? You home from school already?" Addie asked, walking across the living room toward the kitchen. "I didn't hear you come in."

"I came through the back door," Luke answered, the ball anchored on the floor under his high-top-clad foot, his head stuck inside the refrigerator.

"What do you want?" Addie asked, joining in the search.

"A couple of pops. Do we have any?"

"Two?" A smile teetered on her lips. She pushed him aside and pulled out two glass cola bottles from the back of the shelf.

"One is for Dante."

Addie nearly dropped both bottles at the mention of the name. "Genna's brother?" She swallowed, handing him the drinks.

"Yeah. He's waiting for me in the driveway. We're gonna shoot a few hoops."

"Oh. Don't you have practice today?"

Luke shook his head. "Nope. Coach Ames fell off a ladder at home yesterday. Guess he's pretty busted up."

"Oh, that's awful news."

"He's okay, I guess. Just needs to rest. Anyway, Dante was going to join us. He's a ballplayer, too, but had to quit when his family moved. Tough break." Luke opened both sodas with a church key and tossed the caps onto the counter. "He's trying to get on with a college team. Lucky for him, he doesn't need a scholarship," he added.

Lucky, yeah. His folks can afford to send him wherever he wants to go, Addie thought. "So you guys are just playing around?"

"He told me he's a bit rusty. Since practice got canceled, he asked if we could throw the ball around for a little."

"Well, you're always ready for a pickup game," Addie managed to reply, hoping for a casual, disinterested tone.

"Yeah." Luke laughed. "He wants to get back in shape and try out for some college coaches this summer. Might get a last-minute recruitment offer. Dante's dad thought that would be a good idea."

Addie stepped toward Luke to get a closer look at his face. His expression showed no signs of anger or resentment, only the innocence she hoped he'd retain. "Son, about the other day with Shari. I want to apologize for—"

Luke shook his head. "Mom, he's waiting for me." He gathered the ball in one hand and clacked both sodas together in the other. He turned to leave just as Dante came through the door.

"Mrs. Burhan," he said.

She put out her hand, and he accepted, gently shaking hers. "You must be Dante," she said. "I've heard a lot about you."

"Thank you, ma'am. I've heard a lot about you... Well," he said, gesturing with an open hand across the room, "most of Mom and Dad's friends from Keystone. That's pretty much all they talk about. How great it is to come home."

Addie smiled tightly. *They're happy to be back. Of course they are.* Nora had bounced on her toes like a girl at a sock hop when they ran into Addie at the store.

Maybe the nasty rumors were just that, nasty rumors. Folks, as they age, get melancholy for their family ties.

But to uproot the entire household so suddenly—or what seemed sudden to Addie. Pulling their son out during his senior year, that was unheard of. The school year ended in two months. Why couldn't they have waited until September when Luke would have been in South Bend?

Nothing Dante revealed gave Addie leverage with Barry. If anything, this information might have made things worse. If what their son said was true, the Gallatins simply returned for the bucolic life that was found in their corner of southwestern Pennsylvania. Nothing sinister or underhanded about that. How could she coerce Barry to leave if she didn't have something to prod him to do the right thing?

She pointed at both boys. "Sit down at the table and drink your pop. Let's catch up."

"Mo-om," Luke complained, "Dante's not here to visit with you. We wanna play—"

"It's okay," Dante interrupted. "We can sit for a minute. I'd like to talk to my parents' friends and hear about how they were when they were kids."

Addie eyed him. Dante was a perfect blend of Nora and Barry. His coloring was so similar to her own son's. The Gallatin genes ran strong in both young men. The colors added from Nora's

Italian heritage and from Addie's own Lebanese roots made up the difference between the two.

Same father. Two mothers. How could no one see that they were brothers?

Perhaps no one had wanted to—including Addie—until Genna appeared.

Luke and Dante had a lot more in common than their interest in basketball. She wondered if in the depths of their souls, the two teens sensed a deeper connection, a blood bond linking them in ways they couldn't imagine.

"Good. Sit then. We'll visit for a minute." Addie pulled up the chair across from Dante. "I'm curious. After all these years of living in the big city, why did your family move back to Podunkville?"

"Well, I wouldn't call Keystone a podunk town," Dante defended. "Mom says it's the county seat."

"True enough," Addie agreed. "But most folks never look back once they move. Only visit at Christmas, maybe to see Grandma and Grandpa."

Dante quieted. "We'd come back every year to see Nana, especially after Papa died. Now, it's even better because I can stop over anytime. Have you ever tasted her oatmeal cookies?"

Addie couldn't help but grin. Those oatmeal cookies had been making kids happy for two generations. "Yes. They are the best," she agreed.

"Sounds like I need to get some of those," Luke joked just as the telephone trilled.

Probably Barry's office, Addie hoped. "That's a call I've been expecting. I'll answer it in the other room. Nice meeting you, Dante. Enjoy your game," she said over her shoulder as she left.

"Hello...yes, this is Addie Burhan. Wednesday at ten? That will be fine."

It will have to be.

"Where is Barry—I mean, Mr. Gallatin's office?" She scribbled the address and slipped the scrap of paper in her pocket. "Fourth floor. Okay. Thank you."

Addie hung up and turned to see Dante standing a few feet away.

"Oh. Honey. Do you need something?"

"Sorry, Mrs. Burhan, I need the bathroom. I thought Luke pointed this way."

Addie corrected his misdirection, escorting him to the downstairs bath and flipping on the light.

"Thank you," he said, closing the door.

Addie stood, an uneasiness sweeping through her.

How long had he been standing there? Was he spying? Maybe for his parents?

Addie shuddered. Perhaps she wasn't the only one searching for answers.

Chapter Fifteen

Addie woke before sunrise and ran her thumb over the tip of her forefinger, the rugged, uneven nail scraping against her skin like sandpaper. She grimaced at this visual side effect of anticipating tomorrow's meeting with Barry. Her queasy stomach turned somersaults at the sight of food. She refused the coffee that Ahren had brought her an hour ago and opted for toast, no butter, to tame her topsy-turvy nerves before heading out to help with the bazaar.

Addie hadn't been home for five minutes, preparing for her afternoon piano lesson appointments, when Mabel called in a panic, pleading for her to return to the church hall. This was the last thing she needed after a morning of digging through other people's discards—another complication to an already problematic day.

"I just left," Addie complained. "I have to get to the Naders in a few minutes. Can't Ed or Father Yusuf help?"

"No. They're not here right now. Besides, I need *you*. I'll explain when you get here," Mabel promised, refusing to supply additional details.

Several minutes later, Addie stopped inside the hall entrance, halted by the sight of her dear friend. Mabel, donning an unplugged GE toaster on her hand like a mitten, sent her convulsing with fits of laughter. "This could only happen to you," she said in between guffaws.

110

"Now you see why I couldn't explain this over the phone. Get over here and help me," Mabel implored.

"You're lucky no one donated a four-slicer. You'd have both hands stuck."

"Laugh if you will but help me. I think my wedding ring is snagged on the heating coil," Mabel said, wiggling the entire toaster to no avail.

"The last thing I told you was to shake out the crumbs, wipe the outside, and add it to the appliance table," Addie reminded, still chuckling at Mabel's predicament.

For the life of her, she couldn't understand her friend's unrealistic cleanliness standards. People didn't expect a used toaster donated to a charity fundraiser to be in pristine condition. That didn't matter. Mabel scrubbed everything like she was auditioning to be Mrs. Clean. In a pinch, someone could substitute the chrome on the sides of that toaster for a mirror and put on their lipstick.

"I couldn't do that," Mabel said, her horror seeping through. "Someone is going to buy that for their home."

"True, and they are the ones responsible for the deep cleaning, not you. Seriously, Mabel." Addie shook her head, surveying the dilemma. How in the heck *had* she gotten her hand wedged inside the bread slot?

"Hang on." Addie set her purse on a nearby chair and returned to her friend.

She sized up the situation, lifting the toaster and examining the underside to see if there was a lever or some other way to release Mabel from its clutches. For her trouble, a powder of stale breadcrumbs escaped, sprinkling her eyes.

"Ow!" she shouted, cursing under her breath. "That hurts."

"Sorry," Mabel said, shoving a handkerchief at Addie with her free hand. "I told you this toaster needed cleaning."

Addie scowled. "Thanks for the tip." She wiped the grit from the corners of her eyes and blinked until soothing tears appeared.

"Can you see?"

"Yes." Addie bit the word. A renewed vengeance to conquer the errant appliance sparked. "If I tug up on the lever on the side, maybe the metal thingamajig will pop up like the toast is finished," she theorized. "Then I'll put some butter and jam on your palm and have you with my tea."

111

"All right. I get the message. I'll stop overdoing things. Just get me out of here," Mabel lamented, swinging the toaster away from Addie, her hand still firmly trapped in its jaws.

"Let me try something," Addie said as Mabel yelled out in pain.

"Ow. Ow. Ow. That's making it worse. You're pinching my finger!"

Several minutes later, with the aid of a pair of donated salad tongs, generous dabs of hand cream, and a wide-tooth comb, the toaster finally released Mabel. Her ring was still intact, but her skin boasted semipermanent indentations from where the bread rack had compressed against her hand.

All this nonsense made Addie late for Macy's piano lesson.

In her hurry to set up in their living room, she knocked over a glass of grape juice Ethel Nader had set out for her, even though she had politely declined the gesture. Her stomach punished her for considering drinking, but the lasting penalty was the splashed-pattern stain the juice left on her just-purchased "Rock Around the Clock" sheet music. *There's twenty-five cents wasted,* she sighed, wiping off the paper with a rag as Ethel mopped up the rest of the spill.

Macy, her nose a flaming fuchsia, scooted onto the bench next to Addie and spent half of the lesson sneezing. In between praising her daughter's musical abilities, her mother lamented her daughter's allergies, but Addie wouldn't be surprised if she came down with a cold, or worse, in the next day or two. *Why can't people just cancel if they feel sick?*

When Addie finally got home, she flung her valise onto her double bed and watched in horror as every piece of sheet music spilled from the unsecured insides and slid across her chenille spread, cascading onto the floor. She grimaced at the realization that she had failed to zip the satchel closed.

"What else today, dear Lord," she muttered, now on her hands and knees retrieving the printed works of Mozart, Beethoven, Irving Berlin, and Cole Porter strewn across the parquet floor. A purple-stained copy of Bill Haley's hit crinkled as she shoved the sheet back inside her case. She swallowed, wondering if she imagined a scratchy throat taking hold.

"You'll be fine."

Addie startled at hearing a man's voice coming from down the hall. It was too early for Ahren to be home, and she hadn't seen his truck parked outside. *Maybe in a few minutes or so,* she thought, looking at the clock on her dresser.

She stood to listen and recognized Luke's voice.

"It was such a stupid thing, Coach. I don't know how it happened."

Luke shouldn't be home from practice yet either, but that definitely was him speaking. A growing anxiety planted itself inside her ribcage. Something terribly wrong had occurred for him to be home now and with his coach.

"Tell your folks to put ice on your ankle tonight, and keep your leg elevated," Bill Ames said as Addie burst into Luke's bedroom.

"Oh my, what happened, Luke? Are you okay?" she asked, pivoting her stare from her son to Bill.

"Mrs. Burhan." The coach stood and bowed slightly.

"Coach Ames, what are you doing here?"

"I called the house, but no one answered. Luke had a little accident during practice, so I thought it best to drive him home."

"An accident?" Addie panicked. "What kind of accident?"

"Just a minor sprain. He's sure to be okay in a day or two," Bill said in a soothing tone, but she wasn't comforted.

"A sprain?" Addie turned to her son. "Are you in a lot of pain?"

"Nah." Luke winced. "Well, a little bit."

"The trainer says to keep the leg elevated—"

"I overheard the medical instructions," Addie snapped at Bill. "How did this happen?"

"Me and the guys were clowning around," Luke finally replied after exchanging a glance with his coach.

"That's right, ma'am. That's what I was told. I didn't see the incident."

"You weren't there?" Addie asked, outraged that he would leave the team unsupervised. "Are you still recovering from your fall?"

Coach Ames shot a glare at Luke before answering. "I was in the gym along with Bud, our assistant coach. We were finishing up. I gave the guys some layup drills, and well, the next thing I knew, your boy here was on the ground grabbing his ankle."

"Just like that?" Addie said.

Coach Ames attempted to clarify. "Seemed like he and the new kid crashed into each other."

"Dante?" Addie questioned, a menacing throb soaking her already-compromised gut.

113

"We crossed signals, that's all," Luke defended. "He doesn't know our drills yet, and he...he went up for the ball and came down on my ankle."

Addie cringed. "With his full body weight?" she hesitated to ask.

Both Luke and the coach agreed.

"We need to keep the swelling down tonight, and he can't be walking on it."

Addie peppered the coach with questions. "Could the ankle be broken? Did you get an X-ray?"

"Don't think the bone is broken but can't be sure. Anyway, I'll stop by tomorrow and check it out. If the swelling hasn't gone down and old Luke here isn't feeling better, an X-ray might not be a bad idea."

"X-ray for what?" Ahren asked, joining them around Luke's bed. "What happened, son?"

While Coach filled Ahren in on the details, Addie pulled up a chair near the bed. "Can I get you anything?" she asked, instinctively running her hand gently down his shin, careful to avoid his ankle.

"Maybe some water," Luke said.

"Anything else?"

"That's good, Mom. Well..." Luke stuttered. "One of the assistant coaches from Notre Dame is coming next month to watch me work out."

"That's not a problem, is it?" Addie asked. "You've already accepted the scholarship."

"If I'm not healthy enough to play, they can take the scholarship away, can't they? Or make me sit out my freshman year?"

Fighting to maintain calm, Addie pulled at Luke's blanket and carefully tucked the ends around him. "Right, we're concentrating on healing your ankle," she said in her best comforting tone. "Let's not spend needless worry on something that won't happen."

"That's sorta what Coach said. But..."

"Is something else wrong? What's bothering you?" Addie asked, her gaze fixed on Luke.

"Nothing really, except..." Luke looked away. "I got the feeling that Dante pounded me on purpose."

Coach Ames and Ahren stepped forward, now listening in on Addie and Luke's conversation.

"What do you mean?" Ahren asked.

"He could have avoided hitting me. A couple of the other guys said so," Luke admitted.

"He did this to you intentionally?" Addie barked.

Luke looked away. "I don't think it was an accident."

"That doesn't make sense," Coach Ames said. "You're his friend. You're the reason he's allowed in our practice."

"I don't want to think that, but he had no business being under the rim jumping for the ball. He apologized and all, but I felt like secretly he was glad to see me in pain. Almost like he thought I got what's coming to me."

The doorbell chimed, and Ahren excused himself. Moments later, he re-entered the bedroom. "You have a visitor." He pointed over his shoulder.

"Genna," Luke said, surprised.

"Oh, Luke." She wended her way to his bedside.

The last person Addie wanted to see was the cause of her grief. Well, the daughter of the cause, at any rate.

"Dante told me what happened. I'm so sorry. Does your leg hurt?"

"Not too much," Luke answered, bravado fighting the reality of his injury. "I'll be fine in a couple of days."

"Thank God." Genna exhaled.

As much as she didn't want to, Addie stood and offered her chair to her.

Genna took her place next to Luke. "He's so upset that he did this to you," she continued, shifting closer. "Said I should come right over and see how you're doing. He thought you might be mad if he came."

Addie slid back toward a bedroom corner where she could observe all the characters as this new drama unfolded. She noted Coach Ames standing on the opposite side of the bed, his arms crossed and his face stern, in deep discussion with Ahren.

She felt fairly certain the coach was making a cover-your-butt excuse for his negligence, and she hoped her husband wouldn't agree to anything. Ahren, mirroring the coach's stance, listened, and responded noncommittally.

She released a small sigh of relief and turned her attention to the kids.

She reined in her focus on her son who, she thought, had miraculously inflated into a roguish, shiny knight when Genna first appeared. The contrast of his previously slack posture, now strong and erect—even in these awkward circumstances—was evident as he spoke to Genna, portraying the worried damsel to perfection.

She watched the young girl console Luke, her tone sincere and soothing.

What adolescent boy wouldn't fall head over heels for this pretty miss?

As Genna bent closer to Luke, Addie became struck by the similarity of their hair. The texture, even though Genna's wavy tresses gathered about her shoulders, matched Luke's swoop pompadour identically. She examined their faces, startled by the shape of their narrow chins, one masculine, one feminine, both originating from the same bloodline. The same genes.

The same parent.

Brother and sister. Siblings. Yet their nuanced differences camouflaged what was so transparent to Addie. Different last names, different stations in life, different sexes. But surely Barry had noticed the similarities between Dante and Luke when her son called on his daughter. Did he suspect, and that's why he had agreed to meet? Or did he deny the truth before his eyes?

Addie stood stupor-like as the scenes of this movie flicked in front of her, grainy and disjointed, like a 1930s gangster film. Lost in the spectacle, she jumped when Ahren placed his hand on her shoulder.

"Coach is leaving. We should see him to the door and let Luke get some rest."

"Yes, of course," Addie said, noticing Luke squeeze Genna's hand before she stood to go.

"I'll stop by tomorrow," Genna said, and quickly turned toward Addie and Ahren. "If it's okay with your parents."

"Of course," Ahren said as Genna headed toward the staircase.

Coach Ames followed. "We'll see you then," he said.

Addie waited a beat for the room to empty. "I'll bring that water you asked for. Is there anything else?"

"Just the water. Thanks, Mom," Luke said, suddenly appearing drained. "If I'm asleep, just leave the glass on my nightstand."

Addie left the room, dread intensifying. How did she ever think this day wouldn't come? She would be forced to tell Luke that his girlfriend was his sister.

That Barry Gallatin, not Ahren, was his father.

She swirled that idea around like a sip of wine with an acidic bite but a smooth finish. With all the horror and turmoil this revelation would wreak, being the child of Barry Gallatin could turn out to be useful. Once Barry acknowledged Luke as his oldest son, he'd quietly speak to Genna and, of course, Nora.

Addie would explain things to Luke and Ahren separately. She'd tell Ahren first, she decided, so that they, as a couple, could clarify this familial shift to Luke. They were his parents, the only ones he knew. Nothing would change on that front. Ahren would still be Dad.

Of course, the confrontation would be ugly at first, but it was possible that this unbearable situation could strangely benefit Luke.

He wouldn't have to fret about his college scholarship being revoked. In fact, once he became one of Barry's heirs, Luke wouldn't worry about money again.

Her dread melted into a surprising peace as she joined Ahren on the front porch, where he and Coach Ames were recapping the night's events.

"Where's Genna?" Addie asked.

"She left," Bill answered. "And I should, too."

A short while later, they exchanged good nights. Ahren waited until Bill was in his car before he guided Addie inside.

She closed the door and rested her back against the solid wood for support, quelling her mind from shooting off more fireworks.

There were too many ramifications, too many unknowns, but maybe, just maybe, things might work out. She hated when people claimed that everything happened for a reason. But perhaps, in this case, they were right.

"Why are you smiling?" Ahren interrupted her momentary reprieve. "Are you okay?"

"Yes, of course. I was just thinking about… Anyway, I better get Luke his water."

Ahren wrapped his arms around his wife and kissed her quickly. "You're taking this well."

Addie shifted her weight, attempting to wriggle free of Ahren's embrace. "You seem surprised."

"Guess I am. Anytime something happens to Luke, you basically go crazy, but today you seemed to be handling this setback very well."

"Huh. Some setback. Our son is in bed with what may turn out to be a broken ankle, a new friend assaulted him on purpose, and his chances of him going to Notre Dame might be disappearing." She turned to step away.

Ahren grabbed her wrist. "That's why I expected you to be a puddle of worry, but you were calm and levelheaded, not getting Luke all wound up."

"Well thank you for the critique of my mothering," Addie snarked.

"I was giving you a compliment. You're handling this like a champ. I'm proud of you. Luke will be okay, and you not showing your worry..." Ahren said, tipping Addie's face to his, "...when I know you're worried, will hasten his recovery."

A telephone bell pealed, echoing through the house, giving Addie the excuse she needed to end this conversation. "I'll get that," she said to a disappointed Ahren.

"Let it ring. They'll call back," he said, tugging her toward him.

"It might be important." Addie broke his hold and scurried to the phone. "Hello," she said, placing the receiver against her ear. "Oh, hi, Beth." She signaled to Ahren that she'd be a few minutes, hoping he'd move on. Instead, he stood under the arch of the door, waiting for her to finish.

Addie nodded, listening to Beth's account of the events. "Well, yes...so nice of Genna to stop by, especially since her brother is the reason Luke is laid up. Listen, sis, I need to go get him a glass of—"

Beth interrupted.

"What do you mean?" Addie asked, astonished.

She glowered at Ahren and mouthed *gossip*. He slowly retreated to the living room, and Addie waited until she heard the television click on before angling her body away so he couldn't hear her next question.

"What do you mean he hurts people?"

***

Beth hesitated sharing what Ruby had told her earlier that day. But after her conversation with Ruby, and Genna's brief visit, she couldn't wait to warn her sister about Dante's volatile, perhaps callous, personality. As she dialed the familiar two letters and five digits, Beth became resolute that she was doing the right thing. *Addie should know who she is dealing with.*

The line rang for what seemed like forever, and Beth worried that Addie and Ahren might have rushed Luke to the hospital in an emergency. Maybe her nephew's condition was worse than what Genna had conveyed. She let out a relieved sigh at the sound of Addie's hello.

"I heard that Luke had an accident," she began, evening her breaths. "How is he?"

"He'll be fine, I'm told."

"I'm so glad," Beth said, forcing artificial cheerfulness into her voice.

"It appears that bad news travels fast. How did you hear about the accident?" Addie asked.

"Genna came over after she left your house and talked to Ruby. I sort of overheard them chatting. Nice of her to visit him," Beth said, fishing for words.

Addie agreed that the gesture was kind but repeated that Dante had been responsible for Luke's injury.

Beth sensed Addie's desire to hustle her off the phone, so she cut in. "Genna was genuinely upset at what happened to Luke. Seems like this is a pattern with Dante. People around him get hurt."

Beth shook her head at Addie's question. How should she answer?

"What do you mean he hurts people?" Addie repeated after a few beats.

"Well," Beth replied, choosing her words carefully. "You remember Ruby had a crush on him around the time of Joel's confirmation?"

"Yes," Addie replied, a cloak of confusion in her answer. "What does that have to do with…?"

"I'm getting to that."

"For the love of God, Beth," Addie muttered. "You're watching too many television shows. Just tell me the facts. I need to check on Luke."

"Okay, okay. In a nutshell, Ruby liked him until she found out, in her words, that Dante is a jerk."

"Like a nitwit?" Addie asked, and Beth knew she was attempting to make sense of this.

"Ruby says he's not nice to people. Especially people close to him."

"Physically close to him?" Addie questioned. "Or related to him?"

"Possibly both, but what I was told is that he's mean to his sister and his little brother."

"Like teasing them? Everyone teases their baby brother or sister. You're a great example of that!" Addie grunted, obviously losing interest in Beth's anecdote.

"He is always causing damage and then playing off his actions as harmless pranks. According to Genna, Dante's bad behavior is the reason why they left Pittsburgh."

"Are you sure? I would have guessed that Barry was the problem. You know, chasing the secretaries, making passes at waitresses. Something stupid like that."

Beth retold the story of how Ruby had listened in on Nora's conversation, and Genna's confession about the nasty tricks Dante had played on her and Roman. "Apparently Barry and Nora have had to clean up after Dante a lot," she concluded and waited for Addie's response. A full minute passed. "Are you still there?"

"I'm here," Addie acknowledged. "Dante told Luke and the coach that what happened was an accident. But Luke thought Dante hurt him on purpose. Like he wanted to get even about something."

"That's crazy. Luke's been nothing but nice to that kid."

"I know, to the detriment of his own well-being." Addie's words carried a newfound heaviness.

Crushed at this revelation, Beth fretted that if she had said something sooner, perhaps Luke wouldn't have been friends with Dante. She knew that was naïve and unrealistic. These details had only come to her attention a few hours earlier.

Her nephew was dating Genna. Of course the two boys' paths would cross, in school or somewhere else. Now Addie knew what to watch out for.

Prepared was always better than being surprised.

"Do you think Genna ever talked to Luke about her brother's...peculiarity?" Beth ventured to ask.

"I don't know. Maybe," Addie answered.

Beth knew by the deliberate way her sister responded that Addie's mind was somewhere else, her thought process revving into high gear. "Will you tell Ahren about all this? He can forbid Luke from being friends with Dante and have him end things with Genna...just like you wanted."

Addie's huff vibrated through the phone line. "I'm not sure I should say anything to Ahren yet. He's famous for giving the benefit of the doubt to people long after there is no doubt they've screwed him. You know how he is."

Beth nodded, realizing her sister couldn't see her, but Addie continued before she could say anything.

"But..." she paused as though preparing to deliver a powerful edict, "...you can be sure that I'll give Barry an earful tomorrow."

"You finally got hold of him. Good for you," Beth said, enjoying this first moment of relief in their tense exchange. "The sooner you put this whole thing to rest, the happier we will be, even if we have to pull away from our friendship with Nora."

"Do you mean that?" Addie shot back.

"Of course I do. Blood is thicker..." Beth imagined Addie's coy smile on the other end of the call.

"Thanks, sis. I'll stop by your house after my meeting, sometime around eleven."

"That would be great," Beth said. "Seems like it's best for Luke to stay away from Dante and Genna too."

"The best thing for everyone is to stay the hell away from the Gallatins," Addie said.

Beth agreed.

Chapter Sixteen

Addie pushed the floor button and waited for the elevator doors to close. She sighed, swiping at the bags under her eyes with the pad of her forefingers. It would take more than a bit of cosmetic tugging to remove the sag and the puffiness she saw reflected in the elevator's mirrored walls. She hadn't slept well, getting up every hour or so to check on Luke, who had snoozed like a stone.

Straightening her back, she stepped off onto the tenth floor. A girl—now a woman—from her childhood made a beeline toward her.

"Adele," she greeted. "I saw your name on Mr. Gallatin's schedule and wanted to say hello."

"Becky," Addie chirped, "I had no idea you worked for Barry."

"Yes. We reconnected a few months ago. Right before the move. He offered me an office position, and I set up this satellite headquarters," Rebecca Smithson said in what seemed to be a bragging tone. "He is waiting for you in his office. Let me show you the way." Rebecca extended her arm in an invitation to follow her.

Can you have a satellite headquarters, Addie wondered, but didn't bother to inquire about the oxymoron description of the space. Instead, during the short walk, she took in the extravagant trappings of Gallatin Coal and Fuel's newest command center. Franklin Tower, with its neoclassical porticos and columns, was an iconic mainstay in the center of downtown, and GCF now encompassed the top floor.

Barry's décor, however, lent itself more to the Art Moderne style of the late 1940s, with a streamlined, simplistic approach. Before Addie could compare the two, Rebecca had ushered her inside an expansive corner office at the end of the floor.

Barry stood at his desk with most of downtown Keystone in view behind him, sparkling through a bank of arched windows. Of course his office faced south, offering him the best natural light for most of the workday.

"Thanks, Becky," he said and pointed to a chair where Addie should make herself comfortable. She remained standing, though, until the door closed behind them. Barry, always the gentleman, or he pretended to be, remained standing as well.

Addie avoided his eyes, choosing instead to take in the mahogany-paneled walls dotted with photographs of local and national politicians. She recognized Barry and Nora in snapshots with a few of her favorite celebrities as well. Just over his shoulder, she spotted family portraits clustered on the credenza. A couple of the kids, one family shot, and a picture of Nora striking a Sophia Loren-type pose. Just like in the movies.

"Seriously, you have Becky the Boozehound working for you?" Addie snarked, recalling a Friday night party at Barry's parents' house where Becky had consumed nearly three bottles of Bordeaux by herself. The rumors were that she threw up the entire weekend and was grounded for the next two weeks. Barry's folks were incensed as well because the girl had imbibed with their most expensive varietals. Barry, of course, unscathed by the event, had nicknamed her Boozehound.

"Wow, you have a memory." Barry scratched his chin as though recalling a long-ago fact. "You have to admit, for a teenager, Becky had good taste in wine. Anyway, she's about to be a grandmother in the fall."

"Young mother. Younger grandmother," Addie said, enjoying this rejoinder at the expense of someone else's reputation.

"We are getting older. And hopefully wiser."

"You're so magnanimous in your twilight years," she goaded.

"I was darn lucky to hire her," Barry continued. "Someone with her skills and local connections made this move so much easier on Nora and me."

"So Nora knows?"

"About hiring Becky? Of course. For some of us grown-ups, high school shenanigans were just that. Shenanigans. Seems like you're the only person who hasn't gotten over them."

Addie narrowed her eyes at his assessment.

"That's one of the reasons I wanted to talk to you. But first, can I get you a glass of water, a cup of tea… a glass of Pomerol, perhaps?" Barry offered jokingly.

"It's a bit early for me, but don't let that stop you or Becky," Addie replied.

She licked her lips. *A glass of wine might be what I need to take the edge off.* She slipped an embroidered handkerchief from her purse and dabbed the perspiration gathering under her nose. She needed to appear relaxed, even though her insides churned like the 1956 Olympic gymnastics competition was taking place inside her ribcage. *Of course I haven't gotten over everything that happened in high school. I wake up to the handsome face of my shenanigans, make him breakfast, and send our son off to school.*

"A cigarette?" he continued.

"I quit," Addie lied and crossed her legs at the ankles. "But please, enjoy one yourself if you like."

Barry flipped open the lid of his Winston hard pack, fished out a cigarette, and tapped the filter end on his palm, packing the tobacco. "I'm trying to quit, too. See?" He turned the box so she could read the word LIGHTS printed in blue under the brand name. He lit up and inhaled a couple of times. She wondered if he was going to swallow all that smoke.

He finally released the white-gray stream in the direction of the wall of celebrity photos before angling toward her. The pleased smirk of a young lad plastered on his churlish face was unnerving.

"So wonderful to see you…and Beth too. Well, everyone here in town. Who said you can't come home again?"

"Thomas Wolfe."

"Huh?"

"Thomas Wolfe, the novelist. And I think he's right."

"I can tell you're not happy to see me. Or Nora. Any of us," Barry said. "But listen. I have Ahren's personnel file here, and I'm sure there are some strings I can pull. Maybe shift him into a supervisory role. We're growing old, as you know, and well, Ahren's not getting any younger." He laughed. "Anyway, a supervisor position would pay about seventy-five dollars more a month. There's also a bonus program that could be worth as much as five hundred dollars a year. That would help, wouldn't it?"

Addie stared at Barry. He had believed her when she said she wanted to talk about Ahren's career.

Was this all a play to get into her good graces?

That wasn't a bad move on his part since the additional money would make a huge difference in their budget and their lives. Still, she couldn't let this diversion obstruct her objective. She had to be straightforward about her motives right now—and demand that he fix this mess he had left her with so many years ago while he sailed into wealth and prominence on his daddy's coattails.

Her urge to get this meeting over with suddenly waned. Perhaps probing a bit more would be prudent. Patience was a skill Addie had never mastered, but the stakes were too high to follow her impulsive instincts like she usually did.

She could spare a moment or two learning what was going on with Barry and the company. Maybe she'd hear something she could leverage once she wised him up to her demands.

"I had no idea that your business had grown so much," she commented, hoping he'd elaborate.

"We've been in the local papers; GCF's expansion into West Virginia. That's why I'm working out of Keystone now instead of Pittsburgh. I'm closer to the outskirts of Wheeling, where our new mines are being explored."

He moved back for legitimate reasons. Addie pondered this and wondered if perhaps Barry had manipulated work circumstances to camouflage his personal folly. If he wanted to be closer to West Virginia, then why didn't he take up residence in the Mountain State?

"That's where our new opportunities are appearing," he continued. "Ahren could be a part of this latest endeavor. The promotion would require some travel and long hours, but he'll find the work challenging with a financial payoff."

"You've really put thought into this," Addie said, surprised that she had become ensnared in this conversation.

"It's important to have loyal people on my staff. I can't think of anyone more loyal than Ahren. Sure, I'm not his favorite person, but I've always known him to be reasonable, levelheaded, quick on his feet, and trustworthy. All skills I'm willing to pay dearly for." Barry rocked a bit, appearing pleased with his summation.

"All that sounds fine, and I suspect that Ahren would be interested in hearing your offer. You see, Ahren's the one who grew up." Addie curled her lip just enough to convey her annoyance at his earlier barb. "He doesn't live in his high school memories like you seem to suggest his wife does."

Barry laughed. "You still have that quick tongue. You twist a word just like you'd twist a knife into an enemy's gut."

"That's harsh," Addie retorted, rearranging herself into a more comfortable position on the overly upholstered client chair.

"I don't know anyone who can put someone in their place quite the way you can, Adele Frances Bernadette Reuben." Barry punctuated his sentence with her litany of names.

She swallowed. *He's using my middle and maiden names. And how on earth did he remember my confirmation one? I'm supposed to have the endless memory.*

"I recall the day you told me you picked St. Bernadette as your patron saint," Barry answered as though reading her mind. "We were sitting on the curb in front of Puleo's. Beth had just bought two cents' worth of shoestring licorice, and you couldn't decide what to spend your nickel on. I called you wishy-washy."

Addie smiled at the surprisingly happy memory, and that made her uneasy. She couldn't get sidetracked by playing *remember when* with Barry.

"Wow, I was only twelve, and you were what, fourteen?"

"You yelled at me and said you weren't wishy-washy. That you were like St. Bernadette. That you stick to what you believe in, and you can make decisions anytime you wanted to."

"Why are you bringing this up?" Addie asked, hoping to disrupt this nostalgia trek, but Barry was undeterred.

"Then you marched off and came back with a candy necklace and four caramel creams because you got two for a penny. So proud of yourself for having a penny left over."

"You remember all this? Honestly, I can't imagine why."

Barry grinned and continued. "On the walk home to your house, you told Beth and me that you admired St. Bernadette because she died so young but still accomplished so much good."

He had lit the torch illuminating that deep place inside Addie where unwritten memories were stored and—for almost everyone—usually forgotten. She couldn't help but reflect on those carefree days when the three of them would play until the streetlamps turned on, and the dark night sparkled with lightning bugs. How they would scour the alleys searching for glass soda bottles to exchange for treats, making certain they had one bottle for each of them to cash in at the corner grocery store.

"I was always taken with how no one believed her, yet she stayed true to what she knew was right. Even at my young age, I knew that was a rare quality in a person," Addie said.

"So I got the story right? See, I remember things too. Insignificant, yet important, details."

"Something can't be insignificant *and* important," Addie corrected, feeling that old connection she once enjoyed with Barry.

"Who says?"

She stiffened. This friendly banter wasn't getting her where she wanted to go—where she desperately needed to be. "It's nice reminiscing, but all that was a long time ago. We were kids. Right now, we need to get back to the reason I asked to meet you in the first place."

"You asked to meet me? Huh," he stewed.

Addie stretched her smile tight, like a rubber band about to snap out of control and sting her finger. "Does it really matter who asked first?"

Barry shook his head.

Addie continued, "I said I wanted to talk to you about Ahren's job, and everything you've said sounds wonderful. He'll be thrilled to be considered for such a trusted position." She took in a deep gulp, propelling her toward what she needed to say next. "But that was just a pretense. I really want to discuss—"

"Our children," Barry declared and sat back in his leather chair. "We do have some details to iron out."

Addie gulped. *Our children. Does he mean our child?*

"Yes, I want to talk about Genna and Luke too," Barry said. "That's one of the reasons I approached Beth the other day. I also wanted to apologize for the little accident that Dante caused. How is Luke feeling? Is the ankle better?"

Addie's heart pounded so furiously she could barely concentrate. *Focus.* "He's better," Addie replied, not giving any additional details.

"That's great," he said after waiting a few beats for her to elaborate. When she didn't, he continued, "Let's finish with Ahren." Barry held up a manila folder not much thicker than a nail file. "From everything I read in here, he's a damn good worker. All his coworkers think highly of him, which isn't surprising. From all measures, he's the ideal employee, and he's way past due for a promotion. I want to correct that right now."

"I made a mistake in talking about Ahren's job. You should have this discussion with him, not me," Addie protested.

"I don't disagree, but I need help in convincing your husband to move up the corporate ladder, so to speak." Barry opened the personnel folder on his desk and shuffled through the few papers inside. "You see, Addie, the funny thing is, he never applied for a promotion of any kind. Ever. If I'm reading between the lines, it appears that he shied away from any opportunity or situation where he could shine."

Addie wished he would get to the point faster so she could finish what she came there to do.

Barry jabbed a finger against the thin stack of papers. "There's nothing in here to indicate that he wants to do anything more than deliver coal."

"Really, Barry, you're talking to the wrong person. You and Ahren figure that part out."

"You must know why he doesn't want to move up. To make more money."

"Maybe the right job never came his way. Maybe he's not into advancing his career. Maybe there are things more important to him," Addie said, knowing that everything Ahren did was to be a better provider to her and Luke.

Perhaps he didn't want a job that would propel him further into Barry's world. Bad enough he saw the Gallatin name twice a month scrawled on his paycheck. Delivering coal in sleepy Keystone had kept Ahren in his own galaxy, safe from the man his wife had once been in love with.

Addie stood, forcing Barry to look up at her. She huffed, mad at herself for allowing him to take them so far off course. "Let's talk about Luke and Genna. About their dating."

There, she'd said the words. She prayed the rest of her plea would come easier now that the floodgates were open. She'd explain the extenuating circumstances, and Barry would fix things.

Just like he told her twenty years ago when she had cried about their breakup. "Hearts mend," he had said, "and besides, Addie, you can always fix things. That's what you do. Fix stuff."

There she stood, trying to fix things, proving once again that all those years ago, Barry was right.

"Yes, I want to discuss that, too." Barry rose to his full six feet, two inches. He leered down at Addie, the gold flecks in his eyes firing the same way Luke's flamed when he was mad. Addie had hazel-green eyes, too, so the eye color was explainable. But the flecks...those were wholly Barry's. There were no points of light in Ahren's onyx-colored eyes. No hint of light of any kind.

"I'm hearing a lot about our kids being friends. Mostly, though, I hear from Genna, complaining that you don't like her because of me. Well, because of what we once meant to each other."

"That's ludicrous. I'd never—"

"I thought so too when I first heard. That Genna was too sensitive, taking things too seriously. My old friend Addie wouldn't purposely hurt anyone, especially not my child or anyone's child. Then a day or two later, Genna came home from school crying. She said you forbade your son from seeing her. There were a couple of other stupid stories of you setting Luke up with an ex-girlfriend and you blackballing Nora from joining the ladies' group, but those rumors seemed too ridiculous to even mention today."

Barry towered over Addie now and pressed on, not giving her an opportunity to explain herself or defend her actions. Sadly, everything he had said was true. She had no excuse, except that she was acting in the best interests of both Luke and Genna. He'd have to understand that.

"I didn't peg you as a meddling momma. The Addie I grew up with was better than that, way more caring of a teenager's feelings."

Fury charged through Addie like wild stallions through an inferno. All this had gone too far, exactly as she predicted. *Just tell him and get this part over.*

"Our fling was a hundred years ago. You're the one who chose Ahren before I proposed to Nora."

What did he just say?

Addie shuddered with rage. "That's how you remember things?" she nearly shouted incredulously at his faulty recall. This from the man who remembered even the insignificant details, like two for a penny caramels.

"I'm just saying, let the kids have their fun. Your son is leaving for college soon. He seems like a nice young man. Anyway, Addie, you of all people know how these things flame and then burn out. Before long, they'll be on to other crushes."

"You don't understand. We can't simply wait, hoping they get bored with each other."

"So you *are* meddling," Barry bellowed. "I told Nora that you'd never do something so cruel and small, but here you are, the personification of an interfering mother."

"I am not!" Addie defended.

"Then Luke must be a momma's boy." Barry drew the conclusion as though he were declaring clouds white.

"That's a horrible thing to say. Luke is—"

"A fine young man." Barry finished her sentence. "I think so, too. But then why are you acting this way? Is my daughter not good enough? Not good enough for even an innocent springtime romance? I never thought I'd live to see you grow into a hateful old woman. Not the young girl with the ideals of St. Bernadette."

"It's not like that at all." Her temper ebbed, realizing how insulting all this must seem to Barry and Nora. "The reason our kids can't date each other has nothing to do with me not liking Genna. I'm sure she's lovely. The thing is… What I'm trying to say is they're—"

The intercom buzzed, and Barry waved his hand, cutting Addie off. "Just a second." He flipped a switch. "Yes?"

"Dante is here," the secretary's voice boomed through the speaker.

"Ask him to wait a minute," Barry directed before releasing the toggle and turning his attention back to Addie. "Sorry. I have no idea why he's here now. But let's finish. You were saying…"

Addie also wondered why Dante would show up at his father's office unexpectedly. She hurried to complete her thought before anything else interfered. "What I want to tell you—"

"Hey, Dad."

They both turned to see the teen yank open the door and barrel into the office. His brown hair uncombed, a white T-shirt and loose blue jeans hung from his skinny, tall frame. Luke stretched maybe an inch taller than his unrevealed younger brother, but Addie suspected that neither boy had finished growing. They would both top their father's height by two or three inches.

"Hi, Mrs. Burhan," he greeted, stooping slightly to bow his head. "I saw your car in the parking lot and thought I'd stop by to say hi. That's a sweet convertible, cherry red. I'd love to burn rubber on those wheels."

"Shouldn't you be in school?" Barry asked, apparently as perplexed and exasperated as Addie.

"Yeah, probably. But I told Mom I wasn't feeling well," Dante answered and turned to face Addie.

"So you're here instead?" Barry asked.

Dante stuck his hands in his pockets. "Just wanted to say I'm sorry about what happened to Luke the other day."

What happened to Luke! Addie bristled at the phrase as though Dante, a mere spectator, watched the accident unfold instead of being the perpetrator of the injury.

"I hope he's getting better, and he'll be back on the court soon. Told Coach I wouldn't come to practice until Luke was healthy and playing again."

"That's big of you," Addie said, gritting her teeth. "Your father and I were about to finish—"

"Don't let me stop you. I'll just sit over here and wait." Dante moved toward a divan on the far side of the office.

"This is something private," Addie continued, flashing a pleading glance at Barry.

"Oh, I get it." He paused in mid-action and straightened his frame to what appeared to be a height taller than when he first entered.

Addie now believed he had Luke by an inch. In seconds, the casual demeanor of a carefree teenager clearly morphed into an angry young man. The creepiness of his manner, akin to walking through a spiderweb, forced her to rub her arms.

"Didn't mean to break up the rendezvous with the old girlfriend," Dante sassed.

"Watch your mouth," Barry ordered. "I'll not have you disrespecting Mrs. Burhan or me—or your mother, for that matter. Apologize right now."

Dante pushed a chunk of his hair in place, forming the front of his unkempt ducktail. "Sorry. Seems I'm saying *sorry* a lot since we moved to this backwater town."

Barry strode around his desk and stood in front of his son. "I don't know why you're here, but I have an appointment," he said, gesturing toward Addie. "You and I can have our daily row after Mrs. Burhan and I have finished our business. Wait with Becky until I call you in."

"You gonna ask her why she gives Genna the royal shaft?" Dante raised his eyebrows *à la* Groucho Marx. "Does she know she makes my sister cry?"

"Is that why you hurt Luke on purpose?" Addie accused, jumping to her feet. Engaging in this conversation was only delaying the inevitable, but the mother in her couldn't let this scuzzball think he was fooling anyone. Especially her.

"Addie, you'd better leave. We'll reschedule," Barry said, moving to stand between his son and his former friend.

"This is too important to wait. I have to tell you…" She wanted to say, *"Luke is your son too."*

"Tell him what? If everything is so innocent between you two, talk to Dad with me here. Or are you afraid?" Dante badgered.

"Stop." Barry placed his hand on Dante's chest. "Addie and I are old friends, that's all."

"Well if she's not here for some backseat bingo, then she's here to make trouble for me because of that mix-up on the basketball court." Dante stepped closer, forcing Barry to remove his hand from his son's chest. "You heard her, Dad. She blames me," Dante stammered hanging his head.

"He purposely injured Luke so badly that my son may lose his scholarship," Addie stated the facts, incensed by Dante's outburst. *How can he see himself as the wronged party? Luke is the one at home nursing a sprained ankle.*

"It's always the same, no matter where we go. People are against me," Dante sobbed, reverting to the facade of a child in need of his father's defense. "Everyone is against me."

Barry gathered him into a hug and peered at Addie over Dante's shoulder. "We need to finish our conversation later. Now's not a good time."

"What in the world is he talking about? Who's against him?" Addie shouted.

Barry shook his head, staring at her with a mournful plea. "I'll call you, and we'll finish our discussion. I promise." He rubbed Dante's back, his son's face buried against Barry's gray flannel suit. "Right now, I need to be here."

Addie began to argue but realized her efforts would be in vain. An unusual dynamic, almost a ritual, between father and son took place before her eyes. One that she guessed Dante had staged many times before. She didn't really care to know the details. The only fact that mattered was how easily he had prevented her from revealing the truth to his father.

She nodded goodbye to Becky typing at her desk and headed toward the elevator. On her way to the parking lot, she couldn't shake the feeling that Dante's visit wasn't happenstance, but rather a planned assault.

He claimed to recognize her car in the parking lot, but why was he in the area at all?

He had been listening in on her phone call the day Luke brought him home. What or who was he trying to protect?

The knot in her stomach tightened at the consequences of delay. With every passing hour, the possibility of Luke and Genna playing their own version of backseat bingo grew closer. How much longer could Addie afford to let this charade go on?

***

Just before leaving for Helene's, Beth popped four TV dinners in the oven and asked Opal to pull them out when the timer dinged. The easy meals were a smash with her children and an even bigger hit with Beth, who hated dreaming up food ideas every day. In fact, of her most-detested duties of all her hated housewife tasks, weekly menu planning topped the list, only taking a backseat to washing endless laundry and dusting the venetian blinds.

Practically since Beth first heard of Swanson's, she had added them to their rotation. Before long, the tinny trays made a regular appearance as the dinner of choice for Thursday Sewing Circle night. Ted, a bigger fan of home cooking, especially when all he did was the eating, didn't argue. His fried chicken supper was on the table when he got home, and at fifty-nine cents each, he couldn't complain about the price. And possibly the best part—Beth didn't have to listen to Ruby and Opal argue about doing the dishes.

"Come on already. We'll be late," Beth yelled out the driver's window after waiting a full ten minutes since the last time Addie had hollered from her second story window, "I'll be right down."

Beth had been looking forward to tonight's game all week, and now because of her sister's perpetual tardiness, they would be late. That meant they wouldn't get to play a full complement of hands because Helene would insist on the girls eating one of her fancy dinners. Usually her ideas for frugal yet elegant repasts came from the *Woman's Day Calendar of Money-Saving Menus*. Beth didn't mind, of course. Having dinner made for her, even Helene's experimental turkey à la king with parsley lima beans, was a welcome treat.

Ted wasn't home by the time she left. He hadn't called to say he'd be late, which meant he had knocked off early and gone to the Red Stone for a cold beer or two. Friday was usually his lightest day of the workweek, so he'd often take advantage on Thursday nights. Beth thought this was less coincidence and more preplanning on Ted's part, so he could jumpstart his weekend boozing.

She didn't worry about leaving her children home alone. They would feed themselves, finish their homework, and watch *I Love Lucy* if Ruby were in charge, or *The Real McCoys* if Joel had his way, before heading off to bed.

The car door slammed, snapping Beth out of her daydream.

"Sorry, I should have been ready the first two times you honked." Addie grinned at her sister. "But Ahren got home, and we started talking. I wanted to make sure he knew what to do for Luke while I'm gone."

Beth hit the gas and steered the station wagon down the street. At the first stop sign, she paused and took in Addie. "Oh, sweetheart. I should have asked. I've been thinking about Luke all day. I know accidents happen, but—"

"If it *was* an accident," Addie snapped.

"Do you really think…?" Beth signaled a right turn, checked her rearview mirror, and waited for an answer.

She hadn't said a word about Luke's condition when they met earlier in the day. The only news she mentioned was that Dante had interrupted her meeting with Barry.

"I'm pretty sure," Addie answered. "Especially after yesterday's little melodrama in Barry's office."

Addie had stopped by and relayed the strange events. Beth couldn't provide salient insight, but she did agree. Dante Gallatin was the common thread.

"What did Doc Kelly say about his ankle?"

"The X-ray doesn't show a break, but Doc thinks the ligaments might be torn. Hopefully a mild tear, so we'll start seeing improvement in about ten days."

"And if the injury is worse?" Beth hated to ask.

"Could be as long as five weeks, in which case, we'd have to tell the college. Doc says to wait a bit. Since Luke is in such good physical shape, he believes the tear will heal quickly." Addie fidgeted with the clasp of her handbag. "It's bad enough that Luke is hurt, but when I think about who did this, I want to scream. Ever since I heard that kid's name, my life has gone to hell."

"Aw, sis, that's not true."

Addie scowled. "How can you say that? You of all people should know. You've had a front-row seat for this freak show."

"Things are still okay with Luke's scholarship, right?" Beth asked, hoping to sound supportive instead of meddlesome.

"They haven't been in touch. In fact, they may not even be aware. There's no reason to tell them until we know something for sure. So we sit and we wait. Seems like that's all I do anymore. Wait. And hope nothing else blows up in my face." Addie gulped back tears.

"Honey, all this will work out. Things will be okay. You wait and see." Beth placed her hand on Addie's arm. "Luke will be better than fine and break all the Notre Dame scoring records, just like he did for Keystone."

Addie sniffed, unable to resist her sister's indomitable penchant for the positive.

"Luke is talented. He will rise above this and soar. He's made of tough stuff. You and Ahren are an unbeatable combination." Beth recoiled, wondering why she had emphasized Luke's pedigree.

Addie ignored the comment. "He's such a good kid. This shouldn't have happened to him, and I can't stop blaming myself. I knew the Gallatins were no good. I should have barred him from having anything to do with them—mother, father, sister, brother."

"That's a silly thing to say. You had no way of knowing about Dante; well, not until recently, and that was after Luke got injured." Beth reinforced what she believed to be true. Still, ever since she first laid eyes on that boy, she understood what Addie's heart held, a secret that now threatened to break free.

She should have realized sooner that Luke's basketball body wasn't a product of Burhan genes, but from his natural father's influence. Had things between Barry and Addie been that serious? She couldn't remember. Those times were so long ago, and the particulars blurred in her mind. She was busy falling in love with Ted and starting a life of their own. He wasn't drinking then. Well, not like he did now. She was on top of the world being married to the man of her dreams, tangled up in her own romance, eager to start a family.

Truth was, she had been a little jealous of Addie getting pregnant before she had, giving Frances and Del their first grandchild. She wouldn't have Opal and Ruby until nearly a year later, but she remembered Addie teasing that Beth always had to show her up, this time by twice as much. That had been a running joke between them. But what else had Addie been hiding? Had Beth been too busy or too selfish to see what was going on around her? Or did she not want to see?

The whole Addie-Barry-Nora triangle had played in the background as her own life unfolded. She hadn't bothered to get involved. Rather, she purposely stayed out of that spectacle—a no-win situation. Her sister and her best friend in love with the same man. Had she overlooked the tumult of Addie's emotions when Barry chose Nora? Or had Addie picked Ahren first?

As wedding plans were made, their discussions revolved around the color of bridesmaids' dresses and should she get Ahren's mother orchids or roses for her corsage. No discussion of her being intimate with Barry, much less pregnant by him. Luke had been born a few weeks early, but that happened all the time, their mother had declared, comfortable with the thought that if her daughter hadn't saved herself for her wedding night, she had married the baby's father.

But had Addie? Beth's certainty diminished by the minute.

She pulled up next to the curb a house away from Helene's, killed the engine, and held on to the keys. Luke had to be Barry's. When would Addie admit that fact to her...well, to everyone?

"You sure you want to play tonight? I'll run in and tell Helene you're not feeling well, and I'll take you back home." Addie didn't reply. Her sister remained still, a ghostly pale washing over her face. "What? Are you sick?" Beth stuck the key back into the ignition.

"Whose car is that?" Addie pointed to a cream-colored Oldsmobile with a red roof parked in front of Helene's.

Beth turned to take in the vehicle she had never seen before. "Wow, that's nice. Maybe Helene got a new car."

"Don't think so," Addie said, her eyes fixed on Helene's Rambler positioned up the street.

"Maybe it's Adam's," Beth volunteered. "Why does it matter?"

"I've seen that car around town."

"Where?"

Before Addie could answer, the slap of a screen door crashing against the aluminum siding made them turn their heads.

They saw Helene running madly down her walkway toward them, her apron fluttering. "Hey, you two, come on. You're already late!" she hollered. "I have fabulous lamb chops with parsley potatoes in the oven."

"I knew something would be parsleyed," Beth cracked.

Addie gave her a quizzical look. "Parsleyed or creamed."

They both laughed.

"And creamed peas," Helene added, now standing in front of their car.

"We're in for it now." Addie reached for the door handle.

Helene waved her arms wildly as though landing a jet plane. "Hurry or we won't have time to play."

Beth and Addie joined her on the sidewalk, and Helene threaded her arm through Addie's. "And that's not the only surprise," she said.

"Don't tell me," Addie speculated. "Flaming baked Alaska for dessert."

"No, you two sillies. I made cherry cobbler, but that's not what I'm talking about," Helene admonished. "It's a bigger surprise, and you'll both be so happy."

The trio flooded through the front door, Helene pointing them to the dining room, where the Sewing Circle ladies usually gathered. Mabel and Peg were already seated at the table and next to them, Nora Gallatin.

A mixture of joy and alarm swept through Beth as she gazed at her longtime friend. Nora's face, so obviously filled with delight and excitement, warmed her. *Nora, and she wants to make amends.* Even though this meeting was unexpected, Beth convinced herself that they would overcome.

Then she saw the shock and irritation punctuating Addie's ashen face, and every ounce of hope blasted away.

Chapter Seventeen

What in the world is going on with Helene? Addie thought, placing her belongings on the living room sofa. *I've never seen her so animated. She acts as if Mamie Eisenhower was joining us for a hand of cards.*

She tousled her curls and followed her sister to the dining room, where Mabel and Peg waited, a deck and their coin jars nearby ready to play after indulging in Helene's feast, of course.

"Hello, Beth," Nora greeted.

Addie froze in the doorway, her legs immobilized. She knew that voice, that syrupy-sweet intonation. Wholesomeness to camouflage the blackness of her soul. But why was she here? Who would have been so cruel to invite her? Her closest friends, even Beth, had betrayed her.

The icy chill of past wrongs crashed headlong into the reality of the present. Addie swallowed and took a moment to regain her composure before moving forward. She fought to appear calm and refined, yet inside she wanted to scream, *"Go home, Nora! You can't take my friends too!"*

"This is a surprise. Look who's here, Addie," Beth said, obviously shocked. A warning tone textured her words. Beth directed her stare toward Nora and appeared as stunned as Addie. Perhaps she hadn't been behind this. Addie hoped so. The idea of losing her sister to the other side might push her into an irretrievable darkness.

"Honestly, you two are always late," Peg teased. "You know Helene won't let us play until after we eat. You need to get here early on the nights she's the hostess."

"Sorry," Addie said. "I wasn't feeling well. Took me longer to get ready. But since you're here, Nora, I won't feel bad about excusing myself from the game."

"Addie, darling, what's wrong?" Mabel said, rocketing to her side. "You were fine earlier when we were finishing up at the church."

"Yes, well, something seems to have upset my stomach." Addie turned away, realizing she wasn't lying. Suddenly in the throes of nausea, she rubbed her midsection, where an eruption of acid gurgled wildly. "Mind if I take your car?" she said to Beth. "Maybe one of the girls can drive you to my house to pick it up later?"

"Well, no, I don't mind. I could drive you home if you like," Beth said.

"I've already delayed everyone. I can drive myself," Addie said.

"Well, not if you're sick," Helene said. "Beth, we'll wait until you get back."

Nora stood. "There's no need to hold up this lovely dinner. Clearly I'm the reason Addie feels she must leave. Let me go instead. That way *your* Sewing Circle can continue just like it has all these years while I was away." She gathered her pocketbook and turned to Helene. "Everything is just wonderful. Your home and your hospitality. I'm sure dinner will be delicious as well."

"You don't have to leave," Helene insisted. "Does she, Addie?"

"Really, Nora, stay," Addie said. "I wasn't feeling well on the way over. Beth offered to take me home, but I didn't want the game to be a player short... Now that you're here, well, I don't have to worry about that."

"You never were a good liar," Nora said, now standing inches in front of Addie, as though inciting a fight.

"No, I guess I'm not." Too tired and unprepared to battle her elegant nemesis, Addie grabbed the keys out of Beth's hand and turned toward the door. "I'm sorry."

"Nothing to be sorry for. If you don't feel well, that can't be helped," Helene said.

"Addie, wait," Beth said. "I'll take you."

"No need. I'm fine, just not up to—"

"Spending time with me," Nora accused.

"I don't know what's going on with you two girls, but now's not the time to start a squabble. Nora. Addie," Peg said, extending an arm toward each of them. "There's no reason to behave this way. We're friends and have been for decades."

Peg was right. Now was not the time to clear the air with Nora and assuage her guilt. Let the beautiful Mrs. Gallatin enjoy being the long-suffering victim a little while longer. She'd know the truth soon, anyway. There was nothing to be gained by making a scene.

Addie turned to leave, but Adam, Helene's husband, blocked her way.

"Don't blame Helene." he said. "I invited Nora over without asking."

"But why?" Beth asked.

"Because I asked him to. I've been in town for more than two months. I've reached out, and you've all ignored me," Nora said, looking each woman in the eye. "In deference to Addie, I suppose, for the horrible wrong I didn't know I had done to her two decades ago."

"Nora, stop," Beth pleaded.

"No. I have to say this, right now. Might be the only time I'm allowed to be in your presence and say my piece. I'll grow old and die waiting for Princess Addie to allow me to rekindle our friendship. Well, I'm here now, bowing down to Her Royal Highness, asking to be allowed back into her kingdom."

"Apologetic and remorseful doesn't suit you, Nora," Addie taunted. "Your style is two-faced and backstabbing."

"Ad-die!" Helene shouted.

"No one holds a grudge quite like you can," Nora shot back. "I'm here extending an olive branch. I tried that day we ran into you at Kresge's. You met with Barry yesterday, yet you won't give me even the slightest courtesy. Addie, please…"

Addie blinked. She had to get home, get away from Nora, or she couldn't be held responsible for what she would say. "I'm not feeling well. Will you excuse me?" she said, wanting to step around Adam, still in between her and the front door.

"I hoped after all these years, after all we meant to each other growing up, that maybe…you would have forgiven me, and we could be friends. I guess some wounds never heal. But before you go, I want you to know I never meant to hurt you." The flood of tears filling Nora's eyes matched the buckets invading Addie's vision.

"Are you through?" Addie asked, blinking rivulets away. "Can I go now?"

Nora shook her head to knock the tears away and to deny Addie's departure as well. "I didn't know that you and Barry... I mean, you two were always like brother and sister. He didn't tell me until later about the fling. And by then, you had married and had a son and we had our three. And, well…life had moved on."

A fling. Addie wanted to bellow. *He told you we had a fling!*

Instead, she replied, "Yes, life has moved on. I'm not the little sister following you and Beth around anymore. I'm a grown woman. A grown woman who at this moment needs to lie down."

Without glancing at Nora, she pushed past Adam to make space for her exit. Addie trooped out his front door as Nora fired her parting shot. "Our children are paying for our sins."

You have no idea.

***

"Give me those."

Addie jumped to see Beth standing behind her, holding out her hand.

"I can see myself home," she replied, tightening her grip on the keys.

"I don't think so." Beth shifted her weight but left her arm extended. "Not with my car."

"Really. I'm not as sick as I sounded in there." Addie gestured toward Helene's house. "I just had to leave."

"You might not be physically ill, but there are many sicknesses that are just as bad as having the flu or a migraine. Like getting ambushed by your past." Beth smiled, and Addie was comforted by the warmness of understanding. She sighed at Beth's knack for reducing trouble into a nicely folded sheet of stationery that could be slipped securely into an envelope, never to be mailed.

"That's pretty much what happened in there," Addie said. "I wasn't prepared to talk to her."

"I know," Beth said, her hand still outstretched. "Everyone knows, including Nora."

Addie finally placed the station wagon keys into her palm and waited for Beth to unlock the passenger door. She tugged on the handle, but before she could climb inside, Beth stopped her.

141

"You have to tell the truth before this pulls you and your family apart."

Addie cast her eyes to the asphalt and fingered a run in her stocking where the toe peeped out. "Tell what?"

Beth put her hand on her hip and huffed. "Honey. I know."

Addie leaned against the fender to steady herself. *If Beth figured this out...* She climbed in on the passenger side and braced herself.

Her sister strode around the car and slid in behind the steering wheel. Slicing her gaze to Addie, she continued, "Anyone with two eyes and the willingness to open them can see that Luke is a Gallatin."

"How long have you...?" Addie stammered.

"Maybe always, but never seriously until last week when Dante came past our car at the Italian Club. For a quick second, I mistook him for Luke."

"Now you understand why I'm so desperate. Luke can't fall in love with his...sister. But if you caught on, maybe everyone else will. Then I won't have to be the one to—"

"Confess what you did," Beth finished her sentence. "You can't take the easy way out. You're the reason this happened, but you're not to blame for how Luke's and Genna's lives intersected."

"Had they only stayed in Sewickley," Addie lamented, knowing wishes were a poor substitute for proper action. Still, she couldn't let go of the dream that she would have gotten away with this secret.

"I wonder if they would have settled back here had they suspected this would be the outcome." Beth faced Addie, her face a pucker of angst.

"I can't sit back and hope this will work itself out. They're at the age where hand-holding leads to kissing fast. And we both know what comes next." She shuddered, anxiety lacing her every word.

"Calm down." Beth patted her hand. "Even with this new generation, I don't think things have gone that far that fast."

"You might be right, but I don't want to have to count on Genna being a slow mover."

"Do they still call them that?"

"God knows," Addie answered. "I have to tell Barry, so we can put together some sort of plan. One that hopefully doesn't include telling Luke he's been calling the wrong man Daddy."

Beth started the car and shifted into drive. "No matter how this turns out, Luke has been calling the right man Daddy his entire life. Ahren is his father in all the ways that matter."

Addie nodded.

Beth pulled away from the curb without a word.

Several minutes later, Addie broke the heavy silence. "Remember when we were kids, running around the backyard catching lightning bugs?"

Beth slid her glance to Addie and back to the road. "Of course I remember."

"I'd chase after the fireflies holding an empty mayonnaise jar, and you'd swoop them in using a net. Then we'd watch the few we caught, spellbound as they flitted, flashing their tails." Addie sighed.

"I remember how they sparkled, dancing across the sky. We never seemed to catch many, though." Beth cast a smile in Addie's direction. "Mostly, I remember Mom yelling at us to come inside and go to bed."

"There was that, too." Addie chuckled. "Back then, I felt like fireflies could make every wish come true. That they held a special magic."

Beth wrinkled her forehead. "Why are you bringing up fireflies?"

Addie paused. "Because that's how I thought life would be if I married Barry. Magical, innocent, beautiful, filled with twinkling lights and possibilities."

Beth huffed. "A princess for the rest of your life, huh?"

Addie stared into the growing darkness of the Pennsylvania night sky, not a single lightning bug to be seen. "I'm so naïve."

"Not naïve, hopeful maybe. Trusting, definitely," Beth responded. "Every young girl has those dreams. Then you grow up."

Addie sensed that Beth referred to her own shattered dreams of happily-ever-after.

"Well, instead of the fairy tale," Addie continued, "instead of glimmering fireflies and wishes coming true, I created a tangle of hurtful secrets and devastating lies."

"It doesn't have to remain that way," Beth said.

"I know." Addie released a huff of exasperation. "I tried to tell Barry yesterday, but just when I was about to, Dante showed up and put on his little tantrum. If that boy were mine, I'd take him over my knee and give him what for."

"He's a little big for your lap," Beth joked. "Maybe borrow Sister Mary Philomena's paddle."

"Huh, that's an idea." Addie smirked. "Someone needs to take a strong hand with that kid, or there will be real problems ahead. He gets away with murder."

A foreboding shiver tingled down her spine. She had been tamping down the notion, but that nagging dread sprang to life anytime Dante's name was mentioned.

"I nearly told Nora halfway through her rant, just to shut her up," Addie confessed.

Beth grinned. "Love that woman, but she does go on and on."

"Always has for as long as we've known her."

"Her rambling just made you madder and madder."

"I'm not mad at Nora. I'm not mad at Barry," Addie defended. "If anything, all this upheaval has forced me to take a good, hard look at my choices."

"And…?"

"And, I've made some damn good ones. Not always perfect, but the right decisions about the important things. I'm quite happy with my life, my husband, my son. Just didn't realize how good my life is. Why does it take catastrophe to make you appreciate what you have?"

"You never want a drink of water…" Beth chimed in with the old adage.

Addie agreed, even though clichés did little to help her cause. "Obviously, this has gone on too long. First thing tomorrow morning, I'm talking to Barry," she said, satisfied with her decision.

"The sooner he knows, the sooner you can rectify this before something…unnatural occurs."

Beth only meant to console, but her phrasing of the obvious caused a knee-jerk reaction in Addie to spit a foul taste from her mouth.

Unnatural? Yet that was the truth. *Incest* was an ugly term. A small ribbon of relief passed through her, thankful that Beth hadn't chosen that word.

"This is as much his problem as mine," Addie declared. "If what Nora said is true, she didn't know he and I were…well…involved, then she'll flip her lid when she finds out."

"You've already come to the crossroads, sis. Many people will be affected once this news is common knowledge. You're choosing the lesser of two awful outcomes," Beth said. "I know, though, that once you've said your piece and all this is out in the open, things will get better. Folks will accept the truth and move on with their own lives and secrets."

"Not before a great deal of discussion, judging, and condemning is served up," Addie said. She was committed to doing the right thing, albeit close to twenty years too late. Still, she regretted the stigma that certainly would be attached to Luke. And, of course, to Ahren. Addie couldn't muster much sympathy for Genna, Nora, and Barry, although they were surely to be the butt of the rampant criticism and gossip as well.

One way or another, everything would be out in the open. That was the only path forward.

***

Ted's truck wasn't parked in its regular spot when Beth arrived home; in fact, she didn't see the truck anywhere when she scanned the street. *Still out drinking,* she supposed. She quietly turned the doorknob and snuck into her house, surprised that the usual blare from the television set was replaced by quiet.

Upstairs, lights were on, but no voices filled the hallway. She hoped her trio was getting ready for bed. With any luck, Joel would already be asleep. She softly tiptoed into the kitchen, wishing no one would hear and run down the stairs to check on her. The evening with Addie had drained her sensibilities, leaving her too exhausted to explain why she was home earlier than normal.

She bent close to the clock on her range to where she could make out the hour hand. *Must be quarter past nine.* Good to know they turned the TV off at nine, like she had instructed.

Beth had never been home before ten on card night, leaving her to wonder what really went on with her brood when they were left alone to supervise themselves. Now she knew.

A satisfying peace many mothers could only ache for grew inside. Her children followed the rules.

Delighted with this newfound knowledge, she kicked off her shoes and turned to make her way into the dining room. A hand reached from across the darkness and grabbed her.

"Ohhh!" she yelped, panic now replacing her fleeting peace.

"*Shhh*, baby girl. We don't want those pesky kids coming down here, do we? I just sent them upstairs not five minutes ago. All that noise and ruckus coming from the TV, I could hardly think."

She smelled the liquor before she recognized the voice. "Ted! Let go. What are you doing?" she said, half angry, half afraid of his answer.

"Doing?" He stood and kissed her. "That's what I'm doing. I came home early 'cause I missed my wife. Forgot tonight's damn Sewing Circle and you'd be out with the *hags*. Then lookee here, you're home a tad bit early, too." He kissed her again, this time thrusting his tongue halfway down her throat. "What do they call that? Kismet?"

Beth stepped back and wiped her mouth. She couldn't tell if his last drink was whiskey or beer. Could have been both. He always enjoyed a boilermaker.

He grabbed for her dress and toyed with the pearl-size buttons on the front, his hand clumsily brushing against her breasts. "You look awfully pretty in the moonlight."

She shifted toward the counter and turned on a switch.

Ted shielded his eyes from unwanted illumination. "Don't!" he shouted, causing her to flip the light off. "Come over here and give your old hubby some attention."

He spun her toward him and slobbered another compliment. Or maybe he mumbled a baseball score. She couldn't tell because he buried his face into the bend of her neck and trailed kisses up her earlobe and back down her skin. The heat of his breath caused the tiny hairs to lift, not from sensual excitement but from dread.

"Oh baby, I've missed you," Ted whispered as he kneaded her breast.

Both nipples pebbled at his touch. The natural desire of a man and a woman flamed. Still, the last thing Beth wanted was sex and not with a drunken bully. She dared not push him away, though. She'd learned over the years what a dangerous and painful mistake that would be. Still, if she could stall for a few minutes, this ravenous tiger would change into a drowsy puppy.

This pattern surfaced most times when Ted had been at the bar for hours. There was a window, somewhere in between drinking too much and passing out, when he turned into the horniest man alive. Often, if he ate, he'd fall asleep before his romancing turned into physical abuse bordering on brutality.

Beth knew how to play along. To act interested and aroused, hoping that he'd pass out before forcing himself on her. In spite of his drinking, she loved her husband but not when he came at her like an animal. He was not the man she wanted in her bed.

"I didn't see the truck," she commented.

"Left it at Red Stone," he said, unfastening her top two buttons. "Need you to run me down there in the morning. I have a call at eight thirty."

Thank goodness he didn't drive drunk again. "Did you eat?" she asked in an effort to stall for time and find out if Ted was operating on alcohol alone or if there was some TV-tray fried chicken in his system.

"That's not what I'm hungry for," he growled, undoing a third button, revealing the satin of Beth's rocket bra.

His hands moved down her sides and the folds of her dress lifted. Ted's fingers played with the waistband of her panties. With a masterful swiftness, both of his hands cupped her ass, and he yanked on her underwear until her panties dropped to the floor.

He hurriedly unfastened his pants and unzipped his fly, keeping one hand between her legs as a placeholder.

"Ted, not here. Let's go upstairs," she suggested, hoping he'd pass out on the bed if he made it that far. She reached to pull her lingerie into place, but Ted swatted her hand away and tugged, freeing her legs from the underwear.

"Right here, honey. And right now," he ordered, his pants pooling around his ankles, constricting his movement. "What's the matter? Don't you want me?"

"Don't be silly," Beth defended. "I always want you, just not in the kitchen when the kids might still be awake."

He grabbed her between her legs and moved his finger back and forth inside her. "They're not coming down. I told them to go to bed and not show up before breakfast."

He bent down to kiss her again. "You're getting interested." He grinned, wiggling his finger.

He anchored himself against the counter and grabbed Beth with both hands. "Come here, doll face," he said before hoisting her around him. With one motion, he was inside her. "Wrap your legs around me, baby. We're going for a ride." He thrashed against her until he moaned in ecstasy.

Ted went limp quickly, and Beth knew if he didn't shuffle off to bed in the next minute or two, he'd be snoring in her arms.

"That was good. Ahhh, so good," Ted said, his liquor-laced breath assaulting her senses. He untangled himself from between her legs and pulled his pants up. He dangled her lacy underwear from a finger. "Put yourself back together." He kissed her chastely on her forehead and left.

Tears streamed down Beth's cheeks, but she remained in the kitchen for several minutes until she was certain Ted had fallen asleep. Finally, she quietly made her way to their only bathroom, where she kept iodine, baking soda, and the fountain syringe the kids thought was a hot-water bottle with attachments. She sat wide-legged on the open toilet and flooded her insides with the homemade concoction, allowing the returning fluid to drip into the toilet bowl. The combination stung, but the alternative was worse.

A good Catholic practiced the rhythm method, but Ted wasn't a man to be dictated to by calendars and clocks. And she definitely couldn't trust him to pull out if it was her fertile time of the month. She had read recently about an oral contraceptive being approved by the FDA for menstrual disorders that would also prevent pregnancy. She marveled at the thought of something as simple as taking a pill as the solution to this time-worn dilemma.

Even if a magic pill were in the future, that couldn't help her tonight. So Beth cleaned her insides with a disinfecting mixture, a testament to her mother that an extra bit of prevention was better than a mountain of cure. Blessedly, so far the douching had worked.

She neared an age where biology would render her too old to become pregnant, but her body hadn't begun the change. A change she welcomed but knew was several more years in the offing.

Three children were plenty. She couldn't lovingly welcome any more. And financially, well, that wasn't even a discussion. On the rare occasion when she and Ted considered their children's futures, their hope was for Opal and Ruby to marry well. Joel, of course, would take over the plumbing business, although he showed little aptitude for water pipes, much less for connecting gas stoves.

The only person they knew who had brighter prospects and a chance at college was her nephew, Luke. After the occurrences of the past few days, his possibilities might be in danger as well.

Beth stepped into the tub and turned on the shower, a luxury most homes in Keystone had yet to embrace. Ted had surprised her a year ago when he replumbed their house, affording her this glimpse into 1960s bathrooms. His real purpose—to use theirs as a model to show potential clients this new plumbing breakthrough in action.

This modern convenience was catching on, and Beth thought she might know why. Most folks, like her, preferred the lingering relaxation of a bath, but the efficiency of showering had won them over. Everyone in her own home was ready for school in record time with minimal complaints and fighting over bathroom hogs. What family wouldn't want that?

Happily, Ted installed enough showers in the past few months that Beth didn't have to find that part-time job he had threatened her with needing if his business didn't pick up.

She toweled off and pinned her hair in finger curls before finally climbing under the bedcovers. She stared into the darkness with only Ted's boisterous snores to mark the time, waiting for sleep to arrive. She'd be up in less than five hours with breakfast on the table, ready to send her kids to school and her husband off to work. She remembered that she'd have to make time to drive him to the bar where he had left his truck.

Ted needed to stop drinking before he killed himself or hurt her. She knew that to be true.

Also, she knew that unwelcome rough sex was not the norm for married couples, especially couples wedded as long as she and Ted had been. But she couldn't begin to formulate solutions or ask for help to remedy either problem. She took solace in getting through tonight without a new bruise.

She'd face her difficulties soon. She couldn't allow her daughters or her son to view their parents' relationship as typical. Husbands didn't drink to excess; wives didn't submit to sex for fear of being beaten by the men committed to loving them.

But before she could muster the strength to make that happen, she had to be there for her sister. And for Ahren and Luke once they learned the truth.

The Burhans were a family worth keeping together. And so were the Jacobsens. She knew that to be true. But for the first time in twenty years, she entertained the thought that perhaps Ted wouldn't be a part of that family picture.

Chapter Eighteen

Addie let herself into her home and paused to offer a prayer for strength to do what she knew she must. Ahren appeared before her holding a glass of milk and a plate with a peanut butter and jelly sandwich.

"You're home early," he said.

"A bit." Addie and Beth had sat in the car in front of her house for a half an hour discussing possible solutions to her seemingly unsolvable predicament. With no easy answers magically appearing, Addie said good night to her sister, eager to go inside and check on her son.

She angled toward the staircase. "How is Luke feeling?"

"Hungry." He lifted the plate to emphasize the point. "This is the second sandwich I've made for him. And if he's asking for seconds of *my* cooking, well, he must be famished."

Addie grinned. "I don't believe constructing a PB and J constitutes actual cooking. You didn't use the stove at all. Nothing was cooked," she joked.

"Best I can do," Ahren said. "Just happy he has an appetite. And boy, his mood has improved too. He's been on the telephone, talking with that Genna girl, I think. He sure lights up when he's with her."

Addie reached for the plate to divert Ahren from noticing the involuntary grimace overtaking her face. "I'll take that."

Ahren surrendered his culinary creation willingly. "Hey, I'll be in the sitting room. I'd like to talk for a minute after you've seen Luke."

Addie climbed the stairs. *What could be on Ahren's mind? Did he finally notice that Luke resembles Barry?* Her stomach seized at the thought. Perhaps coming clean with Ahren first would be the better plan.

"Mom, is that you?" Luke called out just as she reached the second-floor landing. "Can you ask Dad where my sandwich is?"

Addie stepped into the room and noticed the black handset near his ear. She rested the plate on a TV tray and waited.

"Hey, I gotta go," he said into the mouthpiece. "Okay, bye." He hung up, and handed his mother the desk set phone, an extra-long cord dangling from the backside.

"I didn't know the phone would reach from our room to yours," Addie said.

"Dad figured out a way to add a longer cord, so I didn't need to get out of bed."

"He's been taking good care of you," she said, picking up the plate holding his snack. "Even making you a meal."

"The first one was really good." Luke grabbed for the uncut sandwich and took a bite. "This one too," he said, bits of peanut butter hindering his speech. Addie handed him the glass of milk, and he took a gulp. "I don't know when I've been so hungry."

Addie scooted Luke's desk chair nearer to the bed. "How's the ankle?"

"So much better. The swelling has gone down a lot."

"Are you still putting ice on?"

"Naw. Coach Ames said I didn't need to anymore. Just made me promise to stay off my feet for another day or so. I'm sorta hopping on one leg to and from the bathroom."

"Sounds like progress to me," Addie said, absentmindedly tucking at the corners of the blanket covering Luke, grateful that the doctor hadn't found a break in the bone.

"It will be a few more weeks before I can go back to practice, though. I'm going to be so rusty. Coach says not to worry. That I'll bounce back just fine."

Luke's hard stare sought her agreement. Did she believe the yarn Coach Ames was spinning? She certainly wanted to.

151

"I'm sure your body will bounce back, and you'll be stronger than ever," she said, attempting to boost his spirits. "You're young enough to overcome this setback quickly."

"I think so too," he said in between bites.

"You know, Luke, we need to talk about what really happened the day you sprained your ankle," Addie said, changing direction and laying the groundwork for the revelation ahead. "And just what kind of friend Dante may be. And that Genna—"

Luke folded his arms and rested against his pillow, stiffening his entire body. "I know what you're going to say, Mom. I'm just not ready to think about that right now."

Addie lowered her head. Coming down on Luke wasn't something she had been good at. In fact, if there was any discipline necessary, she happily punted that parental duty to Ahren. But today, she had to be the one to redirect her son's actions and prepare him for the changes that would blow like a tempest through his life before the next day ended.

If things went according to her plan, by this time tomorrow, Luke would know why he and Genna couldn't be boyfriend and girlfriend. And the reason had nothing to do with Addie's narrow-mindedness.

Would he hate her for what she had done? Resent her for having been a reckless, irresponsible young woman? Would he reject Ahren as his father and possibly want nothing to do with either of them?

Causing the breakup of his romance with Genna might be the least of her sins. She hoped, in time, he'd come to understand and forgive the foolish actions of his naïve mother. Luke had to know that her every decision since before he was born was made with what she thought was best for him.

Could this loving, wonderful young man she watched scarf down the last corner of his sandwich not judge her present by what she had done in her past?

"Mom. Mom." Luke prodded Addie's arm. "You don't need to cry."

Lost in her thoughts, tears had pooled in her eyes. She looked into Luke's expectant face. "I'm sorry, I didn't—"

"I'm going to be all right," he continued. "I'll go to Notre Dame. I'll score a lot of baskets. I'll end up with a business degree and get a great job. You'll be proud of me, I promise."

"Son, I am already so proud of you. You couldn't possibly top that," Addie said, tousling his uncombed hair.

"I know. But now you and Dad won't have to worry about me and about money. I can take care of myself," Luke bragged, and Addie thought she saw him puff his chest a bit. "Heck, I plan to do so good that I'll be taking care of you." He flashed that glistening smile sons reserve for their mothers when they were up to something. She wiped a tear away.

"I'd get you a tissue, but ya know, I'm not supposed to be walking around," he teased.

She poked him gently on his shoulder. "Sorry, honey. I didn't mean to cry. Well, not in front of you."

"It's okay, Mom. I know you cry. I know you and Dad worry about me."

"That's our job," Addie said through clouded eyes. "And that's why you need to listen to me about Dante. He intentionally caused your injury. Nothing accidental about it."

Luke pushed against the mattress, struggling to sit up, suddenly deeply interested. "The thing is, I don't understand why he'd want to hurt me. We got along so well. Even if I wasn't dating Genna, Dante and I would still have been friends. I can't put my finger on it, but we connected, ya know? We have a lot in common."

Addie fully understood the inherent bond between siblings. She suspected that Dante already sensed this link. Maybe that's what had made him strike out against Luke. Some twisted jealousy that he wasn't his father's firstborn. She couldn't afford to let her mind wander down the convoluted road of possible motives.

"What happened to make you change your mind?" Luke asked.

"I thought more about what you said. That got me questioning the behavior of the entire family. So I did a little digging. I asked around."

"And...?"

"I've learned more about Dante's pattern of treating people badly, including Genna."

"Genna?" Luke said, disbelievingly. "He adores his sister. He'd never hurt her. Who told you that he did?"

"Doesn't matter who. Ask Genna herself. Find out straight from the source. I'm sure she'll tell you."

"Tell me what?"

"Whatever she thinks you need to know about her brother and his tendency for hurting people under the guise of innocent fun. Apparently, there is a long list of victims, some of whom are his immediate family." Addie emphasized the last two words.

Luke remained quiet. He took a gulp of milk and licked off the accompanying white mustache. Instead of defending Dante's reputation as a callous tormentor, he seemed to be debating how much to disclose to his mother.

Addie believed that none of this was news. Luke was a good judge of character, and he had probably witnessed something that Dante dismissed as playful teasing.

"Honey, your dad and I must protect you from anyone who means you harm. Look at me," she directed.

Luke faced her with an anxiety-riddled expression, the look of someone who had lived through horror and still hadn't accepted the ghastly result.

"I don't want to believe he'd hurt me, but deep down, I knew he meant to punish me. But for what, Mom? What did I do?" Luke croaked. "We were friends. Almost like brothers."

Addie gulped and turned her head to block Luke from seeing the fright pulsing through her. *He is your brother. That's why you feel loyal to him.* A simple explanation that would sprout more questions than it ever could answer.

"Sometimes we just have to walk away from people we care for. It's hard, I know, but in this case, what's best for you is to sever ties with Dante and everyone in that family."

"Mom, you can't blame Genna for what her brother did," he snapped.

Luke's defense of Genna caused Addie to startle. His feelings ran deeper than she already suspected. Or did he share the same loyalty he obviously held for Dante? In either event, she was pulling this relationship up by its roots none too soon.

"I don't blame her for anything. Nonetheless, there is a problem between you and Dante. From the little bit I've learned, Dante has problems with a lot of people."

"Who said that?"

"I told you before. It doesn't matter," Addie defended.

"Well, you pretty much only hang out with Aunt Beth, so one of the twins told you. What did Ruby say?" Luke sputtered.

"I have a feeling you already know. Where either of us got the information isn't important. The fact is, you're starting college soon. You'll be in Indiana, playing ball, studying, meeting new people... preparing for your future." Addie stopped to make certain she had engaged Luke's attention.

He looked up in silence. His wavy locks, usually controlled with Brylcreem, bounced freely on the top of his head.

Her teenage son on the cusp of manhood, one foot planted firmly on each side. Addie recalled that confusion and angst when someone realized they were no longer a kid. When stepping into adulthood means leaving the carefree parts of childhood behind. The hardest change—she believed—was the inevitable surrender of simplicity for complexity.

Luke was learning that from here on out, nothing would be easy. Up until now, a hard decision had been choosing between chocolate or vanilla at the malt shop. His life was about to snowball from one hurdle to another. Addie ached that she was responsible for adding to his challenges.

She offered the wisest advice she could muster, the same advice she told herself many years ago. "Best to put this behind you now." She patted his hand. "Leave with a clean slate."

"I can't leave Genna, Mom. I just can't."

***

The coal-black darkness of her bedroom comforted Addie as she kicked off her shoes and flopped onto the bed. Every inch of her body ached with a hollowing regret and shame.

Tomorrow, the day after at worst, Luke would find out that, in fact, he could leave Genna. He'd have to. Staying as friends would be too difficult. Such a harsh lesson to swallow.

Maybe in time, they could reconcile as a family. Brother and sister. That would take maturity on both their parts and years of healing. And the threat of Dante would overshadow any chance of normalcy.

Addie must have dozed off. She woke when Ahren switched on the nightstand lamp. Startled, she sat up, rubbing her eyes. "Oh, please, turn the light off," she cried.

"I've been waiting in the living room for you, Addie. We need to talk," he said, storms of displeasure dripping from his words.

"Not tonight, Ahren. I'm so exhausted I fell asleep in my clothes." She climbed off the bed and undressed, intentionally

155

ignoring the plea in his voice. She grabbed a nightgown out of her bureau, slipped it on, and turned to get under the covers.

"This is something that can't wait," he groused in a tone he used only when he discovered their checking account overdrawn.

Addie stifled a yawn. "What can't wait until the morning?"

Ahren frowned, deepening the worry lines etched in his forehead and outlining the frame of his mouth. "We can't talk up here. No privacy." He slid his gaze in the direction of Luke's room.

He knows.

Addie's stomach dropped like an elevator whose cable had broken, careening wildly until crashing at the bottom. She laid a hand on her abdomen and breathed steadily in an effort to fortify herself for what was about to explode.

Ahren tossed a robe in her direction that landed at her feet. "I'll be downstairs," he snapped. "*Waiting.*"

She lingered until the sound of his shoes hitting the hardwood faded before bending down to retrieve the dressing gown. Every ounce of her wanted to run away. But what good would that do? Ahren had already unraveled her deceit.

She crept down the steps, careful not to make any loud noise as she passed Luke's room. This was a conversation their son shouldn't hear.

Addie surveyed her husband tipping forward in the chair by the window, his elbows propped against his knees, his fingers laced. He jutted his chin toward the matching chair across from him and waited for her to sit.

She perched on the end of the cushion and watched Ahren lick his lips, as though harnessing courage to bring up a misery buried for nearly two decades. There was forgiveness in his eyes, a longing she had witnessed sporadically during their marriage. She placed her hands in her lap and exhaled, no longer bracing for the worst.

She recognized that expression.

Ahren's love.

"I know I wasn't your first," he finally said. "But I took pride and comfort in knowing that I am your last. Your only lover."

Addie gathered her robe tighter around her middle and tugged on the belt. The mention of the word *lover* made her feel exposed; somehow dirty, even though she knew Ahren wasn't using the word in a shameful way.

"That's how I can go out each day and work hard. Because I know my wife loves me and only me." Ahren tilted his head to one side and then the other, eliciting popping sounds from his neck.

Addie sighed at the familiarity of his favorite method of stress relief. How many years had she watched these stretches and listened to the subsequent crunching and cracking of his joints? The hum comforted her as she debated what she should say.

Before she could reply, Ahren continued, "I love you, Addie. And I'm in love with you. There is a difference."

Addie's eyes flooded with tears, and she hastily swept them away. "I love you, Ahren. You must know that. I love you more each day."

"But are you still in love with me?"

"What? Why are you asking?"

"It's a simple question. Are you in love with me? Crazy, mad, silly, toe-tingling love because that's how I feel about you. It's more than loving you," Ahren said, untangling his fingers so he could use one hand to comb through his hair. "We love lots of things, but I believe you can only be *in love* with one person... So I want to know, Addie Burhan, are you still in love with your husband?"

Addie stared at Ahren, considering his question. Loving and being in love were two different things. She hadn't made the distinction between the two.

"Were you ever in love with me?" he questioned, tears gathering at the corners of his eyes. "Maybe I should start there."

"Ahren, of course I love you, and I'm in love with you. More than I ever realized." She cast her gaze down, rattled by what she had just admitted. Her eyes followed the odd striated pattern in the wood flooring, and she pondered her revelation.

Addie couldn't say when or how, but yes, she was passionately in love with the man she had married, the man she built a life with.

He sighed, relieved at her answer, but tension hung like a dense fog refusing to lift.

Addie blinked through tear-drenched eyes. "You are the only one who makes my toes tingle."

Ahren laughed.

"Why are you asking me this? Why now?" Addie insisted.

"I had to know where I stand, what I mean to you. You know why. We didn't start off as the unblemished couple. When you married me, you were still in love with Barry."

Addie clutched her sides tighter. He'd always known, even from the beginning, even as she stood beside him in church and vowed, "I do."

"I made peace with this years ago. I chose to marry you, hoping that my being in love with you would be powerful enough for the both of us." He moved to where she sat and extended his arms.

Addie clasped his hands, allowing him to lift her from the seat. "And it was enough, more than enough," she said, wondering where this was leading.

"We grew to be a family," Ahren continued, "and you understanding that makes what I have to say now a little easier. We can move forward."

"Did you think I didn't love you? That I was planning to leave you?"

"I thought the life we've built was strong, but I needed to hear from you that this is the life you still would pick in spite of..."

"In spite of what?"

"I know that our son was fathered by Barry," Ahren said the words without inflection or emotion, as though he were a tour guide pointing out a sixteenth-century castle or a sports announcer reflecting on Bill Mazeroski's batting average last season.

The matter-of-fact way he recited details that would devastate most men took Addie's breath away. He knew Luke wasn't his son, not in the normal way a man claims paternity, yet he was revealing this fact as easily as discussing the price of gasoline.

Addie was convinced that no child had a more loving father than the man Luke called Daddy. Blood didn't make that connection, caring did. Showing up every day, being a shoulder to cry on and a leg up when you needed one. That's who fathers were. Always there. Always reliable. Always proud of their children. Ahren continued to be those things to Luke.

A peace wafted through her at the realization that nothing would change between father and son. She wished she had the same confidence in her relationship with Luke. He would see her as the cause of this façade and he might never forgive her for her dishonesty.

She started to defend her indefensible actions, but Ahren held up his hand. "When I saw him playing basketball with Dante, I knew for certain that Barry was the father. I'm not bringing this up now to upset you. I would never have told you I knew the truth, hoping someday you'd tell me yourself." Ahren toed the hardwood floor as though delaying what must be said next.

"Ahren, I—"

"I started wondering pretty much from when we brought Luke home from the hospital. How he was born just seven months after we married. Your mother said he was premature, but he weighed a good eight pounds. Nothing premature about that," Ahren bragged as though recalling the memory with pride.

"Please, Ahren, I can explain," Addie pleaded.

"Let me finish," he said, his plea stronger. "When Luke was two or three, we really tried, you remember. But you couldn't get pregnant. I saw how much that hurt you—not being able to have another baby. So I went to the doctor to see what was wrong. That's when I found out that I'm sterile. Something about having mumps when I was a young boy."

"Why didn't you tell me?" she asked, vacillating between relief and anger. "All these years you…"

"Addie, really, it doesn't matter. I love Luke as my own. But I am sad that I couldn't give you another child. You're a wonderful mother, and I had hoped we'd have lots of kids. I'm the luckiest man alive to be married to you and get to raise Luke. Still, I always felt guilty for not giving you that daughter you wanted so badly." Ahren broke away and wandered the room a bit.

Addie reclaimed her seat, aching at the pain she knew Ahren endured. If he had already known or suspected the truth, perhaps the sharpness of this revelation would have dulled in time. She prayed this was true.

"We might have lived our entire married lives without ever talking about this, but then they moved back, and everything exploded. I immediately understood why you've been so crazed to interfere with Luke and Genna. The boy can't date his sister. But mostly, I was worried that you'd want Barry."

Addie pushed against the armchair, propelled herself toward Ahren, and stood toe-to-toe with him. "Are you out of your mind? Why in the world would I want him? What I want is for Luke to be happy and not find out the horrible thing his mother did so many years ago."

"Was it really so horrible? You married me. We had a son and gave him a good life. We'll continue to give him a good life, and if we're lucky, he'll supply us with a passel of grandbabies." Ahren wrapped his arms around Addie and kissed the tip of her nose. "You know we have to tell him, right? You can't keep hoping that Barry and Nora will pull up tent stakes and move back to Pittsburgh. And even if they moved, that doesn't mean Luke and Genna won't keep seeing each other."

"That would be the easiest answer," Addie confessed. "If they just relocate somewhere else and let all of us go back to our normal life."

"Honey, there's nothing easy or normal about any of this. We both know what needs to be done," Ahren said.

Addie frowned and stepped back. "We have to tell Luke."

"I don't see any other alternative. Barry's not moving east. Gallatin Coal's future is moving toward West Virginia."

"How do you know that?"

"That's all everyone at work talks about, the expansion into Wheeling. They're all jockeying for new positions. Some of the fellas say they'd move if the job opportunity is good enough."

"Did Barry talk to you…about job opportunities?" she asked, worried he might be offended that she had meddled in his career.

"Not directly, but I've been requested to submit an application for section chief. Never heard of that before—'request to apply' was what Boots Tucker said. Seemed a bit snippy when he handed me the application."

"Boots is always snippy, like his shoes are too tight or something. How he got to be manager of the delivery drivers is beyond," Addie snarked. "What the heck is a section chief?"

"Don't know for sure. Pays a dang sight more than what I make now. More than Boots earns, too, I suppose."

"Well, are you going to apply?" Addie asked.

He shook his head. "Don't think so. The extra money would be nice, but I've spent most of my adult life avoiding Barry Gallatin. He and Nora living fifty miles away suited me fine. We didn't run into either of them, even when they'd come back to visit her momma."

"It's a good opportunity in spite of the fact that Barry's involved. You wouldn't have to work directly with him, would you?" Addie asked, hoping Ahren didn't dismiss this chance for the wrong reasons.

"This job would put me smack-dab in the middle of his highway. Only a matter of time before our two cars collided."

"But you're really good at avoiding collisions," Addie teased. "Once this news gets out, our relationship to the Gallatins will change. In a positive or a negative way, time will tell. Maybe you should hold off making any decisions just yet."

"You're probably right. Best thing is to wait and see, but I have a feeling that I should start looking for something else." Ahren hooked his thumbs under his armpits and poked out his chest. "Lots of businesses can use a hardworking guy like me," he bragged.

Addie bent toward him for a kiss, and Ahren complied. He was a hardworking man. She gazed into his eyes, realizing she had never loved him more than she did at this moment.

After their lips parted, she asked, "Will you be there when I tell him why his daughter can't date Luke?" hoping he would say yes. The thought of them confronting Barry as a couple appealed to her and lessened her anxiety. *Yes, Barry, biologically Luke is yours. That's why you need to keep your daughter away.* She fantasized saying those words with Ahren by her side, holding her hand, supporting her. Defending his family.

"If that's what you want," Ahren said. "He might already suspect, though. Barry's a snake in the grass, but he's one smart snake."

"He's smart about financial matters and business dealings," Addie said. "But when it comes to personal matters, he's dumber than a rock. He can't see what's right in front of him. I got a little taste of that earlier tonight from Nora."

"Nora! Where'd you see her?" Ahren asked.

"She was a surprise guest at Sewing Circle. Hijacked the entire evening. That's why I came home early." Addie pursed her lips. "I couldn't sit and make courteous small talk like nothing had ever happened between us. All the girls think it's water under the bridge, that I should forgive and forget. Frankly, I have. I was happy to forgive and forget as long as I didn't have to talk to either of them. Now that's an impossibility. I'll have to confront them, and I will, as long as you'll be with me."

"Of course I'll be there. But I don't think this news will come as a shock to Barry or Nora, for that matter. They've interacted with Luke and seen him with his other kids at their house. The resemblance among that group is obvious. Frankly, Addie, I don't see how they don't already know."

Addie considered this and hoped he spoke the truth. But if Barry and Nora knew, why weren't they doing anything to end this relationship?

Addie couldn't take the chance. Tomorrow was the day. A new beginning. No more dark secrets.

"I'm through guessing at what people might be aware of." An anger edged Addie's words. "And I'm through pretending. All that pretending cost me and you. Now Luke will pay the price. I'm so very sorry about that. I'm sorry about a lot of things, but my biggest regret is not being honest with you before we married. And I'm overwhelmed and humbled by how you understand and have forgiven me," she said, running her hand across his chest.

"I wouldn't say I've always been understanding. I've been dealing with this a long time, trying to make sense of what's been going on. I was hurt, angry, and felt betrayed when I first figured things out. Remember when I slept on the couch? I told you it was because I was putting in so many extra hours or some nonsense. I needed space to think—to decide whether I should stay or not. No, honey, the calm guy standing before you was pretty much a ranting lunatic for a long time."

Addie watched Ahren's gaze flit across the room and slice back to her, as though seeking to quell a growing pain. His hurt ran much deeper than he showed. But that was Ahren's way. She never really knew when worry weighed him down.

She recalled the period he referred to as one of the darkest in their marriage. Not having his body to snuggle against in their double bed made her wonder if he had fallen in love with someone else. The worst part was that she couldn't blame him if he had. That may have been the beginning of her recommitting to their relationship.

"But today's not redemption day. Maybe soon, once we've gotten this all straightened out, perhaps we can talk. You see, Addie, you're not the only one keeping secrets."

Her stomach knotted. *He had had an affair,* she thought, wiping a tear from her cheek.

"Maybe we'll take a trip, a second honeymoon of sorts, and tell each other of our failings and foolishness and seek forgiveness."

"Do you regret staying with me?" Addie squeaked, barely able to form the thought.

"I'm married to the perfect woman," he replied.

"I married the right man," Addie said, "and I'm miserable that I wasted so much of our time questioning that."

Ahren tilted her chin up, and she looked into his gleaming eyes. "That's in our past. For our future, neither one of us will waste any more time. We have each other, dare I say through better or worse, to enjoy the rest of our lives together."

Addie fell against his chest and let his embrace envelop her. Every fiber of her being pulsated at the drastic changes her life would absorb in a few hours, but at this moment, the security of Ahren's hold calmed and soothed. His touch cleared her mind of doubt, and she felt at peace.

Ahren kissed the top of her head. "And now, once Barry knows, I... Well, if I don't find a different job, as crazy as it sounds, I could be working for Luke one day. After all, he'd be Barry's firstborn."

"No, he wouldn't," Addie said, although a part of her wanted Barry as a financial backup should Luke ever need him. "Fathering a child and being a father to one are two distinct things. Luke is your son, born to us as a married couple. If Barry has any claim, it won't be to take Luke away from us and finish his upbringing as a Gallatin. He may accept the truth, but I guarantee he won't be looking to expand his family."

"Maybe not, but they could give Luke more than we can," Ahren confessed.

"More what? Money? I guess. But not more happiness, more confidence, more love. Those are the important things you've secured in him over the years. He's ours, and he will find his own path, on his own. He won't require a thing from the Gallatin family," she finished.

Ahren took her hand. "We better get to bed," he said. "Big day tomorrow."

She followed him up the steps as a foreboding chill seeped into her soul. The premonition floated in like fog on a San Francisco night, and she silently gasped at the thought.

If Ahren thinks Luke would supersede Dante, maybe Dante does as well.

Chapter Nineteen

"Coming, I'm coming!" Beth yelled at the ringing phone greeting her as she walked into her kitchen. "Why doesn't anyone else ever answer this thing?" she shouted in the direction of her children lollygagging upstairs instead of getting ready for school.

As soon as breakfast was finished some thirty minutes earlier, the trio had disappeared to their rooms, eager to avoid additional interaction with their father. Beth drove Ted to the beer garden to retrieve his truck from the night before.

He muttered something about a clogged drain at Mrs. McAbbie's and scooted himself out her car door. He was equally pleased to escape. The peck on the cheek he left her with barely acknowledged the trauma from the night before. Usually there was some sort of apology or contrition, followed by promises of improved behavior that he never intended to carry out.

Did he not remember, or was this a new game of pretending to forget? No matter. As soon as this mess with Barry was straightened, Beth would turn her energies to her own troubles.

"Addie. My goodness, you're phoning early," Beth said into the receiver. "Is everything okay?"

"Yes. Just wanted to ask if you could come over for a couple of hours and stay with Luke."

"Well, of course. What time do you want me there?"

"Before ten. I'm meeting Barry and Nora at their house after their kids have left for school."

"When did you set this up?"

164

"Late last night. I called and told him we needed to talk. That I'm bringing Ahren, and he should have Nora there as well," Addie said.

Beth couldn't believe the nonchalance in her sister's voice. "Ahren! What? How! Did you tell him?"

"I didn't need to. He figured it out."

"Is he upset? Are you okay? Oh, my God, Addie. Should I head over now?"

"Everything is fine, or will be. Look, sis, it's a long story, and I'll fill you in later. Just get here before nine forty-five."

"Mom! Mom! Where's the blanket?" Ruby's question screeched through the doorway from the living room before she did.

"Hold on, Addie." Beth placed her hand over the receiver and shouted, "I'm on the phone!"

But Ruby, who never practiced patience, pushed through the kitchen's swinging door, nearly knocking her mother over. "Mom. The blanket. The one we take on picnics. I can't find it anywhere," she moaned, panic vibrating through her announcement. The smallest inconvenience amounted to a crisis in Ruby's world.

Beth waved her daughter off. "I gotta go, Addie. I'll be at your house in plenty of time."

"Thanks," Addie said before hanging up.

"What is wrong with you? Don't you have any regard for other people?" Beth scolded.

"Sorry, it's just that—"

"And what do you need the picnic blanket for anyway?"

"Some of us are going to the crick after school, play some Wiffle ball and goof around," Ruby said.

"Who's some of us?" Beth quizzed, hands firmly on her hips. "This is the first I've heard of your plans."

"Genna and me and Dante. Opal's a spoilsport. She doesn't want to go, but maybe some of the other kids from school will. Not sure yet."

"Oh no. I don't want you anywhere near Dante. And well...cancel your plans with Genna, too. I need you home right after your last period. Do you hear me? Straight home," Beth said, knowing what news was about to be unleashed, and the effect it would take on the entire Gallatin family. Genna needed to be home with her parents, too. No telling how she'd react.

"Aw, Mom, you're always telling me what to do."

Beth laughed. "And…?"

"It's not fair, that's all. Genna's mom doesn't boss her around." Ruby's whine made Beth's ears hurt as if granules of sand were rubbing inside.

"You have no idea what goes on between Genna and her mother. And even if you did, it has nothing to do with us." Beth stared hard into Ruby's eyes. "Do you understand?"

"Yes, ma'am," Ruby answered, although Beth knew her daughter was not convinced.

"Get upstairs and finish getting ready. Be in the car in ten minutes. I can't be late today because you can't find your algebra book or you lost your tube of ChapStick." Beth turned away. She spun back, sensing Ruby still standing there. "I am not changing my mind. Get moving!"

Ruby pushed the swinging door so hard, she had to put her hand up to prevent the wood from bouncing back and smacking her in the face. Inwardly Beth hoped it would, just a little. Someone or something had to smack some sense into that girl.

"Hey!" Opal screamed. "Watch it! You almost took out my front teeth."

"Sooorr-reee," Ruby said and stomped past.

"Guess you're not letting her go picnicking," Opal gloated, coming into the kitchen.

"Where does your sister get these crazy ideas?"

"Beats me. I told her not to go, especially after the Dante news, but does she listen? Nope," Opal said. "Hey, Mom, I need to take four eggs into home ec this morning. What can I put them in so they won't break?"

"Four eggs?" Beth questioned, calculating the cost at about twenty cents to replace them.

"We're making soufflés. Mrs. Bond says every girl should know how to master them," Opal said. "Someday you'll impress your mother-in-law. Not sure what she meant by that."

"She means, once you're married, you'll be doing things your husband's mother can take pride in," Beth explained. "She's preparing you to be a good housewife. Definitely not something you need to worry about today. And I question the focus on soufflés. Maybe Mrs. Bond should pay more attention to how to stretch a pot roast into leftovers your children will eat."

"Mom, you teach us that. No one pinches a penny tighter," Opal said. "And I mean that as a compliment."

"Do you?" Beth asked, a slight smile dancing around her lips. Making delicious soufflés was not the key to a happy marriage. She would have to have a serious conversation with both of her daughters soon. A conversation that would include the importance of self-reliance, not culinary magic.

"Whatever. If I bring in the eggs, I get extra credit. Can I put them in one of your Tupperware containers so they won't break? I'll bring it back tonight," Opal promised.

Beth fished out her oldest piece from a cupboard and held the plastic bowl for Opal to fill before sealing and burping the lid.

"Tell your brother and sister they have five minutes," Beth called out as Opal left the room. She plopped onto a chair and picked at a spot on the seat cushion where the white cotton padding peeked out from a corner seam of the secondhand kitchen set. *The chrome legs could use some polishing,* she thought, willing her mind to focus on tasks she could succeed at.

Not teenagers and the inevitable conflicts mothers were certain to endure.

Battling with Ruby left her drained. That girl had been bumping against her boundaries harder and more frequently these past few weeks. Beth couldn't tell if it was the Genna influence or the normal stage of a teenage daughter.

Beth sent up a quick prayer of gratitude that her twins weren't exactly alike. Fortunately, Opal didn't incessantly test the limits and question Beth's authority. Opal rarely rocked the boat. While Ruby was looking for ways to get into trouble, Opal sought chances to earn extra credit.

Beth could only hope that Opal's exemplary behavior would continue and, with any luck, rub off on Ruby. The realist inside knew it was only a matter of time when the twins would join forces in testing their mother's fortitude. And in the years to come, Joel would provide his own questionable actions to the mix.

"Let's go!" she hollered, grabbing her handbag and car keys. Beth headed toward the driveway, firm in her resolve to handle today's worries.

No point in paying interest on a balance not due for troubles that had yet to arrive.

Chapter Twenty

It was well after ten before a maid showed Addie and Ahren into Barry and Nora's drawing room. She offered coffee, which they both declined, and left, closing the door with a promise that Mr. and Mrs. Gallatin would be with them shortly.

Moments before, Addie and her husband had parked on the semicircular driveway, and together they gaped at the two-story Georgian-style home covering, what seemed to Addie, an entire city block. She rolled her eyes at the opulence of the massive red brick house framed with tall windows and white columns that reached for the sky.

A butler, or some other male servant, waved at them. Once he had their attention, he directed Ahren to park farther down the path, alongside the garage. *Guess you can't put a Chevy near the Cadillac.*

From where she sat now, the bank of windows treated her to the expanse of rolling shamrock-green lawns bookended by manicured gardens. In the winter, there probably was little to appreciate, but this was springtime, and the setting boasted a riot of colors. Nora, always a lover of the great outdoors, had to be the force behind this panoramic showing.

Addie recalled the memory of planting black-eyed Susans in Nora's mother's backyard as a birthday surprise. Nora would instigate hikes along the Greene River Trail near the Monongahela, where the girls collected leaves, cones, and buckeyes along the way. Nora's father had once driven them all the way to Ohiopyle to see Cucumber Falls.

Addie couldn't help but note its influence as she observed a waterfall fountain, as tall as the second floor, cascading into a small lake in the center of the grounds. No doubt all this had to be maintained by a professional, or a team of professional gardeners. With lantana borders and waves of hollyhock and delphinium—a few flowers Addie recognized by name—she imagined Nora occasionally sneaking in after the gardeners left to plant bluebells or snip the heads off dead roses. Nora's gentle touch blazed through in the design, the varied selection of flora and their calming effect offered anyone lucky enough to pause at this viewpoint.

Addie sucked in a few breaths, grateful for the peacefulness filling her, knowing in moments that her serene aura would evaporate like water drops on a hot skillet.

Ahren sat alongside her, wordless and not interested in the botanical view. He appeared more taken with the gun collection exhibited in a case against the far wall. The juxtaposition of gardens and guns was not lost on Addie. She wondered why Nora would allow Barry to keep his locked cherrywood gun cabinet in this chamber used to receive guests. Perhaps every room had a similar breathtaking view, although she doubted that.

It struck her odd that among the line of firearms on display, one of the felt-lined holders lay empty. Before she could ponder this inconsistency, the doorknob turned and Barry walked in, Nora by his side.

"Please don't stand," Barry said as Addie and Ahren shot up as though their chairs suddenly pulsated with electric bolts. They remained standing as he came toward them, extending his hand for Ahren to shake. He offered Addie a brief hug. Nora simply nodded and retreated to sit in an overstuffed wingback chair adjacent to Barry.

Addie and Ahren reclaimed their seats.

"Did you care for coffee or tea?" Nora inquired.

"No, thank you. The maid extended your hospitality," Addie said. "Your landscape is stunning. I especially love the variety of flowers you've planted."

Nora accepted the compliment. "I was lucky that the previous owners shared my love of gardens and allowed me to inherit these." She gestured toward the windows. "I just tweaked them a bit."

"A bit!" Addie demurred. "They are magnificent. I can see your green thumb everywhere I look. And the waterfall...that is definitely a Nora original."

"My way of honoring Cucumber Falls," she said, obviously recalling the same memory.

They had shared such a wonderful history. Happy childhoods, girlhood secrets, laughter until their bellies ached. And love. So much love between friends until that summer. A summer that now brought them to this moment.

A deep silence fell, neither of the couples ready to say out loud what they knew in their hearts. Addie fidgeted with the clasp on her pocketbook, each click ratcheting up her courage to speak.

"I'm glad you wanted to see us," Barry began, "but I suspect this isn't a social call. Especially since you're here, Ahren. You took the day off work, from what I understand. Something you've never done in all the years you've worked for our company."

Ahren nodded but didn't speak.

"When Addie called last night, I hoped you were responding to the job opportunity I extended. But now that the four of us are here, we all know why you wanted to see us." Barry bored his stare into Addie. "But instead of me guessing, tell us what's on your mind?"

"Yes, please," Nora added, a cavalier tone to her voice. "You hardly had a kind word for me last night at Sewing Circle. You couldn't get away fast enough, and well, when Barry said you phoned...I think we know why."

Addie swallowed. Telling the truth, especially when the truth would be best for everyone involved, shouldn't be hard. Still, she struggled to get her voice operating.

"Cat got your tongue?" Nora goaded. "Go ahead and make your apology. We'll accept. Say your piece and get it over with. Then we can move ahead with our lives."

"Apology?" Ahren blustered. "Addie's not here to apologize to the likes of you. She's got nothing to be sorry for. Why, she's been—"

Addie waved him off. "It's okay, honey. I'll tell them what I came for, and we'll be on our way." She licked her lips and noticed that, for the first time, Nora's demeanor shifted from casual to concerned.

Had she really the hubris to believe that Addie came to apologize for being hijacked by their friends? The Nora she knew wouldn't think so highly of herself. The Nora she once loved always put her friends first. That was until the time she didn't.

Addie held her purse as though the bag were an amulet giving her the power to speak. As long as she kept it in her grasp, she could continue until everything necessary had been said. "I wouldn't be here today if there was any other way, any other solution to this…dilemma. You have to understand that. What I'm about to say is for the best for both of our families."

"Both families?" Barry questioned. "We thought you came to apologize for the way you've been treating Nora."

"I am sorry that Nora's feelings were hurt last night. That wasn't my intention. If you'll let me finish, you'll both understand."

Nora glanced at Barry and leaned against her chair. A haughty air of superiority seemed to rise around her as an invisible guard, shielding her from the words about to be unleashed. "Please continue, by all means," she encouraged, clipping each word.

Addie licked her lips, now chapped and dry. She wished she had accepted a cup of tea or a glass of water. "In a sense, if you hadn't moved back to Keystone, it's likely that today wouldn't have come. I mean, we wouldn't be here discussing our children."

"Our children?" Nora repeated. "What exactly are you trying to say?"

"I don't know how you can't see it for yourselves," Addie continued, wishing Barry would make this easier on her. "You have to see the similarities. I mean, you'd be blind not to."

"The similarities between our kids?" Barry asked.

"Oh, for God's sake," Addie said. "Yes. How much they look like each other. How Luke and Dante—"

"Could be brothers," Nora stated.

Addie pursed her lips. There. She had said enough. Barry and Nora would fill in the rest.

But neither continued her train of thought to the obvious conclusion. She stole a glance at Barry, eager to see his reaction and if he'd follow the string to its inevitable finale.

A ghostly pale washed over his face as though he'd never considered the possibility that the two boys shared genes.

Addie shifted her gaze to Ahren, who remained motionless. His hands folded, he tilted against his elbows anchored on his thighs, staring at the floor. She ached at hurting him this way.

If Ahren would allow, she'd spend every hour showing him that he'd never have to doubt her love again. For now, it was enough to own a heart filled with gratitude for his strength.

Finally she turned to her girlhood chum. Nora's narrowing eyes and laser-like stare forced Addie to blink before returning the gaze. She was received by a hideous scowl coloring Nora's normally docile features.

Addie shifted uncomfortably in her chair. Was today the first time Nora had considered this possibility? Addie guessed not. Her old friend had arrived at this street corner much earlier.

Barry's voice broke the silence. "Are you saying that Luke is not Ahren's son? That he is mine?"

Addie turned to see that he stood less than a foot away. Before she could respond, Nora bolted to his side.

"That's why you've been so against Genna. Not because she is my daughter, but because..." Nora placed her hand against her mouth to muffle the yelp. Her eyes filled, and she fell against Barry's chest, tears consuming her.

He wrapped an arm around his wife and patted her back gently. "All this time we thought you were being childish, small about their romance, as a way to get back at us," he said to Addie. "But in reality, you've been working to break them apart for their own good. You were doing the right thing, the honorable thing."

"Like she always has," Ahren interjected.

The three turned to where Ahren sat, as though just remembering he was there.

"Luke is my son in all the ways that matter," he confirmed. "But one. He cannot fall in love with Genna. He cannot pretend that Gallatin blood doesn't flow through his veins. In every other way, he is a Burhan and will continue to be."

"So now do you understand why you need to move? Separate Genna from Luke before they go too far and..." Addie couldn't bear to say out loud, *"Before they have sex and Genna gets pregnant."*

"You want us to move?" Barry asked in disbelief. "I don't see how taking Genna away from here would prevent them from seeing each other."

172

"Distance. Simple geography," Addie said dismissively. "It would make it harder for them to see each other. Luke will leave for college in a few months, and they will drift apart." Her voice rose an octave in pleading with Barry to see things her way. "Don't you see, none of this would have happened if you and Nora had stayed in Pittsburgh? They never would have met. No one would ever have to know."

"None of that matters now," Ahren said. "We have to deal with the way things are, not the way we wish they could be."

Barry paced. "Moving wouldn't solve the problem. They'd see that for the ploy it is," he said after contemplating the situation. "If anything, being apart would make their forbidden romance all the more alluring."

Nora pulled away from Barry and wiped her eyes. "He's right. They'd see themselves as a modern-day Romeo and Juliet, with Burhan and Gallatin substituting for Capulet and Montague."

Barry sighed, still holding an arm around Nora. "We have to tell them, Addie. You've known all along we have to tell them the truth. Luke deserves to know who his father is."

"He knows who his father is," Addie barked. "You're just the man who fathered him."

Ahren moved to stand behind Addie and put his hand on her shoulder. "There will be plenty of time to defend me." He kissed the top of her head. "Right now, we need to stay focused. This won't be easy, but Barry is right. We need to speak to Luke. They need to speak to Genna, Dante, and—"

"Roman," Nora supplied, assuming Ahren had forgotten—if he'd ever known the name of their youngest child.

"Yes, yes. Roman. Both families need to accept this change, try it on for size, and..."

"And what?" Addie bounded to her feet. "Go on like nothing ever happened after telling Luke his entire life was a lie?"

"No less a lie than the one Barry and I have lived. You had no right to keep this from us. From Barry. How could you be so careless, so selfish, so...*irresponsible!*" Nora screamed. "You didn't give anyone else a vote. Anyone whose life would be permanently changed, possibly ruined. Not me. Not Barry. Not even Ahren."

"Leave me out," Ahren said.

Nora's breath, hot and dense, brushed against Addie's skin with each word, each insult she hurled.

"Look, Nora, you can judge me today as a grown woman if you like," she said, stepping to face her, "but know that I made this choice nearly twenty years ago as a young mother. I chose my child's happiness, my child's security. I chose this life before I had ever seen Luke's precious face because I knew the world he would battle if I didn't. He would always be tainted goods. Not quite worthy. I couldn't bear to have him bounced back and forth, called a bastard or worse. This decision was my sin, not his."

Barry wedged himself between the two women. "Calm down. Your decision wasn't a sin, Addie. And Nora, this isn't a reflection on you. I love you, and I chose you for my wife. What Addie and I…shared…was a long time ago and pretty much died by the time you and I got serious. So if you're going to be angry, be angry at me."

Nora sulked, but Addie recognized her body language. Nora didn't really want to bully her, but Addie suspected that she needed to defend her pride, her nest she had lovingly feathered over the years.

Addie grinned. Funny, Ahren hadn't succumbed to pride, at least not in front of her. He was the cuckold in this tragedy, the man who should be livid with Addie for marrying him under false pretenses. Of course she hadn't told him everything, but still, Addie knew that their marriage wasn't a charade.

Even though she had been pregnant, she took her vows seriously. The day she said "I do" in front of St. Gregory's altar, she meant those words with all the love and commitment she possessed. Ahren was always her Mr. Right—then and now. Somehow, working to keep the truth of Luke's paternity a secret had muddled her vision. Until today.

"I made choices based on what was best for me and my child. I didn't care how those choices might affect you. I didn't care then, and I don't care now."

"Well that's evident," Nora snipped and sauntered toward the windows facing the gardens. She crossed her arms and turned her back on Addie, but it was apparent that she was listening.

"You're a grown woman with an established life, Nora. Nothing will destroy that. What I care about is Luke, a soon-to-be man about to embark on life. Just starting out. And Genna, too. A young girl, all moon-eyed with her first boyfriend. I see a bit of myself in her, but I didn't have the wisdom to avoid careening down the wrong track. We have that wisdom right now. We can see their road ahead. We can't let their lives crash."

"And telling them the truth will make them crash?" Barry asked.

"Not telling them will lead to far worse repercussions. And you realize things have a way of making themselves known in this town. Even I had wondered when we first moved back but dismissed the idea. It didn't occur to me that you would have kept this secret for so many years."

"But if there was a way to keep them apart," Addie tried, "A way to separate them without the stigma of Luke learning that I've deceived him. There has to be another way. A way that I don't lose the love of my son forever. That he doesn't lose respect for his parents."

Her chest pulsated with agony she could no longer contain, a fact that could no longer remain secret. Finally, the tears she'd locked away, refusing their existence, crashed through. "Please don't tell them. Let's find another way."

Addie crumpled to the chair, all options narrowing, all hope snuffed out like the remains of a burnt candle. She had known this day would come, but she hoped it would be after Luke was grown, married with children of his own. Then she could explain, and he'd understand. Understand the love and sacrifice of being a parent. How you'd cut off your arm if it meant your child would be safe and not suffer. How you'd do anything for the life you brought into the world. That's what she had done. She'd done everything for Luke—except tell him the truth.

"Hey." A small voice sliced through the momentary silence. "What's all the yelling about?"

The four swung around to spot Roman standing inside the room, near the door.

"When did you come in?" Barry asked.

"Just now," the boy stuttered, realizing he might be in trouble.

"Son, you need to leave," Barry ordered.

He turned away, lowered his head, and slunk toward the doorway, but before he left, he asked, "Why are you yelling at Luke's parents?"

"No one is yelling," Nora admonished. "We're discussing something important, and... Why are you in here anyway?"

"I didn't know where you were, and I'm hungry," he moaned. "I finished the toast you brought me. Can I have some applesauce?"

Nora hurried to her son. "Yes, of course. Come with me. I'll put you in bed and fetch your applesauce."

"With cinnamon?"

"If that's what you want." Nora combed a curl hanging in front of Roman's eye.

"I don't have a fever anymore," Roman volunteered, grabbing his mother's hand to touch his forehead. "See? I'm not warm. I'm feeling tons better."

Nora agreed. "You're much cooler, but we'll take your temperature to be sure."

"Kept him home from school," Barry informed Ahren and Addie. "He was throwing up last night, and we thought a virus—"

"Or the three hot dogs he ate for dinner last night," Nora finished.

"You'll be fully recovered by Monday, ready for school," Barry said, turning back to Roman. "Go with your mother now. I'll check on you in a few minutes."

Roman tramped alongside Nora. "Why is Luke's mommy crying?" he suddenly asked, turning to face the room.

Addie wiped her eyes. "Aw, honey, don't worry about me. I'm fine. Your parents and I were just sharing some memories of when we were kids growing up. You know."

Roman raised an eyebrow, not fully convinced, but not interested enough to pursue the story. "Uh-huh."

"Come along, honey. Let's get that applesauce." Nora herded him toward the exit.

"Can I get a lot?" he asked.

"We'll see," she said, her hand firmly on his back.

Roman wormed out of her grasp. "Mommy, why did Genna take a suitcase with her to school today? Is she going to sleepover at Ruby's?"

Nora grabbed Roman by both shoulders. "Suitcase? What are you talking about?" she asked and glanced at Barry, who now stood next to her. "Genna's not going anywhere tonight. No place that she would have to pack for, anyway."

"Okayyyy," Roman said in a singsong voice. "Then what did she need a suitcase for?"

"You must be mistaken," his father said.

"She had that green one you gave her after she finished sixth grade," Roman continued, not being talked out of what he saw. "The one you said she should use when she comes to visit Noni. When we still lived in Sewickley."

"I know what I said," Barry chided, obviously exasperated with this change in events. "You saw her with that suitcase this morning when she left for school?"

Roman nodded. "I watched her put it in Dante's trunk."

"Dante!"

"Excuse me, Mrs. Gallatin." The maid reappeared, interrupting Barry's quizzing of Roman. "Beth Jacobsen is on the telephone. She wants to talk to Mrs. Burhan. Says it's urgent."

Addie jumped to her feet. "Beth is staying with Luke while we're here. Dear God. I hope everything is all right," she shrieked, searching the room.

"We don't have a telephone in here," Barry said. "Irma will take you to the extension in my study."

Addie followed the maid, willing her legs to move faster across the polished marble floor. When she finally reached the room and grabbed for the receiver, her knees nearly buckled at Beth's words.

"Addie, Luke's gone."

Chapter Twenty-One

"Gone?"

Beth listened to Addie's tiny voice on the other end of the line, filled with defeat and angst.

"What do you mean he's gone? He's not able to walk very well on that sprained ankle," Addie said as if that detail would change what had just happened. "Where could he be?"

"I don't know," Beth confessed. "A few minutes ago when I went up to check on him he asked me to make him some food. Seemed odd since you had made him breakfast."

Addie's sobs poured out and her anxiety surged through the telephone line. "I fed him before we left," Addie relayed, a heaviness burdening her every word. "He was in bed, said he was tired and that his ankle bothered him."

"That's what I thought, but if he was hungry, I wanted to feed him. So I went downstairs to make him the eggs and toast he asked for," Beth said her heart breaking as she told her sister.

Beth could hear a man's voice but wasn't able to make out what he was saying.

"Ahren wants to know what time you last saw Luke," Addie asked.

Beth gazed at her watch. "Maybe ten, fifteen minutes ago. He was standing by his window. He didn't look like his leg was bothering him then. I left, thinking maybe he was extra hungry since he was healing and all. When I went back to his room, his window was open, and he was gone."

"He climbed out of a second-story window?" Addie sounded incredulous.

"Looks that way. God knows how he fumbled down the side of the building with his bum leg." Beth scratched her head. She had received a strange vibe from Luke earlier. He seemed preoccupied and didn't question her about where his parents were or why she was babysitting him.

"Addie, are you there?" Beth asked after a few moments of silence. "What do you want me to do?"

"I have no idea," she said, her voice cracking.

"Beth. Hi, it's Ahren. There's really nothing you can do right now. You might as well go home."

"I feel terrible, like I let you and Addie down. I never suspected—"

"None of us did," he interrupted. "Apparently Genna left this morning with a suitcase too. Put it in the trunk of her brother's car."

"Dante?"

"He'd be the one. Hey, Beth, do you have any idea if Luke got picked up? I mean, did you see a car around?"

"Well, I thought I heard tires squeal right about the time I took Luke his eggs," Beth said, recalling the sound of a car peeling away down the street just as she had entered Luke's room. "Someone must have picked him up. Didn't see the car, though. Could have been Dante. Do you think those two kids are running away together?"

"I have to hang up. Barry wants to call the sheriff and see if we can locate Dante's car and find them."

"Okay," Beth said. "I'll lock up here and head home. Call me when you hear something."

"I will."

Ahren disconnected, leaving Beth standing in Luke's empty room.

She looked around for a clue of where he might have gone.

That's when she noticed the empty corner where earlier a duffel bag leaned against the wall. She hadn't recognized the bag as a sign of a planned escape. Both the bag and Luke were gone. He had run away. From what and to whom, she could only guess.

Beth was certain her sister's heart was shattered. She was even more convinced that Dante was behind this.

And that meant trouble.

Chapter Twenty-Two

What have I done?

Addie cocooned in Nora's guest chair by the window, no longer enjoying the outdoor splendor. She pressed her palm against her chest as though struggling to keep her heart from escaping her body. She knew this was useless. Her heart had already left and was riding through Pennsylvania with Genna and Dante Gallatin.

Every possible tragic ending raced through her mind, competing for her attention and anguish. A car accident at the hands of a teenage driver.

Or worse, Dante had driven the couple to neighboring West Virginia to elope.

Barry and Ahren separately paced the room, crossing paths in the center every minute or so. They anxiously anticipated a call from Sheriff Wesley Montgomery, who had promised that his deputies would find "those dang kids" somewhere in the commonwealth.

Addie wasn't convinced.

Dante's manipulative actions, disguised as a helping hand, had maneuvered her son and Genna into running away from home.

Addie could only imagine his devious spiel.

"Your parents don't understand," he likely said to Luke. And to his own sister, he would have complained that their folks were so old they don't remember romance. Heck, they were probably never romantic at all. Dante would have piled the lies on thick. "You two

181

kids are in love. Once you're circled, there's nothing they can do. They'll have to accept you as you are."

Would they run off to get married without even telling them?

An involuntary shudder rippled down Addie's back. She clutched the opening of her cardigan and wrapped it tighter around her chest as though warmth would quell the emotional ice surge. Addie couldn't believe that Luke would be so naïve, but if they had built this romance up à la Romeo and Juliet, with Dante's encouragement, he and Genna might be convinced that a wedding would answer their prayers.

The legal age in West Virginia was sixteen, but she thought that was with parental consent. Details like that were easy enough to work around. Especially if shyster Dante were at the helm.

Addie jumped at the gentle caress on her hand and looked up to see Ahren.

"You seem to be miles away," he said. "You've got to stop worrying. They're fine. The sheriff will find them before anything changes."

Addie nodded as a reflex, but she wasn't convinced that the damage hadn't already been done, whether they had eloped or not. Had she been honest with Luke, this entire situation could have been avoided.

"Have you heard anything from Wes?" Addie asked, knowing that if there had been word, Ahren would have already told her.

He shook his head no.

"He's pretty optimistic, though," Barry said, moving toward them. "He figures that they were gone maybe twenty minutes or so before we phoned. They couldn't have gotten far."

Addie huffed. "Only to the state line."

"You mean Ohio?" Barry asked.

Addie stood to stare Barry down. "No. West Virginia, where you only have to be sixteen to get married."

"They didn't run off to get hitched," he said, sounding like he was hoping to convince someone, including himself.

"Even if they did," Ahren said, "they'd need parental consent, and the four of us are here. None of us consented."

"Luke's nearly nineteen. He doesn't need our consent, and—"

"Genna turns eighteen tomorrow," Nora said, now standing in the doorway. She had been absent the past few minutes, keeping Roman at bay with bribes of unlimited applesauce.

Addie ran toward her and grabbed her by both arms. "Her birthday is tomorrow? Oh, dear God. They've been planning this all along."

Nora wriggled out of Addie's hold. "I'll be right back." She scampered out of the sitting room. A few moments later, she returned holding what appeared to be a strongbox with several documents visible.

"What is it?" Barry asked.

"Her birth certificate isn't here," Nora lamented. She held up two papers—Dante's and Roman's birth certificates were intact; Genna's was missing. "Can you find out if Luke has his birth certificate?"

"Not without going home," Addie said, "but maybe that's something we should do, Ahren? And see if any of our suitcases are missing?"

"Yes."

"Perhaps we should leave. Wait for some news at our house. Wes can call us there," Addie said, picking up her pocketbook from the floor where she had laid it earlier.

"That's true," Ahren agreed. "We're not much help staying here and staring at the walls."

"Beth didn't say anything was missing from Luke's room." Hope fueled her response.

"Would she have even noticed?" Ahren asked, turning to leave the room. "I'll check with her. Do you know if she went home?"

Addie nodded. "But call our house first. She might still be there."

A few minutes later Ahren returned. "Apparently, Luke was as prepared as Genna," he said. "His duffel is gone. Beth checked on the birth certificate too. It's missing as well."

"Damn it to hell!" Nora yelled and stalked to the far corner of the room.

Ahren stated what no one else would. "They're listening to Dante, who only wants the worst possible outcome."

"I'd argue with you," Nora said, "but what you're saying is true. I love my son with all my heart, but frankly he's the most insecure and jealous child I've ever known. He resents everything and everyone. That's why we left Sewickley. He had pulled one too many pranks at the private school. Even the Gallatin money couldn't buy our way out of his last "

"That's enough, Nora," Barry cautioned.

"I'll say," she spat back. "You have a child with Addie. And now that child has run off with my Genna. You know Dante has something to do with this, don't you? He's caused so much grief, Barry, that I want him out of our lives. He couldn't possibly let anyone be happy. He's so miserable. He's so…"

The words caught in Nora's throat just as a gush of tears flooded her eyes.

Addie's long-ago friend had been suffering for a while. She shifted enough to encircle Nora in an embrace. "We love our children," she whispered into Nora's ear. "That's what mothers do. You loving Dante isn't wrong. I don't know what the solution is but to stop loving him isn't the answer."

Nora wiggled out of Addie's hold. "You don't understand. You don't know all he's put us through. And now this. I'm sure he convinced Genna and Luke that he wanted to help. But the only person Dante has ever helped is Dante."

"Is there any chance he knew that Luke is his half-brother?" Ahren asked, a perplexed look overtaking his face.

"Anything is possible, but I don't know how he could have found out. Unless you told him." Barry looked to Addie.

Addie clutched at her collar. "Me? Told him? Of course not. I didn't want to tell anyone. Even you. I'd been working on a way to separate those two without…"

"Without hurting me and Luke," Ahren defended.

"Not entirely," Addie confessed. "I wanted to protect you both, that's true. But I didn't want to admit my mistakes either. I'm not saying that I regret having Luke. It's not that. But, hey, a single girl pregnant back in 1940 wasn't just a scandal, it was a disgrace to the family… I couldn't do that to Mom and Dad."

"Times haven't changed all that much," Nora added. "It's still the woman's disgrace. Her problem to resolve without many options to choose from." She took a deep breath. "I admire your amazing strength, Addie. You could have picked a simpler path, gave your baby up for adoption secretly. The church handles those placements all the time."

Addie was taken aback. She hadn't considered any other option. She wouldn't have ended the pregnancy in some back alley outside Pittsburgh, like she heard other teenage girls had done. She wouldn't have given her child away, either.

She recalled clearly thinking the only way forward was to marry Ahren and make a life with him, a safe home to raise her child. She was no heroine. Addie simply had followed her heart and never looked back—that is, until Luke met Genna.

"No, my dear, you took the harder, selfless route, and you are blessed with a wonderful son. Don't doubt yourself. You did the right thing," Nora concluded with a gentle pat on Addie's shoulder, then moved to stand next to Barry.

Addie appreciated the encouragement Nora generously offered in the midst of her own tragic revelations. Remnants of a little-spoken-of sisterhood carved out long ago still remained. Addie could rely on this foundation constructed among the Sewing Circle gals, even if she hadn't allowed Nora full membership.

A connection each of them had counted on time and time again.

"You're kind to gloss over this for me, Nora, but there's no excuse. Until Luke and Genna became...friends, I was willing to continue the charade. I had lived with my lie for so long that I couldn't expose myself to the shame and judgment that comes with being an unwed mother." Addie diverted her gaze to Ahren. "I was afraid of what my folks would have said. They would have been furious and hurt. I took what I thought was the easy way out, not wanting to bear the pain of their disappointment."

Ahren reached for her. "We can't know for certain what Frances and Del might have done or felt. They were loving, kind people. They wouldn't have shunned you," he said, referring to his in-laws.

Addie blinked back a tear, and Ahren continued, "It doesn't matter to me now, and it wouldn't have mattered then. You could have saved yourself so much grief and—" Before he finished his thought, Addie buried her face into his neck and wept. He held her for several minutes as Barry and Nora looked on.

Finally she pulled away and wiped her eyes, not caring that mascara lines ran down her cheeks. "If I had the wisdom of today yesterday," she said and attempted a tiny grin.

Nora stepped toward Addie. "We all would have done so many things differently. We've caused each other too much sadness when we could have stayed united in our friendship."

Addie hugged her. "I was so frightened and angry and confused, I could only hold hate in my heart for you both."

"You were young. We all were," Barry said. "We have to focus on today. What's happening with our children right now. How we can fix this and cause the least amount of damage."

"That's why I asked about Dante." Ahren looped back in. "This escapade may not be about them getting married. That wouldn't help Dante. But…"

"But what?" Barry encouraged.

"I can't help but think, from Dante's point of view, of course, that if Luke is out of the picture—"

"What are you saying!?" Addie sputtered. "That Dante wants to kill Luke?"

"It's not the conclusion I want to jump to, but everything points in that direction," Ahren answered, reluctance in his voice. "We have to be realistic about what's going on and tell the sheriff what we think."

"And?" Addie questioned.

"I'm guessing, based on what you've said here and other stories I've heard, that Dante isn't good at sharing. He certainly won't want to divide his inheritance with a Johnny-come-lately half-brother."

Barry scratched his chin. "Ahren makes sense. If Genna and Luke get married, that brings Luke into the family. No benefit to Dante."

"Except that he's helped them defy their parents," Addie said.

"Yes, that's true, but we know Dante pretty well. There is a more concrete upside for him, something that aids him directly. He's cruel, but every one of his antics, whether he embarrassed a teacher or cheated on a girlfriend, always ended with a tangible gain for him." Barry paused, giving the impression that he was considering every bit of information. "He's after money, power, loyalty. A payback or an advantage he could use to influence his desired outcome or help himself."

"Good Lord, Barry. He's figured out how to use people? Hell, he's not even out of high school yet." Ahren shook his head.

"He's very smart," Barry said. "A miscreant operating at genius level. The frustrating part for Nora and me is that we couldn't guide his actions toward good. So brilliant, but he only wants to use his brain for evil. If he's stumbled onto the fact that Luke is biologically my oldest child…"

A surge of dread pulsated through Addie. "Are you saying that Luke's life might be in danger?"

No one answered, which confirmed her deepest fear. "We have to find them right now! Do you hear me? We have to find my son before something happens. If Dante wanted to hurt him, Luke couldn't even fight back. He couldn't run away on his sprained ankle. He couldn't protect Genna," she said slowly, as though the full picture were coming into focus.

"We're jumping to conclusions," Ahren said calmly. "All we know for sure is that the three of them are together. Luke and Genna took their birth certificates and some clothes. Facts that point to eloping—or trying to. There's nothing that leads us to a dire ending."

"Don't you see?" Addie lamented. "Luke and Genna prepared for the story Dante told them. They believed him. Dante's plan is the one we need to worry about, not theirs."

"What is taking Wes so long? How hard is it to spot our Studebaker?" Barry said, his frustration evidently rising.

"Unless they're not riding around town or on the turnpike," Nora said. "Maybe they're parked somewhere the cops wouldn't know to look."

"Why would they do that?" Addie said.

"I don't know. Waiting until dark or…"

"I know," Roman chimed in.

"Know what? Why are you down here again?" Barry scolded. "Go right back to your room."

"Wait," Nora said. "Roman, do you know where Dante is?"

"Sorta."

"Then tell us, son," Barry said, "and right now."

Roman swallowed. "Dante said if Genna wanted his help leaving town, she would have to be ready early and do exactly what he said. That if Luke wanted to go, he would need to be ready early, too. That's all I know. Dante saw me, and I left before he punched me in my arm."

"Did you hear where they were heading?" Addie asked.

"Nope. I ran to my room." Roman paused. "I did hear him warning Genna to stop asking questions or else."

Addie and Ahren exchanged panicked looks.

Or else from Dante Gallatin meant her worst fears coming true.

***

187

The clock on the mantel indicated that only a few minutes had passed since Beth returned home. She busied herself with mundane household tasks, interspersed with prayers that Luke would be found soon and safe.

She chided herself for not being aware of what was going on under her nose. She should have recognized the signs. Luke's jumpy behavior while he was on the phone, a packed bag near the window, a double breakfast order from a rail-thin fellow. All the red flags lined up, but she hadn't recognized them.

Luke took advantage of the perfect opportunity to run while his mother and father were otherwise occupied. They could be halfway to West Virginia, she guessed, just as their house phone rang.

"Hello, Addie?" she asked, a little breathless hoping she'd hear good news.

"No. It's me," Ted snapped. "Hey, listen, this is probably nothing, but I'm over here at the Silverwing Motel fixing another one of Bert's backed-up toilets. Really, he and Mabel need to invest in new plumbing. Anyway, I'm calling 'cause I thought I saw a boy who looked a lot like Luke with that girl who hangs around with Ruby. They were checking into a room."

"What!?" Beth shouted, nearly dropping the receiver.

"No need to yell. There's a third kid, too. Tall like Luke. They look like they could be brothers or somethin'."

"Did you talk to them?"

"Nah, I was across the way. I called over to Addie's, but there's no answer. Anyway, thought I should tell someone, so I'm telling you. Ain't those kids supposed to be in school?"

"Yes. Well thanks, Ted. I know how to get hold of Addie, so I'll let her know. Can you tell if they're still there?"

"Barry's old green Studebaker is parked in front of 132. He drives a Caddy now, I hear. So, unless they ditched the car and are hoofing it, they're still in the room. Want me to knock on the door and scare the crap out of them? Old Uncle Ted there to bust up their fun." He guffawed, but Beth knew, if anything, he'd be bringing them booze and smokes to add to their party, not snuff it out.

"No, don't do that. Are you calling from the office phone?" she asked.

"Yep, and Clarence here is about to throw me out. Wants his ancient toilet repaired ASAP, don't cha, Clarence?"

Beth heard mumbling that she guessed was coming from the motel manager.

"Know anything about those kids in room 132?" Ted questioned.

"Just that they's of age and paid in cash." The response came clearly.

"I put the receiver out for you to hear. Gotta go."

"Wait!" she yelled. "Is Mabel or Bert around?"

"Nah. Clarence is running the show today. Says Mabel might turn up later. What's that?" Ted asked. "Oh. She's supposed to bring some new sheets. Hell, you guys need new pipes. Hell."

"Ted!" Beth shouted through the line. "Can you do me a favor? While you're there, keep an eye out to see if they leave and call me. Okay?"

"Yeah. Okay. I'll be another forty-five minutes or so."

"And if Mabel shows, have her call, please. I'll get hold of Addie right now."

"Will do, baby. See you tonight." Ted clicked off, and Beth immediately dialed Barry's number. What were those kids doing in a hotel room when they were supposed to be heading for the state line?

Maybe that wasn't the plan after all, she decided, just as the maid answered the phone.

The seconds passed like hours as she waited for Addie to pick up. Finally her sister's voice, quavering and tentative, came across the line.

"Beth?"

"Hi, Addie."

"Has something happened? Are you still at my house?"

"No, I'm home, but I do have news. Ted's out at the Silverwing Motel doing some plumbing. He called to tell me he thought he saw Luke, Genna, and Dante checking in."

Beth could hear Addie sharing this development loudly with Ahren, Barry, Nora, and whoever else was in earshot.

"That's Mabel and Bert's place, off Route 21, near Winter Ridge?"

"Yes, that's the one."

"Near the West Virginia border?" Addie continued, "There's a river that runs behind."

"More like a crick or a stream," Beth said.

"And that big state park is there, just behind Mabel's motel."

"Well, yeah, I suppose. What are you asking?"

"Not sure. Thought they'd hightail it across the border. Why are they staying in Pennsylvania?" Addie asked.

"Maybe they're waiting for something? Or someone?"

"I suppose. Anyway, thanks, sis. We're heading there now. Thank you. Thank you."

Before Beth could offer a *you're welcome*, Addie hung up. An excited mixture of worry and relief pulsed through her. This could be good news, she hoped. A lead that could bring Luke back home safely.

She dropped into a nearby chair, reached into her skirt pocket, and pulled out her rosary. She fingered the beads nervously as the worry mounted, outweighing the relief of moments ago.

Whatever evil Dante is plotting, please let Addie and Ahren get there before he can carry out his plan.

"Hail Mary, full of grace…"

Chapter Twenty-Three

As Ahren opened the door to the backseat of Barry's Fleetwood, Addie estimated the drive to the Silverwing would take nearly twenty minutes. That was nineteen minutes too long as far as she was concerned. The thought of Luke being under Dante's power overwhelmed her with dread, making each breath an effort to get oxygen into her lungs.

"What things did Dante do that forced you to move?" Addie asked, not sure she wanted a truthful answer. She would find reassurance if Dante's missteps had been harmless pranks. But if people had been injured, the way Luke had been after the basketball incident, then her level of panic would climb like a thermometer held over an open flame.

Nora turned to face Addie. Her complexion so drained of color caused Addie to gulp. The squint of her brown eyes clashed against her powdery pale skin. Addie knew this was not the setting to discuss Dante's sins. Nora had no intention of reliving those chapters.

She could only share her hope that a new scene of horrors wasn't being written now.

"Should we have notified Wes?" Addie asked, shifting topics to one that might help their immediate situation. "Maybe he could get a deputy there before we arrive."

"Probably would have been a good idea to call when we were still at the house," Barry said. "Keep an eye out for a phone booth and I'll pull over."

The four stayed quiet for the next few miles until Ahren pointed out a gas station with an adjacent phone booth. Barry had barely pulled to a stop before Ahren popped out of the car, fishing for a coin in his pocket.

"I got this," he said, jogging toward the booth.

Moments later, he tumbled back into the vehicle and Barry hit the gas.

"I spoke to dispatch," Ahren reported. "Said they'd get the message to Wes. Also advised us not to take any actions. Said we should wait until they show up."

"What? We can't go tap on the door?" Addie asked. "That seems ludicrous."

"I thought so, too, and said as much," Ahren grumbled. "The dispatcher said when the original complaint came in, a pistol was also reported missing."

Nora turned to Barry but remained silent.

"It's probably nothing, honey," Barry's voice soothed. "I noticed a Browning missing from the gun cabinet when we first joined Ahren and Addie this morning. I told Wes just to cover all our bases. There are no bullets in the chamber. I keep those locked in our bedroom. I'm the only one with the key," he said, taking his hand off the wheel for a moment to pat his vest pocket.

Addie gasped, and Ahren reached for her hand. "Dante took your gun?" he asked skeptically.

"Don't know. Where my son is concerned, I stopped guessing a couple of years ago."

"So there's a good chance he took the gun to hurt Luke? And what about Genna? Would he harm her too?" Addie stuttered her questions. Getting bullets wouldn't be difficult, but was this kid of eighteen, barely a man, capable of using a weapon against her son? On his own sister?

"Probably not," Barry said. "We just need to find the three of them and explain the complicated relationship they now share."

"If he already knows Luke is his half-brother..." Addie trailed off.

"We solve the problem of Luke and Genna running off. But once he learns there's another sibling, well, I don't know how he'll take that news," Barry said.

"You're assuming he doesn't already know; that he didn't figure this out," Nora scolded. "Dante is many things, but stupid and naïve aren't two of them." She shifted in her seat to face Addie. "I don't think he'd harm either Genna or Luke. But I do think he'd put a huge scare in them to get what he wants."

"What does he have to benefit by frightening them?" Addie asked.

"That Luke won't want anything to do with the family, with his sister...or his father," Ahren offered. "I agree with Nora. He knows and probably has for a while. Maybe around the time he started being friends with Luke, separately from Genna. That's what nailed it for me—seeing the two of them together. You couldn't miss that they're related. Could be cousins, but knowing the background, brothers is the obvious choice."

"Luke doesn't want anything from Barry," Addie defended. "He's moving ahead on his own, with his own talents. He has a father. He doesn't need to horn in on Dante's."

Barry huffed, and the car sped faster. "Logically speaking, you're right," he said. "But when you're in Dante's world, logic doesn't take the front seat. Whether Luke is a threat or not doesn't matter. What matters is if Dante believes he is."

As Addie slumped against the upholstery, shards of panic attacked every corner of her being. She stared out the window, aware that her grip on Ahren's hand had turned her knuckles white. A moment later, a sheriff's patrol car sped past, lights flashing and sirens blaring. Addie spun her head just in time to see to see the tail lights.

A tinge of relief puffed through her bones, only to be replaced by mounting terror. She had caused Luke to be in jeopardy. A shroud of grief lay across her like a blanket of spiderwebs, covering her in ultimate responsibility. The harder she fought to get free, the more ensnared she became.

We have to get there before Dante does anything to hurt Luke. So I can fix this, make Luke understand.

Ahren untangled their fingers, pulled her toward him, and laid her head against his chest. "Everything will be all right," he whispered in her ear.

"This is all my fault. I should have—"

"Stop," he said, gently placing a finger across her lips. "We got lucky. We know where they are, and Ted is watching to make sure they stay there. Luke is safe."

"I don't feel lucky, and I don't want to entrust Luke's well-being to Ted. He's a drunkard and an abuser," Addie said as tears welled in her eyes. Beth had endured so many terrible things at the hands of her husband, and all Addie had been able to do was listen and maybe comfort her a little. She couldn't stomach that Ted might turn out to be the hero in all this. But she knew if he were, she'd be grateful. Addie would be grateful to the devil himself if it meant Luke was safe.

Barry pulled into a parking spot near the motel office. Through the large-pane windows, Addie saw Mabel behind the desk talking to Wes. She turned, and the car they thought was Dante's came into view, a dark green expanse of wilderness in the background.

Two sheriff's vehicles were stationed on both sides of room 132. There was no sign of Ted or his plumbing truck. *He's already left. Typical Ted. Stupid to think we could rely on him.*

Although her every urge was to race to the motel door and pound until she saw Luke's face, Addie forced herself to remain in the car. There was little comfort in Barry's claim to have the bullets, but she felt reassured that Wes and his deputies would handle the situation. Until they did, and she was certain that Luke was safe, Addie would follow their orders and wait. She couldn't be the cause of Dante panicking and shooting the gun.

"Looks like the coppers got here first," Barry said. "Everybody wait in the car while I go into the office and check."

"Wes said to wait," Addie protested.

"He said not to approach the room until he got here. He's here. We need to find out what's going on." Barry slammed the car door closed.

"I'll go with you," Ahren said, giving Addie a quick peck before climbing out of the backseat.

Addie watched as Ahren hurriedly stepped to catch up to Barry. She couldn't make out what he said, but she saw a distinct look of concern on Barry's face. The pair headed into the office and out of sight.

"What do we do now?" Nora said.

"We wait, I guess," Addie replied, snottier than she meant to sound, but she didn't care. There was enough blame to go around, and she was determined that Nora would eat her share.

"I don't mean about the kids. I mean about each other?"

"Each other?"

"Yes, you and me," Nora clarified. "After all this comes out, we'll both be painted with a soiled brush."

"Really, Nora. Aren't you too old to worry about what people think?" Addie couldn't believe that while Dante held their children against their will—well, what Addie believed to be against their will—Nora was worried about what people would say.

"I don't mean that. I mean how will we move forward? Barry is the father of both of our children."

"Yes, he certainly fathered them, but he is not Luke's father. Ahren has earned that right and distinction. If you're asking me what we should do next, I suggest you and yours move back to Pittsburgh where one more juvenile delinquent won't be noticed."

"I've never known you to be so catty," Nora said. "I'm truly concerned about how we face this as two families with a uniting factor."

"Barry? Hell, he's the opposite of a uniting factor," Addie huffed and yanked on the door handle.

"We were told to stay here," Nora barked.

"And of course you always do what you're told," Addie snarled.

"Well one of us needs to follow the rules, and apparently, Adele, it's never been you." Nora turned away just as Barry and Ahren returned to the car.

Both Addie and Nora hurried out of the vehicle, but Addie saw the defeated look in Ahren's eyes. Barry cast his stare to the pavement. "They're not here," he said. "One of the maids thought she saw them heading toward the crick." He pointed to the forest behind the strip of motel rooms. "Ted's gone to look for them."

Mabel appeared, wrapped an arm around Addie, and nodded with concern at Nora. "I didn't know they were here until Ted told us. Clarence, he doesn't know your kids, or he would have said something to me. He feels real bad."

Addie nodded. "Not his fault," she muttered, turning to face Wes, who joined the knot of distraught parents. "Can we go search, too?"

"I don't advise it," Wes said. "Ted left before I had a chance to stop him. My officers are forming a search party right now. The best thing you can do is wait here. They can't get into too much trouble with a couple of fishin' poles."

"If, in fact, they were really going fishing." Ahren spoke as though he were deciphering a secret code. "Wes, can I ask you something? Private?"

The sheriff nodded, and both Ahren and Barry stepped away from the group. Addie watched even though she couldn't hear.

She saw Wes press his lips together in a sorrowful fashion.

She knew what question had been posed, and the answer devastated her.

They hadn't found the gun in the motel room.

Chapter Twenty-Four

It had been about an hour and two rosaries later when Ted came home, Beth assumed, to have lunch. She glanced at the mantel clock. *Half past twelve.* She rushed to the kitchen just as the screen door slapped shut.

"Damn, people are crazy," Ted hollered.

"What are you talking about?" Beth asked.

Ted headed for the refrigerator. "Ain't nothing in here to eat," he complained, his head stuck inside.

"Sit down," she said, shuffling him to a nearby chair. "I'll make you a sandwich from last night's roast."

"Any soup to go with that?" he asked.

"Sure, I can open a can of chicken noodle. Tell me what's going on," she pleaded, the air nearly expired from her lungs with worry.

"What's to tell," he said, using a church key to pop the cap off a pop bottle. "Those kids were there when I called you. I saw Addie and Ahren make a big scene at the motel looking for 'em."

Beth carved the roast beef paper-thin, the way Ted liked, and laid several slices on a piece of bread.

"So you talked to Addie. I've been calling her house, but she doesn't answer. I might head over there after you're done eating."

"No point. She ain't there." Ted took a swig of pop. "She's at Mabel's waiting for the sheriff to find Luke. He went fishing before the cops showed up."

Beth dropped the knife and turned to face her husband. "Gone! You mean they haven't found Luke?"

197

"Nah. Not the other two either," he said.

"Weren't you keeping an eye on them?" Beth asked, a bitter dread expanding in the bottom of her stomach.

"That car didn't move. Still parked there, last I looked. Those kids snuck out the back way, along the crick. No one saw them leave, except for a maid. She said they were carrying fishing poles. That's how we know they went fishing," he finished, apparently pleased with his detective work.

"Fishing! They're acting like they're on a lark, a vacation with no one out looking for them." Beth dropped Ted's sandwich plate, and it clattered against the table.

"Once I heard what happened, I set off searching along the back side of Deerwood but came up empty." Ted sounded sorry for losing track of Luke, but Beth couldn't take time to console him. The fear of what might happen to her nephew had shifted to a mounting anger.

"Deerwood?" she barked.

"Yeah. The state park is out that way. Lots of open land and wilderness. Butts up alongside the Silverwing. Don't think it's fenced in. Lots of kids sneak in that way."

"You think they're somewhere in a state park?"

"It's a guess. I told the sheriff what I thought when I got back, and he shooed me off. Said his deputies would take over, so I came home." Ted took a bite and chewed. "Your sister's pretty upset. Maybe you should drive out there. Calm her down. She's talking crazy. They all are."

"What do you mean?" Beth asked, worried she wouldn't like Ted's response.

"I overheard Barry say something to Ahren about a missing gun. Don't need no gun to fish," he said. "You still making me soup?"

Beth shoved a pot and a can into Ted's hands. "Warm it up yourself." She threw her apron on the counter, then opened the phone directory and frantically paged through.

"Who you calling?"

"The motel," Beth snarled. "Maybe they've found Luke by now. You've been gone how long?"

"Half an hour or so," Ted replied.

"Busy signal." Beth slammed the receiver back into the cradle. "I've got to get out there."

"Not much you can do by being there 'cept to comfort Addie," Ted said, standing near her.

"You just said I should go and calm her down."

Ted contorted his face. "Is he in some sort of danger?"

Beth nodded, ready to bolt for the door.

"Look, honey," he said, his voice low. "I know something more than a couple of kids ditching school is going on. And I know your sister doesn't think much of me. But if you tell me what the heck's happening, I can help. I know the streams inside Deerwood better than anybody."

Beth surveyed her husband. He had many faults, most of which affected her, but he did love family and would do anything for Addie and Ahren. And Luke. He was always in the bleachers cheering at every game, offering encouragement when the score didn't reflect the solid effort their nephew exhibited on the court.

Sure, Ted could get his ego involved and his nose out of joint, but if he could help find Luke, none of that mattered. She pointed for him to sit in the chair he had just vacated. Ted placed the unopened soup can and aluminum pot on the counter before obliging.

"We don't have a lot of time, so I'll give you the short version," she said, nervously tapping her shoe. "The reason Addie has been so adamant about breaking up Luke and Genna is because Barry is Luke's father."

Ted huffed. "I used to wonder about that. Seemed they got pregnant pretty quick and hadn't dated that long. Figured they played around and got caught."

"It's none of our business what Addie did before she married Ahren. Or even after, for that matter," chided Beth.

"Guess everything blew up when Nora and Barry moved back," Ted speculated, shaking his head. "What's that have to do with Dante and a gun?"

"They think Dante figured out the truth. That Luke is Barry's firstborn son. He may be jealous enough to hurt him. Maybe even Genna." Beth shifted toward the door. "I gotta go."

"What would hurting...?" Ted stopped. "Don't matter. Let's go."

"You just left there," Beth said, surprised. "You want to go back?"

"I was in the way then, but now that I know… Anyway, you're in no condition to drive." Ted stuffed the remaining corner of his sandwich in his mouth. "Get your handbag. I'll get you there in less than twenty minutes. Who knows, maybe by then, everything will be sorted out."

Beth hustled out of the kitchen toward the front door, Ted behind her.

The unfairness of what was happening overwhelmed her, and tears leaked down her cheeks.

Ted wrapped an arm around his wife, and Beth coiled into him. Together they walked to the station wagon. She handed him her keys and wondered how she could love and hate him at the same time. How he could be two distinct men. Sober and drunk.

They stayed quiet for the ride, except for Beth asking Ted to press on the gas pedal a little harder. He gunned the engine whenever he could.

She ached to be by Addie's side. To know that everything was all right.

Luke's life couldn't end at the hands of Dante. If anything happened to her nephew, that would be the end of Addie, too.

Beth couldn't let another Gallatin ruin her sister.

Not in this way. Not ever again.

Chapter Twenty-Five

To burn off her anxious energy, Addie paced inside the motel office no larger than a camping trailer. Mabel and Ahren looked on.

Thirty minutes earlier, Barry had asked for a room so Nora could lie down until this matter was resolved. Mabel handed him the key to 129, a few doors down from where their children were checked in. Apparently Barry needed to rest as well because he hadn't returned.

Resolved! Addie still fumed. *This isn't an acquisition waiting for bank funding or contracts to be signed. Our children are out there somewhere. We don't know if they're alive or dead.*

Some two hours had passed since four sheriff's deputies began their search along the banks of a stream that ran behind the Silverwing Motel into the heart of Deerwood State Park. Under Wes's command, the officers had spread out, two to the east, two to the west.

Three park rangers were recruited to assist. Addie had watched as they trundled off north into the depths of the reserve. She wished the men had shown urgency in their mission instead of appearing as though they were out for a summer stroll.

Wes counseled her and the rest of the parents to remain behind in case the kids circled back. He reassured anyone who would listen of his certainty that the three were out skipping school and goofing off, like teenagers were so likely to do these days.

"All that James Dean rebellion everywhere you look." He rubbed the back of his neck. "Rock and roll music and renegades, that's what we're raising nowadays, Addie," he declared before patting her hand and wandering off to join the search party.

Addie hadn't seen any of the delinquent-teen movies Wes referred to, but she danced to the upbeat music of Elvis Presley and Little Richard that Luke and his friends listened to. Her son's behavior was not an example of kids revolting against their parents. This was far more serious, more dangerous, more sinister. Even if Luke disagreed with Addie and Ahren, he wouldn't run away. He wouldn't be so cruel.

But he had packed his duffel bag, evidence that he planned to leave, totally contrary to Addie's assessment of the situation.

Dante must have convinced him to go. What power does that wicked boy have over my son?

Luke, a trusting soul, took people at face value, naïvely believing them—until proven different. The pain of his sprained ankle had taught him Dante played dirty. Surely Luke wouldn't have trusted him after realizing how cavalierly Dante inflicted pain.

But Genna…

Luke would have trusted her limitlessly. He would have listened to her and believed what she said. Would she have knowingly led Luke into danger?

The only plausible explanation that came to mind was Luke had left the house because of Genna and didn't know Dante was behind the entire scheme. Or he believed Genna was in danger. Maybe that made the most sense.

She slid a glance at Ahren. He offered a thin smile, more of shared grief than encouragement. He remained quiet, no longer able to comfort her by repeating, *"Everything will be all right. He'll be back soon."*

Addie turned away, unable to absorb Ahren's pain along with her own. She traced her finger across a dirt-dusted window for a clearer view. Still no sign of Luke or the deputies. What looked like Beth's station wagon pulled into the lot and parked next to Barry's car.

Her brother-in-law had left in a bit of a snit after Wes admonished him for going out alone to search for Luke. Ted, genuinely worried about his nephew, had offered to join the official search party. Wes declined his help with a "Let the professionals handle this" snarky dismissal.

To be fair, Wes probably worried that if Ted were drinking, he'd get underfoot and make things worse. The sheriff was smart to refuse his help, but he could have handled the rejection with more tact.

A bell hanging above the door tingled as Beth and Ted returned into the already-cramped quarters. Addie raced into Beth's open arms.

Her sister smoothed the hair stuck to Addie's forehead. "You okay, honey? Have you heard anything?"

Ahren took two short steps to meet them. "They've been gone about an hour and a half," he said. "They set out right after you left, Ted."

"How can we help?" Beth asked.

"Sit and wait, like Wes told us," Addie said, gesturing toward a pair of foldout chairs. "Or…"

"Or what?" Beth nearly jumped down her sister's throat at the possibility.

Addie took her seat and waited for Beth to join her before continuing. "Luke wouldn't have run off if he knew Dante was involved. That boy purposely tried to break Luke's ankle. My son is too smart to trust him again. Luke must have gone along to protect Genna." She glanced quickly at Ahren for encouragement before returning her gaze back to Beth. "She told your girls that Dante treated her horribly, so it doesn't add up that she'd leave with him voluntarily *and* get Luke to go, too."

Beth nodded.

Addie continued, "But this morning, Genna's little brother told us he saw her willingly get in the car with Dante. Heard them plan the whole getaway last night. He said she didn't seem scared. So, Dante must have told them some half-baked tale. Maybe that he's helping them be together. Hell, I don't know."

"What are you saying?" Ahren interrupted.

"Beth should talk to Opal and Ruby and find out what they know," Addie said. "Maybe Genna confided in them, swore them to secrecy. You know how the kids do these days."

"That's a great idea," he answered. "Why didn't we think of that sooner?"

"They'd be finishing lunch and heading to their last period. English, I think," Beth said. "I'll call the office and ask them to be pulled out of class."

"Seems like we should talk in person," Ted interjected. "Don't think we'd get much more than a couple *I don't knows* over the phone."

"But that's a twenty, twenty-five-minute drive back into town. They'll be home by the time we get there," Beth protested.

"Ted's got a point," Addie said. "If the girls know something, it would be easier for you to get it out of them face-to-face."

Ted nodded. "She's right, Bethie. Talk to them at the house without me. If Ruby and Opal are holding Genna's secrets, they'll confess them to you."

"Especially after they learn their cousin may be in danger," Ahren added.

"You'll crack 'em like a walnut." Ted smiled. "I'll stay here."

"If you think that's best," Beth said, gathering her belongings.

Ted squeezed her hand. "I do."

"You going to be okay until I get back, Addie?" Beth asked.

"There's a good chance the twins know something. Well, Ruby anyway. If Opal had wind of this, she'd have told you." Addie patted Beth's hand, directing her toward the exit. "Go. I'll be fine. Mabel will keep me company."

Mabel held up a teapot. "Promise."

"This is my third cup," Addie said, pointing to a teacup three-quarters full of cold Tetley. "I can't drink anymore."

"Maybe a sandwich," she offered.

"Later. I'm not hungry," Addie said, shifting to the chair she had occupied for the last few hours.

"I'll call as soon as I can." Beth turned and nearly knocked Barry over.

"Call about what?" He snapped the door shut, rattling the bell. "Is there news?"

"Beth is going to talk to her daughters. Maybe they know what's going on," Addie supplied.

"Great idea," he said.

Barry extended his hand to Ted before turning toward Ahren. "Sheriff took off downstream?"

"Yeah. Sent some boys upstream. A couple of rangers are on the hunt inside the park, too," Ahren said.

"Sounds like Wes is covering a lot of ground," Ted said.

"He is. Still, I don't understand why he wouldn't let you go with them. You know these parts better than anyone," Barry noted.

"Thanks. Sheriff is used to seeing me drunk on my ass. He has lots of reasons to not trust my judgment. But I do know the fishin' holes around here. If in fact those kids are fishing."

Shocked that Ted publicly owned up to his self-absorbed, addictive behavior, Addie swept a glare to Beth. Her sister stood near Barry, her face stoic, not offering even a wrinkled brow of commentary to Ted openly admitting his drinking problem. Instead, she bussed her husband's cheek and moved past Barry.

"Call us as soon as you can with what you found out," Ahren directed.

"Will do," she said.

"Maybe you and I can wander a bit outside," Ahren said to Ted once Beth left. "Get some fresh air. You can show me some of your favorite spots to cast a rod."

"And go against Wes's orders?" Addie questioned.

"We don't work for Wes, so he can't order us around. No law against going to a fishing hole," Ahren protested.

"He's in charge of the search." Addie stated the fact, although she was looking for a loophole to crawl through.

"Yeah, but he's operating on the wrong premise," Ted said. "You said so yourself, Addie. This isn't your average teenage runaway."

"Besides, Ted and I won't approach the kids or do anything crazy. If we spot them, we'll head back and call the sheriff on his walkie-talkie. Beats sitting here while we could be actually doing something to get our son back."

Addie's body surged with Ahren's pain. She shared his remorse of a parent left with no options to help their child. "You're right, of course," she said, hoping he understood the shared terror lodged in her eyes.

Ahren reached for her hand. He kissed her quickly, as though instilling courage, grabbed his hat, and followed Ted out the door.

"Wait! I'm going, too," Barry declared.

She watched the three men march away, a determined bounce to their gait, one that was sorely missing earlier from the authorized search party. She eyed the light green Studebaker still parked in front of the hotel and took solace in the trio's resolute strides.

Claire Yezbak Fadden

The sun, barely beginning its wane into the west, offered a shortening glow. There were only three or four hours of sunlight left.

Surely, they'd find Luke before night fell.

206

Chapter Twenty-Six

By the time Beth arrived home, Opal was curled on the living room couch, a half-empty bottle of Chocolate Bunny soda pop on the coffee table. "Where's Ruby?" she asked by way of a greeting.

"Upstairs," Opal answered without looking up from her copy of *The Good Earth.*

"Is that for junior English?"

"It's extra credit. I finished *Catcher in the Rye.*"

"Stay here. I need to talk to you and Ruby together before Joel gets home."

"No prob. I'm not going anywhere. Can't say the same about my sister."

"What's that supposed to mean?"

Opal frowned and turned a page.

"Ruby!" Beth stood at the bottom of the staircase and shouted. "Come down here, please."

No response.

"Right now."

"Okay, Mom," a voice bellowed. "Didn't know you were home." Moments later, the girl appeared, a small suitcase in tow.

Beth folded her arms and watched her daughter tromp down the steps, visibly pale. "What's that for?"

"The suitcase? Well, I was going to ask if it's all right to spend the night at Genna's. Tomorrow's Saturday, and..." Ruby let her plea fade. "I'll have the car back in the morning. What?"

"You're not driving my car anywhere," Beth barked. "Take a seat by your sister. I need to ask you a few questions."

Ruby dropped the suitcase on the floor and sulked as she made her way to sit on the sofa next to Opal. "What did you tell Mom?" she sniped.

"Nothing." Opal tossed the book onto the coffee table. "What do you think I told her?"

"*Shhhhh!*" Ruby hissed.

Beth sat in the armchair across from the girls. "Do you want to spend the night at Genna's, too, Opal?"

"No," Opal said before turning to Ruby. "Is that what you're doing? Staying at Genna's? She wasn't even in sch—"

"Mom," Ruby interrupted, "what do you want to ask me? I told Genna I'd be ready in fifteen minutes."

"You did? And when did you talk to Genna?"

"She phoned a few minutes ago," Ruby stuttered, obviously spinning a web of lies as fast as her brain could produce them.

"You didn't cook up this plan at school today?"

"They couldn't have," Opal said. "Genna wasn't—"

"Will you shut up? Mommy is asking *me* questions, not you."

Opal retrieved her novel from the coffee table. "Fine," she commented, searching for the last-read page.

"Well, Ruby?" Beth pushed. "When did this plan come together? How did you speak to Genna when she wasn't at school today?"

Ruby stood as though emphasizing her innocence. "How do you know that?" she asked, eyeing Opal, convinced her sister was the source.

"I know a lot of things. Believe it or not, I wasn't born old. I was your age once and thought I knew everything about everything. None of that matters right now because your cousin Luke may be in danger. You have to tell me what you and Genna have been talking about."

Opal clapped her book shut with a wallop. Her eyes wide, she gaped expectantly at her mother and sister.

"I don't know anything," Ruby chirped unconvincingly.

"Well, here's what I know," Beth said, summarizing the day's events.

Ruby listened, then made her way back to the sofa and crumpled next to Opal, apparently ready to confess her part in the scheme. "The sheriff is looking for them?" Ruby wavered, disbelief in her voice.

"Not just Sheriff Wes, but a lot of deputies and some men from the Forest Service. Dad and your Uncle Ahren are out looking for your cousin, too," Beth added.

"They're not doing anything wrong. They just want to be together," Ruby said, a mixture of regret and justification to her voice. "Dante promised to help them, that's all."

Beth, now standing, locked a hard stare on Ruby. "And are you helping, too?"

"It's not fair. Auntie is jealous of Mrs. Gallatin. That's why she's so cruel to Genna." Ruby spit the words, as if they had the magic power to correct all the wrongs piling up at her feet.

Beth huffed. "We can debate this later. Right now, both Genna and Luke's parents are worried sick. Half the county law enforcement formed a search party because we believe they might be in peril."

"From Dante?" she smirked, as though Beth had declared *Romper Room* was dangerous and Miss Nancy public enemy number one.

"You have a crush on him," Opal said.

"Not anymore."

"You've heard Genna complain about the mean things he's done to her and their little brother, yet you still want to think he's Prince Charming," Opal added.

"I do not!" Ruby defended. "He's a jerk. But Genna's my friend. I have to help her."

"But this isn't helping, Ruby. You have to tell me where Genna is or where they're headed to," Beth insisted.

Ruby pouted.

"You must know. You're headed to meet them, aren't you? What are you supposed to bring?" When Ruby didn't respond, Beth scurried to where her daughter had discarded the suitcase and crouched to stand the case upright. She slid the button on the brass clasp, but the hasp latch didn't pop open. "It's locked. Give me the key."

"I…I…"

"Give me the key. Enough of this stalling. Don't you understand how serious this is? Your cousin's life might be in jeopardy. For all we know…" Beth's effort to keep the rage, fear, and frustration from her tone failed. The longer Ruby dawdled, the angrier Beth grew.

"You better tell her everything," Opal said, "and fast. This isn't you coming to your best friend's aid and finding a happily-ever-after ending."

Ruby reached into her skirt pocket and withdrew a thin silver key. "I thought I was helping," she said, handing her mother the key. "Dante said they needed me."

"Dante is a lying, conniving sonofabitch, and you were stupid to believe anything he ever said!" Opal cried.

Beth snatched the key from Ruby's hand and slid it into each of the locks. She flipped open the clasps and slid aside a pair of pajamas and a few of Ruby's panties.

Underneath the clothing, a pile of gemstones glittered.

Incredulous, Beth blinked as if clearing the view. "Where did you get those?"

"Wow," Opal said, now standing next to Beth. She reached in and held up her hand filled with a tangle of necklaces. She fingered through the jumble, touching the stones, inventorying the contents remaining in the case. "Diamonds, emeralds, rubies. Some rings, a few bracelets. Several ropes of pearls." Opal gaped at her twin. "This looks like the real deal."

Ruby turned toward the front door as though wishing she could escape.

"Well?" Beth demanded.

"Genna gave some of them to me yesterday at school," she confessed.

"Some of them?" Beth wrinkled her forehead, trying to understand.

"Well, yes. She's been giving me a few every day for about a week or so. She asked me to stash the jewelry in a safe place, so I put them in my suitcase and tossed some of my clothes over them…"

"In case Mom looked inside," Opal said, finishing Ruby's sentence.

"You've been collecting these for a week? They've been planning this getaway for a week!" Beth couldn't believe what she was hearing.

Luke, Genna, and Dante didn't just cook up some harebrained scheme; they'd been patiently plotting this escape. Gathering valuables to pawn. Biding their time.

"They had to wait until Genna turned eighteen. Tomorrow's her birthday." Ruby took the jewels her sister held and placed them back into the suitcase. "I was supposed to bring them to Luke last night, but I didn't get the chance. You wouldn't let me leave the house, remember?"

"Damn good thing," Beth said.

"Genna's really mad at me. Says I've messed everything up. Because of me, they're stuck in a grimy motel until I get there."

"You may have saved your friend and your cousin from a lot of problems." Beth headed toward the telephone to call Wes. "What are they going to use them for?"

"Hock 'em, I guess, and get the money. Genna's been taking a couple of pieces from her mother's jewelry box every day or two, hoping she wouldn't notice."

"This has been in the works for a while," Beth stated.

Ruby nodded.

"And the three of them needed that much money?"

"They're running away to get married. They don't have cash of their own. Dante said they'd need something to live off and that Mrs. Gallatin didn't use any of the fancy jewelry."

"So this was Dante's idea?"

"Not all of it, just the taking-the-necklaces part." Ruby hesitated. "And the eloping part, too, I guess. He said it was the only way to get the parents to accept them as a couple."

"Stealing Nora's jewelry isn't helping anything. In fact," Beth continued, waving the phone receiver she held around like a baton, "it makes everything worse."

"They didn't steal all her jewelry," Ruby protested.

"You could be arrested as an accomplice! Are you absolutely out of your mind?" Beth's voice rose with each word until she screeched.

"I didn't take anything. Genna gave them to me."

"They aren't hers to give. Don't you see? You're involved in a burglary. You are in big trouble."

"But, Mom—"

"I can't believe you'd be this gullible. First, to hold on to someone else's property, and second, not tell me what's going on.

As soon as I finish with Wes, you're telling me every detail about this whole caper."

Beth dialed as Ruby cried. Her sobs did little to weaken Beth's rage over her daughter's misguided behavior.

As soon as Wes answered, she spilled her words. "Ruby was on her way to the motel to bring, well, to bring some of Nora's jewelry to Genna... I don't know exactly. She said they were going to pawn some after they got married." Beth described a few of the pieces and then listened for instructions. "Yes, we'll be there as soon as we can. I'll bring Ruby...and the jewelry," she said and hung up.

Beth stood in the hallway gathering her thoughts at the realization that instead of being an enabler to a lovers' rendezvous, Ruby might be charged as an accessory to grand theft.

Once again, Dante had preyed on the weaknesses of others.

Fully aware that no one would be left unscathed, she blinked back tears, praying Ruby would be spared for her part in this illicit charade.

"Pick up that suitcase and get in the car," Beth ordered. "Opal, you wait here for Joel to get home. Dad or I will phone you later."

Without waiting for a response, she flew out the door, Ruby at her heels. She would have plenty of time to regret confessing her daughter's role in the heist.

Chapter Twenty-Seven

Addie and Mabel played dominoes on a rickety card table, neither woman with their mind on the game. The sixty minutes since Ahren, Barry, and Ted had left to search the stream running through the forest crawled like army ants across a desert. All Addie had to show for the passage of time was another hour closer to sunset.

Another hour without any word of Luke's whereabouts.

She jumped at the sound of the bell jangling as Ahren entered, holding a random selection of poles and a net, Ted and Barry behind him.

Addie ran to his side.

"We stopped at a couple of Ted's favorite spots and found this stuff at the last one," Ahren said. "Seems to be left behind."

"Or abandoned on purpose," Barry said. "Either way, there was no sign of the kids."

Addie melted into a pile of worry and despair. "Where are they?" she wept against Ahren's chest just as Wes, toting his Stetson hat, wandered into the office.

He acknowledged the group but addressed Addie. "We're calling off the search in about an hour's time," he said. "It will be dark, and we won't be able to see, even with flashlights in those woods. Won't be safe for my men."

"But—" Addie's voice cracked.

"We checked the stream where the guys found the fishing equipment. Two of my deputies are still there, combing the area now."

"Don't know why you wouldn't let us continue helping with the search," Ted complained. "We're the—"

"I know, Ted. You just have to trust me." Wes turned his head at the ringing phone.

Mabel answered and reached the phone toward him. "It's for you, Sheriff."

He tossed his hat onto a nearby counter. "Sheriff Montgomery," he barked in a professional tone meant to convey his command of the situation.

"Yes, Beth… Jewelry? I see. How many pieces… Well, I don't know how that plays into this, but yes. Bring her and the items… Great." Wes returned the receiver to Mabel, his brows knitted in puzzlement.

"What did Beth say?" Addie asked. "Does she know where Luke is?"

Without responding, Wes turned to Barry. "Can you phone Mrs. Gallatin and have her come here?"

"Well, yes, but why?"

"Seems we've come across some of her jewelry," Wes said.

"Jewelry!" Addie shouted. "What do Nora's baubles have to do with finding my son?"

"Calm down, honey," Ahren soothed. "Sit by me, and let's listen."

"Listen to what—a wild goose chase? Wes, I demand that you keep looking for Luke, Genna, and Dante. Nora's jewelry be damned."

Wes remained still.

Addie swiveled to face Barry. "Is Nora missing some of her valuables?" Her question was laced with anger.

Barry scrunched his face questioningly, as though the prospect confused him as well. He turned to Mabel. Before he could ask, she had already dialed Nora's room and handed him the phone.

"Nora—No, we haven't found her yet… Can you come to the office? The sheriff has some questions. I'm sure the kids are fine. Um…they've found some of your…jewelry." Barry listened carefully. "I'm not sure of anything. When you get here, the sheriff will tell us more."

"Ask if she's missing any valuables," Addie prodded.

"I'll raise the questions," Wes sniped. "Just have her join us. And quick."

"Come here so we can straighten this out... I know. I'm worried, too." He clicked off. "She's on her way."

Barry rubbed his hand against the stubble sprouting from his chin. "I have to agree with Addie. I don't understand what Nora's jewelry has to do with this. Or, for that matter, how Beth came into possession of it."

"Don't know," Wes stated, "but she's on her way with Ruby and a suitcase full of what seems to be Nora's property."

"Nora's property?"

"Necklaces, bracelets, rings. We may be getting closer to some answers. What's going on may have less to do with romance and more to do with finance," Wes sneered.

Addie stepped forward. "What are you talking about?"

"This whole thing may have been a ruse to steal. People do stupid things for love or for money. I have a hunch that, this time, cold cash is the motivator, not young love."

Addie turned on her heels to greet Nora, who obviously hadn't rested at all. Her hair, combed with a hand instead of a silver-handled brush, was flat on one side.

"What is this about, Wes?" she asked, stepping inches away from the sheriff.

"Sit down, Nora." Wes retrieved his hat and ran his fingers down its folds as though stalling for time.

Addie wondered if this was an interrogation technique used to make people antsy. If so, he was succeeding because she could barely stay inside her skin. *"Ask her about the jewelry, for God's sake,"* she wanted to yell.

"Just got off the phone with Beth Jacobsen," he said.

"I know Beth," Nora piped, giving Ted a glare. "We were best friends once."

"Of course, of course. Now the thing is, Beth was at home when she found her daughter with what appears to be a suitcase full of your jewelry." Wes made the accusation carefully and without judgment.

"My jewelry?" She swept her view to Barry. "What is he talking about?"

Wes answered. "Ruby will be here soon to tell us herself. Seems like Genna was swiping pieces and giving them to Ruby for safekeeping. A sort of nest egg for after she and Luke got hitched, I'm guessing."

"What! That's the craziest thing I've ever heard. Barry, tell him. Our daughter wouldn't run away to get married, and she certainly wouldn't steal from us," Nora insisted. "Not your mother's jewels. They'll be Genna's someday, anyway."

"But not today," Wes answered. "And today she needs the cash they would raise so she can elope with young Burhan. That's the story we're expected to believe."

Addie stood, arms wrapped tightly around her middle, and rocked side to side. "That's the second time you alluded that something else is going on," she said, not bothering to disguise her impatience. "What are you trying *not* to say, Sheriff?"

"Ma'am, I've been in this business a long time." He paused, sending an understanding look in Ahren's direction. "Long enough to know that things aren't always as they first appear to be. Gotta consider all possibilities, other motives. That's my job."

"You didn't have an open mind a few hours ago. And now you're coming around to my way of thinking," Addie crowed. "This isn't a case of rebellious teenagers out for a joyride."

Wes narrowed his eyes in Addie's direction. "What I'm saying is, as more details are revealed, I'm able to entertain additional possibilities. The fact that the items were taken without Nora's knowledge leads me to believe that one, if not all three, planned this getaway. Down to the fact of how they would get money."

"You're pretty sure that they took Nora's stuff as a stash, a way to get cash on hand?" Barry asked.

"It appears that way. We'll know more when Beth and Ruby get here. In the meantime, tell me about the pieces," Wes continued.

"Which pieces?" Nora answered, appearing beleaguered and exhausted at the prospect of describing her possessions. "What did Ruby say she has?"

"Necklaces, brooches, some rings, a rope of pearls, I think. I don't know specifically, but she collected a suitcase full," Wes replied.

"A suitcase! She must have taken nearly everything Mother Gallatin left. Oh, Barry, your mother's heirlooms tossed about like cheap costume jewelry," Nora cried, nearly toppling over. Barry clasped her by the elbow and helped her to a chair.

"Mom wouldn't care about the jewelry. But she'd be devastated that her grandchildren snatched them," he said, taking the seat alongside her. "The important thing is that Beth got the goods before Dante could hock them."

"You've been through this before?" Wes probed.

"Not with Nora's jewelry, no. But with other things he has pawned to get some pocket money on those rare occasions that we told him no," Barry replied, not making eye contact.

"Do you have insurance on the jewelry?"

Nora glanced at her husband as though seeking permission to answer. "We do." She squeaked her response, obviously uneasy about discussing their private dealings.

"How much is the policy for?"

Nora didn't answer.

Wes rephrased, taking what seemed to Addie to be excessive steps to be discreet. "How much is your jewelry worth?"

Addie huffed at the ludicrous line of questioning. *Get to the point. Ask them what we need to know, for heaven's sake.* She slid a glare to Ahren, who remained stoic through the entire scene. Addie knew that his passive demeanor on the outside camouflaged the mounting anger brewing inside.

"You mean how much could Dante get from a pawnbroker?" Barry answered.

"Well, yes. In a manner of speaking," Wes confirmed. "I'm wondering how much money they thought they'd need to fund their departure. How much cash could they raise?"

Nora fidgeted with the buttons on her cashmere sweater.

Barry sent a cursory glance at Nora as though beckoning her to keep her composure. He then turned to face Wes once again. "We don't insure all the pieces, though, so it's quite possible, depending on what they took, that the street value is close to two hundred thousand if they sell everything."

"That's plenty of money for three teenagers to start out in another state," Wes said more to himself than to anyone in particular.

Addie wailed, her throat closing at the seemingly valid prospect of not seeing Luke again. "They could have enough money to leave and never come back? Never need us again?" Addie cried, exchanging her panic about Luke's safety for the painful reality that he may have chosen another life, one without her.

"But they didn't get away with it," Ahren reminded her. "Ruby has the jewelry."

"We know that Ruby has *some* of Nora's jewels," she spat. "What if they stole other pieces before this? They could have thousands of dollars' worth of gems. Plenty to move somewhere other than here." Addie swallowed, willing saliva down her throat, now suddenly dry and constricting.

Wes put his hands out in a calming gesture. "We don't know what those kids have in their possession. Nora, do you have an inventory of what you kept in the safe?"

Barry answered, "I'm not sure how up-to-date it is, but there's a catalog sheet in a file at home along with the insurance policy. I can go get it if you want."

"Let's wait until Beth and Ruby get here and see what they have. The actual list may not be necessary if Nora can visibly account for what's present," Wes said.

Nora wiped both eyes with the heel of her hand. "Some of the pieces are priceless to me. Your great-grandmother's brooch, for example. Money couldn't replace them. Dante would know that. He wouldn't have taken those," she said to Barry, her words filled with hope.

Barry remained quiet as though telling his wife *don't bet on it.*

Addie's heart hurt for Nora. Next to not knowing if your child was safe, realizing your child had deceived you, stolen from you, had to be the worst pain. She couldn't help but feel empathy for her friend. All the discussion about thousands of dollars' worth of treasures exploded her mind. She couldn't imagine a life with so much wealth.

Today, that didn't matter. Addie focused on one true, undeniable fact—all the money in the world couldn't compensate for the love and well-being of your child.

Addie had spent the past few days knotted in her own drama. Angry at Barry and Nora for forcing this issue, causing her to have to confess to Ahren the depth of her duplicity. There had been little space left to comfort an old friend's broken spirit.

She regarded Nora's sunken eyes, hollow cheeks, and hunched appearance. Those drained features had been piled upon Nora for weeks, months, maybe years. Addie had been wrong to freeze her out of the comradery of the Sewing Circle. Nora needed their unwavering sisterhood, their enduring friendship that Addie and each of the women relied on to pull them through hard times and to celebrate the good ones.

Nora deserved these friends. She had earned them. Addie's selfishness, arrogance, and shame had stripped them from her. The guilt enveloped her like a worn-out shawl.

From Addie's naïveté and youth, Luke was born. That was an amazingly good thing, a miracle that she had wrongly turned into an embarrassing mistake. She closed her eyes in prayer. If God would grant her this blessing, if Luke returned safely, she would never intentionally cause hurt or suffering to another human being.

"What's keeping Beth?" Ted asked, moving toward the bay window overlooking the parking lot. "She and Ruby should have been here by now." He opened the door and stepped outside. Moments later, he returned. "No sign of 'em. The Gallatins' car is still here, too."

Wes walked to the registration desk and motioned to Mabel for the telephone. "What's your sister's number?" he asked Addie.

She uttered the numbers by rote and waited for someone to pick up. Opal or Joel, perhaps.

Wes stood with the phone ringing in his ear. "No answer," he said.

"If Beth said she was on her way, she wouldn't have dallied. She'd be here by now," Ted said, worry invading his presence. "And Opal would have answered."

Ted returned to the doorway and watched for a sign of a familiar car.

Addie glanced at the clock hanging on the wall behind Mabel.

Where are you, Beth? She placed her palms against each other and prayed, pushing down an overwhelming premonition that something was horribly wrong.

Inhaling a deep breath, she closed her eyes, and implored that any second Ted would announce Beth's and Ruby's arrival.

Chapter Twenty-Eight

In her haste to leave, Beth nearly toppled over Genna, standing even footed on her front porch. She released a yelp and after a moment, regained her balance.

Sizing up the girl, Beth stepped back and immediately turned to gaze across the street. Dante and Luke stared back, leaning against a black T-Bird with a white roof. A stark contrast to the seafoam-green Studebaker she had seen in the motel parking lot. Both young men locked their gaze onto Beth as though awaiting her next move.

She turned to Genna without acknowledging either boy.

"You practically bowled me over. What in the world are you doing here?" Beth demanded, already knowing the answer.

"I came to get this." Genna grabbed for the suitcase Ruby held.

Ruby, standing directly behind her mother, kept a tight grip on the handle. Beth remained wedged between the two girls and slid her gaze toward the street.

"Hi, Luke," she said, infusing a calm into her voice to combat the panic pulsing through her veins. "You're supposed to be at home in bed."

Luke jutted his chin in greeting but remained silent.

"You made me look really bad to your mom. Like I can't even keep up with a hobbled nephew," she said, face revealing a tense, agitated state.

"Sorry, Aunt Beth. I had something come up." Luke displayed his perfectly straight white teeth. He moved toward her, Dante alongside.

"I need Ruby to let go of the suitcase," he directed.

"Luke, you're nearly nineteen, but that doesn't make you a man. Your life isn't some teen-tragedy movie with you and Genna cast as star-crossed lovers. Believe me when I say, there's a lot more to the story," Beth said.

"I know you mean well, Auntie. I love you, but this is none of your business."

"Luke, I—"

"Aunt Beth, stay out of this!" Luke boomed, his voice switching from respectful to threatening in a sweeping stroke. "Give me the suitcase."

"Luke, what are you doing?" Beth asked, fully aware of Ruby being sandwiched by Genna and her nephew. Dante stood back, although Beth guessed he was waiting for the right moment to pounce.

"Getting what belongs to us. Just hand over the suitcase," Genna said, "and we'll be on our way."

The front door clicked open, and Opal filled the doorframe. "What's all the noise out here?" she asked before realizing there were visitors on the porch. "Hey, Luke, Genna. What are you doing here?" When there was no reply, Opal looked past her mother. "Oh, Dante. Well that explains a lot," she huffed.

"Everyone inside," Dante ordered, storming up the steps and herding them toward the front door.

In his hands, he held a pistol and pointed it at Beth.

"Oh, my God." Beth gulped.

"Get inside!" Dante yelled, this time using the barrel to nudge her along.

"Just grab the jewelry and let's go," Genna beseeched.

"Genna's right. We don't have to do this," Luke said. "We'll be over the state line in less than an hour, and they won't be able to come after us."

"Shut up!" Dante howled. "Just shut up! You both talk too much. You know that? Get in the goddamn house and keep your mouths shut."

Luke reached for Genna's hand. "Come on," he said, nodding to both Beth and Ruby to follow. They pushed past Opal.

Dante trailed behind, his gun pointed at everyone and at no one. "Get in the living room," he directed. "Luke, close those venetian blinds. Don't need the nosy biddies butting in."

Luke did as he was told and returned to Genna's side.

Beth observed her nephew and understood that Luke had gotten himself into a situation that he couldn't get out of. While Dante would hurt anyone to achieve his goal, Luke would not. She watched him assume a protective stance, basically a barrier separating Genna from her brother.

"Can't we just take the jewelry and go? That's our plan," Luke reminded Dante.

"*Was* our plan, you idiot!" Dante snapped back.

Beth recoiled from the crazed look in Dante's eyes, his pupils dilated, wild with fury. She wondered if he had been drinking or was using dope. What did the kids call it? Wacky weed.

Beth shifted closer to Ruby and Opal, providing her own protective shield, worried that Joel would bound through the front door at any second.

"God, I can't believe what a dipstick you are. Don't you know that your aunt will call the fuzz as soon as she can?"

"Aunt Beth wouldn't call the police, not on me," Luke defended.

"Bullshit!" Dante screamed, spit flying from his mouth.

He paced the room, and Beth marveled at how he resembled a trapped animal, desperately looking for a way out. She had to point him in the right direction, persuade him to trust her. Inside she quaked at the monumental task. The young man threatening her may have never trusted anyone.

"She'd get the heat on us in a heartbeat," Dante continued, painting a bleaker picture. "They'd track us down like dogs. You two would never get married. Look how unfair they've been to you all along. They don't want you to be together. Don't you get it?"

He ping-ponged his gaze between Luke and Genna, finally settling on his sister. "You can't think that suddenly they're going to treat you fair. I know for sure that they won't."

Genna looked away.

"I'm trying to help," Dante continued, attempting to regain her support. "You've got to believe me. We have to make sure these folks don't rat us out. That way you and Luke can be together, like we talked about. You'll have it made in the shade. You want to get married, don't cha?"

"Well yes, I guess…but…Luke and I don't want anyone hurt. We just—"

"You saw those fools at the motel, watching Dad's puke-green car, waiting for us to come back so they could nab our asses. Such chumps," Dante sneered. "They don't know about the T-Bird, and that's what's giving us time to get away. Until your dumb *girlfriend* screwed everything up."

"I-I-I didn't mean to," Ruby defended. "I was coming over when…"

"Stop right there," Beth scolded. "You are not apologizing to anyone, especially this kid, for not delivering stolen goods. Do the three of you know how much trouble you're in? Burglary is a felony. When the theft is in a home, it's a first-degree felony. Do you know what that means?"

"Yeah. Yeah, we're felons. Stop your bullshit. It's my granny's jewelry, and my folks won't press charges. No one is going to prison, so knock off trying to scare us," Dante taunted, offering an exaggerated shudder as though he were frightened.

"We're wasting time," Luke interrupted. "Let's get the stuff and burn rubber. Yelling at my aunt isn't helping." He sliced an apologetic gaze at Beth.

"You're right. But we have to take care of this glitch first." Dante shifted closer to Ruby. "If only Little Miss Half-Ass had held up her part of the bargain…but unfortunately…" He gestured with his gun-toting hand dramatically. "We've got to clean up her mess. You guys got any rope?" he asked Beth, looking around the room.

"Rope?" she questioned.

"Yeah, rope."

"You're gonna tie us up?" Opal said, incredulous. "You're turning this into a really bad B movie. Take your stuff and leave my family alone."

"And something we can use as a gag to shut this one up," Dante said, leveling his gaze. "You've always been a pain in the ass, Opal."

"You are an A-one loser," Opal snarked.

Dante shoved her against a wall. "Shut up or you'll be sorry!"

Opal huffed but complied.

They jumped at the ringing phone.

"Don't answer that," Dante ordered.

"It will just keep ringing," Beth said.

"So what? Let it ring."

"They're wondering where Ruby and I are..." Beth let her words trail off.

"They who? My parents? Too bad, so sad," Dante mimicked. "Let them wonder. Where can I find rope?" His voice rose, and he stepped closer, now in a hurry to finish.

Beth gritted her teeth, glad she had stopped herself before saying too much. And glad that Dante was so full of himself that he didn't realize they had called the sheriff.

"We don't have rope," Beth volunteered, putting herself between Dante and Opal. "But there's a clothesline out back. You could cut it down, I suppose."

"Now there's a woman who wants to cooperate." Dante grinned. "Luke, go cut some rope."

"With what?" he asked.

"Do I have to think of every little thing?" Dante barked. "Figure it out. Find a knife in the kitchen, some scissors, your uncle's hedge clippers. I don't damn well know. Just get back here with some rope PDQ."

Luke scurried toward the kitchen without making eye contact with Beth.

"Everyone into the dining room, where we'll be more comfortable," Dante directed. "Genna, pull out a chair for each of them."

She did what she was told, a mixture of terror and confusion on her face.

"No, not like that, you stupid bitch. Don't put the chairs close together," Dante scolded.

Genna moved each chair farther apart.

"That's better. Auntie," he said sarcastically, "you sit here. Ruby, you sit over there."

"Where do you want me to sit?" Opal pestered, one hand on her hip.

"On my lap," Dante shot back, "but I guess that will have to wait for another day. Sit in the corner over there where I can keep an eye on you." He pointed to the far side of the room.

Once everyone was seated, Dante stomped to where the desk set telephone lay on a nearby stand. The caller had finally given up. He yanked the cord from the wall.

"No more calls," Dante declared. "And once you're tied up, no visits to the neighbors to borrow their telephones."

"Sorry we used your clothesline, Aunt Beth," Luke said, returning with a snarl of rope in one hand and a pocketknife in the other. "I cut several pieces in different lengths." He handed the jumble to Dante.

"Why are you giving them *to me*?" he shouted. "Tie up your aunt and your cousins. Then we can get the hell out of here."

"Is this really necessary?" Luke asked again, apparently reluctant to truss up his family.

"It is if you don't want your folks to stop you from marrying my sister," Dante replied.

Luke nodded. He sent an apologetic glance at Beth and began binding Ruby.

She watched him grab his cousin and fix her to the chair before he turned his attention on Opal. Out of respect, he would tie up his aunt last.

Would telling Luke the truth make a difference? He should hear this news from his mother, but desperate times had changed her preference.

It struck Beth that Luke and Genna weren't lovers. Seemed more probable that he was there to protect Genna from Dante; almost like a big brother saving his little sister from a bully.

Maybe this scenario was what Beth hoped for, seeing facts the way she wished they were. She had to stop Dante or slow him down. But how? In a minute, she'd be anchored to her ladder-back chair. Dante would gladly stuff a gag in her mouth.

Surely Addie and Ted must be wondering where I am. They've probably been calling the house. Now they'll get a busy signal. Will they think Opal's on the phone? Maybe they'll reach out to Mrs. Doyle to check on us.

"Get the suitcase. I want to see what's inside."

Genna scurried to where the case lay and pushed the buttons to release the clasps, but they didn't budge. "It's locked," she said.

"Ru-beeee," Dante said, clearly not amused by another delay.

"I have the key," Beth said soothingly. No reason to get him more hopped-up than he already was. "I put it in my handbag."

Genna scampered to where Beth had discarded her purse, and riffled through it, locating the luggage key. She took a moment to slide it into each of the two keyholes before flipping up the clasps and opening the case. "Looks like it's all here!" she hollered, holding up various pieces for Dante to see.

Dante glanced over his shoulder. "Great news," he said. "Close the case and put it by the door." He turned toward Luke. "Now, go get something to gag them, and then we'll hit the road."

Chapter Twenty-Nine

"Now all I'm getting is a busy signal," Addie lamented, leaning against Mabel's counter. "You sure it was ringing before, Wes?"

"Yes," Wes answered, not bothering to hide his exasperation.

"Well, Opal couldn't be on the phone for almost half an hour."

"Sure she could," Mabel said from behind the registration desk. "She's a teenager, isn't she?"

Addie frowned. For most girls this would be true, but not Opal. She would have her nose in a book, not spending time chatting endlessly on the phone about fingernail polish. Certainly not when her cousin was missing, and her sister was found with a suitcase full of stolen jewelry.

Maybe Mrs. Doyle was the one chatting. Damn party line.

Addie dropped the receiver on the cradle with a *thump*. "Something is wrong. I feel it. Even if she had a flat tire, Beth would have figured out a way to call so I wouldn't worry. Beth knows I worry."

Ted, who hadn't moved from the doorway since the news about the stolen jewels nearly fifty minutes ago, scratched his head. "That is true," he said, glancing quickly at Addie. "I've never seen two sisters who worry more than you and my Beth."

His eyes seemed far away and cloudy; they possessed a longing Addie hadn't seen in them before. Ted was worried, too.

"Do they have another car?" he asked anyone who was listening.

Barry moved toward Ted and put his hand on his shoulder. "I thought about that, but I don't know where they would have gotten another vehicle unless they borrowed one. Nora, do you know anyone who would loan Dante their car?"

Nora shook her head.

"Maybe Dante owns a car you don't know about," Addie stated. "You said he'd stolen things from you and pawned them to get cash. Maybe he saved up for one."

"That sounds like a crazy idea," Ahren said. "But based on what you've told us, is he conniving enough to pull that off?"

"Conniving?" Barry waited a beat before continuing. "Conniving, yes. Add brilliant, manipulative, and devious to the list."

"So it's possible that they have another getaway car," Ahren summarized.

"And we're watching a parked one while they're heading for the West Virginia border." Addie widened her eyes, horrified at the prospect. "They went to Beth's, grabbed the jewelry, and now—"

"Calm down, Addie, you're letting your imagination run wild."

"How can I be calm? We have nothing. No Luke. No Dante. No Genna. No Beth. No Ruby."

"And no case filled with pawnable jewelry," Nora finished. "Once again, they've played us for fools. Wes, can you send a car by Beth's to see what's going on?"

Wes reached over the reception desk for Mabel's phone and dialed.

"Shoulda done that when you first spoke to Beth," Addie snapped, anger now overtaking worry.

Wes frowned, but didn't reply.

They listened as he dispatched two officers to the home of Beth and Ted Jacobsen.

"Call me at the Silverwing as soon as you get there," Wes instructed the person on the other end before hanging up.

"I'm not sitting here cooling my heels." Addie reached for her handbag. "Let's go to Beth's," she said to Ahren.

"We're going, too," Nora agreed.

"Someone has to wait here in case we're wrong," Wes admonished.

"We're not wrong!" Addie shouted. "But if you think we are, then you wait and keep watching the sedan. I'm going to find my son!"

Barry fished his keys from his front pocket, saluted Wes mockingly, and the foursome filed out of the motel's makeshift lobby.

"I hope we're not too late," Barry said to Ahren, unlocking the vehicle.

Too late for what? Addie wanted to ask. Instead, she swallowed her words and scurried into the backseat of the Cadillac behind Barry and wondered if he could drive across town in a lot less time than the usual twenty-five minutes.

***

Beth watched as her nephew froze in his steps, his eyes wide at the vision of Genna tied to a chair near Ruby.

"All I could come up with was some socks and Uncle Ted's neckties," Luke said, returning to the dining room.

Dante stood by an empty one waiting for Luke's return. "Put that stuff down on the table and come sit," he directed, once again using the gun barrel as a pointer.

"What is this about?" Luke stuttered.

Beth couldn't help but have sympathy for her naïve nephew. He and Genna had trusted Dante's charismatic charm. That was one of their many mistakes. She knew they would recount their actions for years to come, and the scars of this deception would haunt them well into adulthood.

"Sit down," Dante ordered. "I don't have time to waste."

"But you're taking us with you," Luke protested, still not accepting the reality.

Dante shoved him into the seat and quickly immobilized Luke's hands by binding them to the wooden armchair.

"He didn't plan to take you anywhere," Beth said. "This was a ruse to get some fast cash. This time, he's trading his grandmother's jewelry to get him out of a jam. Who are you in trouble with, Dante? Who's coming after you?"

"Just shut up, you old biddy. You don't know nothing." He cinched the rope around Luke's legs and tugged on the knot, making certain the cord was secure.

"I know you've been nothing but trouble for your family. That you treat everyone as a means to your ends," Beth continued.

"What I don't know is what makes you do it. What makes you hurt those who love you most?"

"You never shut up, do you? Just like my mother." Dante grabbed a sock and a necktie from where Luke had put them. "Here, let me help you close your trap."

Dante shoved the sock hard and deep into Beth's mouth, forcing her to gag while he secured it with a silk paisley tie, the one the girls had bought Ted last Father's Day. Her daughters gulped at the savagery.

"You don't need to be so rough," Luke protested.

"Yeah, yeah. Thanks for the tip, Mr. All-American." Dante moved toward him. "You're next, then you two babes." He turned toward Opal and Ruby. "Stop staring at me like that," he said to Opal.

"Like what?" she sniped.

"Like you just ate a bug or something. I'm not going to hurt anyone," he claimed, finishing with Luke and approaching Ruby. "I have to get out of town."

"And I'm supposed to believe you," she retorted. "Just like you didn't hurt Luke. And now, look what you've done to my family. To your own sister."

Dante stood over Opal. He forced open her mouth.

Beth shuddered at the thought that he was about to violently kiss her. Strangely, she found herself relieved when he placed the sock in Opal's mouth with more care than he used on the others.

Beth couldn't help but wonder if, under different circumstances, Dante might have pursued Opal.

"Look, Genna, I can't take you where I'm going," he said, moving toward her chair. "I have to leave PA, but I'm not going to West Virginia. If, after all this settles down, you and Luke still want to get married, you'll be able to. You're both old enough."

Beth thought there was a blush of regret in his voice, almost as though he held an iota of compassion for them. But her attitude changed a moment later.

"But I guess you won't be wanting to. Right, Auntie?" Dante taunted, rounding on Beth.

His devilish stare changed her empathetic warmth into an icy surge flaring down her arms. He paused as though taking pride in the scene he had created.

"Cat got your tongue?" Dante laughed. "So glad I'm moving far away from this hick town, to where no one can find me. Unless I want to be found. It's funny that none of this would have happened if I had been the son Daddy wanted me to be," he bragged.

"What are you talking about?" Genna demanded. "Untie me and Luke. We're going with you. Drop us off in West Virginia, then go wherever the hell you want. You owe me that much."

"I. Don't. Owe. You. Nothing." Dante's voice climbed. "Silly sister, you still don't understand. You're never going to marry this guy." He grinned, looking at Luke. "They will *never* let you. As smart as you are, I can't believe you don't see what's right in front of you."

"What are you saying? Of course we'll—"

"Wish I could wait around and watch that drama unfold," Dante crowed. "Be here when Mom and Dad tell you the truth."

"What truth? Dante, you're talking crazy. Untie us so we can leave," Genna insisted, struggling against the ropes strapping her wrists together.

"Hey, Mom? Ruby? Opal? Where is everyone?" Joel's voice echoed from the kitchen.

"What the hell?" Dante nearly yelled but swiftly moved behind a wall near Genna, who he hadn't as yet gagged, and waited. "Is that their kid brother?"

She nodded. "He must have come in through the back door off the alley," she said barely above a whisper.

Dante bent over to reach her ear. "Stay quiet," he warned in a low voice.

"Mom, I passed my history test. Got a B-plus," Joel shouted to the empty air. "Where are you?" He turned the corner into the dining room. "What in the—"

Joel didn't finish his sentence. The blow from Dante sent him crashing to the floor unconscious.

A muffled shriek belched from inside Beth as she watched her youngest child crumple to the ground. She fought against the ropes binding her hands. She couldn't prevent what had happened, and she couldn't rush to Joel's side and make certain he was all right.

"Sorry about that," Dante said, "but I didn't hit him that hard. What a wimp."

He stared at Genna, then walked toward her. He paused and kissed the top of her head. "You were always too soft. Gotta toughen up, sis." He stuffed a sock in her mouth, anchored in place with a tie. "Goodbye, everyone."

Dante grinned and made a sweeping farewell motion with his hand still cradling the gun. With the other hand, he grabbed the suitcase and hustled out the front door, to freedom.

Freedom from what, Beth wondered. Inside, she knew whatever that young man was running from, he was taking with him. Trouble always followed.

She couldn't be concerned with Dante's problems right now. Somehow she had to get loose, call the sheriff to capture him before he drove out of the county jurisdiction and into a new state.

Beth started lifting up in her chair and banging down against the parquet floor, praying the noise would wake up Joel. With any luck, he'd come to and untie them. If what Dante said was true, her son was just temporarily stunned, not permanently injured. She hoped that this once, Dante could be believed.

Luke, Opal, and Ruby caught on to Beth's scheme and began squirming in their chairs, making their own commotion.

Joel's chest rose and fell, but there was no other movement, not even the flutter of an eyelash. Beth mentally implored her son not only to be okay, but to be their knight in shining armor. To free them. Eventually they would be found, but would it be too late? She needed Joel to regain consciousness now.

Outside, the T-Bird's engine roared, and the car squealed away.

Beth's sense of urgency intensified as the rumble of Dante's driving diminished. She looked at the three girls and her nephew and motioned frantically to continue their clattering and clunking.

The noise seemed overwhelmingly loud to her ears, but her son didn't budge.

Wake up, Joel, honey. Baby, please wake up.

Chapter Thirty

Some of Addie's happiest memories—before Barry fell in love with Nora—were when they were a couple. On Friday nights, he'd borrow his dad's convertible, pick her up, and they'd speed through Keystone to the outskirts of the city. Addie would tie her hair with a scarf, but the effort did little to tame her chestnut curls from blowing wildly in the breeze.

It was on one of those Friday nights when they first made love, and Addie foolishly believed they would always be together.

In those days, local law enforcement knew about Barry's hot foot, and more often than not, he'd be pulled over for speeding and released with nothing but a warning. No one wanted to alienate the senior Mr. Gallatin.

Barry, now the senior Gallatin, must have left his hot foot in Pittsburgh because he was driving at a snail's pace. At this rate, it would take them more than thirty minutes to reach Beth's. Thirty minutes they couldn't spare.

"Can you step on it?" she demanded, punching the back of his seat.

Barry jumped at the command, nodded, and increased his speed, but not by much. "No point in getting into an accident," he said.

Addie licked her lips in annoyance. She wasn't asking him to drive recklessly, the way he did twenty years ago. Instead of his distracted response, she wanted him to share her urgency. Obviously, he was in no hurry to collide with Dante.

Was he mulling over his own priorities in preparation for confronting his son? Maybe devising a plan of his own.

Addie huffed, folded her arms, and pushed back against the overstuffed leather seat. She remained quiet, although every pulsing nerve inside wanted to shout, *"Go faster!"*

She should be in the driver's seat. That was her usual role, making things happen while others stalled in their tracks, afraid to take any action, perplexed as to what to do next. Ahren, her beloved Ahren, was such a man. He waited for direction, permission, approval.

Did she love him or hate him for that? At this moment, she couldn't tell.

"Getting to Beth's any faster won't matter," Barry moaned.

"How can you say it won't matter?" Addie growled.

Nora answered, "What he has planned is already in motion. And he won't hurt his sister or Luke."

"How can you be so sure?" Addie gulped. "Look at the trouble he's caused already."

"Because we know our son. Because we've been dealing with him for a long time," Nora said, glancing at Barry before turning to face her. "Because…"

Addie watched as tears filled her friend's eyes. Tears caused by more pain and disappointment than today's events triggered. These were tears gathered over months. Years, perhaps. Tears of a mother mired in desperate worry for her child. Addie knew this truth because those same fret-filled tears pricked her own eyes.

"Dante has a problem," Nora continued. "We've tried everything to help him. The best doctors, the best hospitals, the best programs. Nothing worked. That's why we moved back to Keystone. To get him away from the bad influences in Pittsburgh." Nora shifted to face the road ahead. "But he brought the bad influences with him. *He* is the bad influence."

Addie's heart cracked a little at Nora's declaration. Accepting the truth that your child was not the man you raised him to be was the cruelest parenting burden.

"Luke is everything Dante isn't," Barry continued. "We hoped that when Luke started hanging around, some of his good judgment would rub off. That maybe all Dante needed was a friend to put him on the right path."

"And it seems that worked for a while. They were friends. The three of them would do things together when Luke came over to see Genna," Nora added. "You'd think a teenage boy courting a girl wouldn't want her brother around, but Luke wasn't like that."

Barry agreed. "It was the craziest thing. We never caught Genna and Luke kissing or cuddling or even holding hands. But we attributed that to Dante always being around. Then something shifted. There was a growing distance between the boys. Like Dante learned something about Luke that made him not want to be friends."

"You don't—" Addie said.

"I hadn't at the time," Barry said. "But now, it seems possible that he figured out that Luke is my son. The good son, the achieving son. The son who doesn't disappoint his parents. That could have pushed Dante over the edge."

"And caused all this?" Addie asked.

Nora nodded. "That's a big part of it. The other part is…"

"Dante's drug problem," Barry said, finishing her sentence. "And when he's on God-knows-what, things go from bad to worse. We have to be cautious as to how we confront him, so he doesn't…well…doesn't make any bad decisions."

Addie blinked her eyes in disbelief. Her family was being tossed inside a kaleidoscope, and Dante turned the cylinder, changing one horrific image to another.

"Are you saying that if he's hopped-up on something, he'll get violent?" Ahren asked the question Addie couldn't bear to pose. "We need to get to Beth's sooner, not later, if that's the case."

"He only gets confrontational when he's cornered. That's why Barry and I wanted to come along and make sure that we approach him the right way. Prevent anything irreparable from happening." Nora placed her hands in her lap as though finishing the last direction in a recipe, and all she had left to do was set the timer and wait.

"Have you two been discussing this possibility without telling me or Ahren?" Addie demanded.

Nora nodded again.

Addie stuck her head between the bucket seats to get closer. "What else haven't you told us?"

"We're just figuring things out ourselves," Barry said. "We want to do what's best for everyone involved, for both of my sons, so calm down."

"Calm down! You have a lot of—"

"Barry!" Ahren shouted. "Do you have a black Thunderbird?"

"No. Why?"

"What the hell does that have to do with anything?" Addie yelled at her husband, incensed that he'd interrupted.

"I saw Dante driving a black T-Bird heading in the other direction."

"What?" Addie angled her body over Ahren's lap to look out the window.

"The car that just flew past us. I'm pretty sure Dante was behind the wheel."

"Could you see anyone else?" Addie asked, desperation dripping from her question.

"No, I don't think so. Just Dante."

"Turn around, Barry. Turn this car around now!" Addie hollered.

"Are you sure it was Dante?" Barry asked. "We don't own a T-Bird."

"Looked like him," Ahren said. "Since the sheriff is already sending men to Beth's, I think Addie's right. We should follow Dante."

"And do what?" Nora snarled.

"If nothing else, keep track of him until we can call Wes," Ahren answered, composure coating his reply. "At some point, you two will have to stop running interference. Dante is a grown man, responsible for his own decisions and mistakes. Covering for him will only make things worse."

Barry huffed loudly, and Addie interpreted his response as *easy for you to say*.

Anger inside of Addie struggled against newly-uncovered sympathies for Nora. Every parent wanted to make things better for their kids. What's the harm in smoothing out a little wrinkle here or there?

But in this case, Barry and Nora violated even the most liberal of parental boundaries, covering for Dante at every turn, never holding him accountable for any of his actions, paying off whomever they needed to make things right. Not much different from Barry's dad getting him out of speeding tickets.

"Dante is in real trouble," Addie said, "and he needs you both to be strong for him. Show him how to be an adult."

"Dante can't continue to live this way, and frankly, I don't see how the two of you can either," Ahren added.

Nora and Barry exchanged an exhausted glance. Perhaps they needed this small push, to not give up the struggle when the stakes were so high.

Barry hit the brakes and made a U-turn, this time punching the accelerator like he meant it. "Hang on!" he shouted.

"Can we catch him?" Nora asked, obviously embracing the new plan. "That car was going pretty fast."

"So are we," Barry declared. "Keep a lookout. Make sure he hasn't pulled over and we drive past him."

The four remained silent for the next several minutes as Barry swerved in between cars and cut off a city bus in his haste to make up ground. A loud, sustained honk, courtesy of the bus driver, saluted them as they slid back into position ahead of him.

Unaffected, Barry drove faster.

That's how I remember you, Addie thought, allowing herself a moment of respite from the dire situation.

"Up ahead! That's him," Ahren called, craning his neck for a better vantage point.

"I see him," Barry said, easing off the gas.

"Why are you slowing down?" Addie demanded.

"I don't want him to know we're following him. We can't get him to pull over, so we'll have to wait until he stops or something."

"If you go any slower, that bus is going to pass us," Addie said in disgust. "Can you get close enough to see if there are other people in the car?"

"Not without him spotting us, and then who knows what he'd do," Barry said. "As much as we don't want to, we need to hang back and be patient."

"Is he headed back to the motel?" Nora asked.

"I don't think so," Ahren said, pointing behind him. "The turnoff for the Silverwing was back there. He could be heading to West Virginia, but that doesn't make sense either because he would have taken the Seventy-Nine South. Seems like we're going north, northwest. Ohio, maybe?"

"What's in Ohio?" Addie wondered out loud.

"Not sure," Barry said. "Maybe a route to Canada?"

Nora yelped and buried her head in her hands.

"He's leaving the country? Seems like overkill for taking his grandma's jewelry," Ahren said. "He has to know you won't press charges."

Barry shrugged. "Dante isn't running away from Nora and me," he said finally. "He's running away from people who don't forgive or forget."

Chapter Thirty-One

Dante had been gone maybe twenty minutes when Beth heard the doorbell ring and saw the front doorknob jiggle.

"Anyone home?" a male voice called before identifying himself as law enforcement.

She and the kids made as much commotion as possible, hoping the officer would hear their clatter. She could decipher the silhouette of a second man outside her living room window. He walked around the perimeter, approached the dining room side, and peered through the glass.

"Over here, Jim!" he shouted. "Folks tied up."

Beth gestured for them to continue around to the back of the house, where she guessed Joel hadn't locked the door. She was right.

Within minutes, the five were cut loose. Beth rushed to Joel's side and gently nudged him. While one deputy checked his pulse, the other officer handed her a glass of water and suggested dabbing a bit on Joel's lips to help wake him up.

After several swipes of water and Beth's insistent pleas to be all right, Joel came to.

"What happened?" he asked, rapidly blinking his eyes and reaching for the back of his head.

"Oh, thank God." Beth sent a grateful prayer to the heavens before lowering her gaze to her son. "Are you okay?"

"I guess," Joel said, still massaging the sore spot. "Someone hit me!"

"Dante," Luke said, standing near Genna.

"He did all this," Opal added, gesturing with both arms. "Always knew he was a bozo."

Joel frowned and made his way to the couch, where he fell back and closed his eyes. Beth followed close behind, assessing his gait. She joined him and waited for her heart rate to orbit closer to normal.

Once she was satisfied that Joel had suffered no permanent damage, she called to Opal.

"Get your brother an ice pack," Beth directed, "while Ruby and I talk to the officers."

The taller deputy was interrogating Luke and Genna. Jim, the older one, waited in the far corner of the dining room for his chance to interview Beth and Ruby. The pair relayed the events as accurately as they could remember. Beth described the car Dante drove away in, emphasizing that he was heading for the state line with thousands of dollars of stolen jewels.

Along the way, Beth interspersed their story with a few of her own theories. Jim nodded encouragingly, yet seemed unimpressed. Just as they finished, he advised Beth to take Joel to a doctor, even though he appeared fine.

Beth stared at Joel, ice pack pressed against the back of his head. "I'm calling Dr. Cataldo's office. But I have to go next door to use Gladys's phone. Will you be all right until I get back?"

Joel nodded.

"I'll sit with him," Opal volunteered.

Beth turned, nearly slamming into Luke's chest.

"I'm sorry about all this. About Joel getting hurt," he said, hanging his head.

Beth hugged him. "None of this is your fault, honey. The worst thing you've done is trust a friend."

"Dante's no friend," Luke declared. "What can we do now, Aunt Beth?"

"We sit and wait for the sheriff to capture Dante. They'll find him, and all this will get straightened out."

"I don't know how any of this will ever be okay," he insisted.

"It will. Trust me. How are you holding up?" she asked, realizing how upset he must be.

"Still trying to understand what's going on. I don't know why Dante would have pretended to help us if all he wanted was to steal some jewelry. He could have done that without any help," Luke muttered.

"True, but this way he could implicate you and Genna," Beth said.

"But why? He's Genna's brother, for God's sake. Who'd hurt their own family like this?" Luke buried his head in his hands and swiped up to run his fingers through his mop of hair.

Beth heard no crying, and that made the scene harder for her to endure. Soon enough, Luke would be getting the answers to these questions—and others he didn't even know to ask.

She placed her hand on his shoulder. "Your parents will be here soon, and they'll explain the rest."

Luke lifted his head and stared.

The would-be bridegroom, now simply a confused, broken boy.

Chapter Thirty-Two

Addie stared out the window waiting for a miracle to appear. The foursome had ridden in stillness for several minutes, a silent prayer to bring an end to this nightmare without anyone being hurt. That possibility seemed implausible. Still, she held on to the hope.

After several minutes passed, she cleared her throat. "What did you mean when you said Dante is running away from people who don't forgive or forget?"

Barry didn't answer.

Nora turned slowly to face Addie. "Our son has a big, expensive drug problem. Drugs that are turning him into this hateful being. They've taken our son and made him someone horrible, someone cruel, someone unrecognizable."

"That's enough, Nora. Addie and Ahren don't care about our problems," Barry cautioned. "They're only interested in Luke's well-being."

"That's not fair," answered Addie, "or true. I do care. We care about the both of you and your family, no matter what our past grievances have been."

Barry snorted loudly.

"Okay, that's justified. I've behaved terribly, acting like a teenager. Old wounds heal slowly, especially ones my mind embellished over the years."

"And ones that never really happened," Barry sniped.

"Blame me if it makes you feel better. I'm sorry for what I've done. I'm sorry I didn't tell you about Luke. I'm sorry I deceived Ahren. Mostly, I'm sorry for the lost years."

"We'll have plenty of time to swap apologies," Ahren said. "Right now, we need to keep following Dante."

"You don't care about Dante," Nora said accusingly, "or what happens to him. After all this is over, he'll be just another delinquent who lost his way. For Barry and me, though, he's our son, and we won't walk away from him."

"Addie and I don't expect you to turn your back on Dante. In fact, we'd be disappointed if you did. We understand about loving a child so much that you'd gladly exchange your welfare for theirs."

Addie slid her glance to Ahren. He truly, deeply loved Luke and had pretty much from the beginning. And he loved her so much that he went along with her vengeful charade. A charade that had caused them much pain and suffering.

"Hold on. Hold on." Barry broke into the silence. "Maybe…" He straightened in his seat to peer over the steering wheel. "Look, over there." He pointed up ahead, toward a filling station on the right side of the highway. "He stopped for gas. This may be the break we've waited for."

Barry slowed the car to a crawl and pulled off the highway and into a parking lot adjacent to the gas station.

"The attendant is pumping gas, but Dante's not in the car," Ahren said. "Maybe he's using the bathroom."

"No!" Addie shouted pointing. "He's in the phone booth. Who could he be calling?"

"Doesn't matter," Nora said. "We need to stop him."

"How do we do that?" Addie asked.

"Block his car. Hurry, now, before he sees us," Nora directed. "Park so he can't get away. He always leaves the keys in the ignition. I'll grab them, and then maybe we can talk to him, plead with him to come back home, so we can straighten this whole mess out."

"He needs to tell us where Genna and Luke are," Addie piped from the backseat.

"Later," Barry answered and followed Nora's orders. He pulled his Cadillac diagonally across the driveway and parked, careful not to squeal the tires and alert their son. They watched Nora scamper toward the T-Bird, then turned their attention to Dante, some twenty-five feet away gesturing animatedly to whoever was on the other end of the phone line.

"Things might get a little hairy," Barry said, bending to look at them. "You two wait in the car."

"You're kidding, right?" Addie said.

"Not in the least. Let Nora and me approach first. It will make things go smoother. We'll find Luke and Genna, I promise. Just let me do this my way."

Addie took in Barry's beseeching plea and shuddered at the enormity of pain Dante had caused his parents. Relenting, she dropped back against the seat, folded her arms, and nodded.

Barry exited the car and quietly angled the door behind him, not bothering to close it completely.

Addie immediately slid her gaze to Nora, hunched beside Dante's car. She watched her attempts to fish out the keys through an open window. Once Nora had them, Addie let out a relieved sigh. Both women darted their eyes to Barry.

Addie scrutinized every painstaking step he made toward the phone booth. He moved as though the pebbles underneath his shoes were shards of glass, each with the power to pierce through his soles.

After what seemed like an eternity, but was more likely less than a minute, Addie couldn't wait any longer. She reached for the door handle, but Ahren placed his hand on her knee. "Give them a minute, honey. Let them talk to their son."

Addie acquiesced but rolled the window down farther to hear better. She wedged her upper body through the opening, her eyes ping-ponging between the phone booth and the T-Bird.

Finally, Barry was close enough to tap on the glass pane but didn't. He stood motionless as though waiting for Dante to finish. Finally, Dante turned toward his father, eyes wide and wild with panic, still clutching the receiver. Barry shifted to where his body blocked the exit.

Dante hung up and pulled the folding door open. Barry stepped closer and placed a hand on his son's shoulder.

Dante twisted away. "I'm leaving forever! So move, old man!"

Barry's reply was soft and controlled, forcing Addie to stretch farther out the window. Still, she couldn't hear what Barry said or see the expression on his face.

But she did see Dante's features contort into an aggressive, angry puzzle. He attempted to shove his father out of his way. Barry pointed, and Dante's eyes followed the direction of the outstretched hand until his gaze landed on his mother propped against the car, keys visibly dangling from her fingers.

"You brought Mom? You son of a bitch!" Dante yelled and ran toward her. "Give me my keys and get the hell out of my life." His words blasted like bullets and landed against Nora's chest, puncturing Addie's heart as well.

"He's out of his mind," she said to Ahren. "How could he speak to them that way? They love him so much."

"He's saying the words, but he's not the one speaking," Ahren said.

Confused, Addie turned. "What in the world are you talking about?"

"It's Dante's voice, but the drugs are talking. That boy is in a great deal of pain. I'm not sure anyone or any amount of money could help him."

She quickly pivoted back to see Nora. Her friend stood contrite and defeated, a set of keys suspended from her clenched hand as she surveyed her son.

The depth of anguish Nora's posture telegraphed exploded inside Addie. She blessed herself, thankful that Luke had never put her and Ahren through what she had witnessed in the past few hours.

"I need to hear what they're saying," she told Ahren, reaching for the door handle. "I'll give them space, but I need to know where Luke is."

"Just be still. This is their family. We need to respect that."

A few seconds later, Dante grabbed his mother.

"Dear God, he's wrestling Nora for the keys," Addie shouted, pulling the lever and fleeing the car.

Ahren yanked his door open, joining his wife to aid Nora.

"Don't come a step closer," Dante warned, pulling a handgun from inside his waistband.

Ahren reached for Addie and reeled her toward him. "Do what he says."

Addie squeezed Ahren's hand and shifted closer to him as though presenting a united front. The pair maintained a generous perimeter from where the war Dante waged unfolded.

"What are you doing? Put the gun down!" Nora cried.

"Son, we're here to help. Let us," Barry pleaded.

"I don't need your lousy help. Just let me go. Give me the keys, Mom, or somebody's going to get shot. And I don't damn well care who." Dante stood to his full six-foot height and slowly pointed the pistol at each of them, finally stopping with Addie. "Might be fun to start with you," he added, glowering at her. "You damn busybody."

Addie clutched her neck and willed breaths to continue through her dry, tight throat. Ahren pushed her behind him. "Don't say anything to antagonize him," he hissed out of the corner of his mouth.

Addie nodded, not that Ahren could see. Dante Gallatin's threat went deeper than she ever imagined. She was way out of her league and cowered in shame of her know-it-all attitude toward Nora. Addie's brand of mothering was useless in this situation.

Barry and Nora had been dealing with a problem so severe, she didn't know how they were still standing. And all she had done was add to their misery.

"Leave her alone," Barry said. "Addie, Ahren, get back in the car."

"Stop! Don't any of you move!" Dante ordered.

"You're not going to shoot anyone. Not today and not ever," Barry argued, forcing him to look in his direction and away from Addie. "You're my son, and I love you. You're a better man than that. Let us help you."

"They're not here to help me," Dante replied, returning his focus to Addie and Ahren, his finger on the trigger. "They only give a crap about Mr. All-Star Basketball. Why in the world would they give a flying damn about me?" Dante rattled off the words so fast that he needed to pause and suck in air.

No one moved or challenged his opinion. As long as Dante held a loaded gun—they assumed it was loaded and didn't want to chance that it wasn't—he was in charge.

His bloodshot eyes darted from his parents to the Burhans and back as though he were scoping out his target. His intense glare landed on Barry. "And maybe that's why you're here, too, dear old Dad. You're worried about your oldest son. And I don't mean me."

"Dante!" Nora shouted.

"You know, Mom. We all know that Dad here has three sons. You, on the other hand, have only two."

"Shut your filthy mouth," Nora said.

"It's true. You know it's true. Everyone knows."

"We can talk about this later," Barry said, inching closer to Dante.

"Stay back! All of you stay away," he shouted. "Give me my keys. That's my car. I paid for it myself."

"With money you stole from your mother and me," Barry accused.

"Money you owe me, *Daddy*," Dante taunted.

Nora stepped back so the car formed a barrier between her and Dante, his keys still in her possession. "Where will you go? What will you do?"

"Doesn't matter. I'm leaving this fleabag town and not looking back. You'll never have to worry about me again," Dante said with more bravado than Addie thought necessary.

His exaggerated declaration pealed as a cry for help. *This kid didn't want to go anywhere.* Instead, she believed he was looking for an honorable way out of the maze he'd ensnared himself inside. She prayed Barry and Nora could convince him that they were his only way out.

"Never worry about you again? Do you think that's what will happen?" Barry's words rang out. "Your mother and I will never stop worrying and caring about you. How do you not know that?"

Dante huffed.

"Well, maybe you don't give a rat's damn about me, but your mother, Dante. Your mother has always been there for you, in your corner, always your champion, no matter that the evidence pointed otherwise."

"Don't you see? I'm doing this for her," Dante argued, jutting his head in Nora's direction. "For you. For everyone. Everyone will be better off without me causing problems, making trouble. That's all I've ever been good at." He threw his shoulders back and attempted to regain his composure.

Addie surveyed the intensity set deep in his eyes, a panicked countenance sprouting from the demon possessing this child. Dante acted out of fear, but of who or what she could only suppose.

Addie lurched forward, not able to control her intense fear any longer. "Did you hurt someone? Did you hurt Luke?"

"See? I told you." Dante chortled. "She's only interested in Luke. Well, he's fine. They're all fine. Just dumb. A bunch of dumb kids trusting me."

"Where are they?" Addie asked, pressing toward him.

"Don't come any closer," Dante threatened. "They're tied up at your sister's house. And they're okay. But you...you I could hurt. You're the reason for my problems. If you just...just...shut up!" Dante shook uncontrollably, like a small child preparing to throw a tantrum.

Addie stepped back to her place beside Ahren, every nerve in her body on high alert.

Did he really leave Luke and Genna unhurt? What about Beth and Ruby? And Opal and Joel? She whispered a prayer that Wes's deputies were at Beth's, and everyone was as Dante described—fine.

"What do you mean, tied up?" Barry's eyebrows arched.

"Yeah. I had to so they wouldn't do something stupid. Genna wanted to come with me, and I couldn't have that. If that stupid kid hadn't come home from school, I would have been gone already. No one would have been hurt," he added.

"Joel? You hurt Joel?" Addie quickly asked.

"Didn't want him trying to play the hero. Had to keep everyone contained."

"Contained!" Addie's exasperation was getting the better of her.

"Enough talking. I'm the one with the gun, remember?" Dante boasted, his voice taking on an air of finality and desperation. "Give me the goddamn keys, Mom."

Addie guessed the end of his rope neared. Would he snap? And what would that shattering entail?

"We're supposed to let you go, just like that," Nora said. "And not look back, not worry and fret about how you're taking care of yourself? You underestimate me, Dante Michael. How can you take me for a fool?"

"I don't... Look, Mom, I have to leave. I can take care of myself," he answered, his tone softening.

"Hah! You don't even have a high school diploma. What kind of job will you get? Or will you continue your career of thievery?"

Nora finished, and Addie noted that she appeared to stand taller. Were these words she'd wanted to say to her son for a long time?

"I'm not a thief," Dante defended, the gun in his hand trembling with each word.

"You stole Grandma's jewels." Barry's words crashed against his son from the other side of the car. They rang harsh and factual, forcing Dante to face him. "You've broken our hearts. What's left to take now? What else can you strip from your mother and me? Our family?"

"You're the one cheating and lying and—"

"We can talk about my shortcomings later," Barry interrupted. "Right now, our concern"—he swept his arm around to indicate Nora, as well as Addie and Ahren—"is you. Taking care of you."

"I'll take care of myself. You two, move closer to them so I can keep my eye on you," Dante said, jutting his chin in Addie and Ahren's direction.

"And when you run out of things to hock," Nora chimed in, still positioned on the other side of the Thunderbird, "what then? You're being stubborn and stupid and, frankly, dangerous. I don't know what mess you've gotten into this time, but your dad and I will help you figure it out. Get you the counseling you need to beat this monster living inside you."

Dante studied the gravel near his sneakers as though waiting for an answer to appear. "I've really screwed up, Mom. You can't help me. Not this time. No one can. Just let me go." He spoke in a plea.

"Addie, you and Ahren take my car to Beth's. Nora and I will stay with Dante," Barry said.

Ahren grabbed Barry's keys and directed Addie back into the car.

"Wait a minute," she blurted. "I'll leave, but not until he tells us what the hell he was doing. Why he was—"

"Helping them elope?" Dante volunteered.

"Yes."

He laughed. "We all know that wasn't going to happen. Well, all of us except Luke and Genna. It's against the law to marry your sister, isn't it, Dad?"

Barry stared blankly but didn't reply.

"How did you...I mean, who told you?" Addie asked.

"No one," Dante answered, seemingly insulted at the suggestion. "Doesn't take a brain surgeon. Hell, just look at the two of us. Luke and I look more like brothers than me and Roman. Deep down, Luke knew, too."

Ahren reached for Addie's hand and held on tightly, as though steadying her for the hail of pain about to rain down. "What do you mean?"

"If they were really boyfriend and girlfriend, they would have acted that way. They would have…you know, made out or something. But they never did, just sat around all the time. Didn't even hold hands. I mean, the dude never tried to get to first base, much less—"

A siren's whirring stopped Dante in midsentence. He raced around the car and dove toward Nora, grabbing at her closed hand. He quickly wrestled the keys from her, but not before shoving her to the ground.

Without looking back, he raced to the car, put the keys in the ignition, gunned the accelerator, and backed out just as a sheriff's squad car pinned him in. He nearly slammed into the side panel, then put the car in drive, and attempted to pull forward, but his dad's car had blocked the only other exit.

"Turn the engine off and put your hands where I can see them!" Wes shouted.

Dante froze.

"It's over, Dante. Turn the car off," Wes repeated. "We can do this the easy way or the hard way."

Nora scooted to the driver's side, putting herself between the sheriff and her son. "Let's end this before anyone gets hurt," she said softly.

Dante hesitated before finally killing the engine.

Addie released a loud exhale of relief. When Dante turned to face his mother, a stream of tears rushed down his cheeks.

Barry stepped to where Nora stood and wrapped his arm around her. "Come on, son. We'll go home and figure this out."

"I'm afraid that Dante will be coming with me," Wes spoke slowly and without emotion. "This isn't a speeding ticket we can kick aside." Wes tugged Dante's wrists as he secured them inside handcuffs.

"When can we see him?" Nora asked, her voice quavering.

"Have to let you know. Might not be until Monday, after Judge Beacon is back in town. It wouldn't be a bad idea to talk to an

attorney in the meantime. I hear Adam Maddock is a good one."
Wes turned Dante around to face his parents. "Say goodbye."

Addie watched Barry and Nora speak to their son, assuring him
they would be there as soon as bail could be arranged.

After a deputy collected Dante and herded him toward a patrol
car, she raced to where Wes stood. "The kids? Where are the kids?
Are they okay?"

Wes stepped toward her. "They're at Beth's. Everyone is fine,"
he said, patting her shoulder. "A little shook-up, perhaps, but
okay."

"I need to see Luke," Addie implored. "Can you take me to
him?" she asked the sheriff.

"Take my car," Barry said. "Ahren, you have the keys. We will
be along shortly to see Genna. That is if Sheriff Wes will let us take
Luke's car."

"Don't see why not," Wes answered. "We checked the license
plate. It's registered to him. Might be the only thing the boy didn't
steal."

Addie saw the scowl form across Barry's face. A father could
disparage his son's behavior, but it stung to listen to others do the
same.

Ahren tugged her arm. "Let's go."

She nodded and climbed into the Cadillac's front seat without a
word. Addie didn't look back. She was certain the sight of her
friends, now a broken family, would crush her heart. Instead, she
stared forward, mustering all her strength to face the scene that
waited for her across town.

She prayed for strength to master the right words to tell Luke
the truth. And she prayed for grace to accept the fallout of her
actions. Ahren and Luke deserved that much.

Chapter Thirty-Three

By the time Addie and Ahren reached Beth's, police cars clogged the street. Neighbors milled along the sidewalk guessing at what had happened in this normally sleepy neighborhood. What appeared to be a reporter, notebook in hand, weaved among the crowd, hoping for a juicy tidbit before tomorrow's edition went to press.

The din reminded her of a beehive she saw once as a young girl near a neighbor's grapevines. Lots of noise and activity, but it seemed to Addie nothing was getting done.

Addie spotted Ted's truck a few houses away. The relief that washed across her chest, knowing he was home with Beth and their children, surprised her. They had butted heads often, mostly because of the way he treated her sister. But today, she was grateful to her brother-in-law. If it hadn't been for him, they wouldn't have uncovered Dante's scheme as quickly as they did. That delinquent would have put Luke and Genna in harm's way or ditched them somewhere in West Virginia.

"You okay?" Ahren asked as he slid the Fleetwood's gearshift on the column into park.

She nodded and gently touched his arm. "Let's see Luke," she said, pulling the door latch and jumping out.

Ahren took her hand and steadied her as they approached the house, avoiding anyone attempting to engage in conversation. One of Wes's men recognized them and waved them through.

Addie kept her head down, both to avert eye contact with the neighbors, especially Mrs. Doyle, and to offer a small prayer. It was through the grace of God that she was walking up Beth's path on her way to hug her son.

As soon as they reached the porch, an officer opened the front door and ushered them inside. Addie hesitated before entering, looking around and spotting Luke before he saw her. The sight of him made her legs go weak, forcing her to cling tighter to Ahren to take another step. Luke stood alongside his aunt who appeared to be comforting him.

Beth noticed Addie immediately and pointed across the room.

Luke turned to see his parents. "Mom! Dad!" he yelled, racing to where Addie and Ahren stood. They opened their arms wide, and he enveloped them in a hug.

The trio embraced for several minutes, Addie savoring the warmth and strength of Luke's arm around her. She blinked back tears before reaching to touch his hair, his cheek. A relieved sigh escaped from deep inside her chest. Addie hoped the exhale would release the colony of moths fluttering in her throat preventing her from speaking. *I must tell him, but not here; not now.*

The thought had barely formed in her mind when Luke said, "Mom. Oh, Mom. I am *so* so sorry. I wish…I wish…"

"Hush, honey. We'll talk later. Right now, what's important is that you're okay. That Genna and…well…that you're all okay."

Beth joined the circle and gently herded the family to the living room. "*Yinz* sit in here and gather your thoughts. Wes is keeping us around for more questioning, and then I'm sure you can go home. I'll get some water," she said, disappearing into the crowd of law enforcement.

Addie glanced over her shoulder to the dining room, where Beth's children and Ted gathered around the table in deep discussion with who she guessed was a plainclothes detective.

She looked away, immediately training her gaze on Luke. It remained there, unbroken. The two sat on Beth's divan, holding hands, while Ahren occupied a nearby chair.

"I don't know how to apologize," Luke said. "I was stupid, stupid, stupid."

Addie allowed a telling grin. If anyone knew about being stupid, it was her. Soon Luke would know, too. He'd understand the choices you make as a teenager in love fall under another name.

Not quite stupid, perhaps, but naïve, maybe. Or gullible. Love painted an enchanted picture.

"How are you feeling, son?" Ahren asked.

"Fine. The ankle is pretty much back to normal." He smiled shyly at his mother. "It's been pretty good for a while now, but Dante said to keep milking it to buy us time. How could I have listened to that guy? He's such a weirdo. Damn it to hell, he even tied up his own sister. Sorry for cussing."

Addie laughed. "You cussing is the least of my worries. I need to know that you're all right."

"My body is fine. My pride and common sense took a massive hit, though." He tipped his head back, making a hank of hair fall into place. "I thought I was a good judge of character. This guy played me. He played me so he could steal from his parents. Never cared about me and Genna," Luke said, sliding his gaze to where she sat alone on the far side of the dining room. "In fact, he said you'd forbid us to be together. Said he wanted to watch when his parents told us the truth. What was he talking about?"

The nest of moths returned, flickering faster inside Addie's chest. She swallowed hard. *Now or never,* she thought, looking to Ahren for support before digging deeper for courage. "Luke, we do need to talk about this. You see—"

"Mr. and Mrs. Burhan," a deep voice called out.

"Yes?" Ahren responded.

"Detective Parris would like a word," the officer said, pointing to the dining room where Ted, Opal, Ruby, and Joel were exiting. "You too, Luke, now that your parents are here."

"He's a nice guy," Luke volunteered. "I talked to him earlier."

"You've spoken to the detective? What did he say?" Ahren asked, moving toward his wife and son as though he were a protective shield.

"Said I probably won't be held responsible for the stolen jewelry. He doubted if charges would be filed. But he wanted to wait until you guys got here to formally interview me and get my side of the story. Aunt Beth thought that best."

Addie nodded.

"Shouldn't Genna's folks be here, too?" Luke asked.

"They're with Dante," Ahren said, "and Sheriff Wes."

"I heard they caught him before he got outta town." Luke punched his fist into his palm. "He didn't get away with anything. Damn that feels good. I hope he's grounded forever."

"Things are a bit more serious than that. He'd be lucky to get grounded," Ahren said. "Let's not keep the detective waiting."

Addie nodded and led them into Beth's dining room.

Wasn't she playing cards with the gals here a few weeks ago? She had sat in the same seat the detective now occupied. Addie rubbed her eyes in disbelief at how much had changed in the short time since the Gallatins reappeared.

She looked at Luke, knowing that soon his life would be upended, permanently and completely. Her son, her only son, would never see her the same way. His mother who kept secrets, important secrets, other people's secrets with the ultimate power to shatter lives.

"Detective Mike Parris." He offered his hand, and Ahren shook it. Addie smiled tightly and took a seat, with Luke sandwiched between them. As Detective Parris outlined what she and Ahren already knew—the facts they had lived through, Addie nodded compliantly, not bothering to correct some of Parris's fuzzier points.

He told them Dante had been arrested and taken to the county jail. He would be arraigned the next day, but because of his age, the detective was pretty certain the judge would set bail and release him into his parents' custody.

"What were the charges?" Luke asked.

"Don't know all of them. If you want me to guess, I'd say false imprisonment would be the biggie. Can't get him for kidnapping. You and Genna came here willingly. But he did hold you and the Jacobsens against your will. Four counts there." Parris totaled the number using his fingers. "Assault on Joel. Possession of stolen goods, illegally possessing a gun. Not sure if he stole that T-Bird… Probably more but—"

"We get the idea," Ahren said, seemingly eager to move on and not wallow in the laundry list of troubles awaiting Dante.

"There will be some discussion with you and Genna about the jewelry. It will depend on whether the Gallatins and the DA want to press charges, but I'm sure that will get worked out." Mike Parris winked at Luke.

"What I want is the specifics of the plan, how it unfolded and mostly, Luke, how you were roped in." Parris leaned back and waited.

"*Used* would be a better word choice," Addie began, before Luke had a chance to reply. "Dante preyed on both my son and his own sister for reasons known only to him. Luke is in love, or he believes he is. And Dante took advantage of that romance."

Addie turned slightly, her eyes softening at her son's profile. "You remember how it is to be in love, don't you, Detective?"

Parris remained silent. Addie continued, "Well I know about being in love. And I know what it's like thinking you're in love."

"Mom, this isn't the time," Luke interrupted. "No one wants to hear about how Mr. Gallatin broke your heart."

"Listen to your mother," Ahren said. "She understands more than you could imagine."

"She knows about having her heart broken by Genna's dad. That's all she's cared about through this whole thing. If she had been even the least bit supportive of me liking Genna, none of this would have happened. I care about Genna, sure, but it was the way Mom was so against her that made me want to be with her. And then I got to know her better. It was like we knew each other from another life or something. Dante and Roman, too. I can't explain it."

"I can," Addie said, turning her chair to fully face Luke. "I can explain all of it as soon as we're finished with the detective."

Some thirty minutes later, Ahren asked, "Is there anything else you need from us?"

Parris licked his bottom lip and glanced at his notebook. "That's everything for now. You don't need me to remind you not to leave town," he said, somewhere between serious and joking. "Sheriff might have more questions."

"We live here," Ahren said. "Not going anywhere, right, son?"

Luke nodded.

***

From the corner of the living room, Beth watched as Addie, Ahren, and Luke spoke with Mike Parris, still holding court around her dining room table. She was too far away to hear, but if past experience meant anything, Beth knew his questioning would be thorough. She had first met Mike several years back when Ted was arrested for drunk driving. He was Deputy Parris then. Nice to see him move up the ranks.

She appreciated how he pretended not to recognize her. In fact, he seemed genuinely pleased when he interviewed Ted about his part in the events and made no mention of Ted's past run-in with the law.

Ted snaked his arm around Beth's waist. "What're you lookin' at?" he asked as his eyes traveled the path of Beth's gaze. "Oh. Him."

She twisted to face Ted. "What?" Beth answered a bit too defensively. "I'm wondering what he's asking Addie. And I'm wondering when she's going to tell Luke about Barry."

"You don't know that she hasn't already," Ted said.

"They wouldn't be sitting there so calm, so contained if…well, if Luke knew the root of all this."

"You're quite the detective yourself, yeah? You always took a shine to that guy. And now, look, he's—"

"He's what? Doing his job?" Beth snapped.

She couldn't help it. This day crawled by like it had thirty-four hours and still hadn't ended. She had reported Luke missing some ten hours ago. Enduring the minutes that folded into hours was like riding an unending rollercoaster.

And now Ted was starting a fight, after all the good he'd done that day. How he'd raised his esteem in others' eyes, even Wes, at his relentless pursuit of Luke and Genna. He'd been a hero of sorts, and he just couldn't shine in that moment for even a little while.

"Hey, baby, I'm sorry. I was kidding."

"You've always been a kidder," Beth said, not convinced. "Guess I'm just not in the mood for jokes."

Ted bracketed her hips with his hands, just like he had done that night in the kitchen, but today his touch was gentle, not threatening. She looked in his eyes and tenderness stared back.

"I remember him from that night. How upset you were and how he soothed you. Just sat in my craw, that's all. I was drunk on my ass, but I wasn't blind. He flirted with you, in front of me."

"Flirted! He was comforting me because you had just crashed the truck and—"

"I know. I messed up. I've messed up a lot, but maybe I learned something today. Something about myself. Something about you.

Not saying I'm perfect or nothing, but I can be better. I want to be better, and I want to be better with you. For you...and the kids."

Beth blinked aside a few tears and looked away. She'd heard this story—or a similar one—many times before. Ted was an alcoholic. He wasn't going to magically change. Sure, the day's events had been stunning, but enough to stun him sober? Beth didn't think so.

"Now's not the time to discuss this. My sister's family is about to be torn apart."

He reached for her hands and held them as though if he let go, Beth would fade away. "Sure, it's going to be rough," Ted said. "But trust me, those three won't fracture. That is a strong family. Like ours. You and Addie are the backbone. You gals keep all the gears working."

Beth laughed.

"I'm serious. What Addie did to preserve her family. Hell, what you put up with every day to keep ours together. Spines of steel, that's what you sisters have. And I've been overlooking that for—"

"Excuse me. Mr. and Mrs. Jacobsen."

Mike Parris stepped closer.

"Yes, Detective?" Ted answered as Beth turned.

"Just wanted to say thank you for your hospitality. Me and the officers will be leaving shortly. Think we have everything we need for now. Sorry about some of the items we took as evidence. I understand one of those ties was a Father's Day gift." Mike smiled. "Not sure if and when I can return it."

"The girls will get me another one come June," Ted replied.

"You're a lucky man," Mike said, a smile trailing his lips. "Here's my number in case you have any questions or you remember something important."

Ted snatched the card from Mike's outstretched hand before Beth had the chance. "Think we told you everything we know." Ted returned his arm around Beth's waist.

"What's all that about?" Beth asked, pulling out of Ted's possessive grasp after Mike had walked away.

"Just showing him where I stand," Ted replied. "And where he doesn't."

Beth shrugged. "You're making something out of nothing."

"And that's just how I like it. Nothing." He gathered Beth in his arms. "It's going to take more than talk," he whispered, "but I meant what I said. I've taken you and our family for granted. After what I've seen today and knowing what the next few days hold for Addie and Ahren, I will never do that again."

Beth remained still, not certain if she should agree. Not certain she possessed the will to make her marriage work. Ted stopped talking and held her, his head nuzzling her neck. She looked up to see Addie reach for her handbag.

"Addie's leaving," Beth said, stepping back. Ted turned just as Addie and Ahren approached.

"We're heading home. Just wanted to thank you both for everything you did for us today," Ahren said.

Addie leaned forward to hug her sister. "We would not have made it through without you both. Ted, I'll never be able to thank you, but I will try." She gathered him in a bear hug.

"Wow! You got some strength, girlie," he said once she released him. "I love Luke and you guys. Just glad I was able to help."

"Uncle Ted. Auntie Beth." Luke moved closer. "I am so, so sorry for everything. Absolutely everything I put you both through. Good thing I'm your favorite nephew."

Beth laughed. Luke was her only nephew, but no matter if she had ten, he would still be her favorite.

Beth escorted her sister to the front door. "Are you up to telling Luke the whole story?"

"Tomorrow, probably. I don't want to overwhelm him today after all that's happened. But no matter when he learns the truth, he will be overwhelmed."

Beth nodded.

"That detective said Barry is on his way to pick up Genna. I really want to be gone before he gets here. I'll have to face him soon, but I can't take any more today."

The sisters hugged briefly, and Ahren followed Addie out the door. Beth gazed across the room to see Luke holding Genna's hand. They exchanged a few words, he kissed her cheek, and left.

"Would you like something to drink while you're waiting for your dad?" Beth asked, crossing the room to where Genna stood.

She shook her head. "He'll be here in a few minutes. Then I'm really gonna get it."

Beth reached for Genna's hand and patted it gently. "You've been through a lot. Your parents may surprise you. They understand more than you think."

"You're probably right, Mrs. Jacobsen. I really just want to get home and go to sleep," Genna said.

"Sounds like the best plan," Beth said. "A good night's sleep makes everything clearer. Problems become possibilities." She pointed to the divan. The two sat in silence and waited for Barry Gallatin.

Beth wondered if what she told Genna was true.

Would she see her life more clearly in the morning? Could her problems turn into possibilities? She prayed they could.

Chapter Thirty-Four

Early the next morning, Addie busied herself rearranging knickknacks and fluffing sofa pillows. *When would Luke wake up?* She mentally rehearsed the words to tell him about Barry, but no practice would make the conversation easier.

A nervous energy pulsed through her as she flitted around the living room, the feather duster in hand, swiping at any nearby surface when the phone rang.

Addie glanced at the mantel clock. *It's not even eight. Who would call this early?*

"You gonna answer, or do you want me to?" Ahren asked, now standing in the doorway.

"I'll get it," Addie responded, moving toward the telephone. "It's probably Beth. Hello?"

"Have you told him?" Barry's voice boomed from the other end of the line.

"Are you crazy?" she snarled into the receiver and flashed a frown to Ahren.

"Calm down, Addie," he said.

"I will not. Why are you bothering us, Barry?" she barked, alerting Ahren to who was on the other end of the line. "Ahren and I barely–"

"I wanted to catch you. I mean Nora and I wanted to... Well, we think it's a good idea to be there when you tell Luke," he stammered. "We want to tell Genna and Roman at the same time."

Addie tossed the feather duster across the room. "I couldn't care less what you and Nora want. This is not your decision. You're not controlling this situation."

"I didn't mean it like that. We just think—"

"Fine. You and Nora keep plotting and planning. In the meantime, Luke's father and I will explain everything to him. Then once he has the chance to absorb how is life has changed, he can decide if he wants to talk to you."

"He's a boy. He doesn't know—"

"Just stop! He's a young man capable of making his own decisions. This time, Luke has the choice." An unfamiliar finality rang through Addie's voice and gave her strength.

"A choice about what, Mom?" Luke asked, wiping sleep from his eyes, and dragging himself farther into the room. "Hi, Dad," he said to Ahren hovering near Addie.

"Luke, honey, you're awake." She smiled and placed her hand over the mouthpiece to muffle the sound.

"And hungry. Who you talking to?" he asked.

"No one. I'll get your breakfast going." Addie lifted the receiver to her lips. "I have to go. We'll talk later."

"You have to tell him soon." Barry's words seemed dipped in warning. "We're telling Genna and Roman today."

"I understand," she said, forcing a neutral voice. "I'll get back to you."

She carefully placed the handset on the cradle and turned to Luke, mustering every ounce of calm she had left. "Pancakes? Eggs? Bacon?"

"Sounds good. But…"

"But what?" Ahren asked. "You'd rather me whip up one of my famous PB and Js?"

Luke laughed. "It's not the pancakes. They'll be great. It's just like… Well, I don't know. I feel like something is going on. Like there's a secret everyone knows except me." Luke looked from his mother to Ahren and back.

Addie remained silent and glanced at Ahren. He nodded.

"Well," she said. "There is something your father and I need to talk to you about, but we were waiting for the right time. Seems like this might be it." Addie motioned Luke to sit.

"Oh. It's that *kind* of news. Are you and Dad splitting up?" he asked, a renewed dread coloring his face.

Ahren touched Luke's shoulder. "Of course not. Your mom and I are fine. We just need to… Well, your mom should be the one." He stepped back.

"Is someone dying?" Luke guessed. "They're rescinding my scholarship?"

"Sit. It's none of those things. In fact, this could be good news, in a way," Addie said, forcing a smile. "What I have to say will explain a lot, so I need to just tell you."

Luke plopped onto the sofa. "Tell me what?"

Addie shifted to face Luke, so close their knees nearly touched. Ahren remained standing, but now he was behind Addie. Both parents had their eyes trained on Luke.

"Where to begin?" Addie raised her hands in the air and let them fall to her lap. On a large inhale, she continued, "Honey, I understand why you think I'm a stubborn, nasty woman. You believe that I've held a flame for Genna's dad all these years. That I wanted to break the two of you up out of spite. None of that is true. Or even close to the truth."

"But everything—"

Ahren signaled stop with his hand. "Just listen."

"What is true is that once, a long time ago, I was in love with Barry Gallatin. So in love that…well, we…" Addie stared at her hands, nervously entwining her fingers.

"You what?" Luke insisted.

"We had a child," Addie said, now looking at Luke. "A handsome son. A son I didn't tell Barry about. Instead, I married your father and pretended the baby was his. I didn't confess the truth to your dad until a few weeks ago."

"That baby is me?" Luke's eyes widened, and then he shifted his surprise to Ahren. "I'm a Gallatin? Barry Gallatin is my real father?" His words were coated in disbelief.

"Hell, no," Addie said. "You are a Burhan. Ahren Burhan is and always was your dad. Barry Gallatin fathered you."

Luke didn't reply. He leaned against the tufted sofa back and folded his hands behind his head, as though giving himself space to process all he'd just heard.

Addie watched as though looking through a kaleidoscope as her son's emotions rearranged themselves. She wanted to reach out and hug him hard enough so that the only thing real was her and Ahren's love for him.

Instead, she remained still and waited.

After what seemed to be an eternity, Luke said, "Genna is my sister?"

"Your half-sister," Ahren corrected.

"And that's why..."

Addie nodded.

"I couldn't let you fall in love with her. And I was so afraid and selfish that I couldn't tell you and your dad the truth. I kept hoping another solution would bubble up. Another way to fix things without you ever knowing how your mother acted so selfishly, keeping this secret from you."

Luke leaned toward Addie, shaking his head. "By giving me life and raising me in the most wonderful home? With a dad all my friends envy? If that's your sin, then, Mom, we all should want to go to hell."

Addie swiped at his hand. "Don't talk blasphemy."

"Sacrilege or not, this is the truth. You've given me the best life, the best father, the best chance to grow up loved and secure. Every kid should come from a home like mine."

Luke hugged Addie and hung on to her for several beats before Ahren leaned over to join them.

"Dad." Luke rose, tugging Addie along with him, and the trio embraced.

"I wish you would have told me sooner," Luke said, pulling away, "but I totally get why you didn't. I'm guessing Genna didn't know either, but I bet Dante did. Who told him?"

"We think he figured it out," Ahren said. "But really, Luke, if anyone saw the two of you together, they'd see the resemblance. Even with you and Genna."

"The problem was, no one was looking. And for a long time, I was grateful for that," Addie confessed. "And no one would have known if Barry and Nora had stayed in Pittsburgh. Or moved anywhere else."

"But Dante, well he's a different story," Ahren added. "He paid attention, always looking for an angle. That kid has a chip on his shoulder the size of—"

"Don't be so hard on him, Dad. When I would go visit Genna, Dante and I would talk. He did have a 'chip' as you say, but he wanted to get past that. The guy just didn't know how. He always seemed to me like he thought he got a bad deal. Being the son of a rich man and all. I didn't get it. Didn't sound so bad, but…he acted like he had the worst life in the world. That if he could just get away from his folks, everything would be better. They were holding him back. Always changing the rules, moving him away from his friends."

"That boy made some bad decisions and then waited for his parents to get him out of whatever jam he got himself into," Ahren corrected.

"If you'd listen to his side—"

"There are a lot of sides to this story," Addie said. "More than we want to know. The simple truth, the truth that hasn't changed is that Dad and I love you. You are our son. What has changed— what may be a gift in disguise—is you have siblings. It's up to you to get to know them better. Get to know Genna in this new light. You make the choices from here on out. Dad and I will stand behind you." Addie released a deep sigh; one she had held for several minutes.

"You don't have to make any decisions today," Ahren said. "Or tomorrow. Or even next month."

"What Dad is saying is that you haven't lost anything, Luke. You've gained. And you can pick and choose what you want to add to your pretty amazing life. All of it. Some of it. Or none of it. This is a lot to take in. A lot to swallow in one big gulp."

"Does Genna know?" Luke asked.

"Possibly by now. That was Barry on the phone, nagging us to tell you. Wanting to be here when we did."

Luke nodded and returned to the sofa. He placed his elbows on his knees, a faraway look owning his expression. "I sensed something was off. I just couldn't put my finger on it. Thought there was something wrong with me."

"Wrong with you?" Addie asked, staring down at him.

"Well, yeah. I really liked being around Genna. She's pretty and funny and smart and easy to talk to. All the things you want in a girlfriend. It's just that…I never wanted to kiss her. I didn't feel about her the way I had for Shari. I tried to pretend, but it just didn't happen. Even holding hands felt more like friends than, well—"

Addie scooted to sit next to Luke. "I know, son. You felt a connection. A strong bond, just not a romantic one."

"I was so confused. How could I want to be with this girl and not want to kiss her...or anything else? Now I just feel yucky that I tried to change my feelings. Genna told me not to worry about it. That we just had to get to know each other better. She sensed the weirdness, too."

Luke hung his head as though it suddenly weighed a ton.

Addie patted his knee but remained silent. *He's got to work all this out himself,* she thought, blinking back a flood of tears. *Luke will walk a long path to healing. We all will.*

"Now when I think back on it, Dante kept trying to push us together, but then he'd always say something mean like, 'You know you two will never get married.' It all makes sense now. Everything makes sense now."

After several minutes of quiet that hung like a dense fog, Addie rose. "Let me get you some breakfast."

"Don't feel hungry anymore, Mom. I'm going back to bed to think, maybe sleep for a bit." Luke stood slowly, his tall frame now appearing bent and weakened.

"You do that, son," Ahren encouraged. "Mom and I will check in on you in a couple of hours. We'll have breakfast then."

Luke nodded and trudged toward the staircase. Before he was out of their line of sight, he turned. "I know what you did is because you love me. I'm not angry, I'm... Well, I don't know what I am. I need to sort out my feelings." He resumed his walk toward the second floor and ultimately his room. "I don't want to talk to anyone right now," he concluded in what seemed to Addie to be an afterthought, and he was gone.

Ahren put his arm around her. "We need to let him be," he said.

"I know. I know." Addie buried her face in Ahren's chest and released all the tears that have been threatening to flow for the past several hours, months, years.

Chapter Thirty-Five
Fall 1958

Beth stood on the riverbank, watching Ted string Joel's fishing pole for what might be the tenth time in the past hour. Opal and Ruby sat nearby, poles in hand, but neither was paying enough attention to catch a cold, much less a fish.

It had been Ted's idea to take the family to this peaceful spot alongside the stream in Deerwood State Park, not far from where he had found the fishing gear left behind by Dante, Genna, and Luke, some three months before.

"What's the old saying...teach a man to fish," Ted said, approaching Beth now seated with her feet tucked under her on an old patchwork quilt reserved for these occasions. "Well, it's a damn good thing we don't have to count on our kids to feed us." He curled alongside her on the blanket and dug for a sandwich inside the wicker picnic hamper Beth had filled hours earlier.

Ted took a bite. "The girls wouldn't even touch the bait. And Joel, well, he's more of a shooting-fish-in-a-barrel kind of fellow. Not the least bit of finesse to that one," he said in between chews. "Still, those three are my world."

Beth swallowed hard at the sound of Ted's voice dropping. A force of seriousness permeated the air as his eyes bore down on her. "Bethie." He scooted closer. "I've made some really dumb decisions in our marriage. You don't have to agree with me." He smiled. "I know this to be true. But I have to tell you those few hours we spent with Addie and Ahren when they didn't know if Luke was alive or...well. All that got me thinkin' about us. About our kids and what I would do if anything happened to them or you."

Beth blinked but didn't speak. She knew Ted had mapped out this speech. He'd been mentally practicing for a while. She'd let him meander down this path, however long it took, but inside she prayed that his final destination would be to stop drinking.

He put the half-eaten sandwich on the waxed paper and set it aside before reaching for her hands. "I've been going to these meetings for the past two weeks. I didn't want to tell you about them until I was sure they would help. And well, that I'd actually go."

"Meetings?" Beth asked. What in the world was he talking about? Crestfallen that she misunderstood their conversation, she sat up on her haunches. "What kind of meetings?"

Ted licked his lips as though stalling. "Meetings with people like me. People who have trouble with the drink." His eyes darted away from her face, and she watched him stare just beyond her shoulder. "The meetings are for folks who don't want to be alcoholics anymore. Not that I'm a full-blown alcoholic, but I know if I don't change, I'll be one soon."

"I don't understand," Beth said.

"I've joined Alcoholics Anonymous. It's helping me to stop drinking. I just wanted you to know."

Beth had heard about the organization founded in neighboring Akron, Ohio, a mere two-hour drive from her home. But she never knew anyone who had joined.

She resisted the urge to touch Ted, to encourage this commitment. He needed her support, but she had heard his promises of quitting before. And every time she was devastated when he inevitably fell off the wagon. But today, his words rang differently. There was a resolve that had been absent before.

Still, Beth wouldn't get her hopes up. If anything, she banked on the secretarial course at the local adult school as her ticket to stability. Instead of playing cards on Thursday evenings, Beth attended class to increase her typing speed. She was closing in on eighty-five words per minute. Her instructor claimed she would be job-ready before Christmas.

Now that her kids were old enough to be left alone while she worked, the idea of leaving Ted wasn't a pipe dream. Beth could be home every night and her weekends would be free. She didn't have to live her life with a drunkard.

"Are you going to say something?" Ted asked. "You've wanted this for a long time, Bethie. Me not drinking our future away. I finally get it. I'm ready to stop, but I need your help. I need to know that you'll stand by me."

Beth reached into the grass and plucked a dandelion, its seedhead in place with dozens of fluffy white parachutes ready to take flight. She glanced to where her children sat, the murmur of insults and bragging among siblings exchanged like ping-pong balls. Closing her eyes, she blew hard, making a secret wish, a wish she barely had the courage to think, much less hope would come true.

Ted reached for her hand. "What did you wish for?"

"Oh, the usual things. World peace. Healthy kids. Lose ten pounds." Beth observed him from the corner of her eye. Was he serious, really serious this time? Or was this another tactic to keep her home? To keep her dependent on him? Could she risk letting more time pass, only to find out that she had wasted another chance to be happy?

Well, maybe not happy because her heart still tugged for Ted. Love be damned. She wanted to close her eyes at night with no fear. No fear of a drunken husband...

"I can't do this without you. I have no reason to change unless you and the kids are with me in this." Ted hung his head.

"I don't know much about the program," Beth said, thinking about a long-ago conversation she'd had with Peg after one of Cal's rages had left her friend with bruises along her arms and a broken pinkie toe. Peg mentioned Alcoholics Anonymous and how she had pleaded for Cal to give it a try. The last time Beth checked, Cal was the same miserable, angry drunk he'd been since she'd met him. It would take a miracle for him to change.

But Ted? Maybe he was a different story. Maybe he was ready to change. "What do you need from me?"

"To know that you'll stick with me. You're the reason I'm doing this," Ted said.

"I'm pretty sure that's not how it works. Ted, you need to make these changes because they will make *your* life better. You can't do this for anyone else, even me," Beth said, the words pouring out harder than she intended.

"You're right. I am doing this for me. I'm working what they call the twelve steps," Ted said. "I want to be sober. I want to be here for you. For Opal, Ruby, and Joel."

"I want that too," Beth said, smiling at him. "I'm just afraid that—"

"I'll screw up," Ted finished.

"Well." Beth blinked back tears. "You don't have the best track record."

"That's why you're going to secretarial school? Because you can't trust me."

"Ted, I…" Beth gulped, fearful of his reaction.

"No, it's true, and I deserve it. And I don't blame you for making plans. In fact, I'm proud of you and the example you're showing our kids. I want to show them a better example too."

"You're not mad?" Beth could hardly believe Ted's reasoned, rational response.

"Probably would have blown my stack several weeks ago, before I took a good hard look at myself. AA helps with that, too. Doesn't let you believe your own bullshit."

Ted lowered his head to peer at her under his thick eyelashes, offering the brown-eyed puppy dog look she couldn't resist. "What I'm telling you right now, Bethie, is that I've changed. I'm changing. I'm getting better. This program gave me a map. Sadly, pretty much every road leads back to me and the bad choices I've made…and the unfairness of those choices for you and the kids."

Beth listened, trying to keep a clear head. Was this real? Was Ted returning to the man she had fallen for some twenty years before? Could she trust him one more time, or was this just a pretext to get her to drop night school? And how did he find out about that, anyway?

"Hey, Mom!" Opal's voice rang out. "Ruby pushed Joel in the crick."

Both Ted and Beth looked across the way to the river's edge, where a wet Joel stood, yelling at the top of his lungs at his sister, before they both fell to the ground encased in laughter.

"What the heck?" Opal said. "They were just fighting tooth and nail. Ruby took his last worm."

Ted frowned and called down to the children. "We have lots of worms, Ruby-doobie. No need to punish your brother."

They looked up, echoes of laughter still bracketing them. "I know," Ruby said. "We just wanted to see if Opal would go running to you and tattletale. And she did."

"Well!" The embarrassment and disgust rolled off Opal's words. "You did all this to show me up?" she hollered, racing down to the water. Ruby and Joel stood alongside one another, still laughing. Beth and Ted followed.

"You owe me fifty cents," Joel boasted.

"I know," Ruby said.

"You took my side?" Opal asked her twin. "You bet I wouldn't tattle?"

"Of course I took your side." Ruby grinned. "I'm never on Joel's side."

The sisters exchanged a glance and simultaneously shoved Joel back into the water.

Beth started toward them, but Ted held her back. "They're kids. Our kids, figuring stuff out. Heck, we're adults, and we're still trying to get things right. They'll be fine and so will we." Ted circled her with his arms and held her close.

Beth allowed herself to lean into him, inhaling the familiar menthol and oakmoss of his Aqua Velva.

Would they be all right?

Could she trust him again?

The only thing Beth knew for certain was that she wouldn't quit night school. She'd get that certificate and find a job.

Even if Ted stopped drinking.

Chapter Thirty-Six

Addie stood in front of the same large windows where she had observed Nora's gardens some months earlier. Only today, the bright promise of spring foliage had muted into the browns, oranges, and yellows of autumn. She soaked in the sun-dappled vista; southwestern Pennsylvania's Indian summer in all its glory.

The Gallatins' maid had opened the double doors, ushering her and Ahren into the drawing room ten minutes ago. The steady ripple of Nora's three-tiered water fountain provided a bucolic, peaceful backdrop in direct contrast to the unsettling tremble relentlessly vibrating through Addie's nerves.

Where was Luke?

Her son had left home that morning to meet Barry and Nora. It was the first in-person conversation since he learned of his true paternity. Luke had been very private about this visit, refusing her and Ahren's offer to accompany him.

Around five o'clock he phoned, asking if they would drive out to the Gallatins' home for dinner. Addie had said of course, but before she could ask any questions or garner a detail or two—like had he spoken to Genna—Luke had hung up.

"This is the last place I'd ever wanted to come back to," Addie declared, her back to Ahren. "Why are we here again?"

Ahren walked to Addie and turned her to face him. "You know the simple answer," he said, gathering her hands into his. "Luke asked us to."

She peered into his deep brown eyes. Strength, love, and resolution reflected back. Addie had been so wrapped up in her own feelings that she paid very little attention to Ahren's. These past few months couldn't have been easy for him. Waiting and wondering if the boy he raised since birth would still call him Dad.

"Mom. Dad." That familiar rakish voice boomed. *Luke.*

They turned to see their son enter, Genna and Roman at his side. Not far behind, Barry and Nora sauntered in, completing the picture. The extra-wide doorway framed the five of them like a *tableau vivant* ready to be hung above the living room fireplace.

Addie fought the tightness crushing against her heart at the sight of Luke nestled among this beautiful family. A family waiting for him to seamlessly take his place with them. Was this where he belonged, flourishing with the wealthy and elite?

Being Barry's son would open every door. Luke would never worry about money. They could give him much more than Ahren and she ever could. Each realization pierced through her like a poison-tipped arrow. How could she not want that safe, secure life for him?

Luke crossed the room in what seemed like two strides and hugged them both. Addie soaked in his embrace, more grateful than usual for Luke's occasional displays of affection.

"I've just polished off a plate of *pizzelles*," Luke said, releasing them. "Nora said they were your favorites when you were little."

Addie smiled at the memory, the flavor of black licorice dancing on her tongue. A decade or more had passed since she stuffed her face full of the lacy, crispy cookies. She fought the urge to dust the traces of powdered sugar from Luke's lips.

"We usually make them at Christmas, but today was a special occasion," Nora said, following Barry to one of the two sofas in the room. She gestured to the matching one across from where they sat. "I'll send some home with you, the way Mom used to," Nora added.

The three Burhans, with Luke in the middle, wedged into the overstuffed upholstered sofa to face Nora and Barry. Genna and Roman stood near their parents, almost as though the two families had chosen sides, then lined up for a seated game of Red Rover.

"We used the time to get better acquainted, huh, Luke?" Barry asked, continuing without waiting for a reply. "We had a lot of catching up to do before he heads to South Bend."

Addie listened to the innocuous topics being thrown around as conversation, while quelling the excitement mounting inside her chest. Luke referred to them as Barry and Nora. Not Dad. Not Mom. Or any other euphemism for endearment like Papa Barry or Momma Nora.

She had panicked for nothing. Luke knew who his parents were, and he loved them. Nothing would change that, just like nothing would preclude him from a relationship with the Gallatins. And of course, there would be one. A strong and full connection where her only son could enjoy a bond with his siblings. Every child deserved a sibling or two. In Luke's case, three, even though restoring a relationship with Dante would take time.

But Addie knew, there was always time to forgive. Time to learn. Time to understand.

"Barry's a basketball fan," Luke gushed. "Said he played hoops in high school and hoped to play in college, but his dad wanted him to finish his degree and start working."

"Pop thought being on the basketball team would be too much of a distraction from my studies," Barry added. "He was right. I never could do two things at the same time. But Luke here, well he can shoot a jumper and ace his exams practically at the same time, right, buddy?"

Luke chuckled. "Guess we'll find out."

"You're ready for the next step," Barry stated. "The Irish are lucky to get you."

"Luke's prepared his entire life for this opportunity," Ahren said.

Addie detected pride lacing her husband's words. *We've prepared him well. But have we prepared him to accept a second family?*

"And that's why I asked my parents to come," Luke said. "Since I leave next week, I wanted everyone together to sort of, well, figure out where we stand."

Addie patted Luke's knee gently, wondering where this speech was headed. Was he building a bridge?

"I mean, it's weird finding out your girlfriend is your sister and that your younger brother...hates you. Not you," Luke added, sliding his gaze at Roman. "It's going to take some time for my mind to get hold of this. And for us to see how we fit. But that's the thing, I know that we fit."

A thickness hung in the air. The kind of silence borne of politeness and courtesy. Luke stood and moved to the middle of the room. Genna and Roman joined him as though presenting a united front.

"It's like Genna and I talked about. Things were weird when we tried to be a couple, but somehow we knew we belonged together, just not in a romantic way. I wanted to spend time with Dante and Roman, too. And when I hung out here, I discovered that I liked Barry and Nora." Luke scratched his head as though helping an idea form in his mind. "Things felt right, in spite of all the dumb stuff Dante pulled. And as odd as it may sound, learning that we're related was a relief. It made everything make sense."

Addie willed away tears and smiled at her son.

Truth would be their way forward, a path to rebuild trust with Luke, with Ahren, with Barry, with Beth. And with her cherished friend, Nora.

"This is weird, I know, but it doesn't have to be. I mean, as long as it's okay with my folks, I want to spend time with Roman and Genna, like a regular brother would and well, get to know the two of you better," Luke said, nodding to Barry and Genna.

Barry gestured to his family. "We want that too. And well, Dante…"

"Don't worry about Dante and me," Luke said. "We started this pen pal thing, writing letters about pretty much everything. Getting a lot of stuff out in the open. When he comes home, we'll have a face-to-face, brother-to-brother clearing of the air about what he did to me and Genna."

"No fighting," Addie insisted.

"But maybe you could punch him a couple of times for me," Roman suggested.

"Or give him a knuckle sandwich," Genna added.

"I'm not making any promises." Luke winked. "But I could be persuaded."

Chapter Thirty-Seven
Winter 1958

Beth picked at a thread hanging from her sleeve, occasionally nodding to wives, husbands, and friends of alcoholics quietly taking their seats in the basement of the Presbyterian church. For the seventh time in as many weeks, she waited for Darlene T., the group's leader, to call the meeting to order.

Ted had been right. The Al-Anon meetings helped.

Almost immediately after the kidnapping, Ted had stopped drinking. He swore this time would be different. And to his credit, so far, his walk matched his talk.

At first, Beth hadn't held out much hope that his recovery would last. She had gone about her daily life caring for her children and continuing her night school classes but switching to Wednesday nights. Secretly she held a back-up plan for her future.

Little by little, though, Beth had noticed small changes. Ted's touch was gentle, not demanding. He no longer asked for cash or reached into her wallet for a *fiver*. Pop bottles took the place of Iron City in their refrigerator, and any hard liquor left over from Ted's drinking days had been given away or poured down the drain.

The physical and verbal abuses Beth regularly shielded herself against, a result of when Ted drank too much, had disappeared altogether. All this seemed like a miracle.

How could he overcome so much in a relatively short time? Or was this temporary?

Sitting next to her, Peg fidgeted with her purse clasp, her normally soft features magnified into a twisted panic by the intensity of the moment. Cal's addictive behavior had become so ingrained in her daily life, that Peg couldn't see any solution. Both women had endured the effects of alcoholism. Sadly, it was often easier to live with what we know instead of taking any small step toward healing.

After weeks of cajoling, Peg finally agreed to join her tonight. Luckily, the hour-long meeting began before Sewing Circle, so Peg could truthfully tell Cal she was going to play cards at Addie's, which they would do afterward.

Darlene T. read the Twelve Steps of Al-Anon, then invited discussion around the evening's topic—the courage to change. Beth couldn't imagine a better theme for Peg's first meeting.

Beth had clued Peg into the premise of Al-Anon. She wasn't going to get any ideas or tips on how to make Cal sober. These meetings were for those who loved an alcoholic and how to find hope and strength for the problem drinker in their life. Even though everything said at the meetings was anonymous, living in a small town made that part of the rules moot. Beth knew several members and recognized even more. Still, they would never bring up the topic of the meetings outside of these surroundings.

"Once you recognize that the old way of doing things isn't working anymore," Darlene T. said before opening the discussion, "that's when you'll be able to muster the courage to change."

A man Beth recognized as the grocery store produce manager stood. "I'm Mike."

"Hi, Mike," the group responded.

"I don't feel courageous," Mike said, "but I knew I had to change when my three-year-old found his mother lying in the bathroom in a pool of vomit. I had to change for her. I had to face the truth."

Beth turned to Peg and watched as she nodded at what Mike said. Several minutes later, Peg's nodding returned, this time listening to an older woman—perhaps a future Peg—sharing a tale of her husband of thirty-five years.

Peg would find the courage to change, not to accept the status quo, not for herself but for her children.

The same motivation that now fueled Beth's choices.

***

Addie peeked through the venetian blinds of her living room window. *Where were they?* she wondered, checking her watch for the tenth time in as many minutes. *Half past six. They know we won't play without them.*

"Hey." Helene tapped Addie's shoulder, causing her to jump.

"Whoa," Addie shouted, grabbing the tops of her unbuttoned cardigan. "I didn't hear you come in."

"Mabel and I have had our fill of your ham salad sandwiches. They're delicious. But we really need to start," Helene said.

Mabel stood next to Helene. "Are Beth and Peg still coming? If not, I'm going to hit the road. Have to get up early tomorrow to meet a county inspector at eight. Some newfangled regulation or other."

"Another new rule for the Silverwing?" Helene asked.

"Seems like there's a new one every other month. This one has to do with the number of occupants per room," Mabel lamented. "They think we're packing folks in, I guess. All these rules 'bout to make Bert and me sell and move to a cabin in the Appalachians."

"It's not like Beth to be late and Peg, well, she's usually the first one to arrive on card night." *Anything to get away from Cal.*

"Are they together?" Mabel asked.

"I have no idea. They're already nearly an hour late," Addie said. "Looks like we will have to cancel."

"Cancel?" Nora walked in, wiping her hands on a dish towel. She had obviously straightened up in the kitchen in spite of Addie encouraging her not to bother. "Let's not. Can we hang out a bit? Maybe they're running late."

"Late from what? There are no church projects to delay them. If there were, they would have phoned and begged us to pitch in," Mabel suggested. "Maybe we should call?"

"Call who? Cal? Or Ted? And open up a whole can of worms? I don't think so," Addie said.

"We could play four-handed stud for a bit," Helene volunteered.

"Let's do." Nora tossed the towel over her shoulder, signaling the matter settled and headed toward the dining room table. "I'm certain they'll be here soon."

Addie watched Nora's jaunty gait as she moved away from her. She smiled inwardly.

With Dante's trial over, her girlhood friend seamlessly slipped back to the generous soul Addie had goofed around with as a child. During the past several months, Addie watched the brick-by-brick transformation as the weight of a worried mother lifted from Nora's shoulders. The proof was clearly evident in the small ways Nora handled herself. She quickly picked up the slack whenever she could, giving the benefit of the doubt to anyone in a questionable situation. The judgmental, snarky tone no longer painted her words.

Speculation about what would happen to Dante Gallatin had kept tongues wagging for weeks and weeks. After all the legal acrobatics had been performed, it appeared to many Keystonians that Dante was getting off easy.

Barry and Nora wouldn't press charges, leaving the grand larceny allegation moot. Originally, Dante had been accused of five counts of kidnapping, with three counts involving minor victims. Since Luke, Genna, and Ruby were initially described as accomplices, those charges were immediately peeled away.

After some masterful maneuvering, and what Addie guessed was a legal fee that could finance opening day tickets at Forbes Field, Dante pled guilty to two charges of false imprisonment with a weapon. The Gallatins' slick attorneys also managed to get the assault on Joel dismissed, claiming the altercation was unintended by the defendant. Dante's plea bargain eliminated the need for a jury trial and mitigated all the negative press that would surely have surrounded the spectacle.

The Honorable James Willis, a longtime friend of the Gallatins, had presided over the punishment phase at the Washington County Court of Common Pleas. In an oratory worthy of Daniel Webster, Judge Willis cited the country's troubled youth, the challenges of coming of age, and television as a vile influence on our young men and women.

For the rest of the world, the 1950s had been the Golden Age with job security, prosperity, and success. Judge Willis, however, drew a different picture, claiming he had to consider Dante's youth and naïveté when he handed down the sentence. In the end, those in the courtroom were left to believe that Dante was a victim, not a perpetrator.

Addie knew this legalese bluster was a convoluted cover for the lenient punishment Dante Gallatin would surely receive. The speech was nothing more than pretext for placing Dante in a juvenile facility instead of state prison. Still, she couldn't stop the sigh of relief escaping her chest when Judge Willis declared two years in the Allegheny Juvenile Detention Center with the possibility of parole after twelve months.

The time between Luke's kidnapping and the sentencing had given her insight and a chance to come to terms with everyone's role in Dante's circumstances, including her own.

"I heard a car door slam," Helene said, rushing toward the front door. "It's Beth. And Peg's with her!"

Addie hurried to open the door. "Well, well. Where have you two been?"

Beth gave her a quick hug, whispering, "I'll tell you later." She grabbed Peg by the arm. "Let's get to shuffling," she said, promenading toward Addie's dining room. "Is there any food left?"

Nora hustled back into the entry, a plate of sandwiches in her hands. "Yes. Plenty. You know Addie. She can't cook, but she can prepare sandwiches for an army."

The ladies clustered as though they hadn't seen each other in years, much less days. Everyone talking at the same time, and no one really listening.

Addie hung back, once again the observer. What had happened during these few weeks impacted everyone she loved. Even her dearest friends had emerged with new confidence and resolve.

Something was genuinely different about both Beth and Peg. Addie could only imagine that it had to do with their alcoholic husbands. She'd get the full scoop later. For now, she breathed in deeply enough to make her back straighten and headed toward the poker game, satisfied with this moment of bliss.

Epilogue
February 1960

"Every time we come here, I get butterflies," Addie said, looking around the expansive Notre Dame Fieldhouse. Rows of bleachers were rapidly filling with fans, and a canopy of steel beams surrounded them. "But today a bunch of woodpeckers took up residence in my stomach."

"Luke will play great. He's been starting all season," Ahren said.

"I know. I'm not nervous for him. Well, not any more than usual. Did Luke get enough tickets?" she asked, her gaze darting around.

"I think so. He left them at will call, just like we talked about. I don't know how he managed to get so many," Ahren said.

"He swapped with other players so we could all come. This is the first time the whole family will be here to watch him play."

Ahren swept his arm around his wife and tugged her toward him. "Nora and Barry made the drive out here a couple of times last season. Genna and Roman too. So by whole family, I'm guessing you mean Dante."

"Well, yes. They have written to each other, but they haven't seen each other since—"

"The hearing," Ahren finished.

"So much has changed, and yet everything is the same," Addie said. "Family is family, and ours grew. Everything I worried about and tried to hide ended up being okay." A tear traced her cheek, and she swatted at it.

"Let's wait over here." Ahren shifted them out of the path of college basketball enthusiasts seeking a good spot to watch the game.

Addie meandered, following him to a far corner. "I wasted so much time, everyone's time," she lamented. "I'm so thankful for this second chance. All I can do is pray that Dante understands and forgives me."

"Forgives you for what? Addie, you were protecting your child, your family," Ahren said.

"I was protecting myself and hiding my shame at that boy's expense. At everyone's expense."

"*Shhh.* Now's not the place to rehash this. You've had months and months to make up for, well...for your choices. Today, let's celebrate Luke and enjoy that both of his brothers and his sister will be in the stands."

Addie glanced at her watch. "Where is everybody? They should be here by now."

"It's forty-five minutes to tip-off," Ahren counseled. "We have plenty of time."

"Mrs. Burhan?" A tentative voice seeped through the crowd noise.

"Yes?" Addie said, swinging around to face a tall young man.

"Looks like Luke is getting ready for the game."

Addie glanced over his shoulder to see her son and his teammates had come out of the locker room. The *thunk, thunk, thunk* of basketballs knocking against the court floor echoed as the players warmed up.

"Yes, he is." Addie turned back. "Are you a friend of Luke's?" she asked, but as the words spilled out, she gasped. "Dante?"

Ahren stepped back, clearing Addie's path.

It took a moment for her to recognize his cavalier grin. A crew cut had replaced his mop of wavy brown hair, and his previously skinny frame now carried an additional twenty pounds of muscle. Clearly he had been lifting weights. She smiled at the familiarity of his sparkling hazel eyes dotted with gold flecks. Just like Luke's.

"It's me. I drove separately. Wanted to get a minute with you alone."

"You wanted to talk to me?" Addie swallowed hard and took a step back, steeling herself for the shower of verbal abuse she knew she deserved.

"Can I hug you?" he asked.

Addie blinked back an ocean of tears waiting to flow. "You want to hug me?"

"I've learned a lot since that day at the gas station," Dante said. "Most importantly, to take responsibility for my own actions. You taught me that lesson. You took responsibility for your choices and look where we are today." He hooked a thumb to point to the basketball court behind him. "I'm about to watch my big brother score twenty points, grab at least eight rebounds, and maybe ten assists."

Addie laughed. "You know his stats."

"I had a bit of time on my hands." Dante grinned. "You gave me a second chance to be a part of this family. A family I was willing to throw away until, well, until you presented me with an example of why it's important to stay and fight for the people who matter."

"I did that? I don't think so, Dante. Your parents did the hard work. They love you so much," Addie said.

"Yes, they do. They've stood by me through this whole ordeal. But you showed me how things can be different. How making a bad decision in the past doesn't mean you have to keep making them in the future. I need to thank you for that."

Addie opened her arms, and Dante bent down to fill them. He hugged her tightly and longer than she expected before pulling back.

"Thank you," he said.

Addie swallowed. "I owe *you* an apology. I should be thanking you."

"Not true, Mrs. Burhan. What I did was, well—"

"In the past," she said. "But there is one thing I'd like you to do for me in the future."

"Anything, just name it," Dante said.

"Would you call me Aunt Addie? Sounds so much nicer."

"I'd like that," he said, looking over her shoulder.

Addie turned to see Barry, Nora, Genna, and Roman approach.

"Your folks are here," Ahren said, rejoining them, extending his hand.

Dante accepted the handshake. "It sure is, Uncle Ahren," he said, winking at Addie before joining his parents.

Addie watched them share a group hug. She laughed as he tousled Genna's hair, causing her to holler at him for ruining her coif. Dante ignored her. Instead, in the spirit of being the big brother, he playfully punched Roman in his upper arm.

When Dante turned to face her, Addie reveled in the image of joy and belonging silhouetted on his face.

"Aunt Addie, everyone is here," he announced.

She smiled. "So they are. Luke got us good seats. A bit right of center court."

"Works for me." Dante grinned, ushering his mother ahead of him.

Nora embraced Addie, her smile gleaming.

Addie swiped a tear sneaking from the corner of her eye. "You know Luke always wanted a kid brother."

Dante bristled at the suggestion. "Younger, yes. Kid, no way. We have Roman to hang that title on."

"That you do," Addie agreed, slipping her hand into Ahren's and following him up the bleachers.

Addie waited for Nora and Barry to take their seats on the bench behind them before asking, "Sewing circle at your place Thursday?"

"Plan on it," Nora confirmed. "I have this new recipe for tiramisu. Helene thinks she's the only one who can bake. Well, I'm gonna show her different."

Addie laughed.

Life wasn't perfect. She never expected it to be. But she knew one thing that was perfect and genuine—the friendship among the sewing circle gals. Not just Beth, but Mabel, Peg, and Helene had stood by her through some dark days. And now they'd expanded to make room for Nora.

As sure as a cluster of fireflies would twinkle against the darkness of a summer night, troubles would arise. Addie would get through them. And she would help her friends navigate their woes as well.

She took in a replenishing gulp of air and focused on center court where Luke faced off against an opponent who was maybe an inch shorter. The referee blew the whistle, Luke tipped the ball to a teammate, and the game was on.

The End

Author's Note

I often say: "It's the journey, not the destination." I stole that line from my best friend and acquired sister Carole Campagna. Carole claimed that half the fun is in the getting there. And she is so right. Along this winding journey, I've been blessed with energetic, spirited women, sharing their laughter, vision, and encouragement as I wander toward those coveted words: *The End.*

My biggest blessing, author Sharon C. Cooper, encourages (read: demands) me to look for solutions when all I see are obstacles. Sharon never lets me give up, always poised to move forward no matter the challenge. Right now, I can hear her asking, "So what's the next book?"

Maggie, without your inspiration, and a hot cup of tea, this idea would have never made it to the page.

Thank you to my early readers, Yolanda Barber, Margaret More, and Kim Yezbak. Your kind words, astute critique, and passion for a well-written book make my novels better. Much gratitude to author Heather Webb for her critical eye, challenging questions, and spot-on insight that directly improved my work. I'm lucky to give my ultimate reader, Donna Greeley, the last word.

Elaine Payne, I'm still signing books with the Waterman you gave me so many years ago. Laura Moore Vickery, because of you I'm an ardent reader.

Lastly, this novel is a work of fiction. Any errors, mistakes, or missteps are my own.

About the Author

Pennsylvania-native Claire Yezbak Fadden lives in Orange County, California with her husband and two spoiled dogs. She spends her spare time playing with her four grandchildren and immersing herself in the words of other authors.

Follow her @claireflaire, email her at claire@clairefadden.com or visit her at clairefadden.com.

Other Titles by Claire Yezbak Fadden

A Corner of Her Heart
Promises To Keep
A Ribbon of Light
Maybe This Time
Woman@Heart

Made in the USA
Columbia, SC
28 June 2024

37838129R00174